CODENAME
FAUST

Gustaf Skördeman was born in 1965 in Sweden and is a screen-writer, director and producer. *Geiger*, his thriller debut, is published in 24 countries, and film rights have been optioned by Monumental Pictures.

Also by Gustaf Skördeman
Geiger

GUSTAF SKÖRDEMAN

CODENAME FAUST

Translated by Ian Giles

ZAFFRE

Originally published in Sweden by Bokförlaget Polaris in 2020

First published in the UK in 2022
This edition published in 2023 by
ZAFFRE
4th Floor, Victoria House, Bloomsbury Square, London, WC1B 4DA
Owned by Bonnier Books
Sveavägen 56, Stockholm, Sweden

A CIP catalogue record for this book is
available from the British Library.

ISBN: 978-1-83877-783-8

Also available as an ebook and an audiobook

1 3 5 7 9 10 8 6 4 2

Typeset by IDSUK (Data Connection) Ltd
Printed and bound in Great Britain by Clays Ltd, Elcograf S.p.A.

Zaffre is an imprint of Bonnier Books UK
www.bonnierbooks.co.uk

For Adelenya

1

Such a beautiful animal – completely oblivious to the fact that someone was looking at him through a telescopic sight.

Gunilla had a free shot. It was as if everything were set up for her first trophy, proof that she deserved to be a member of the hunting association. A splendid buck, beautiful and majestic, and completely at her mercy. Well, her weapon's. It was a Tikka T3 that the hunting store assistant had picked out for her while she had pretended to be interested in the differences between all the guns: sporting rifle, side by side, over and under, drilling. They all had different characteristics, but they shared a common purpose. To kill.

She could taste coffee in her mouth – it was seemingly an important part of hunting. The same thing applied to grilled hot dogs. Hot dogs, kabanos and slices of falukorv – the hunters' looks of pleasure as they chewed their way through their almost meat-free offal. Did it really taste good? Half the sausage burned, half still cold? But it was part of it.

Part of the hunt.

Which she was now taking part in.

Taking a life. Preferably several lives. Every death a victory. Why? For the camaraderie? For the adrenaline kick? To keep roe deer numbers down, so they said. A pretty shaky argument, to say the least.

Didn't the blokes who did this ever suffer from a guilty conscience? These men who had smirked and commented on her presence on the training range and had changed the subject when Gunilla had started nagging to join the hunt. The ones with their walls at home covered in animal horns mounted onto plaques, with gun cabinets filled with rifles worth tens of thousands of kronor. Some, hundreds of thousands. Men who didn't seem to come to life until they put on khakis and fiery yellow weapon slings. As if it were finally their opportunity to be themselves. Or the men they dreamed of being. Maybe it was like drag show performers, finally putting on their sequined dresses and having their moment to mime a song under the spotlights? A transformation number, in protest at what they had been born as? There were no slightly chubby second-raters here, just skilled hunters, warriors, bringers of death – the very survival of our entire species depending on them.

Why had she done this herself? Toiling through the courses to get her hunting licence, serving as a beater for several seasons while constantly nagging to join the hunt. Was it to get to know her husband? To try and understand why he loved hunting so much? To find a common interest?

Or was it for the sake of equality? To shake up one of the most male-dominated strongholds in all of Sweden?

Perhaps.

But she hadn't shaken up a thing.

All she had done was give the blokes something to joke about, laugh at. She had most definitely increased their sense of belonging. She had possibly gone as far as embarrassing her husband, but if that was the case then he was concealing it under a layer of indulgent joking. At any rate, he had agreed to give up his spot for her and was now serving as a beater instead – a voluntary downgrade which had been a long time coming, despite being very temporary in nature.

A doe and a kid joined the buck. She had learned that they were called that. Doe and kid, rather than being a she deer and a baby deer. In this regard, as in all others, the correct terminology was essential – small codes that proved whether you were on the inside or not. A bit like wearing the right brand of jeans in high school.

You never shot the doe first, to ensure that the kid wasn't left motherless. An absurd degree of consideration in the midst of a brutal ritual. We'll shoot your child first so that it isn't left all alone. Aren't we kind?

Slowly but surely, her index finger began to squeeze the trigger. The buck was in the middle of her sight. His final seconds with his family . . . But that was nature for you – or so she persuaded herself. Humans weren't the only animal who killed other animals. But they were the only animal that was capable of doing it from a distance like this. Distanced. Impersonal. Cowardly.

The shot rang out. The three beautiful animals ran, vanishing as if by magic. Trained by evolution to move at lightning pace at the first sign of danger.

The shot caught a tree trunk right by the spot where the buck had been standing, just a few inches from its target.

'Good try,' said Håkan encouragingly.

'Close, but no buck,' Martin said, smirking.

Gunilla didn't care. It was she who had demanded to take part, it was she who had passed judgment on the buck's fate. She accepted the others' comments and had no intention of offering any explanation or pleading for their understanding.

'I suppose any others that might have been nearby have legged it too,' said Håkan. 'Let's move forward a bit.'

'It really wasn't far off,' said Martin in an attempt at comfort that stung far more than the cackle of mocking laughter.

'But we also don't want the animals to end up with gunshot wounds,' said Håkan. 'Anyway, perhaps you should do a bit more practice before you take another shot?'

'Hmm,' she said, but merely nodded.

They continued onwards, the Lang brothers leading the way and Gunilla trailing a few steps behind them. Elegant Håkan with his Blaser R8 and his Mauritz Widforss khakis, while Martin was there in his old clobber bought twenty years ago at the hunting wholesalers, clutching his Husqvarna 1900 as if it were his firstborn.

They followed the small forest trail, rutted with deep tracks left by motocross bikes. Gunilla couldn't fathom how anyone could treat nature this way. Not to mention how much it must distress the animals: elk, foxes, deer and their young, birds sitting on their eggs. The pine forest began to thin out to an expansive open area with power lines, a hunting tower and a small road. Kolbotten, Håkan announced, as if Gunilla hadn't known what it was called.

Parked on a patch of gravel was a big SUV – a Porsche Cayenne from a few years back. The doors were open and two burly men were dragging something from the car up the forested hill, beyond which was Lake Mälaren.

The men were fully occupied with their heaving and hadn't noticed the hunters as yet. Once the trio were close to the dragging men, Martin thought to himself that the two didn't look like men to be messed with, and he felt instinctively that it was best to adopt a matey approach. The plates on the car weren't Swedish either, and Martin felt generally uncertain around foreigners. They were deceptive, hard to interpret. But a smile usually bridged most cultural divisions – that much he knew.

'Hello there!' Martin called out cheerfully, whereupon the men started and looked up. 'Have you seen any deer about?'

Both men dropped their bundle, drew a pistol each and opened fire.

Håkan dropped with a scream, hit in the leg, and Martin instinctively let go of his rifle, turned on his heel and ran.

One of the two men rushed after Martin, while the other took a few steps towards the fallen Håkan.

The man loomed over the bleeding, whimpering hunter as he raised his weapon. A Glock, a shocked Håkan noted. A bloody good gun.

But before the man had time to fire, there was a crack from the treeline and he collapsed across Håkan, blood gushing from a hole in his forehead.

The other man heard the shot, saw his companion fall and turned around, his weapon drawn.

The next second he was hit by a similarly well-aimed shot right in the centre of his forehead.

Not a sound crossed his lips as his body tumbled to the ground.

Håkan, who had been convinced that his end was nigh, shoved the man who had died in his place out of the way and twisted to see who had saved him.

He didn't know whether he was expecting to see that Martin had returned, or the cops, or some other dodgy types who had been after the duo and were going to do away with all witnesses.

Instead, what he saw was Gunilla, Kalle's wife, slowly lowering her smoking rifle while fixing her gaze on her first two hunting trophies.

2

'Where's Karin?'

The rope was tight around his throat, making it difficult to get the words out. He peered down at Rau. They were both much older now. Why was he doing this? Why not simply spend his remaining years in peace and quiet? After all, he had offered him that opportunity, Stiller thought to himself as a sweat formed on his brow. A highly unusual guarantee.

'Of course,' said Rau. 'Karin. Good job you mentioned that. *Danke.*'

Stiller felt Rau placing something in his hands, which were tied behind his back, and his fingertips being pressed against some kind of handle.

'I almost forgot to get your fingerprints on the knife. I must be getting old.'

Rau smiled, as if the mere thought of himself ageing was some kind of absurd joke. Stiller looked at him, unable to tear his gaze away. Grey hair, a deeply-furrowed face, just as old as he was but still so much more attractive. A real man. Stiller had never been that – not in his eyes, and barely in anyone else's either. Rau's posture divulged neither his age nor his tough ways. He was straight-backed and radiated energy and strength.

'The knife?' Stiller said quizzically, even though he sensed the truth. He merely wanted to retain hope until the last moment possible.

'I'm thinking that you'll throw it away in the panic,' said Rau, flourishing a large knife and then casting it nonchalantly into a corner of the kitchen. A regular kitchen knife with a long blade – now covered in blood. Fiskars, if Stiller's memory served. How ridiculous for the brand of the knife to crop up in his head now of all times! It was a knife they'd had for at least thirty years and it worked just fine. Why buy a new one? Bread, steaks, heads of cabbage, it had dealt with everything – no problem. And now . . .

'Where's Karin?' Stiller said again, this time with panic in his voice.

'Well, what is it you call it? The upper salon? I suppose it's customary to give fancy names to dead spaces. A hall that it's impossible to furnish. Well, she's up there.'

'Karin!'

'Good. Shout. If anyone hears you, it will only serve to reinforce the official version.'

'Of what? What have you done to her?'

'Me?' said Rau, sounding surprised. 'I assume you simply lost it after your old spy pals were murdered. Perhaps you were afraid that you were next in line. And there must have been all sorts of feelings of guilt brought to life. You've been living under so much pressure for so long, ashamed of the past that's finally caught up with you. What do I know? The police will be in a better position to figure it all out. You returned home from your early morning walk and then you began to argue, and, well . . .'

Rau paused, looking at Stiller standing there balanced on the tips of his toes on his own kitchen chair. A chair that probably belonged to the vicarage and had been there for several decades. Light pine, which didn't really go very well with the dark-stained gateleg table and the woven table runners and small, bright yellow candles in their own holders. With the moss-green velvet light shade with brown tassels. the copper stove lid, the decades-old spice jar containing thyme, cinnamon and lemon pepper. Pinned on the wall was a supermarket-branded calendar, a wallchart of mushrooms and a couple of hangings featuring Christian messages. 'My soul thirsteth for God, for the living God: when shall I come and appear before God?'

Rau couldn't understand how people lived like this without developing breathing difficulties. Well, actually, breathing difficulties were exactly what Stiller had right now.

'Ah yes, props.'

He left the kitchen and Stiller stared up at the ceiling, as if hoping to see through it to Karin upstairs. Was she still alive? How badly had Rau hurt her? And what was he going to do with Stiller? Was this just a warning? He prayed with all his soul that it was.

Rau returned with a Bible.

'Matthew, right? It has the best version.'

Rau fell silent, as if he were genuinely waiting for an answer. After a couple of seconds, he continued.

'Chapter twenty-seven, isn't it? Verses three to five? *Oder?*' He looked searchingly at Stiller and then he smiled. 'I Googled it. I'm afraid it's not written very imaginatively, but I think it'll do the job nonetheless.'

He opened the Bible to the relevant page and placed the holy scripture on the kitchen table. Then he turned towards Stiller.

'Well, my friend, I have just a couple of questions for you. And how you answer will determine your fate.'

Stiller stared around wildly. The rope was cutting into his throat, and his neck ached from his head being held at an angle for so long. Every breath was a struggle.

'The People's Court versus Jürgen Stiller, who betrayed the revolutionary struggle by surrendering himself to petty bourgeois concerns and revisionist tendencies in order to seek personal gain at the expense of socialist orthodoxy.'

'I confess,' Stiller managed to splutter. His legs felt increasingly numb. He wouldn't be able to hold his balance for much longer. 'I confess . . .'

The smile disappeared from Rau's lips.

'Who have you spoken to?'

'About what?'

'About me.'

'No one.'

Rau reached out with the tip of his shoe and prodded the kitchen chair. Stiller shuddered and tried to parry the movement, which instead made him tip over the other way. The rope pressed against his Adam's apple and for a few endless seconds he was unable to take in any air. Rau watched his struggle with an indifferent look.

'No one!' Stiller shouted, hoping that someone would be passing by on the road outside and hear him. Perhaps he would be able to get out of this after all. He knew that mock executions were a common method used to break people. But at least you survived. 'No one. I promise!'

Rau raised his foot again. He waggled it back and forth, teasingly.

'Why would I?' said Stiller. 'Who would I talk to?!'

'What do you know about Wahasha?'

'About what?'

'Operation Wahasha.'

'Nothing.'

'That's a pity.'

'Why?' Stiller whimpered.

'If you don't know anything then you're worthless to me. *Leider*.'

Rau placed his foot on the chair again.

'Wait! Did you say Wahasha? I can find out. I know people. I can find out about it!'

'Forget it.'

'Please, I won't tell anyone anything. I'm sorry that I . . .'

'Shush . . .' Rau said, going to the fridge and opening it. Herring, anchovies, caviar, yoghurt, Tupperware filled with leftovers, a blue teacup filled with what appeared to be dripping. No food fit for human consumption as far as the eye could see. Rau turned back to Stiller again with a grimace.

'What have you told Sara Nowak?'

'Who's that?' said Stiller.

'The policewoman who exposed Geiger. *Die Polnische*. The one you've called.'

'No, I haven't.'

'You've written down her number without knowing who she was? It's a coincidence?'

Rau held up the small black notebook he had found in Stiller's study.

'Notes for sermons, phone numbers for carpenters and the diocese in Linköping, and Sara Nowak's . . .'

Rau looked up from the notebook. He wasn't smiling any longer. Stiller gulped and sweat broke out on his brow again.

'I . . . I was just going to find out how the Geiger case was going.'

'*Du lügst*,' Rau said, allowing the tip of his shoe to rest on the edge of the kitchen chair.

'I didn't manage to reach her! I swear! I haven't talked to anyone!'

'*Vielleicht*,' said Rau, nudging the chair forward a couple of centimetres. '*Vielleicht nicht.*'

'*Bitte, Otto, ich habe sie nicht . . .*'

'Shush . . .'

Rau looked at him reproachfully, a finger to his lips.

'I believe you.'

Stiller exhaled, insofar as that was possible.

Rau smiled at Stiller, turned around slowly and lifted his black bag onto the kitchen counter. Old cabinets, he thought to himself in irritation as he opened the bag. Probably from the 30s or 40s. Why not buy a modern kitchen, even if the house was old? These people lacked any aesthetic vision. Spirituality was just another name for a complete lack of style.

Through the window he caught a glimpse of the church a few hundred metres away on the far side of a field. The great Bishop Giertz, one of Sweden's most renowned Christian leaders, had once worked there – as a simple pastor early in his career. Rau had naturally Googled Giertz too. Nowadays, all knowledge was to be found on your phone. If he had had time, he would have very much liked to look around the church properly, but things were the way they were. Perhaps he might return on another occasion.

He took what he needed out of the bag. A speaker – a Bang & Olufsen Beolit 17 – offering excellent sound for its size. An LED panel, small but luminescent. An extra lightweight stand to attach the light to. And the video camera. A Panasonic HC-VXF990. An old but faithful servant offering excellent image quality. Of course, he could have filmed the whole thing on his mobile, but then it wouldn't have been possible to play music at the same time. And there was something special about a proper video camera – you couldn't get away from that. He liked his modest kit.

He turned the light on Stiller and switched it on. He was once again impressed by the light the small red metallic box was able to produce. The vicar's tear-filled eyes blinked in response to the unexpected strong glow. Good. That made him look even more afraid.

Then he got out his mobile and selected the music: Diamanda Galá's *The Litanies of Satan*. Not music that he personally appreciated, but he liked the title and the effect the piece had on the people he played it to. As expected, Stiller also responded with great discomfort to the diabolical cries.

Once he had finished rigging it all up, he switched on the video camera and took a moment to admire the scene he had set. Then he went over and kicked the chair out from under Stiller's feet.

It wasn't such a long drop that the neck was broken. He wanted Stiller to slowly suffocate under his own bodyweight – extra torment provided by the twenty kilos he could have done with losing.

A protracted struggle to the death was what he wanted to capture.

Close-ups of the terror in the eyes of the condemned, the desperate attempts to gurgle entreaties for mercy as the neck was sealed by the strong rope.

And the rising panic in response to the irrevocable creep of death slowly taking over his senses.

Stiller was fighting for survival.

Good.

His legs floundered, searching for footing, something to support themselves on. But it was no use.

The choking sounds indicated that he had begun to lose his struggle while also suggesting that he was trying to produce a message, a cry for help.

Where's your God now? Rau thought to himself, before realising that God was, of course, with them. Rau was exercising God's will. That was the only logical conclusion for believers, of which the man jerking and shaking on the rope was one.

God's will was just not what Stiller had been hoping for.

3

He honked.

The bastard honked.

Sara was standing in the loading bay right outside their building's street door on Kornhamnstorg, waving to Martin who was approaching in the rental van he'd picked up from the petrol station. Ebba had wanted them to hire a removal company, but Sara had decided they would do it themselves. There had to be some limits. She had been standing in the bay to keep it free for twenty minutes, but when Martin finally came into sight there was a black Audi right in front of him that wanted to pull into the empty space that Sara was standing in – despite the fact that she was waving at it to ward it off. The Audi simply pulled in closer and closer until the fender struck Sara's shin. And when she didn't move the driver honked. Bastard.

Behind the rental there was now a taxi waiting, and a Volvo behind it. They began to honk at the hold-up. Martin emerged from the van and gesticulated towards Sara.

'Let him in. We're blocking the road. I'll find somewhere else.'

'What did you have in mind? Ten blocks away?'

Sara waved at the Audi driver to move his car and received nothing but another honk in reply.

She sighed and pulled out her wallet.

'No,' said Martin, who realised what his wife was intending to do.

'What? I was only going to try and bribe him,' said Sara, looking innocent. 'If that doesn't work then I'll give up. Get back in the van.'

Martin turned around and began to walk back to the cab. Sara produced her police ID and held it up to the driver in the Audi while simultaneously keeping an eye on Martin in order to conceal her actions if he did turn around. She waved angrily at the moron in the Audi to get lost. When he persisted in his parking attempts, she leaned forward and slammed both her palms onto the bonnet as hard as she could while turning her head to show the left side of her face. The side with the scars and burns. Then she stared right into the eyes of the besuited man behind the wheel with a look that suggested he was next in line if he didn't move his vehicle. Finally he gave in – just an immature little boy in a fifty-year-old man's body. Childishly flooring the accelerator, he pulled away.

Martin turned around in response to the sound of the engine and looked surprised.

'He left?'

'All it took was a hundred kronor,' said Sara with a smile.

She found her double face often came in handy. Without it she would have difficulty even comprehending that it had all really happened. That she had been trapped in the Broman family's burning garden shed while the terrorist Abu Rasil tried to transmit the codes that would trigger atom bombs from the Cold War. Bombs powerful enough to devastate vast swathes of Germany's heartlands. That she had seen the double agent, Agneta Broman, be shot. That she had discovered that her childhood friend Lotta was the spy known as Geiger, while Lotta's father Stellan – the nationally beloved TV personality – had been a monster who had raped countless minors. And had turned out to be Sara's father to boot. A realisation that still disgusted her.

The fact that half of her face was covered in burns reinforced what she had always felt: she had two personalities. One beautiful and attractive, the other frightening and repulsive. A true Janus. Men who only saw the uninjured half of her face still approached her with their usual pick-up lines, just as they always had done, but then they would recoil at the sight of her scars.

Sara had begun to like her two-sided face, partly because it actually divulged something about her inner self, and partly because she realised she wasn't dependent on her face and on being beautiful. She was Sara Nowak, even if she scared the people around her. In fact, she was more Sara now than ever before.

She was scheduled to have plastic surgery, but the doctors refused to make any promises. The scars might be there for good.

She was happy just to be alive. She didn't care that people occasionally stared at her. Given the wounds inside her, the scars might as well be visible on the outside too. Perhaps it was time to take up more space – to stand for who she was. Not just in relation to others, but as herself. Not as a police officer, nor a mother, nor a wife, nor a daughter. But as Sara.

She had decided she was going to let her red hair grow out again. She was no longer an investigator on the prostitution unit, so she didn't have to dye her hair brown to blend into the crowd. And besides, she had found it increasingly difficult to do that – to blend in; to just observe. She had ended up resorting to violence against johns in her custody, which had almost got her the sack. Not that it had got the men in question to reconsider, she thought to herself.

The violence she had been subjected to herself had frightened her. First there was Holmberg, the john who would have beaten her to death if Jennifer hadn't stopped him, and then the fight with Abu Rasil in which she had been both burned and shot. She had been lucky not to come out of it all worse off.

But she was almost more scarred by the violence she had engaged in herself – shooting another person dead without hesitation. Using C.M. the neighbour's expensive shotgun. How would things have panned out if she hadn't thought of that?

She still dreamed of that night. The fire, the sound of the automatic weapon, the pain when the shots hit her, all the blood when she shot Abu Rasil, the aftermath . . .

While she had probably saved thousands of lives, Sara struggled to see herself as some kind of anti-terrorist force taking people's lives without batting an eyelid.

She was grateful that she had found that strength within her, grateful for that side of Sara. But it had almost cost her life. Now she needed to recover. Accept the Sara who sought out calm, who looked inwards. It was time to stop and sum up who she was in life.

For instance, the first strands of grey were beginning to appear amongst the red, though so far she had just pulled them out. She didn't want to be dismissed ahead of her time by a society that had so little respect for age and experience. But she was allowing the fiery red hair to grow out – a fire that before long would spread across her whole head. She looked forward to that. She didn't want to hide any longer.

She'd enjoyed a beautiful summer after being discharged from hospital. Everything had been normal. No spies, no sexual deviants, no one dying. Just Sara and her family. She had slept, swum, read and dedicated energy to completely trivial matters like getting worked up over split infinitives and the unreasonably long pauses between the songs on Depeche Mode's *Ultra*.

She was doing well. And she wanted to continue doing well. That was the most important lesson she had learned from the events of the early summer. That, and that family came ahead of everything else.

Martin had parked and opened the rear doors of the van. Sara peered into the empty interior. How many pieces of furniture had been carted around in here? New apartments, bigger to accommodate a new child, smaller because a spouse had died, two because they no longer wanted to live together. Or a first home. Moves filled with joy and anticipation, or sorrow and resignation.

Sara's philosophising was interrupted by an annoying sound from her mobile: three shrill notes in a rising crescendo. She so rarely heard that sound that she had almost forgotten what it meant. A video call. She had ignored most calls of late, hadn't been up to talking to telesales operatives or her colleagues. It had almost become a reflex to reject calls and then ignore her voicemail. Her best friend, Anna, had told her off on several occasions for this, but Sara wasn't always able to deal with the world around her. Not yet. But this was a different sound, and perhaps this was why she paid attention to it.

'Nadia would like to FaceTime,' said her display.

The only Nadia she had in her contacts was one of the girls down on Malmskillnadsgatan. One of the many to have been lured from her home country and then forced to sell her body to pay off fabricated debts and to ensure that her family back home didn't suffer the consequences if she didn't. Sometimes the threat would be that a little sister would be subjected to the same thing if the woman didn't do as the traffickers said.

While Sara was no longer involved in the prostitution unit, she still felt a responsibility for the girls she had met while working the streets in her former role. She'd had to stop, she knew. To make sure she didn't do anything really stupid. But she couldn't quite escape the feeling that she had let down the people who needed her most. So she wanted to help now, if she could.

Unless Nadia had pocket-dialled her, of course. That would be the most natural explanation.

But when Sara accepted the video call, she saw a bloodied face.

Nadia, battered and barely conscious.

Her mouth was moving as if she were trying to say something.

'Where are you?' said Sara when she realised the gravity of the situation. 'Use the camera to show me.' She swapped to English. 'Show around you!'

Nadia turned her hand and surveyed her surroundings using the phone's camera. She was clearly lying on the ground, by an open expanse of asphalt beside some kind of warehouse. Lots of large containers were stacked on top of each other, all covered in foreign names. Further away there were trees – an entire forest. And the Kaknäs Tower. And a rectangular red brick building with the word 'Frihamnen' on the side. The Free Port.

'I'm coming!' Sara cried out to Nadia. She ended the call just as Martin and Olle emerged from the building carrying a white-painted desk.

'I've got to go,' said Sara.

'Now? In the middle of the move?'

'I'll be back soon!' Sara shouted, running over to one of the taxis on the rank next to the bureau de change. 'Frihamnen,' she said, getting in next to the driver. 'Quick as you can,' she said, flashing her police ID.

With a police officer at his side, the driver wasn't afraid to floor it. Thanks to some risky overtaking manoeuvres, rapid lane switching and speeds of up to ninety kilometres an hour, they reached Frihamnen in just a few minutes.

Using Street View, Sara was able to find exactly where Nadia was, thanks to what the woman had filmed. Sara directed the cabbie to the outer edge of the port, to what was called Warehouse 7.

They passed a gigantic red brick structure housing production companies and an auctioneer. Cars with the names of various TV shows on them in large lettering were parked outside. Sara wasn't familiar with any of them. Warehouse 7 was in an area used for the transhipment of containers for international transportation.

Frihamnen was new territory to Sara and the world was distorted here. The sky seemed high above, but also gave the feeling that it was a lid over everything and the fact that the distances between the huge buildings were so expansive also skewed perspective. It was almost as if you could touch the old warehouses and massive silos, despite the fact that they were hundreds of metres apart. You felt both gigantic and microscopic at the same time.

Sara recollected that, once upon a time, there had been a thriving sex trade in Frihamnen. That had been thanks to seamen on visiting ships, family men who appreciated the seclusion. But that had been before the media companies had moved in. Now there were people working here around the clock and you were rarely alone, except perhaps at the remotest wharves. As far as Sara knew, sex workers were no longer active in Frihamnen. So what could have happened to Nadia?

She caught sight of her as soon as they pulled into the deserted turning circle, lifeless and bloody, behind her the looming wall of containers with the names of different shipping companies. But not a soul in sight. Sara jumped out of the taxi and ran over to Nadia.

Black eyes, bloodied eyebrows, a couple of teeth knocked out, split lips, big bruises on her arms and legs. Internal injuries? Quite possibly – Sara was in no position to assess that. Nadia needed to go to hospital right away. She dialled 112.

'This is Sara Nowak with Västerort Police. I'm in Frihamnen with a badly injured girl. She needs an ambulance right away.'

'Address?'

'Don't know. Frihamnen. Right at the edge. By the containers.'

'We need an address.'

'I don't have an address! Frihamnen! At the edge!'

'You need to calm down or I'll terminate this call.'

'Aren't you listening to me?! She's seriously injured! Do your fucking job and dispatch an ambulance!'

The operator hung up.

'Fucking cretin!' Sara yelled into her phone.

She wondered whether she could head down to the emergency services dispatch centre and find the bitch, but realised it was more important to help Nadia. She turned to the taxi driver.

'She needs to go to hospital,' she said.

'No blood in car,' said the driver. 'You got to pay. Then you call ambulance.'

'I just tried to do that. You heard how it went. And she needs to go to hospital.'

'No blood in car. You know, this my job. If there blood in car, no customers want go.'

'I'll put my jacket under her.'

'No.'

'I'll pay you a thousand kronor extra.'

'You know, if blood in car I can't drive for two days. Must wash car.'

'Two thousand.'

'OK. Get in. But jacket under.'

Sara looked down at Nadia.

'Can you hear me. Nadia?'

It looked like her eyelids flickered, but Sara didn't know whether Nadia was conscious.

'We need to go to hospital.'

A barely perceptible nod. Then her eyes opened a crack. Nadia raised a trembling hand to Sara's burned cheek.

'What happened?'

Sara put her own hand over Nadia's. She felt the rough surface of the burns outlined against her fingertips.

'An accident,' she said gently, and Nadia shut her eyes, satisfied. 'But what's happened to you?'

Nadia tried a couple of times before she managed to reply.

'Peepshow.'

'What do you mean, peepshow?'

Nadia struggled to continue, but before she said any more she looked around.

'My bag . . .'

Sara saw the panic in Nadia's bloodshot eyes. She reached over and picked up the handbag that had been lying right by her.

'This one?'

'In-inside?'

Sara opened the handbag and found a thick wad of thousand kronor notes. She showed Nadia the money and the woman relaxed. She took the handbag and pressed it to her breast.

'Where did you get that cash?' said Sara. She tried English. 'Where is the money from?'

'Warn Jenna,' said Nadia without opening her eyes. 'Please. No good.'

'Warn her? About what? Nadia – about what?'

No answer.

Sara stood up to gather up the items that had fallen out of the handbag – perhaps when Nadia had been searching for her mobile to call for help. Makeup, keys, wallet, throat sweets, condoms, morning after pills, teargas, a flick knife, headphones and a fluffy little cuddly toy. And right by Nadia was her mobile.

Sara paused for a moment's thought and then applied Nadia's thumb to the fingerprint scanner. No good. She had more luck with her index finger. In the contacts there was a number for 'Jenna'. But she got no answer when she tried calling. She tried calling the number from her own phone too. Same result. What if it was already too late?

While looking at the phone, Sara checked the call logs and text messages and took photos of the last twenty-four hours of communications using her own mobile. The previous call had been the evening before, and then there had been a series of unanswered calls during the night and morning, and last of all Nadia's FaceTime to Sara.

Sara examined Nadia's mobile. The same model Ebba had. And they were about the same age. They were just living in completely different worlds.

4

Sara had asked the staff in the emergency room at St Göran hospital to keep an eye on Nadia's handbag and to call her when Nadia was in a state to talk. As she made her way out of the hospital, her guilty conscience began to weigh on her. Once again she had put work ahead of family. And for a job she no longer had. The street prostitution squad had been disbanded and she had decided to apply to something else completely rather than join the newly-formed trafficking squad. She had eventually realised that the job had been eating away at her. The girls on the streets and in the brothels inside regular flats were no longer her responsibility. Well, they were, she supposed; just like they were everyone's responsibility. She had been obliged to help Nadia, for instance, as a fellow human being. But now David would have to take over. Sara had promised herself she would prioritise family life and reduce her commitment to work to normal levels. She called her former colleague while setting off back towards town.

'How are you doing?' David said, right off the bat.

Everyone was being particularly considerate to her these days, handling her with kid gloves. Perhaps because the burns were such a tangible reminder of what she had experienced. At any rate, Sara was increasingly enjoying being alone, avoiding the anxious glances. At the same time, she wanted to be with her family, keeping an eye on them and knowing they were safe. It was a split.

'I'm good,' was all she said, without expanding any further. And then she told him about Nadia and what had just happened. David wasn't aware of a peepshow either, but he said he'd ask around. He was also surprised that a sex worker had turned up in Frihamnen again after all these years. Perhaps a visiting foreign ship was luring them in? But did that mean there was a peepshow on a boat? She gave David Jenna's number and he promised to try and contact her. Then he said he would be in touch as soon as he heard anything and they rang off.

Sara cut the corner of the square at Fridhemsplan and continued along Hantverkargatan.

Right now, she realised, everything felt good.

In some ways, this was perhaps the toughest day of her life, but she was so happy that she could even be part of it that she was able, in spite of everything, to accept the facts.

Her daughter, Ebba, was moving out.

Ebba, who was supposed to have become her confidant, her best friend, the one whom she was going to help through life in her capacity as her mother, with the benefit of all her hard-won experience. But Ebba didn't want her mother's help. It was unclear whether this was because work had taken Sara away for much of Ebba's childhood, or whether it was a personality trait, or quite simply something all daughters did to their mothers: refuse to accept help. Sara had shut out her own mother, Jane, for many years, believing that Jane had ruined her life when she had fled the Bromans' beautiful home beside the water in Bromma, taking her to a drab one-bed flat in Vällingby. When in fact Jane had rescued her from her horror of a father.

What did Ebba make of Sara's pain? Did she think Sara was trying to control her? That she thought of nothing but herself?

When you were nineteen, you had no idea how much you didn't know, Sara thought to herself as she strode up Hökens gata towards Mosebacke. She glanced over towards the large area of outdoor seating for the bar on the other side of Södra Teatern and reflected on how many summer evenings she had spent there when she was young. It still looked just the same, although it had been decades ago. The town was like a photo album for her. So many buildings and streets charged with memories, traces of times gone by. It almost felt as if she could travel back in time to those days, those nights, to join the friends gathered around those tables so many years ago. As if all it would take was to turn around and they would be there.

Up in the square itself, there was at least one thing that had changed – apart from the old phone box now being merely decorative, a new eatery had opened its doors: 'Woodstockholm'. Inventive name, Sara thought to herself ironically. Beyond the restaurant, she saw her mother waiting on the pavement outside the door to Ebba's new apartment block, next to a pair of large cardboard boxes. She was wearing colour-coordinated, neatly ironed work clothes. Purple, pink and white. Sara couldn't help smiling at her mother. As for herself, she had just pulled on a pair of jeans and a T-shirt, Martin's old Joy Division top. He'd never really and truly liked them – that much Sara had determined before depriving him of the right to wear the top with them on it. Parked by the kerbside she saw Ebba's Beetle – the mocha-coloured cabriolet she had been given by Grandpa Eric on her graduation from sixth form. It had three yellow notes tucked under the windscreen wipers. Sara resolved to take robust action with her daughter, her husband and her father-in-law about who was going to pay those parking tickets.

'Didn't we say nine o'clock?' Jane said, instead of greeting her.

'Aren't the others here?'

Sara looked around.

'Martin arrived at ours with the van two hours ago. Have you been here for an hour?'

'Two. I wanted to be on time.'

'Mum! Surely you know what we're like?'

'I never give up hoping.'

'What's this, then?'

Sara looked at the large boxes marked Hästens and Montana, frowning. Expensive bed, expensive furniture. Recipient: Ebba Titus. Invoice to be paid by: Martin Titus and Eric Titus.

'Did you sign for these?'

'Yes.'

Lucky for Ebba that Jane had been there. But doubtless she'd fail to thank her for that.

'You won't believe this,' Jane said. 'Those morons said it had to be Ebba. "She's my grandchild," I said. And they said: "We can't leave these expensive things." "I'll call your boss," I said.'

'And they gave in?'

'Yes? Why? You think I should have given in?'

Jane followed Sara's gaze towards the furniture.

'I wasn't able to give you things like that when you moved out.'

'No, and so I learned to get by on my own.'

'Get by on your own?' Jane said with a snort. 'Why do you need to get by on your own? I had to get by on my own when I was young. It was awful. I would have been happy to help you, however I could.'

'You helped me with the most important thing of all – I just didn't know it.'

'Have you told them?' Jane said, fixing her gaze on Sara.

'About Stellan? No. I'm never going to.'

Jane had badgered Sara to tell her family who her father was. Nothing would have made her more proud when she had been a child, but now it was impossible. Completely out of the question.

'That house is yours too.'

Sara started and looked at her mother.

'Stellan's? Why should I want it?'

'It's yours.'

'I don't want it. Jesus Christ.' Sara fell silent, disgusted by the thought of everything she had found out about her father, but then she looked back at her mother again. She was looking determined in a way that only Jane could.

'Mum, don't tell the others anything.'

'What would I say?'

25

'About Stellan.'

'It's not just your decision. He was their grandfather.'

'Yes, yes. But—'

Martin appeared in the van, driving along Östgötagatan. While he drove around the square to reach them, Sara put her hand on Jane's arm and repeated her plea:

'Promise me!'

'Yes, yes,' Jane said wearily. 'I promise. No problem. If you promise to tell them yourself.'

'Not yet.'

Martin parked up and jumped out of the cab. He still had an energetic, boyish air about him, Sara thought to herself. She was, however, unsure whether it was natural or contrived. Her beloved husband had real issues with his impending fiftieth birthday – she knew that much. A couple of years left, then it was all over. Lately, he had let his hair grow out and changed his blazers for leather jackets, hoodies and boots, and he had been practising more often with his blokey rock band, with the intentionally ironic and droll name C.E.O Speedwagon – selected because all the band members were high ranking executives. Sara often noticed that Martin got looks from women in the street, even far younger ones, so she supposed she ought to be proud of her catch. At the same time, she knew that even the most beautifully wrapped packages could be empty. What was the deal with her husband?

Ebba climbed out of the van, engrossed in an agitated phone call.

'What do you mean "already delivered"?! Where? Well then, to who? "Don't know"?!?' Mobile pressed to her ear, she didn't notice her mother's discreet wave. 'If you've lost my stuff you'll have to replace it! Send new ones. Today! I'm having a housewarming party tonight!'

'Ebba!' Sara yelled, and when her daughter finally noticed her she pointed at the boxes outside the main door. Ebba hung up.

'Oh, great,' was all she said. Then she gave her grandmother a hug. But no hug for Mum, Sara thought dejectedly.

Martin kissed Sara, rounded the van, opened the rear doors and lifted out a moving box filled with clothes. Sara went over to help with the rest, but the van was completely empty.

'Where's the furniture? And all the other clothes?'

'I left them at yours,' said Ebba. 'After all, I need to buy new stuff.'

'Buy new? You've got at least ten boxes of clothes! And your furniture! You've got a whole flat to fill.'

'Kid's stuff. Come on . . .'

'We'd carried it all down and filled the van up when she suddenly changed her mind.' Martin flashed his charming, boyish wolf's grin, just like he always did when he wanted to pour oil on troubled waters. 'We had to carry it all back up again.'

'What are you going to do now then?' said Jane, without paying any heed to the exchange. 'How are you going to pay the rent?'

'Work,' said Ebba. 'And some resits to improve my grades. Then I'm going to apply to the Stockholm School of Economics next year.'

'She's got a job at Eric's,' said Sara. 'On reception.'

'My own trainee programme,' said Ebba. 'I'm going to learn about the whole company, from the bottom up.'

'Here's a tip for you,' said Sara. 'Don't tell the others on reception you think they're at the bottom.'

Ebba shrugged.

'Whatever.'

'Where's Olle?' Sara said with a sigh, telling herself she had to pick her battles. 'Surely you didn't leave him at home?'

'Christ, no. He's . . .' Martin looked around. 'Surely he's still in the van?'

Sara looked into the cab and quite rightly, there was her fourteen-year-old son. He was wearing a pair of big Beats headphones connected to his mobile, and singing along without the slightest sense of timing:

'*You don't know where I've been, you only see the colour of my skin.*'

Sara studied Olle's skin colour – very pale, considering it was the end of summer. But he seemed engaged, so that was probably a good thing.

'*But I'm your brother, I'm your next of kin!*'

Then he sat there nodding in time to the music. It was Martin's way of connecting with his son: letting him do what he wanted, and encouraging everything. More a mate than a dad. But then lots of fathers were like that these days, Sara thought to herself. Olle noticed his mother's presence, paused the song and lowered his headphones.

'Hi,' he said.

'Good song?'

'Bloody brilliant. Uncle Scam.'

'What did you say? Mamma Scan?'

'Uncle Scam!'

'OK.'

At least it was an artist Sara had heard of. Uncle Scam was due to play in Stockholm that week, and according to Martin it was a massive deal. The world's best-selling artist right now: two sold-out nights at the Friends Arena. Getting him to come to Sweden was the biggest thing ever to have happened to Go Live, despite the lad having barely been born when Martin had founded his concert organising company more than twenty years ago. But Sara knew it was a big deal – a real feather in Martin's cap. And she knew that the celebrated rap star spelled his stage name Un¢le $cam, using the dollar and cent symbols. Olle had explained to her that this was complete genius, a crushing criticism of the prevailing hegemony of commercialism in the West. From a twenty-three-year-old who charged a fee for signing his autograph and made millions from selling T-shirts every year.

'Come and help,' Sara said to Olle.

'But there's nothing there. Just, like, a box.'

'And some eye-wateringly expensive stuff your father and grandfather bought for Ebba. Come on, you need to move. You and Dad can carry the bed.'

'Can't. Got to go,' Martin said at that moment, jumping in behind the wheel.

'Where are you going?' said Olle, absolving Sara of the need to ask the same question, which was a relief since she would have sounded far more annoyed.

'To prepare for the party.'

By all appearances, Olle seemed to accept that answer. He pulled on his headphones, turned the music back on and got out of the van, once again bellowing in a tone deaf fashion:

'Don't you know every yang needs a yin, don't you know I'm the original sin, my own evil twin, so let it begin!'

But instead of helping, he merely sat down on one of the large boxes by the door and carried on singing.

'My shelves!' shouted Ebba. She rushed over and yanked Olle off the Montana box. He allowed himself to be shoved aside without resistance, accustomed to his big sister being the one to call the shots.

Sara turned to Martin.

'You need to prepare for the party? Surely you've hired people to do that?'

'Yeah, but they can't do everything. Procedures, checking things are in place, the rehearsal with the band.'

That was what took the biscuit. The band. Martin's band.

'Surely they can wait?'

'Hello! It's a twentieth anniversary. There are going to be execs over from America.'

The idea that Martin was going to play the rock star in front of a bunch of stony-faced management types from the USA made Sara laugh. Martin looked at her uncomprehendingly, but seemed to decide that she was happy at the thought of it.

'When are you coming? It starts at seven, but it's fine if you're there by nine. We won't play until people have got warmed up a bit.'

Before Sara had time to reply, a black Maserati Quattroporte Trofeo pulled over by the van. The passenger-side door opened and Martin's mother Marie stepped out wearing a sporty ensemble in pastel shades with a load of polo players visible in various places on her garments. And a sun visor. The kind dealers wore for poker games and at roulette tables in Lucky Luke cartoons, Sara thought to herself. But she grasped that it was a chic accessory as far as Marie was concerned. Eric was wearing his golf get-up and had his clubs in the back.; he'd probably got up early to have time for eighteen holes before the move.

'Grandpa!' Ebba shrieked, running over to open the door on the far side and giving Eric a hug.

'Housewarming present,' Eric said, handing Ebba a small box.

As if furniture costing tens of thousands of kronor wasn't enough. And an apartment worth millions.

'A new mobile!' Ebba shouted. 'Thank you!'

There went Sara's final avenue for controlling her daughter. She had borrowed Ebba's current mobile and added her own fingerprint, which had allowed her to keep an eye on Ebba's friends and which websites she was visiting. The new model had facial recognition, which would make it very difficult for Sara to get into it without Ebba noticing. What was more, her daughter would be spending the night in her own apartment from now on, so it was probably for the best to accept all that was over. The moorings had been cut loose and the good ship Ebba was sailing away. Leaving Sara behind on the shore.

'And there's one more thing.'

Eric handed Ebba an oblong decal that she applied to the back of his car.

'You're going to have a driving lesson now?' said Sara.

'Yes.'

'What about the move?'

'I'll take over,' Marie warbled in her keenest voice, waving her hand eagerly.

'But you've got your own car – why don't you take that?' said Sara. 'And park it somewhere else to avoid getting more tickets.'

'It's so small. Grandpa's is better.'

'Don't call me Grandpa,' said Eric. 'It makes me sound like I'm a hundred years old. Call me Eric.'

At least Sara knew where Martin had got his fear of ageing from. But then she looked at Marie, who was occupied with checking her makeup, and she realised that he had inherited this disposition from both parents.

'You coming tonight?'

Martin leaned out of the side window, looking expectantly at his father. The son's insatiable need for affirmation, Sara thought to herself, before immediately feeling cruel. Of course people wanted their parents' appreciation, even if they were nearly fifty and heading up a major company.

'Of course,' Marie replied. 'It's your big day. And we're not allowed to Ebba's housewarming.' The grandmother smiled kindly at her grandchild. Sara wondered how she managed to be so happy all the time. What did she run on? Sherry? Lifelong self-deception? Or just a perfect childhood? There was something about her mother-in-law Marie that reminded her of a thoroughbred. Carefully bred and dressed and meticulously turned out to ensure she always put in a top performance. No decline to be seen there.

'It's friends only,' Ebba said, smiling sweetly. 'You can come next time.'

Sara could never make out whether Ebba truly loved her paternal grandparents or whether she was just careful to secure her flow of presents. At any rate, she knew Ebba would have been angry if she had asked the question.

Sara watched the big black car pulling away with Ebba and Eric inside it. Not once had her daughter asked for a lesson with Sara. She probably assumed her mother would be impatient and get angry with her, but in reality it was Ebba who got angry at Sara. She was quite simply at that age where you projected all your anger onto your surroundings. Sara wasn't quite sure that she had ever left that age herself. But she could always hope.

The Maserati turned right down onto Östgötagatan – Stockholmers always pronounced the 'g' in göta wrong. Getting it right was proof you were a country bumpkin.

And then they were gone.

The next time she saw Ebba, her daughter would no longer be living at home.

Her own apartment and a proper job. With her grandpa.

Sara realised she was a little envious. It was too bloody easy to sidle in with presents whenever it suited, while avoiding the constant battles at home. Eric had probably been like that with Martin too – constantly working while Martin grew up, avoiding all the quarrels over getting him up in the mornings, getting him off to kindergarten and to school, getting him to do his homework. And now here he was, proffering his silver spoon again, pockets filled with cash. It was so easy to buy love.

Would she have to fight her father-in-law for her family? Ebba seemed to be lost, but Sara wasn't the sort to give in.

Shortly after, Martin also pulled away, while Olle was completely absorbed in some YouTube clip – probably featuring Uncle Scam. So the men were out of the picture, and the move would have to be handled by the good old matriarchy. Albeit a rather diverse selection of matriarchs.

'Well,' said Sara. 'I guess that leaves Mum and two grandmas to do it all?'

'Martin and Eric did buy the furniture,' Marie said, in defence of the men.

The furniture. Of course. Sara had found loads of decent, second-hand furniture cheaply online, but Ebba wanted nothing but designer furniture. Nineteen years old, in her first apartment – bought for her by Daddy – with a five million kronor price tag. Good God. Sara had really resolved to put a stop to it all and make Ebba sort her own accommodation out, but after the tragedy at the Bromans she hadn't been able to go against her family. All she'd wanted was to show them her love because she had been so vanishingly close to never seeing them again. Now all she wanted was to be with them as much as possible. And that had included, amongst other things, accepting Martin's and Eric's senseless waste. For now, at least.

'Yes, yes,' said Sara, giving up. One advantage to Ebba buying everything new was that there wasn't much to carry inside right now. 'Well, let's get on with it then. Can you take the shelves and Olle and I will take the bed?'

'Why don't we call a removal company?' Marie said, looking around.

'No, we're going to do this. Then we'll get coffee here in the square and christen Ebba's flat without her.'

Jane nodded her assent. And against that united front, Marie could offer no opposition.

5

Sara was really supposed to have started at nine, but she had been allowed take a half day in lieu to help Ebba with her move. Then Anna had called and Sara had picked up, which her friend had lauded her for – not without irony. Anna had asked her to come into work as quickly as possible because there had been a dramatic shootout with three dead and one hurt in Ekerö. Anna had sent her a map with a pin dropped on the location. Sara fetched her car from the car park on Slottsbacken. Martin had his big, bright yellow Lamborghini Urus, but Sara refused to share it with him – the shame of showing up in an inferiority complex on wheels would have finished her. Instead, she got behind the wheel of her nippy little Golf GTI and followed the directions out of the city centre towards the crime scene.

On the way, she realised that she felt a certain reluctance about going to work. She would have preferred to withdraw from it, to be together with her family or alone with her thoughts. But she was eager to make a good impression – more than anything else, she didn't want her boss to regret approving her transfer. Now she got to work with her best friend, and quite honestly she had no idea how she would have managed otherwise. Family, Anna and solitude – those were the three things keeping her going.

She was struck by how rural the landscape became as soon as she had crossed the Nockebybron bridge, just a few minutes' drive from the city centre. On the day that Stellan Broman had been murdered, Sara had gone to Brostugan, the café on Kärsön island, to gather her thoughts, but she had no memory of ever coming further this way than Drottningholm. After the palace, the road was lined with fields and meadows and woods.

But then the idyll was interrupted by a huge set of roadworks: the tunnelling project to build an underground motorway bypassing central Stockholm. Yet another pyramid built with the dynamite of the contemporary era; overgrown construction projects as monuments to the otherwise wholly anonymous bureaucrats of the age. A long tunnel, then several fields and a hillock covered in oak trees. After passing through central Ekerö, the road led up onto a ridge with Lake Mälaren far below. And a beautiful church. Inconceivably beautiful. How could people want to shoot each other dead here?

After passing the exit for Ekerö sommarstad and rounding a sharp bend, she spotted Anna standing on the verge halfway up a long straight section, waving. Sara pulled over and lowered her window.

'I know,' said Anna. 'God, isn't it beautiful?'

'Isn't it just?' said Sara. 'I had no idea.'

Anna jumped into her car and Sara drove behind her up a small slope and into the woods on a gravel track. First there were lots of slender, tall birch trees that must all have been planted at the same time, then an open section for power lines and a hand-painted sign that read 'Unmetalled road, no HGVs'. Then the pine forest grew thicker and finally they reached a new open expanse with hunting towers visible at either end, a turning circle and a sign labelled 'pothole'. Standing on the turning circle was a host of police cars and ambulances.

They got out of their cars and went over to the blue and white police tape and the forensics team in their overalls. On the far side of a wooded hillock, Sara glimpsed Mälaren through the trees, while to the right of her was a parked SUV. One of the few times a set of stockbroker's wheels like this had been driven in proper terrain, she thought to herself.

Beyond the car, up the hill in the direction of the lake, were three bodies that were being photographed and examined by forensics.

One of the bodies had been rolled up in several layers of black plastic that had been unwound by the police.

Sara had never been able to get used to the sight of dead bodies. So incomprehensible, so unnatural. Despite death actually being one of the most natural things in the world, there was something so alien about a dead body. A body was made to live – to work. And the thought that someone had intentionally put an end to a life was still so hard to grasp. Even now, when she herself had killed. That had been in extreme circumstances, and she knew that she had still not fully processed it. Perhaps she ought to talk to a psychologist? At any rate, this was a comprehensible case – an encounter between criminals. Probably drug-related.

'The two not covered in plastic have a gunshot wound each in the centre of their foreheads,' said Anna, putting an index finger to her own brow and nodding in a way that disclosed a certain admiration for the marksmanship.

'Execution?' said Sara.

'Housewife,' said Anna with a smile.

'What?'

'The two without plastic opened fire on three hunters who approached them on foot. One of the hunters was hit and is in hospital right now, one fled, and one shot back. Two shots. Bull's eye.'

'And it was a housewife who took the shots?'

'Her first hunt,' said Anna, pointing discreetly towards a police minibus where a middle-aged woman was sitting beside a female police officer. A little rotund, with a distinctive blunt cut fringe and purple-rimmed spectacles, khaki clothing and a cap with a bright yellow band around it.

'Gunilla Larsson,' Anna said. 'She was out hunting with her husband's group for the first time. Says she's good on the range, but never thought she'd be able to shoot a person.'

'Or two. Who are the dead guys?'

'So far: muscular and tattooed. But no Swedish tattoos. Lots of crosses and Madonnas, and some football team, I think. The car has Polish plates, so I guess that's where they're from. We've sent the registration number and photos of them to Interpol and the Polish police. And we're checking cameras at road tolls to see whether we can find them. But the really awful bit is the guy in the plastic. Young lad who's really been worked over, must be at least fifty cuts and stab wounds. And – wait for it – his fingers have been cut off.'

'Charming.'

'There's still a gold chain around his neck and a mobile in his pocket, so they weren't after money.'

'Were they going to dump him in the lake?'

'We think so. Body wrapped in plastic, and they had chains and other stuff in the car to weigh it down. And one of them had a key to a boat that's down by the shore.'

'They've got a boat tied up? Maybe they've done this before.'

'Shit – thank goodness you said that. We would never have thought of that ourselves. Lucky for us you came to Västerort, otherwise we'd have been scratching our heads.'

It took Sara a moment to recognise the irony.

'Sorry, I didn't mean . . . Well.'

Anna grinned at her.

'Did it go OK?'

Chief Inspector Axel Bielke, neatly turned out as ever in a well-fitted suit and a tie with a Windsor knot, as well as shiny black shoes, was suddenly beside them. His grey-flecked hair was cut short in a military style, and his pale blue eyes were surveying Sara intensely. It was a penetrating gaze – Sara had always thought so. But she liked it. It made her feel seen. Scrutinised, but above all seen. Bielke had a strong presence. The only thing that disrupted the overall positive impression was the signet ring on his little finger. She knew it to be a family ring, but it still bothered her. Or perhaps that was why. What family did she have to brag about? A horrible rapist for a father, and a mother who seemed to think she did most stuff wrong. For a brief moment, her thoughts turned to Agneta, Stellan's wife and a deadly double agent. On so many occasions, Sara had dreamed that she and Stellan were her real parents during the summers she had spent in their luxurious home in Bromma. And the dream had actually turned out to be half true. Sometimes the worst thing that could happen was to get what you wished for, Sara thought to herself.

'What?' she said, pushing these thoughts aside as Bielke looked at her encouragingly.

'The move.'

'Oh, yes. She's finally out. We now have a spare room. Need somewhere to stay? I can offer you a good price.'

There was no laugh from Bielke. Not even a smile. He wasn't the sort to engage in small talk – instead he left it to ring out unanswered and said what was on his own mind. When other people did that, it was all too easy to feel stupid, bleating and frivolous, but with Bielke it was somehow all right. It felt more like he was focusing on what actually mattered.

Bielke was basically the direct opposite of Sara: controlled, thoughtful, faultless. And he was a good boss. Not at all like Sara's last boss, Lindblad, who had more or less managed to get her fired. Sara was grateful that Bielke had approved her application for a transfer to Västerort, despite her being on the receiving end of a disciplinary action for getting her headstrong self mixed up in the murder of Stellan Broman. If she hadn't managed to stop Abu Rasil, she would probably have been dismissed. Perhaps the move to Västerort was a way of getting back to her roots, given everything she had found out about her own childhood. She had grown up in the west of Stockholm – in Bromma and then Vällingby. Or perhaps it was working together with her best friend from the police academy, Anna, that had been the lure. Her BCFF, as they usually put it. Best Cop Friends Forever.

'Might it have anything to do with the motorbike club that's based that way?' said Sara, with a gesture.

'None of them look much like bikers,' said Anna. 'But the guy in the plastic wrap apparently had gang tattoos of some kind.'

'The two meatheads don't look like gangsters.'

'They don't look like maths teachers either. Let's guess a drug lord turf war? Competing criminals, anyway.'

'Do you think the woman who shot them is in any danger? That anyone will want revenge?'

'She's going to receive police protection,' Bielke said.

'For how long?'

'As long as we can.'

Sara knew that wasn't very long. They would just have to hope that the groups the two heavies belonged to wanted to maintain a low profile.

'We were talking about the fact that they seem to have done this before,' said Sara, turning to Bielke. 'Dumping bodies, I mean. Given that they had a boat tied up.'

'I've requested divers. But it's a big lake to search.'

Sara stared across Lake Mälaren beyond the hillock. She wondered what they would find beneath that innocent, mirror-smooth surface.

6

'New kitchen? Get your loan approved instantly! FHO Bank.'

Julius Schönberg put on the reading glasses which were hanging on a chain around his neck and read the text message while the large iron gates in front of the house slid open. He adjusted his bow-tie, slightly absent-mindedly placed his pipe in the cupholder between the front seats and contemplated his home while reflecting on the meaning of the SMS. It was undeniably a beautiful home. The small castle in Pullach Kolbermoor looked old-fashioned with its romantic turrets and ponds filled with water lilies, its carefully laid out parkland and the old stone wall around it all. It was like something from a fairy tale. The original castle had been built in 1430 but it was in no way stuck in the past. In fact, Schloss Pullach was an almost impenetrable fortress with multiple alarm systems, full CCTV coverage including heat cameras and night vision, and a safe room. It featured buried gas canisters whose contents could be released through concealed nozzles across the site, electrified paving and floors that could effectively neutralise intruders. And a respectable quantity of weapons in the hidden safe room.

Whether all these security arrangements were really needed he had no idea, but he appreciated the feeling of assurance they provided – not so much for his own sake, but because he felt it came with his job. It was a sign of his seniority, confirmation of the importance of his work fighting the evil forces that constantly sought to crush free society. It was ironic that those who fought hardest for a free world had to operate in one that was closed and he was glad to have been allowed to keep his systems despite his redeployment. When he retired, they would probably have to be taken away.

The lights along the driveway up to the front of the house illuminated as he approached. If the camera had been unable to read his number plate, powerful floodlights would have come on and dazzled him while an alarm went off inside the house and all doors and windows had locked automatically.

Renate had been amused by the automatic lights and had never had to see the floodlights turned on, as luck would have it. That would probably have made her reconsider the risks that her husband's job entailed, and whether they could truly be lived with.

Schönberg stopped and looked up at the grand building. Twenty-six rooms, three storeys and a splendid tower. A very old building in an austere, classical style. He wondered what it would feel like to live here all alone when he retired in a year or so – a retirement that had been postponed multiple times.

Schönberg reread the text message.

'New kitchen.' That meant that Koch was dead. The chef had been deactivated. 'New car', 'new roof', 'rebuild' and so on stood for a series of old spies and agents. But on this occasion it was the kitchen that mattered.

He parked his Mercedes-AMG G63 and got out, watching the gates close and the stinger strip outside sink back into the ground again. No tails to stop this time either. The motion-detecting cameras followed every step he took as he approached the manor, and the facial recognition opened the door well before he reached it. He knew that it could tell the difference between his calm facial expression and the same face if he were very stressed or frightened. A vital feature to protect against extortion or hostage situations.

He had once triggered the alarm when he had just heard that his goddaughter had been run over and he still didn't know whether she was unharmed. On that occasion, his face had apparently displayed so much mental distress that the system had reacted. Five cars filled with armed personnel had driven over from the old headquarters at breakneck speed, while two helicopters had been diverted to rescue him. At least he now knew that the system worked.

Once inside the echoing, magnificent hall with its shiny stone floor and vaulted staircase to the upper floors, he opened the cloak-room door concealed behind an oak panel. He put the palm of his hand onto the scanner and his eye in front of the small sensor that was almost hidden behind a beam. Noiselessly, a section of the wall opened itself. He pushed his coats aside and stepped into the safe room, which constituted its own structure within the house. It was fully clad in metal, a cocoon that could withstand explosions and fire. If anyone burned down the house, the safe room would remain unharmed amidst the smouldering remains. The cables ran through fireproof conduits straight into the ground – impossible to access unless you moved the entire castle.

There were several rows of screens, some dark but most of them constantly switched on. This represented both the castle's own security system and that of German intelligence – the BND's inter-nal systems – including the part that only those personnel with the highest security clearance were permitted to connect to. Now he was finally able to receive confirmation from his colleagues in the new headquarters in Berlin that the former Stasi officer, Jürgen Stiller, code-named Koch, had been found dead in his home in Sweden.

When Stiller hadn't shown up for a baptism, the agitated grand-father of the child in question had made his way to the vicarage and there he had found him hanging in the kitchen. His wife, it was discovered shortly afterwards, was lying upstairs – stabbed to death. The local police were working on the theory, so Schönberg was informed, that the uncovering of the old spy ring that the priest had been in had triggered old traumas, and that he had either believed his life to be in ruins, or he had simply been so tormented by his guilty conscience that he had taken his own life.

On the floor beside the pastor they had found a bloody knife that had been used to kill his wife, Karin. That he had killed his wife first was interpreted as an attempt to spare her the shame, or else indicated that she had said something that had enraged him so much that he had stabbed her to death with the kitchen knife and then hanged himself in regret.

On the kitchen table there had been a Bible opened to the passage in which Judas takes his own life, which the Swedes had assumed to be a sign that Stiller had felt himself to be a traitor. But Schönberg knew exactly what the message meant. It was an altogether different Judas who had been on the scene. Or rather, it had been a devil.

The important thing, nonetheless, was that it was regarded as a suicide. That was very good.

Hopefully, it meant the end of the BND's operations in Sweden, allowing them to concentrate on other countries – the ones that actually mattered in this context.

And hopefully it meant that Rau's identity remained protected. He just hoped that Nowak woman – not to mention Hedin – didn't stick their noses in. They had been the ones who had tipped off the police about Stiller when the old spooks had begun to be knocked off one by one in the early summer.

Schönberg leaned back in his ergonomic office chair and wondered whether he should do anything about Nowak and Hedin.

He realised he probably should.

7

When they finally wrapped up in Ekerö, they returned to the police station in Solna. Sara's new place of work was in a red brick building situated between Sundbybergsvägen and the commuter train line. During her lunch breaks, she often sat alone in the small empty park behind the Huvudstagrillen fast-food joint, her mobile set to silent. She had been overcome by a strong need to simply sit down and think. And here she was able to do so. She could think about everything she had experienced and the choices that had led her to where she was today. She liked hearing the warning signals from the level crossing and the trains swishing past. The signs of life and movement that the city pulsed with. Sometimes, she heard the sound of chainsaws as tree surgeons in neon vests cut down branches that had grown across the rails. Small, everyday trivialities that made it easier to resurface. She always spent a while standing in front of the small white sculpture known as 'Pregnant', if only because it was a rarity that anyone else did. The body that had borne two children had also been pierced by bullets. Ebba and Olle had come close to losing their mother. And Sara had put herself in that danger. How could she weigh up the happiness of her own children against that of all the people whose lives Sara had presumably saved? And *if* Sara had died, would it have been any comfort to Ebba and Olle that lots of people in another country had been saved? People who would never know how close disaster had come to striking? Sara couldn't escape the gnawing suspicion that she had done the wrong thing, even though it had all ended well.

Once the team were back in Solna and had gathered in the meeting room, they reviewed what they already knew, which wasn't much. The gang crime unit had been sent photos of the badly mauled victim, but hadn't had time to respond yet. Perhaps it was hard to identify a face that badly mangled. Neither Interpol nor the Polish police had been in touch about the photos of the other two deceased persons or the number plates on their car. Sara called those amongst her contacts who were most familiar with the struggle for power in the underworld and asked whether they knew anything about any antagonism between Poles and gangs in the Stockholm suburbs, but she turned up nothing. Of course, the conflict might be brand new. If they could just identify the guy, they would probably be able to uncover the truth.

They followed the usual procedure. They reviewed probable motives and connections, wrote it all up on the whiteboard with question marks appended, distributed assignments and then went home. Now it was a case of waiting for information retrieved from the mobiles of the dead, the identification of any one of them or finding the car on traffic cameras which would allow them to trace it back to a point of departure. There were no doors for door-to-door inquiries in the woods.

So Sara clocked off early, went home, showered and got dressed in her glad rags. For Martin's sake, she put on a couple of the pricy garments he insisted on buying for her from the luxury boutiques on Birger Jarlsgatan. As far as she was concerned, Sara thought it was absurd to traipse around in a layer of fabric that had cost half a month's pay. Martin only bought presents for Sara at Schuterman, Prada or Gucci. Or possibly at the NK department store so that he could show off his black NK card. What was the matter with H&M? Well, Sara knew what it was. The conditions for the factory workers. Well, what about something in between then? She lined up the latest gifts, removing a gold-coloured leather top and a pair of beautiful trousers with a blue and yellow flower print from the reckoning. Her eye was caught by a black skirt with white pearls forming a floral pattern, to which she added a black crepe blouse where the sections over the arms and shoulders were made from a fine gauze, or whatever they called it. The ensemble was suitably dressy for an anniversary party.

How could it have been twenty years since Martin had launched his company – Dunder & Brak Scenproduktion AB? He had done it mostly to create opportunities for himself to perform, since so few people wanted to book him – not as a one-man band or as a stand-up rookie. But when Martin had started putting together bespoke packages of artists, he had discovered that he was shit-hot at finding good acts, selling them and managing the whole thing, packaging tours with catchy names and attention-grabbing concepts. And there were plenty of artists and entertainers who needed help with that bit in particular.

After ten years of toil as an aspiring artist, and five years as a tour producer, Martin had been the biggest concert organiser in the country, and shortly thereafter his company had become one of the biggest artist agencies. And then, all of a sudden, he'd been noticed on the global scene. The entertainment giant Go Live had bought Martin's company for a fortune on the condition that Martin stayed on to lead it for at least another ten years. After that, the pressure on Sara's husband had increased even more. As part of an international conglomerate, the Swedish branch had gained access to the really big names, and most of Martin's working hours were spent entertaining and hanging out with artists, bosses and agents. Lunches, dinners and late nights. Constantly surrounded by young girls who wanted to carve out careers and thought it was the norm to attract sexual attention in order to succeed. Sara had occasionally been overcome with jealousy, but was mostly convinced that Martin wasn't like that. Sure, he wanted attention – a great deal of it – but not like that.

A lot of the money Martin had been paid for his company had gone on the huge apartment they lived in, which covered a full storey of their building on the edge of Kornhamnstorg in Stockholm's old town. Nearly three hundred square metres of creaking parquet, oak panelling, a terrace and their own tower at the top of the building from which they had a view across the rooftops, the water down by Slussen and the German church just around the corner from them.

After all his years of desperately trying to gain his father's attention by performing on stage, Martin had finally succeeded in the same way Eric had: in business. He had single-handedly built up a respected and profitable company, becoming rich in the process, yet it didn't seem to be enough for either his father or Martin. But that was surely how it was for everyone who wanted to show they were good enough? They would never be satisfied, merely struggling more and more. Where this need came from Sara had no idea, but she assumed the old cliché was correct: a father married to his job and rarely at home, and a little boy missing his father. Eric had at any rate compensated for his absence from Martin's childhood with a greater presence in Ebba's. A bit too much if she were honest about it, Sara thought to herself.

*

'Beer? Wine? Cocktail?'

'I'm fine thanks.'

Sara held up her glass by way of proof. The girl smiled and moved on.

'Beer? Wine? Cocktail?'

Sara spotted another one inbound and held up her glass from a distance.

Everywhere there were young girls. On the bar and at the door, mixing among the guests with trays of glasses, and hostesses wandering around and checking that everything was going well, that empties were being removed and that the schedule was being adhered to. The latter were spotlessly dressed in black suits instead of the waiting staff's short black skirts and white shirts. But they were all young girls. Employed by Go Live. How many of them had their own dreams of becoming artists, and how many just wanted to have power over other people's careers?

'Oi,' said Sara, firmly elbowing Anna in the side when she saw her friend's avid gaze taking in the young girls. 'Can't you see how practised their smiles are?'

'You don't know the code. That look was me being hit on.'

'I don't know the code in your world, but I know the code in this world. She probably knows that I'm Martin's wife, and that you're with me, so it may be a shortcut to the boss. Don't be too flattered.'

Sara realised she was a bit downhearted that Anna was with her at the party. Not that she didn't like Anna, she was her best friend – but because when Martin had asked if Sara wanted to bring anyone to the party, she had realised that she only had one friend to ask. She needed to get more friends – but how did you do that as a grown-up?

'Cool!' said Anna, looking around the resplendent garden. 'What's this shindig costing, do you reckon?'

Sara followed Anna's gaze and only now noticed quite how expensive it all was. Flags, pennants, bar tables covered in white cloths, bottles of beer and champagne everywhere, a string quartet on a small podium, and massive, enlarged photos from the company's history featuring all the big artists they represented or had worked with. Paparazzi were thronging outside the gates to document the celebrity gathering, while the guests basked in the attention.

The party reminded Sara of Stellan's and Agneta's many expensive events at which the celebrities of the day had mingled, just as happy to be there as the guests tonight were. Sara had hidden with Lotta and Malin, spending hours spying on the dressed up and madly smiling adults who became increasingly peculiar as the evening progressed. Now she was a guest – indeed, the wife of the host. Just like Agneta had been in her day. Was she becoming Agneta? She couldn't help smiling at the thought that cropped up momentarily.

Sara felt like she was being watched, but reflected that it was probably normal given all the photographers there craning their necks to see who was in attendance. And who *wasn't* there. The guests tonight really did live diametrically opposed lives to the spies that Sara had encountered. The spies did everything to avoid being seen or attracting attention. Some of them even had several layers of false identities behind which to hide, such as Agneta Broman. But the guests here were doing their all to be seen.

'To be without being seen.' The motto of the Wallenberg family popped up in her head. Those that held true power, who governed the world, didn't want to be seen. Regardless of whether they were a spy or an industrialist. That was where the gulf between Martin and Eric was most obvious, Sara thought to herself, looking around for her husband. The son was doing his utmost to be seen and the father was conversely doing all he could to avoid being seen. To run his empire in peace.

'Have they bought the building?' said Anna, interrupting Sara's train of thought.

'It's a lease. There was some university department renting it, but they moved out, and then Martin managed to talk his way into getting the lease. But it costs a fair whack each month, and that's putting it mildly.'

Go Live now had its offices in a huge old mansion on the royal island of Djurgården, just opposite the Nordic Museum. It was a building that Sara had walked past many times when she had been younger, heading for the theme park at Gröna Lund or a picnic further along the island. She remembered how imposing she'd thought the building was, and now her husband's company was based in it. Odd how things could turn out . . .

Go Live had invited twelve hundred guests to its twentieth birthday party, and had received more than one thousand acceptances before being overwhelmed with emails and phone calls from people who hadn't been invited but wanted to try and get in anyway. An open bar, loads of celebrities and in all likelihood a performance by at least one global star. Go Live had plenty of those on its books. A big stage had been built to the rear of the building with a massive lighting rig and sound system that practically screamed superstar rather than cover band.

Sara scrutinised the other guests. Thin, tanned women, either around twenty or over forty years old, standing beside men of around fifty in expensive blazers and big sunglasses, their hair combed back and the shirts that strained over their bellies unbuttoned far too far down. Loud laughter and lots of kissing of cheeks. Every artist ever to have played on a Go Live stage was here. The younger, more impressionable figures naturally became intoxicated immediately. The older ones, chuckling, were all in late middle age, some of them indeed older, and now making their livings from best-of tours for their equally aged fans.

The queues for the buffets were enormous, and guests were loading as much as they could onto their plates. Free is the best flavour, Sara thought to herself, explaining to Anna that they should wait until the queues got shorter.

'Uncle Scam,' Anna said, nodding to a poster emblazoned with the artist's name against a background of countless green dollar bills. 'He's playing here this week.'

'I know. Martin's so proud he could burst. I barely know who he is.'

'Only the biggest artist in the world right now. Do you think he's going to play here tonight? Isn't there supposed to be some secret headliner? A superstar or something?'

'Yes, there's going to be a performance, but I don't know who by.'

'Hoping it's Uncle Scam. Do you think we'll get to meet him?'

'You like hip-hop?'

'I like everything. But my sister's kids would be really fucking impressed. They think I'm a rat for being a cop.'

'If he's here I'm sure we can arrange it.'

'Yay!'

'Aren't you going to have something to eat?'

Martin's mother, Marie, appeared at their sides clutching a plate of grilled asparagus and a glass of wine in a holder attached to the plate.

'The queues are too long,' Sara said, but Marie merely smiled.

'Martin sent off a girl to get some for us.'

Of course. Eric Titus and his wife were hardly ones to stand in a queue. Sara looked around for the great man himself. He had been caught by some gentlemen whose faces were familiar to Sara from the business pages: two men approaching seventy with self-assured smiles and permanent sun tans, one with a wife the same age and the other with a wife half his age. A fairly representative selection of Eric's circle, in other words. There were a lot of executives who liked to rub shoulders with celebrities, and Sara knew that Martin liked to help Eric out by inviting his business associates to big parties and by providing VIP tickets to various concerts. Eric smiled professionally, nodding to the two couples before rejoining his wife.

'How lovely that you could come,' said Sara. 'I'm sure Martin will be thrilled. You've met Anna, haven't you?'

'I would remember if I had,' Eric said with a smile. 'I remember every beautiful woman that I meet.' However, being a gentleman, he allowed Marie to shake her hand first.

'We were at the academy together and now we're colleagues.'

'Hope things have calmed down for you,' Eric said, nodding at Anna in admonition, as if urging her to ensure that Sara didn't place herself in the same danger she had done at the beginning of the summer.

'We take on nothing but the safest cases,' said Anna with a small laugh. 'Lost property, missing cats, stolen bicycles.'

'That sounds good.'

'This asparagus is delicious,' Marie said enthusiastically.

The sounds of a chord being played on a guitar hooked up to a few hundred kilograms of amplifiers made everyone rush to the stage at the rear of the building. No one wanted to miss whichever global superstar was going to play unannounced. The secrecy was a big part of the bragging that would follow.

Anna ran with the others, while Sara sauntered along after her. She realised that her lack of interest was in part feigned – a somewhat pubescent desire not to be visibly impressed, to demonstrate her lack of interest in celebrities and stars.

'Don't worry,' she heard Martin's voice say over the sound system, 'there's some proper entertainment coming soon. But first you're going to have to put up with us for half an hour.'

Martin's employees hooted, probably hoping someone in senior management would notice their loyalty. The rest of the audience smiled politely. They understood this was the price they paid. But they would rather not have bothered.

'We're called C.E.O. Speedwagon,' Martin said on stage, surrounded by his bandmates. 'And when you're a bunch of execs, what better way to start than with a song by the Boss himself, Bruce Springsteen?'

Nicky and Stoffe played the intro to 'Dancing in the Dark' and immediately received polite applause. Martin leaned forward to the microphone and began to sing.

Hands in the air, clapping in time, a small sea of audience swaying along. Martin was glowing. More than a thousand people, and no one could do anything but show their appreciation. Sara saw her husband's gaze seeking out his parents time after time. Their free period in sixth form kept coming back to her. At least once a month, Martin would stand on stage in front of the whole school. Singing, joking or doing sketches. He wasn't much of a leader ordinarily, but his energy on stage meant that despite this he assumed a leadership role in the school. That, together with his appearance, made him the hottest guy there. The one everyone wanted – and the one Sara got. Although that had been a few years later when Sara had been living in Vällingby for some time and when both she and Martin had finished sixth form, so there hadn't been many people to impress by then. But Sara convinced herself that the most important thing was what she herself felt. And she almost always managed to persuade herself that it felt right.

She reflected on their early days as a couple and what happened when you got together with someone. The way you built your own world together. You acquired shared experiences, defined views, decided who you were together. Sara remembered their pet names for each other. It had been so long since they had used them. The names were a secret that welded them together. Pet names weren't something to be used in the presence of others – that would mean the names lost their power. And with a secret pet name, you suddenly became a different person – someone better, someone loved. They had applied new labels to themselves and each other and, as if by magic, simply by stating it, they had become the person they had depicted for the benefit of the other. Shazam – Billy Batson was transformed into Captain Marvel. Although more romantic.

Sara could tell that Martin was brimming over in the moment, which was only right. Although she wasn't at all entertained by parties like this, she was pleased that someone in the family could share his big moment. Olle was too young and was sleeping over at his friend Gabriel's, while Ebba was throwing her housewarming party at her new apartment.

Did Sara have any counterpart to Martin's stage horniness? Was there something that drove her? What was the most fun thing she knew? Sparring with her Krav Maga club was the answer that came to her spontaneously. God, what did that say about her? But she couldn't actually think of anything better. When she thought about it some more, she realised that she was tempted to take her training to a more ambitious level again. The fight at the Bromans' house had made her realise that life might end at any moment, and that she had to be able to defend herself. It didn't have to be international terrorists – all it could take was an aggressive pisshead out on the town who unexpectedly pulled a knife and went for it. It vexed her that she had never got Ebba to do self-defence training.

'Thanks for a lovely evening.'

Marie stopped in front of Sara and Anna and smiled at them. She was heading for the exit, and a little ahead of her was Eric waving goodbye.

Sara gave Marie the hug protocol demanded. Over her mother-in-law's shoulder, she saw that Martin had noticed his parents were in motion. He gesticulated to the others in the band and they quickly drew their number to a close. There was polite but fairly loud applause. Martin was both an important figure in the entertainment industry and a well-liked boss.

'Dad, wait!' Martin shouted into the microphone. Sara watched her parents-in-law and saw Marie stop Eric with a hand on his arm. They turned back towards their middle-aged son far away on the stage. Martin was talking to his bandmates and then he turned back to the microphone.

'Do you remember this one?'

Nicky began to hammer the keys with the introduction to Abba's 'Money, Money, Money' and Martin smiled expectantly as he began.

Eric smiled politely, offered a thumbs up and then turned around to leave. Marie waved to her son and followed her husband.

Martin was left behind, singing about the importance of money.

It was a bit too much for Sara. She dragged Anna round to the front of the building and the almost deserted bar. A couple of glasses of wine to get over the embarrassment, she told Anna.

They raised their glasses and clinked them while the refrain echoed out across Djurgården. 'Money, money, money, must be funny, in the rich man's world.'

*

At around midnight, both Pink and Ed Sheeran had performed and the guests at the party were becoming more than a little sloshed. Sara was due to work the next day, so she told Anna she was going to head home. Martin would be just fine, she knew that. It was Go Live's evening, and in that context she was no more than a walk-on. Anna, however, wanted to stay a little longer, so they said goodbye and Sara left. She walked all the way home. Along Strandvägen, across the Strömbron bridge and then Skeppsbron, and home to the old town.

On the way to a home without Ebba.

Why did it feel so lonely?

The whole apartment had felt so different after the events of the early summer. As if their secure fortress could no longer protect her and her family, or so she had concluded when she had returned home from the hospital with her face bandaged. As if she had let in evil forces after her battle with the ghosts of the past. When she was at home alone, it felt in some diffuse way as if there were something there, something she couldn't quite put her finger on. Anna, who was obsessed with the occult, obviously thought it was the souls of the people who had lived there previously haunting them. Dead people who couldn't find peace or who had a message for Sara – she just had to let them speak. Sara assumed the disquieting feeling came from within. But she didn't know what to do about the problem. The solitude that had always been reassuring in the past now felt more melancholy, at least when she was at home. In other locations, the solitude was helpful for her recovery, but at home there was so much that reminded her of everything she had lost and of the life she had lived before, when she had still felt invulnerable.

'Where is she?'

Sara had just reached out with her hand to tap in the code when a figure emerged from the shadows and lobbed its question at her.

Sara turned towards the voice to be confronted with Malin Broman's wide eyes. Malin – her childhood friend. The youngest daughter of Uncle Stellan, who had been murdered so unexpectedly and brutally in his home, and who Sara had discovered was a monster in human form. She swept her gaze over the woman before her. Malin's usually meticulous makeup was smudged around the eyes and her skin looked pale and washed out, as if it were winter.

'Which one?'

'Lotta. I know where Mum is. She's dead.'

'I don't know where Lotta is. Hasn't she been in touch?'

'She emails.'

'Well, there you are,' said Sara.

'No. It's not her.'

'What?'

'It's not her writing them. It's someone else.'

'What if she's still in shock? There must be a reason she left. Perhaps she took all that stuff with Stellan and Agneta harder than you thought,' Sara said after a brief pause.

'She'd never leave like that without talking to me. Or to Petter. Without saying good bye to the kids.'

'I don't know what to say.'

'And there are people sitting in cars. Out in the street. Outside our house. All night. Who are they?' Malin stared at her, wide-eyed.

'Don't know. Could be anyone. Doesn't have to be anything to do with you.'

'They are. They're watching us. Taking photos when we come and go. They've been there for days now.'

'Probably just photographers from the gossip rags.'

'What actually happened that night?' Malin took a few steps closer to Sara and looked imploringly at her. Sara noticed that the younger Broman daughter was trembling, looked to be on the verge of tears.

'Tell me!'

'What little I know I'm not allowed to tell you. But I don't know anything about Lotta. I promise. Where she's gone, I don't know.'

'They said they found Mum, shot by the same burglar as Dad. But where did they find her? And where had she been? I didn't even get to see her. Why didn't I get to see her?' Malin's voice was becoming increasingly shrill.

Sara didn't reply. She had no idea what to say. She really didn't know a thing about what had happened to Lotta – Geiger, going by her code name.

'Are you absolutely sure that Lotta didn't write those emails herself?' she finally asked. 'Traumatic events can change a person a lot.'

'I've only got her!' Malin said, her voice filled with desperation. 'Mum and Dad are gone. I want Lotta!'

Sara reflected that Malin actually had a husband and two kids too, but she didn't say anything. She looked at her old childhood playmate, remembering all the sisters' malevolence that had resurfaced in her brain lately, but was still overcome by a strong sense of sympathy for Malin. She was so lost now that her usual protectors weren't there to take care of her. She wasn't spoilt Malin, but a little girl who had lost so many of her closest loved ones in one blow and couldn't understand what had happened. All she sensed was that something was dreadfully wrong. And it really was – that much Sara had discovered. But she couldn't tell Malin that, since she'd been forced to sign a non-disclosure agreement. Her childhood friend was oblivious to Sara's presence and significant involvement in the resolution of the Geiger drama at the Broman family home.

'There's one more thing,' Malin said, as if she didn't quite know what she was asking. 'There were a couple of weird cops who came round to the house.'

'Weird? Aren't all police weird?'

Malin didn't even notice the joke.

'A man and a woman, slightly older. They said they wanted to talk about Dad, but they asked loads of questions about Lotta.

Asked whether she'd told me anything about politics and contacts abroad. I mean . . . what's that got to do with Dad's murder?'

'They have to investigate every angle. That means there's a lot of questions that at first glance seem pointless. Did they say where they were from?'

'Just the police, and they flashed their badges. Well, she did.'

'What were they called?'

'I don't know about him. But she was called Brundin. She never gave her first name.'

'Malin . . .'

'Yes?'

A glimmer of hope was visible in the other woman's eyes.

'I promise I don't know a thing about where Lotta is or what she's doing. All I've heard is that she's taking some time out. But I'll see whether I can discover anything.'

Sara was reminded of the glow from the burning shed and how it had illuminated Brundin as she'd dragged Lotta to one of the Security Service's cars before driving off. Sara had seen Lotta one more time after that. One final time – one she could never talk to anyone else about. And that she hadn't really understood.

She didn't know how to interpret what they had done with Lotta.

'Worst case, we have gang warfare in progress.'

Sara was sitting clutching a mug of coffee while listening to Axel Bielke. She felt far more alert than she had feared after some half dozen alcoholic beverages. Anna, on the other hand, looked like she hadn't slept in a fortnight. She was sitting there nodding along and seemed totally worn out. Martin had got home at half past seven in the morning, absolutely hammered and practically euphoric. With Ed Sheeran's autograph scrawled on his chest in black marker pen, and hearts drawn around each nipple. Sara had helped him into bed, given him a kiss and left for work.

Now she was sitting in the white meeting room together with her colleagues. White walls, white furniture and a whiteboard that was far too white; bottles of mineral water and a bowl of fruit. As if a nineties aesthetic was what the Swedish police needed more than anything else. There was, however, nothing aesthetic about the fluorescent strip lighting on the ceiling. Regardless of decade.

'The deceased in the plastic wrap is a guy called Cesar Bekas,' Bielke continued. 'He's a prominent member of a gang in Alby. We don't know who the other two are, but the manner in which Bekas was killed, the way they were going to dump the body and the fact that the duo opened fire on a group of hunters indicates that they weren't exactly law-abiding citizens.'

'Does that mean we can expect revenge?' Sara asked.

'Or perhaps his gang will settle for the fact that the other two men are already dead. Hard to tell, when we have no idea what the conflict was about.'

'What have we got on Bekas then?'

'The usual, I was about to say. Drugs, weapons. He's been questioned on multiple occasions about rumbles between different gangs, but he's never said anything. Went down for the first time as a twelve-year-old when he kept watch while some older boys broke into a corner shop. No punishment at the time, but it meant there were eyes on him.'

'So we should find out more?' asked one of Sara's colleagues, who was sitting beside the sleepy Anna.

'Talk to the other members of the gang, to his friends, family, neighbours. Yes, you know the drill. Ah, yes. The car's been traced. We've been able to map some of their journey. They came via Bromma – it's not clear exactly where they set off from.' Their boss paused and leafed through his papers. 'And the boat. Yes. Apparently it had been there a while, so it's possible it had been used before. I've requested diving assistance, but apparently it's hard to get them out on a Sunday. I'm hoping they'll get started tomorrow. Well, I think that's everything for now.'

Bielke closed his laptop, gathered up his papers and sat down. Sara turned towards Anna, who contorted her face into a grimace.

'How long did you stay?' said Sara.

'Not that long. Until Lina got off.'

'Lina?'

'The waitress.'

'The waitress? The one you said was flirting with you?'

'Yes. And she was, so it turned out.'

'So you went home with her?'

'Not right away. First we had our own crawl of three or four places. Did some shots. Then we went to hers. At about five, half five. I think.'

'So you've had how much sleep?'

'Zero. Not even a minute. You don't fall asleep next to a girl like that.'

Anna smiled, tired but happy.

'What about that TV show?'

Bielke looked up from his papers. It was Ergün who had asked the question. He had even put up his hand like a schoolboy, which looked funny when it was done by a slab of muscle who was one hundred and ninety centimetres tall and weighed in at one hundred and twenty kilos.

'Which one?' Bielke said, looking at him in confusion.

'They wanted to make a show about us.'

'That docusoap?' said their boss, who was either unable or unwilling to conceal his distaste. 'I said no. We're not circus chimps, we're police officers.'

'Pity,' said Ergün, looking genuinely disappointed. 'I mean, not for me, but people are interested. It'd be cool to show them how we do our jobs.'

'They just want to gorge themselves – see people who've been hurt, drunks fighting. I've no desire to encourage such tendencies. It's not the police's job to contribute to public ignorance.'

'It's fun, though,' Ergün said by way of a second attempt. 'I remember watching *Cops* on TV when I was growing up. That's what made me want to join the force. Didn't you watch *Cops*?'

'I'm older than you.'

'What did you like then? My old man says he watched stuff like *Kojak* and *Columbo* in the seventies.'

'I didn't watch Swedish TV.'

Ergün put his index finger to the tip of his nose and Bielke couldn't help smiling.

'No, I'm not being a snob. We didn't live in Sweden when I was growing up. Dad worked abroad.'

'Well, I think it's a shame. People want to see how we do our jobs.'

'I'm sure there are others who will be happy to show off.'

'It's not about showing off.'

'What then?'

'People are just interested.'

Bielke returned to his papers. Sara and Anna got up. Anna did so with some difficulty.

'So can we participate in the capacity of individual officers then?'

Bielke didn't even dignify Ergün's question with a response.

They began with the members of the deceased's gang, in case there was some act of vengeance in the offing. The mobile numbers they'd been given were out of use. These were guys who changed numbers frequently. And on a Sunday morning they were less accessible than usual. The fact that none of them had opened up when Sara and Anna had rung on their doorbells could be because they were paranoid and never opened up to strangers, or because they were actually at war with a rival gang and keeping their heads down, or quite simply because they were hungover and sleeping too deeply to hear the doorbell or someone knocking.

They had the names and addresses of four guys in Cesar Bekas's gang, but no one opened up. And when Sara called the parents she could find details for, all they said was that their son had moved out and they didn't know where he was.

'He might come home for Christmas,' said one father. 'Why don't you call then?' Then he hung up.

They were obviously getting nowhere with the gang members, so they went to the home of the dead man's parents instead – after they had stopped at a hot dog stand so that Anna could buy a fizzy drink and some hangover food.

Devrim Bekas lived on the ninth floor of a block of flats on Servitutsvägen. As far as Sara's prejudices pertaining to the architecture of Alby went, this building was rather tall and drab, reminiscent of her own suburb of Vällingby. On the other hand, it was very well-tended. Just like the shrubs around the building.

Cesar's mother, Devrim, was a woman of about Sara's age, with black hair and a firm, almost strict gaze behind her black-rimmed glasses. She was wearing a black blouse and trousers and clasping a thick book when she opened the door. She looked at Sara and Anna and seemed to realise almost immediately what it was about. She put down the book and greeted them with a curt:

'Come in.'

They followed her into the living room, which was decorated with a mixture of eastern trinkets and IKEA furniture. Gilded mirrors, golden candleholders, tasselled cushions and functional Scandinavian furniture with names like Hemnes and Sollerön. She sat down on the large armchair in the centre of the room while the police officers took the sofa. Devrim waved to someone behind them and Sara turned her head just in time to catch sight of a child disappearing from the doorway back into what must have been a bedroom.

'Your husband?'

'At the university. He's doing research. They're in the final stages now. What's happened?'

'Your son Cesar is dead,' said Sara, letting the words sink in before she carried on. 'And he was murdered. You can call on a talk therapist in the event of tragic deaths like this, and I really would recommend you make use of that help.'

Devrim immediately began to cry. She let the tears run down her cheeks without wiping them away. Sara just sat there, immobile. The woman's eyes were unyielding rather than crushed.

'Who did it?' she said after a while. 'Who killed him?'

'We don't know. Two men were trying to dump the body in Lake Mälaren – that much we're fairly certain of, and those two are also dead, shot by a hunter whom they opened fire on.'

Devrim seemed to be doing her best to digest what she had been told. Sara was unsure whether she had been too detailed. She wondered how it would feel to receive this kind of news herself about her own child. Would she be able to take it in? Would she be able to master her emotions like this mother? Devrim almost seemed to have expected this kind of news, judging by her reaction, or at least she had feared it. For Sara, it had come close to the opposite – one of her colleagues having to come to her home to tell her children that their mother had died. How would the kids have taken it? She had no idea. Would Ebba have been as tough as she always seemed to be? Or would Sara's death have knocked the wind out of her? Sometimes, the person you were angry with was the foundation of your whole life. How Olle would have handled the news she couldn't tell. She didn't know much about the spiritual lives of fourteen-year-old boys. Did they even have them?

'Do you know whether Cesar's gang was at war with anyone else?' said Anna.

'His gang . . .'

'Yes?'

'It wasn't his gang any longer. He'd left it – he wanted to get out of crime. He was good at school. Like all my children. He'd got into an economics degree. Wanted to do his own thing.'

'How did his gang take that?' said Sara, leaning forward on the sofa.

'Not very well. There's so much talk of togetherness, being brothers, loyal to the death. But when Cesar wanted to do his own thing, they got scared.'

'Of what?'

'That he'd succeed. He'd become something.'

'You meant that they . . .?' Anna didn't manage to finish the sentence before the bedroom door opened again and a girl of around five years old emerged clutching a piece of paper.

'I've done a drawing for you,' she said, giving the paper to her mother. Sara caught a glimpse of a shining sun and a princess in a colourful dress. Devrim looked at the drawing and smiled at her daughter.

'Thank you, sweetheart. Isn't that lovely?' Then she turned to Sara and Anna. 'Our afterthought.'

The daughter examined her mother's tears, climbed up onto the armchair and gently wiped them away with her small hands.

'Sweetheart, I need to talk to these ladies. Go back to your room and make me another drawing. Why not a prince or a crocodile? Or a cake! You're so good at drawing cakes.'

'OK.'

The little girl disappeared back into the bedroom and Devrim turned towards the officers.

'Where were we?' she said.

'Togetherness,' said Sara.

'Oh yes.' The woman snorted. 'They show off their cars and watches and weapons and burn through their cash down at the clubs, trying to impress each other and the younger guys, but they're constantly terrified – of being shot. They get paranoid. They numb it with drugs, which only intensifies the anxiety. If they don't get shot, they end up killing themselves.'

Sara and Anna nodded their quiet assent. They waited for the grieving mother to go on.

'They know what's ahead of them. But they can't get out. They say they can't let their mates down. They destroy their chances. Cesar's best friend growing up was an incredible talent on the football pitch. English and German teams wanted to sign him when he was fourteen. Now's he's doing life for shooting someone in another gang. Because his mates told him to do it.' Devrim's voice trembled slightly.

'Are you aware of any specific threats? Has anything happened recently? Perhaps connected to the fact that he wanted to quit?'

'Does it matter? We won't get him back whatever you do. And even if you find out who did this, you won't be able to get a conviction – no one ever talks,' said Devrim, adjusting the three remote controls sitting on a gold platter so that they were all neatly in line with each other. TV, set-top box, Apple TV, Sara thought to herself, wondering why she was bothered by that detail.

'Let us try,' said Anna.

'Why? If you find out who it is, then all it means is that others have to retaliate. You keep the feuds alive. It's absurd, but that's how it is.'

'We're constantly working to break the spiral,' Sara protested.

'I know. You work and you work. But neither you nor we succeed in doing anything about it.'

'"You or we?" You mean parents?'

'I mean us politicians. I'm on the local council in Botkyrka.'

It was the first time Sara had ever encountered a next-of-kin who was willing to share responsibility for gang violence with the police.

'I have to get Ismail to come home,' said Devrim, pulling out her mobile. 'Cesar's little brother,' she explained to Anna and Sara. 'He worshipped Cesar.'

She left a brief message on her son's voicemail. Then she looked at the officers again.

'Would you like us to tell your husband?' said Sara.

'No. I'll do it. Once you've gone.'

Sara understood her and nodded in confirmation. They stood up to leave.

'Have you told Abeba?' said Devrim.

'Who?'

'His girlfriend.'

'No.'

'She's a good girl. She helped Cesar to get away from the gang.' She paused and fresh tears rolled down her cheeks. 'They'd just started planning their wedding . . .'

9

Abeba couldn't stop crying. Her whole body was shaking and the tears just kept flowing as she wailed loudly. It was rare to witness such unbridled grief, Sara thought to herself. It was as if she had feared the worst and built up a huge reservoir of despair, which was now undammed.

She hadn't heard from Cesar in two days, which had made her anxious. She knew the life he led. She knew that he was worried, always looking over his shoulder, always armed, avoiding sleeping in the same place two nights in a row.

Her mother and father held their daughter and let her cry. They appeared to share her sorrow – as most parents did. Sara and Anna stood there, waiting at the bottom of the steps at the threshold to the terraced house. It was a completely ordinary terrace that was home to a completely ordinary Swedish family from Ethiopia, where something very much out of the ordinary had happened.

'Come in,' the father eventually said when his daughter's crying had calmed somewhat. He showed them the way politely with his hand, taking a step back to let the officers in.

While Abeba continued crying, her father explained the family's background. It occurred to Sara that she never felt the impulse to explain her own family history to people she encountered, but she didn't know whether it was she or Ndeme who was unusual.

The Idris family had ended up in Sweden because Ndeme had landed a job with Pharmacia in Södertälje. A couple of years ago, he'd accumulated enough savings to bring over his family, and they had chosen to settle in Norsborg since they had a lot of friends and relatives already based in the suburbs of southern Stockholm. Postängsvägen was a prosperous area of terraces where the residents came from a more diverse set of backgrounds than was the case in many similar Swedish neighbourhoods, Sara noted. People passing by on the footpaths running by the houses seemed to be of Asian, South American and African stock. As well as European.

The hallway was filled with shoes and bike helmets in different child's sizes, as well as scooters, basketballs and footballs. All the coats were hanging on hooks – how on earth had they managed to get the children to do that? Sara wondered to herself as they passed by.

Hanging on the wall of the kitchen amongst the many photos of the five children at different ages were a crucifix and a poster advertising something called the Church of Ascension, or the 'Holy Church of the Divine Resurrection and Ascension of Jesus,' as it said at the bottom. Involvement in the church might explain why it was important for the couple to marry so young, Sara reflected. She had lived in sin with Martin for many years before they had married. When they had actually taken the step, it had merely been to streamline family life in legal terms. Sara realised yet again that she wasn't the romantic type.

Abeba was the family's eldest child, twenty years old, and after graduating from sixth form she had got a job in a consumer electronics store at the Kungens kurva retail park. That was where she had met Cesar. And wedding bells had been ringing. The mother showed them pictures of different bridal gowns they had been considering, and the father produced a list of the names of people they were going to invite. Two hundred guests in a function suite at Heron City. The whole family was going to help foot the bill. Or they would have.

The mother, Rosa, set out coffee and honey-dipped biscuits before sitting down and hugging her daughter again. There was no milk, but there were sugar lumps to add to the coffee.

'Are you up to answering some questions?' Anna asked, and Abeba nodded briefly in reply.

'Did Cesar tell you about anything particular that had happened lately? Any fights?'

Abeba shook her head.

'We gather he was in a gang,' said Sara, trying to catch the girl's eye. 'His mother says he wanted to leave it.'

Abeba nodded, still staring down at the floor.

'Yes,' she said in a hoarse voice. 'He wanted to study.'

'What did the others think about that? In the gang?'

'Don't know.'

'Did he feel threatened? Was he afraid?'

Rosa pushed the plate of biscuits towards Sara and Anna. Sara smiled quickly at the woman and took one, but she didn't want to take a bite while Abeba was talking. Instead, she waited.

'He was getting help. To get out, I mean. One of those networks that help people who want to leave gang life.'

'Which one?' Anna asked, while Sara took the opportunity to take a bite of the biscuit, which was surprisingly delicious.

'Don't know. But I've got the number. He called from my mobile. So his mates couldn't see the number on his phone.'

'Can we have the number?'

Abeba turned towards her father, who stood up.

'I'll get it,' he said, leaving the room.

'But it sounds as if he was afraid they would find out that he wanted to quit?' Anna said in the meantime.

'He hadn't made his mind up,' Abeba said quietly. 'And until then he didn't want them to know, because if he decided to stay they would never trust him if they found out he'd been considering quitting.'

'So he wasn't sure?'

Abeba glanced hastily in the direction in which her father had disappeared.

'His mother wanted him to,' she said. 'She was always nagging him about it – it gave him a guilty conscience.'

The father returned and passed the mobile to Abeba, who scrolled through the call log.

'It must be this number,' said Abeba, showing them the display. 'It's the only one not saved to my contacts.'

Anna took a photo of the number with her mobile.

'Can I try calling from your phone?' said Sara, holding out her hand. Abeba passed her mobile over.

Sara hit redial. It rang five times and then a voice answered: 'Yes?'

'Hello, my name's Sara. I'm calling about Cesar Bekas.'

'Who?'

'Cesar Bekas. I know he was in touch with you from this phone. I'd like to meet you.'

'I don't know who you're talking about. This is a corner shop.'

And then the line went dead.

They didn't get much further and they decided that Abeba's nearest and dearest would be best positioned to help her with her grieving, so they stood up and thanked her for her help. Sara proffered the biscuits to Anna, who felt obliged to take one.

'Delicious biscuits,' Sara said to Rosa, who smiled at the praise before putting an arm around her daughter again.

Ndeme escorted them to the door, and when they stepped onto the doorstep he came with them, closing the door behind him. He shook his head sadly.

'He was a good lad. He wanted to get out of his criminal ways. He'd started coming to church with us. But those gangs ruin people's lives. And now they've ruined Abeba's life too. I warned her about this, but you know how it is – young women don't listen to their fathers.'

A melancholy smile passed across his face, and Sara nodded in assent. She wondered what she would have done if Ebba had come home with a crook of a boyfriend. She'd probably have called her daughter an idiot. Quite how that would have helped matters, she didn't know.

'How are his parents taking it?' said Ndeme.

'They're crushed.'

Ndeme nodded sympathetically, and they parted ways.

'I don't like biscuits,' said Anna, looking at her prize.

'But I do,' said Sara, taking it from Anna's hand.

Once outside in the street, both Anna and Sara tried calling the number from their own mobiles, but they got no answer. Sara left a message explaining what she was calling about and left her own name and number. But she didn't hold out much hope that they would call back.

'OK, so here's the question: was it his own gang that found out he wanted out, or another gang they were at war with?' said Anna as they strolled back to the large visitor car park, surrounded by lock-ups for the residents.

'Perhaps another gang that found out he was going to quit and knew his own mates wouldn't protect him or avenge his death.'

'But he wasn't sure,' said Anna.

'No, it was the mother who was nagging him. How do we interpret that?'

Sara's thoughts were interrupted by Roland Cedermark's 'He's Opened the Pearly Gates' in ringtone form – the one she had childishly assigned to her old colleague, David.

'I managed to get hold of that Jenna,' he said. 'You did want to meet her, didn't you? I've got you a date with her.'

10

Jenna didn't understand what the woman was after. Not really.

And how she had found her in this flat, when not even Jenna knew where it was. The men had said they were in one of the finer neighbourhoods of the city, but Jenna never saw anything of her surroundings, so what difference did it make where they were? All she could think about was that the woman's fiery red hair reminded her of her sisters. They were almost all redheads in her family – Jenna was the exception. A pale brunette in a sea of copper.

The woman said she was a police officer, and that Nadia had been hurt – Jenna had enough English to understand that. But why had she come here? Had Jenna been tricked by the man who had said he was coming? Was she going to lose an hour's work now? When she asked the woman, she gave Jenna cash. So not a cop. Just a crazy lady. Perhaps someone who wanted to wreck things for the people that Jenna worked for? Some journalist who wanted to write about sex work?

When the woman tried to warn Jenna, she pretended not to understand. She pretended that she had never heard of any peepshow. The woman didn't really seem to believe her, but what could she do?

She didn't want to think about how Nadia was doing right now. She knew it was horrible, that it was amongst the worst stuff you could do. But the money would change her life. The others who had been asked had mostly been long in the tooth, all used up, resigned, said yes because nothing mattered any longer. But Jenna was happy to have been asked after such a brief time in the city. It meant she would be able to get out of this while she was still young. She would be able to start over.

No matter how awful it would be, she was still grateful for the opportunity.

Better an intense but brief hell, rather than a protracted one.

All she had to do was put it behind her once she had healed.

Once the woman had finally left, Jenna called Micha and asked whether there were any problems. But he placated her and told her everything was on track.

She didn't need to worry.

She would get her money.

The peepshow was going ahead.

And then all her problems would be gone for good.

11

Apparently she couldn't let go of her old whores, failed existences that didn't even want her help. That suited Rau just fine. Better that she wasted her energy on playing the hero amongst the dregs of society rather than getting mixed up in the big issues, complex connections whose importance she didn't understand. If you couldn't see the road then you shouldn't try to steer.

He squinted towards Nowak as she emerged from the main door of 10 Grevgatan, perhaps the most classic apartment brothel address of all. She was wearing jeans, boots and an old military-style parka, making her look nothing like the girls in the brothel or like a resident. The burns on her face were visible even at this distance. Rau hoped that the injuries meant she had learned her lesson, that she had realised she shouldn't poke her nose in business that didn't concern her. Otherwise things would go very badly for Sara Nowak. Especially if it turned out that Stiller had, in fact, spoken to her, and if she decided to start rooting around in the case.

He followed her with his gaze, seeing her go to her car, which she had left in the disabled bay in front of the main door. She turned around and looked towards the building again, as if she didn't quite know what to do next.

The building was from the functionalism school of architecture, going against the majority of old, magnificent buildings just off Strandvägen. It was the kind of neighbourhood where people believed themselves entitled to pleasures that remained inaccessible or forbidden to others. The right to decide what others should do with their bodies and time. Privileges that Rau also liked to assume. If he were honest, he struggled to understand those people who allowed themselves to be bought. There was always a way to gain the upper hand – he knew that from his own experience.

'Just off Strandvägen,' as they usually wrote in the real estate listings around here. 'Just off.' What difference did it make? It still wasn't Strandvägen. 'Best fake quality' as they liked to say about pirate copies sold in Asia. It was the same here. The whole point was to highlight that you weren't the best option, just in proximity to it. Geographic proximity, which didn't mean a thing. There was no splendid view of Blasieholmen, the Saltsjön bay or Djurgården. No colossal apartments, no celebrated names on the lists of residents mounted in the entrance. Rau had never understood that particular driving force – the heated desire to be in the proximity of greatness, instead of creating your own greatness.

But he appreciated Östermalm. It was calm, peaceful and everyone was too absorbed in their own lives to take any interest in anyone else. There were also a number of embassies in the area, which meant no one was surprised to hear someone in a local bar speaking a foreign language – something which had been particularly useful in the good old days before Sweden had become the subject of interest for foreign tourists. When it had still been just a grey, bureaucratic wasteland full of unassuming nobodies. He glanced towards Il Conte, the restaurant diagonally across the street, where he'd had many meetings over the years. The staff were discreet, friendly, service-minded and not in the slightest bit curious about what took place in the grey areas of society.

But what to do about Nowak?

She had got far too close to him. Without knowing it, of course, which was the only reason for her still being alive. The question was whether he should wait and take the risk that she would end up on his trail, or whether he should be safe rather than sorry and get rid of an unnecessary threat.

He released Nowak from his gaze and looked down to the passenger seat beside him. Lying there was a black sports holdall containing camera equipment. Perhaps he'd twist the little screen around this time, let Nowak watch herself die. If she kept rummaging around in the past, then he would be forced to act.

Nowak's mortal struggle would be particularly interesting to observe. And he intended to make use of something far more extravagant than a mere hanging. She would need to disappear without trace, so he could take his time with her. Plenty of time.

12

Sara stood by her car for a long time, thinking. Jenna hadn't wanted any help. Sara was used to that. But this time, the girl's friend had wanted Sara to intervene and warn her. That hadn't happened before. Nadia was afraid of something that was worse than the revenge of the traffickers. But Jenna didn't seem to have understood what Sara was saying, why she should be frightened. So there wasn't much she could do.

She got into the car, which she had left in the disabled bay outside number 10. Like all the roads around here, Grevgatan was a one-way street. The result was an almost labyrinthine road network that not everyone knew how to escape. Östermalm locals continued to uphold their streets without oncoming traffic. In the case of other areas, the politicians at city hall had decided to open many one-way streets to two-way traffic, but this meant more passing cars and fewer parking spaces. Östermalm had not accepted that. Here, the streets remained one-way. They stood up for their peace and quiet, as well as their parking spots. And they knew the right people, which meant they could influence the decision.

She drove along Kaptensgatan as far as Artillerigatan, turned left towards Strandvägen and continued on towards Gustav Adolfs torg. 'Sophia Albertina Aedificavit,' she knew it said on the façade of the Ministry of Foreign Affairs, but she had forgotten what it meant. Was that still considered general knowledge these days?

As she was driving across Norrbro bridge, her phone rang.

'Hello. This is Herman Cederqvist from the Linköping police. We've got a chap here – well, actually, we don't any longer, I suppose. It's a death, rather sudden and unexpected, and I think it may have a connection to you, if I can put it like that. Well, not to you personally, but to a case that you worked on. It was you who called us about a bloke called Jürgen Stiller at Torpa vicarage down in Ydre, back at the start of the summer, wasn't it?'

'Yes.'

'I thought as much. Well, thought and thought. I did save your number, but then I said to myself, "was it her who called about that pastor?". I only had your name and a number, but I remembered you were working on Uncle Stellan. Well, his murder. Bloody tragedy for it to end that way for him. After entertaining so many people for so many years and spreading nothing but joy. But that's how it is in our line of work – we see a lot of awfulness. Makes you wonder sometimes how you manage.'

'What about Stiller?' said Sara, who was getting slightly impatient.

'He's dead.'

Jürgen Stiller. Code-named Koch, a Church of Sweden priest and Stasi informant. When the others in his spy ring had been executed one after another, Sara had requested police protection for Stiller. Then she had found the murderer, and Stiller had been assessed as out of danger. Until now.

But it couldn't be the same murderer – Agneta Broman was dead.

Sara took all the information that Cederqvist had on the death, thanked him for getting in touch and ended the call.

And then it hit her.

Stiller.

Bloody hell – hadn't he been one of the many phone calls that Sara had rejected of late?

Instead of driving into the underground car park on Slottsbacken, she stopped in the car park outside. With a growing knot of unease in her stomach, she called her voicemail and worked her way backwards through the messages.

And there he was. He had indeed called Sara two days earlier. Several times, in fact. And she hadn't picked up or listened to the message he had left.

'Hello, Sara.' Wheezing breath, a moment's silence before he continued. 'This is Jürgen Stiller. I've got information about a very dangerous man. Please call me as soon as you get this. It's important. A matter of life and death.'

Fuck.

And now he'd killed his wife and hanged himself. Would all that have happened if Sara had picked up? Or if she had at least bothered to listen to the message and return his call? It might be far-fetched, but she was still a little oversensitive after everything that had happened. She couldn't bear the thought of more lives on her conscience. She didn't want to be dragged into any more old conspiracies.

But who was this dangerous man he had wanted to tell her about? Was he linked to Stiller's suicide? And the murder of his wife? Had the fear become too much, meaning he could no longer stand it? Might Stiller's wife have been alive now if Sara hadn't been so self-absorbed? It was impossible to know, but she couldn't shake off the feeling of responsibility. Could she do something for Stiller now, after-the-fact? A bit late, she berated herself.

In the absence of a better idea, she called Eva Hedin, the woman who had told Sara about Jürgen Stiller back when it had all kicked off the first time. Hedin was a retired history professor and the person who had told Sara quite how many of the Cold War's old secrets were still live. She had done research in the old East German archives and after a long legal battle and a Supreme Court judgment, she had been given the right to see the Swedish Security Service's files on Swedes who had worked for the Stasi. Sara had eventually realised that Hedin had been wrong about the identity of the spy, Geiger, but she hadn't told the academic the truth. She couldn't, because she'd had to sign loads of documents from both the German and Swedish intelligence services, promising never to tell anyone about what had happened during that dramatic week in June. Sara had been reluctant to say the least, but it had been the condition for keeping her job given that she had violated most of the police rulebook.

But when she got Hedin on the line, she didn't sound particularly interested in the fact that yet another of the men she had identified was now dead. She agreed to meet, but not at home. She suggested they meet in the Cornelis park. Sara had to put it into her satnav to find out where it was.

A left off Folkungagatan and then on the right at the top of the hill. Sara parked up on Mäster Mikaels gata, passed the primary school of the same name, noting the macabre gesture of naming a school after a hangman, then she walked the few steps it took to reach the end of the street. The cobbled street was lined with small, picturesque wooden houses – as if taken from an Astrid Lindgren story, but right in the heart of Stockholm.

The Cornelis park was just a small patch of open space with benches, but it afforded an incredible view of the old town, Skeppsholmen, the Stadsgården wharf and over to Djurgården. The towers and rides at Gröna Lund were visible – she could hear the distant screams from the free-fall ride, gulls laughing and the hoarse horns sounding from the many white steamers out on the water of Saltsjön. She had a bird's eye view of the green elevator cabin that had served as Carl Anton's art studio in later years. The people passing by down below on Katarinavägen had no idea that Sara was looking at them from above. She felt like Arvid Falk in *The Red Room*, one of the few novels she had read at school and could actually remember parts of.

Hedin was sitting on a green park bench waiting for her, wearing sunglasses and a headscarf, which made her look like someone in a 1950s film.

'Ever been here before?' asked Hedin, and Sara had to confess that she had not. The researcher seemed exhilarated to be the first to introduce the place to her.

'You said he hanged himself?' Hedin continued.

'Wife stabbed to death upstairs, Koch hanged in the kitchen. With a Bible opened to the passage in which Judas hangs himself.'

'A bit blatant, don't you think?' said Hedin with a smile. Sara blinked.

'What do you mean?'

'There are Stasi methods for all kinds of murders, including those that need to look like something else. This is pretty much a textbook example.'

'You don't think it was suicide? The Linköping police do.'

Sara was not at all keen on the idea that it might be murder. That was a dreadful proposition. Because if it were murder, then it was probably the dangerous man that Stiller had wanted to warn her about who was responsible, and that made it feel like the guilt definitely rested on Sara's shoulders, because she had ignored his call.

'Reshuffling the deck was the Stasi's most successful strategy,' said Hedin. 'Confusing the opposition was considered to be a valuable end in itself, even when they didn't truly gain anything from it. But my guess is that this murderer wants to hide the truth for some reason.'

'OK. But which truth? Why would someone want to kill Stiller?'

'To avoid detection, now that everyone else in the spy ring has been killed. He might even have known a name. Or known something we didn't know.'

'He . . .' Sara wasn't really sure she was up to telling the truth, but she forced it out. 'He called me on Thursday and left a message saying he had information about a very dangerous man.'

'That sounds like it might be relevant. What else did he say?'

'Nothing. I didn't listen to the message until just now.' Sara paused. 'Do you think he was referring to the murderer?'

'I don't want to speculate. But it's a pity you didn't speak to him and find out more.'

Yes, Sara agreed. It really was a pity that she hadn't spoken to Stiller. And perhaps saved both him and his wife.

'Who do you think the murderer is then?' said Sara. 'Another spy?'

'Or an employer. Or an old opponent. And we can't forget revenge. The Stasi informants did a lot of harm to a lot of people. Stellan's death may have reawakened old traumas.'

'Or was the murder revenge for the failure of the spy ring?'

Sara reflected that it was actually down to her that they had failed. It felt strange to have stopped a huge terror attack and to have saved the lives of hundreds of thousands of people. And even stranger to never be able to tell anyone about it.

'It's possible it was some kind of punishment – it wouldn't be the first time. But I'm sorry, I can't help you with this.'

'Help me?'

'I can tell you're invested in this from your voice.'

'I just wanted to tell you about Stiller. You're the one who researches these people.'

'But once they're dead, they're no longer of interest to me.'

'OK. I just thought you'd like to know.'

'Here. I brought some new documents for you. They're still piecing together old, shredded documents in Germany. This is a list of names of agents who were active in Sweden and had a connection to Koch, a.k.a. Stiller.'

Hedin passed over a plastic wallet containing sheets of paper. Sara took it and glanced at the contents. The heading on the first page read: 'Files for IM Henker, IM Axt, IM Ritter, IM Faust.'

'But I don't need this,' Sara said, leafing through the pages. Code names, assignments, contacts. There were names with question marks noted against some of them. And then a couple of pages titled: 'Notes from Säpo archives' and a list of what Hedin had been able to memorise from what she had seen of the Security Service's top secret archives on former Stasi collaborators in Sweden.

Sara felt strong reluctance to engage with the case. Getting involved in the murder of Stellan Broman and all the other old connections to the Cold War had led to nothing but a plethora of unwanted insights about her own life and how the world she had grown up in had actually been constructed. What was more, it had almost taken her life from her. And if there was one thing she felt with extreme certainty now, it was that her family was priority number one. She wanted to be with them as much as she could. She wanted to find Martin again, she wanted to get to know teenage Olle, and to make friends with the young woman that her daughter had become.

So she had neither the time nor the inclination to deal with old spies. There was enough unpleasantness in her present, the terrible murder of Cesar Bekas, for starters.

Sara suddenly realised that Hedin was watching her through narrowed eyes.

'What is it?' said Sara.

'What actually happened? That night?'

'They stopped Abu Rasil.'

'They?'

'The BND.'

'How?'

'I don't know. I don't actually have any details.'

'And where's Lotta Broman? I don't believe she's having time out, as I'm sure you can understand. And what happened to Agneta?'

Sara shrugged.

'I know you pretty well by now,' said Hedin. 'You would never have settled for not knowing. I regard that shrug as an insult to my intelligence.'

'I promise, I don't know anything.'

'You're refusing to tell me, but you want my help with Stiller?'

That was the rub.

'I don't want to get involved in Stiller's death. And I really didn't mean to insult you. I'm telling you all I can.'

'You sound like Brundin and her boss.'

Brundin. The spook who had said nothing but 'no comment' to Sara's questions until she had allied herself with the officers of the BND instead.

Would it really be such a bad thing to tell Hedin?

The problem was that Sara didn't know all that much. Nothing about what had happened to Lotta afterwards. And out of consideration for Lotta's family, she had to keep the truth secret. That much she had understood from Agneta's explanation. For Agneta, it had been all about ensuring that her grandchildren wouldn't have their lives controlled by the choices of older generations. She wanted to give them a childhood free of international politics and secret alliances – the opportunities to make their own choices in life. Which Sara could fully understand.

So she had signed all those documents in which she had promised to keep it all a secret. An older German man had shown up at the hospital where Sara was being treated for her gunshot wounds and burns. He was white-haired, wore a three-piece suit with a bow tie, and radiated a quiet authority that appeared as friendly unobtrusiveness. He had smelled of pipe tobacco in a way that no one in Sweden did these days. The man had introduced himself as Herr Doktor Schönberg and said that he was Breuer's and Strauss's boss – they were the two BND agents who had been chasing the terrorist Abu Rasil in Stockholm. Given the prevailing security situation and terrorist threat level, he had told Sara that she had two options to choose from. She could swear life-long silence about what she had experienced or she could quite simply be detained without any contact with the outside world until such a time as her knowledge was judged to be no longer dangerous. Which might be decades. He had also thanked her for her efforts and offered her a medal, even if it would never officially be acknowledged. Sara had turned down the medal, but had signed all the papers that Schönberg had laid out before her. All she wanted was to go home to her family, and more than anything she wanted to forget what had happened to her. So against her instincts, she kept quiet as Hedin asked her questions. The official version would have to do. Lotta Broman had resigned as Director General of the Swedish International Development Cooperation Agency and turned down the offer of a role in the government citing family reasons. Then she had taken a long sabbatical and gone abroad – without her family.

No one wanted people to find out that a possible member of the government had been unmasked as a terrorist and that Säpo had missed this petty detail. The whole imbroglio with Breuer was also hushed up. She was posthumously celebrated in intelligence circles as the person who had stopped Abu Rasil. And Rasil's true identity remained a secret.

Nor could anyone know about Sara's role in the drama. Or the truth about Stellan and Lotta Broman. All that was known to the public was that a garden shed in Bromma had burned down – which generated nothing more than a small story in the local newspaper *Mitt i Bromma*.

Where Lotta was today Sara did not know, and she would probably never know, either.

13

Sara wanted to go for the cheap IKEA crockery, especially since Eric and Marie were coming. But she knew that Martin wanted to lay out the fine china: Versace's Medusa Blue. Not to impress his parents, but so that he felt safe. He didn't want to risk showing a weak spot. If it had been the guys from his band coming to visit, they would all have noticed the crockery being used. Versace was pretty vulgar to Sara's eyes, but was there anything she wouldn't do for her husband? The Riedel wine glasses were worse. Wine buff paraphernalia. Hand-made, costing a thousand kronor a pop, and different glasses for every grape under the sun: Pinot noir, Cabernet, Syrah, Riesling, Chardonnay. How the hell would Sara be able to remember which glasses went with which wines? And who on earth noticed the difference? Of the hundred or so glasses that Martin prided himself on, she selected a few at random – he'd just have to change them if he wasn't happy.

Jane was the first to arrive. Purple blouse, white culottes and with her own pair of indoor shoes even though it was still the late summer and beautiful weather outside. Big gold earrings, and makeup that was slightly too bold to be considered discreet. A scented cloud of perfume enveloped her as she stepped into the apartment. She handed over a small parcel wrapped in gold paper with blue and yellow ribbons around it. She always arrived with a small gift whenever she was invited out. Sara removed the wrapping paper, expecting some framed photograph of herself and her mother, or Jane with Olle and Ebba, but that wasn't what it contained at all.

It was a framed photograph of the king.

Carl XVI Gustaf.

'Instead of those clumsy paintings,' said Jane, frowning towards Sara and Martin's paintings by Cecilia Edefalk and Karin Mamma Andersson.

'Clumsy?' said Sara.

'Yes, exactly. This is better. Suits the flat. Show your pride. He does a lot of good for the country.'

Sara was at least grateful that it was the king in the picture, rather than old Pope John Paul II – the household god of every Pole. Jane had pictures of Pope Karol Wojtyła in every room of her flat in Vällingby. When she had been a little girl, Sara had thought it was her grandfather, given how tenderly her mother referred to 'Jan Pawel'. 'He gave us freedom!' Jane said, by way of explanation for her great reverence. Since Sara had chucked the papal portraits in her bedroom in the bin as a teenager, Jane hadn't tried to palm off any more Catholic idols onto her. Hence the Swedish king now gazing up at her. Neither a Catholic nor a saint, but in full ceremonial uniform. Almost as if Jane had a fetish for men in strange clothes.

'Thanks. It's going to be a hoot hanging the king.'

Jane slapped Sara's arm with an outraged expression. It was always the best fun winding her mother up.

'Hang up his photo, I meant to say.'

The small guest toilet would be the perfect home for the royal phiz.

'Come in,' Sara said to her mother, offering her a tray of canapés. As a protest against Martin's Svenskt Tenn and the silver platters, she had bought a pink plastic tray at Lidl. On it she had lined up canapés made with horseradish cream and vegetarian ham. She really didn't want to lend her support to the brutal abattoir industry, and the vegetarian alternative tasted just as good as dead animal, or so she thought. But she said nothing to Jane about her choice, because she knew her mother would refrain if she found out it wasn't 'proper' ham.

It was Sara who had suggested that the family start eating Sunday lunch together now that the youngsters had started to go their own ways. Ebba had been against the idea and Olle hadn't cared. But when Martin had added that the grandparents would be included, Ebba had cheerily accepted. And Olle had no choice, since he still lived at home.

After some small talk with Jane (when were Sara and the kids coming to visit her in Vällingby? When was she going to see her plastic surgeon to get rid of those awful scars?) Sara fetched a couple of bottles from the wine cellar, which was not in fact a wine cellar at all but a glazed room that had been Martin's forty-fifth birthday present to himself. She returned with two crystal carafes into which she could pour the wine to ensure it was 'decanted'. But Martin would have to deal with that nonsense. Sara wondered whether she should start decanting her diet soda too.

'What does this stuff cost?'

Jane had picked up one of the bottles and was scrutinising it with a sceptical expression.

Sara pulled out her mobile, scanned the barcode on one of the bottles and searched for it in the Systembolaget app.

Nineteen hundred kronor.

Martin really had gone too far this time.

'Two hundred,' Sara said, setting down the bottle.

'Don't lie. When they buy an expensive wine, they want everyone to know it's expensive wine.'

'OK. Two thousand.'

'What an idiot!'

Sara looked at her mother in amusement.

'I do beg your pardon, Sara, but when it comes to money your husband really is an idiot.'

'Tell him that.'

'Are you an idiot when it comes to money too?'

'No. Definitely not. You know that.'

'Stellan had money. And the house is probably worth twenty-five million.'

'What? I don't care about that. You know I don't want to talk about this,' Sara said, frowning.

'One third of it is yours.'

'I don't want any of his stuff! He wasn't my father, he was someone who raped you.'

'Don't be stupid. Think about your children.'

'Mum, we already have too much money. Martin and Eric are spoiling the kids. They're going to turn into ... well, you know. Brats.'

'They don't say brats any longer.'

'What?'

'It's out of fashion,' Jane informed her.

'What would you know about that?'

'I know things. I talk to people.'

'Who? Katryna? She's older than you are.' Sara raised her eyebrows at her mother, who giggled.

'I talk to everyone. Don't you?'

Sara held out her hands. 'OK. I'll stop saying brats.'

'Have you told the kids?'

'About Stellan?' The mere thought of it made Sara feel sick. 'No. Stop nagging.'

She would never soil her children's lives by telling them about the awful man they were descended from.

'You were so angry at me for not telling you.'

'This is different.'

'It's always different when it's you doing it.'

'No one knows about it except you and me, OK? And that's how it's going to stay. I couldn't even inherit from him since he's dead and no one knows the truth.'

'DNA. Before they bury him.' Jane looked at her daughter encouragingly.

'A DNA test? Are you out of your mind? Come on, Mum. Do you really want people to know?'

'Yes. I made a mistake not saying anything. He's your father.'

Sara's father. She now knew who he was, or rather what his name had been and how he had behaved. But who had he really been? At the same time as finding out who her father had been, she had also found out that he had been completely different to what people thought he was like. A monster. How would Ebba and Olle take it if they found out? Or Martin? What would Lotta and Malin say?

Sara's instinctive feeling was that this part of her past had to be erased because it was the only way to move on. At the same time, she couldn't avoid the growing realisation that she really wasn't in control of her own life if she didn't confront and own her own past. If she didn't accept every part of Sara Nowak.

'Hello.'

A worn-out looking Martin appeared in tracksuit bottoms and an old T-shirt with The Pop Group's Margaret Thatcher picture on it under the caption 'We are all prostitutes'. He still hadn't recovered from the twentieth anniversary party the night before.

'So good of you to lay the table. Has the catering arrived?'

'No.'

'You're not cooking yourselves?' said Jane, making Martin fidget awkwardly.

'Hmm, well, they're only bringing the main course. And only today. Since we had the big bash yesterday I thought we might allow ourselves to order in.' A watery smile was followed by a slightly more serious expression. 'But you wouldn't believe how expensive it is. We'll have to make some savings elsewhere this week . . .'

Martin apologising for his caddish habits in front of Jane somehow made it all worse. Him pretending not to have any money just because she didn't have any. As if he really felt sorry for her. It was downright condescending, Sara thought to herself in irritation.

Then the doorbell rang and Eric and Marie arrived, tanned, well-dressed and smiling. With an almighty bouquet of late summer flowers and a contribution to the meal in the shape of a bottle of wine.

Martin showed his parents into the living room, excused himself and went to change, but his hair was still tousled when he returned. In the meantime, Sara had supplied the three parents with a glass of champagne each. Cristal. Only two thousand kronor a bottle. That was Martin's choice too. And it wasn't even the best tasting champagne on the market, in Sara's view.

Before they raised their glasses, Martin rolled up his shirt sleeves to ensure that his big Rolex was fully visible. Sara wondered how rock 'n' roll it really was to have a Rolex, but she had resolved, once and for all, not to question her husband's style.

'Do you want to see the end of the gig?' said Martin, switching on the TV before the parents had time to reply. 'You had to leave before we finished.'

He searched for the clip on his tablet and cast it to the enormous screen. There they were, four executives of around fifty years of age, their rock dreams still intact. The audio from the concert the night before was dire, but that mattered less in this context. 'Sings rather than sings well' had probably never been a more apt description.

Martin watched his father expectantly while C.E.O. Speedwagon continued to play on the screen. Eric smiled his small, polite smile, but hardly seemed amused.

Rich as Croesus, the founder of a successful company, friends with every musician in Sweden and father of two beautiful children, but that wasn't enough. Martin needed his father's approval still – at almost fifty years old. It wasn't enough that he had built up something of his own. He still needed approval as an entertainer too. And, it suddenly struck Sara, it was precisely that need for attention that she had fallen for, once upon a time. Or rather, it had been the result of it – the Martin of high school years had always been the centre of attention, and the one all the girls pined for. He was the one everyone wanted, and that Sara got.

Then she looked at her mother, who was actually following Martin's performance with what resembled a degree of interest. But she hadn't wanted to go to the party. Martin had been a little hurt, until Sara had explained to him that Jane was still reluctant to go to big parties after her years at the Bromans', when she'd had to work so hard during their events. She would probably never be able to regard herself as one guest among the many. From Jane, Sara moved her gaze to Eric and Marie, and she contemplated the differences between her own parents and Martin's. Jane had grown up in communist Poland and fled to Sweden at the age of sixteen, alone and without money or contacts. She had ended up with the Broman family, where she had become a servant, taken advantage of by the master of the house, and she had given birth to Sara, who had then played with Malin and Lotta Broman while patronising her mother the cleaner, eagerly egged on by the girls. Jane had never said a word about it, and she hadn't explained why she had given her notice to the Bromans and moved to Vällingby with her daughter just before Sara was due to start sixth form. Sara had always been angry at her mother for dragging her away from something that Sara preferred to remember as paradise to a depressing, concrete-clad suburb with a rowdy school. Not until a couple of months ago had Sara found out the truth – that Stellan had tried to lure her into the garden shed where he had his way with young girls. Sara would probably always be ashamed of her former rage, and definitely grateful for the rest of her life for what her mother had done.

Eric and Marie were different. Born and raised in Bromma, they had never left. They had been married for almost fifty years, having wed at twenty-three and twenty-one respectively. A happy, stable marriage. They were content and confident in their image. Tanned, wearing exclusive clothes, they had seen the world and eaten at tonnes of Michelin-starred restaurants. They had shedloads of money and therefore had no need to prove anything to anyone. They could even be politely friendly to traffic wardens.

Sara had also met Martin's paternal grandfather before he died, in the early days after she and Martin had got together. Around ninety, a managing director and with noble blood on his mother's side; straight-backed with a firm gaze and handshake to match. He had been born in 1899 – in a different century and a completely different world. In the drawing room of his grand Bromma house, there had been oil paintings of his prominent forefathers hanging on the walls, while the walls of his study had been lined with diplomas, pennants and emblems from various secret gentlemanly orders that Sara hadn't even known existed. Martin had explained to Sara in a low voice which ones they were – at least the ones he knew the names of. The Freemasons, WF, the Order of Svea, the Order of Amarante, the Carpenter's Order, the Odd Fellows. What on earth they actually did, he had no idea about.

His parents and grandparents and the generations before them had given Martin stable foundations, a legacy that must have shaped him and given him the security that Sara had never had. But also a lot to live up to. A certain degree of pressure. All Sara had was Jane. No history, no roots. But on the other hand, she had always been free to be who she wanted to be. She didn't have to show off her performance on a big screen TV.

Once again, Martin's performance was interrupted. This time it wasn't the departure of his parents but the arrival of his daughter. A hungover Ebba stumbled in, gave her grandparents hasty hugs and then collapsed on the sofa.

'Have we got fizzy drinks in?' said Ebba in a tone that suggested she expected to be waited upon.

'Wouldn't you prefer a glass of wine?' said Sara, holding her own glass right under Ebba's nose. She couldn't help grinning when her daughter's face turned a faint shade of green, as if she were about to throw up.

'Rough night?' Eric said, looking nothing but tickled.

'Are you joking?'

'Hope you're feeling livelier tomorrow. You can't welcome people in that state.'

'It's fine,' said Ebba, and it was unclear whether she hoped to recover or whether she thought she might as well work on reception hungover.

'Are you starting tomorrow?' Marie asked.

'Yes. At half seven.' The time was followed by a deep sigh, as if it was an inhumane task she had been burdened with.

'Well, Martin didn't want to join Eric's company,' Marie said, in a slightly accusatory tone.

'I wanted to build something of my own,' Martin objected.

'You wanted to be on stage,' said Eric.

'First you wanted to be an author,' Marie added. 'You used to spend all day and all night writing.'

'Is that true?' Sara said in surprise.

'Yes,' Martin replied. 'Haven't I ever said?'

'No. Do you still have what you wrote?'

Martin shook his head.

'Because after that, it was showing off that was the order of the day,' said Marie.

'Still is, I think.' Sara nodded towards the TV with the now-frozen image of the previous night's performance.

'We were good,' said Martin, looking at his father. 'Pity you missed it. We were good, weren't we, darling?'

Now he turned to Sara. For support, she thought to herself, rolling her eyes.

'Of course. Just like always. Perhaps you should audition for *Pop Idol*?'

'You think?'

Martin looked genuinely flattered.

'I was kidding. You're fifty.'

'Mick Jagger is eighty.'

'Mick Jagger is Mick Jagger. You're Martin Titus.'

At which point they were saved by the bell. The doorbell to be specific –announcing the arrival of the caterers. Martin led them into the kitchen to transfer the food from the disposable containers onto the gold and blue painted Versace plates.

Sara went to fetch Olle. A family dinner was a family dinner. But he didn't reply when Sara knocked, and when she nudged his door ajar she saw her son standing in front of the mirror with headphones on and his mobile phone camera pointed at himself. He was peering towards his computer and clearly practising his 'smooth moves'.

'I'm gospel, I'm blues, I'm Maverick and Goose, I'm Krishna, I'm Buddha, I'm Zeus.'

His timing was about as good as that of Midsummer's Eve revellers at Rättvik at three o'clock in the morning. And when Sara turned towards the computer, she was instantly pissed off. A bunch of stick-thin women grinding almost completely naked. And a bunch of dudes with guns and cash. What a load of shit! Sara stepped in and turned off the video. Olle turned around towards Sara lighting fast, waving his hands at her to leave, while she typed a different word into the search bar: 'Teletubbies'.

'Why don't you watch this instead? And it's time for dinner.'

'Get lost!' roared the embarrassed teenager. And Sara left. Today wasn't the day she was going to overcome the generational gulf.

Instead, Sara returned to the others and told them about her son's show, regaling them with the lyrics as best as she could. *'Homies and whores, show no remorse.'*

'Well I'll be,' said Marie in amusement, helping herself to kale salad.

'It's Uncle Scam,' said Martin. 'He loves Scam. I've promised to take him along both nights at the Friends Arena.'

'That was Uncle Scam?' said Sara. 'With half-nude gyrating women and morons with guns? He's not going to a concert like that.'

'I've promised. He'd never forgive me otherwise.'

'You even had your own stage in the basement,' Marie said. 'Wait, I'll show you.'

Elated by the memories, Marie rooted through her Hermès bag until she found her purse of the same brand and was able to fish out an old, fading photo of Martin as a boy. He couldn't have been more than six or seven and was standing on a small, raised stage with a black hanging behind him. He had his foot on a rather hideous yellow stool with green flowers and in his hand he had a toy microphone that he was singing into, full-throated.

'Wasn't he just the cutest?' said an enchanted Marie to the others before turning to her son. 'Do you remember that? Maybe you should build one like it for Olle?'

'Definitely,' Martin nodded. 'Nowadays, you can do it all for real at home. Record, mix, release on Spotify, film the whole video and share it on YouTube. Anyone can become a star – they just have to want it.'

'And have talent,' said Eric.

'Dad,' said Martin, 'Uncle Scam is the best-selling artist in the world right now. You don't have any colleagues whose grandkids would like to see him live, do you?'

'Grandkids?' Eric said, affronted.

'Well, I thought—'

'You know that out of Eric's old friends, around half have had new families after the age of fifty?' Marie interrupted.

'Well, I-I didn't mean . . .'

'Martin,' said Eric, examining his gold-edged plate, 'in future, why don't you let Sara pick the crockery?'

Sara kissed her father-in-law on the cheek.

14

Sara couldn't sleep. She woke before five, feeling wide awake.

'I can tell you're invested in this from your voice.'

Hedin apparently knew her better than she did herself. At least in this case.

She couldn't stop thinking about the murdered priest and his wife. It felt as if she had another two lives on her conscience, simply because she hadn't felt like answering the phone. As far as Jürgen Stiller went, she could possibly convince herself that he only had himself to blame, given his choice to become a spy for an evil dictatorship. But his wife had, so far as Sara understood, never made such a choice. She had in all likelihood been murdered simply because she was married to the wrong man. And because Sara hadn't listened to Stiller's warning.

She lay there for twenty minutes to see whether there was any hope whatsoever of drifting back off.

There was not.

Especially not with Martin, who was lying beside her, snoring like an elephant with a cold.

An author, she thought to herself as she looked at her husband in the semi-darkness. She'd had no idea. She had always thought he'd been born a diva. She wondered whether he would have written about her if he'd become a writer and, if so, what he would have said. Probably something painful about the emotional decay that crept into a long-term marriage. Or was that what Sara would have written? Hopefully something about how to re-establish a connection to each other instead.

Sara got up and showered. Then she headed for the kitchen to switch on the bright yellow Moccamaster. As usual, the kitchen door was shut, also as usual the big black cat, Walter, was sitting inside. He glowered at her in an accusatory fashion. Martin had done the usual and shut the cat in there for the night so that he would catch rats. Stockholm's old town might be a charming idyll on the surface, but behind those seventeenth and eighteenth century façades there were rats everywhere. In the walls, floors and sewage pipes. And Martin had a rat phobia. Sometimes Sara would emphasise the unsuitability of owning a large apartment in the old town for people who were terrified of these rodents, but Martin didn't want to move. Instead, he put all his hopes in the cat.

Once Walter, a Norwegian Forest cat, had been fed, Sara stood and thought for a while. Her curiosity was struggling against her guilty conscience. Eventually, she resigned herself and went to the hall to fetch the folder that Hedin had given her.

Had she really thought it would stay there? That she would forget Stiller and his connection to Stellan? Her own responsibility for his death?

Of course not.

And of course it wasn't suicide.

Quite how Sara could be so sure of that, from a distance of 350 kilometres and without having ever met the deceased or been to the murder scene, was unclear.

'Without having been to the murder scene . . .'

The words bounced around inside her skull for a while.

No, she mustn't.

She had to stand firm.

She had promised herself for her family's sake, for her kids that she would never again get involved in things that didn't concern her. Never break the rules in the way that had led her all the way into that burning garden shed with bullets whistling past her head.

But at the same time she knew she would never be able to let go of this, never be able to convince herself that the local police had made the right call – detectives who hadn't seen a fraction of what she had in terms of the way that the past still controlled the present, how old alliances determined life and death several decades later.

Sara had herself witnessed how deadly old secrets could be. She couldn't, with a clear conscience, ignore Stiller's death. Perhaps it was the first of a string of deaths . . . just like Stellan's had been.

No, she needed to see the scene of the crime for herself in order to put it to rest, to convince herself that there was nothing she could do, to be sure that the local police hadn't missed something. It was nothing more than that. And, in a way, she could persuade herself that it was actually for the sake of her family that she was doing this: to make sure that it didn't fester and gnaw at her. Because she needed to put this behind her.

So at around half past five in the morning she set off. She drove at well above the legal speed limit and arrived well before nine o'clock, even though the roads were narrow and winding after she had taken the exit for Mjölby. Sara liked these kinds of roads that still followed the old trails used by cattle, roads that had long ago grown into gravel tracks before later being widened and asphalted. They were so essentially different to the soulless E4 motorway which was constantly being rebuilt to make it straighter and faster and keep it further away from built-up areas. She remembered when the E4 had led drivers past Tintomaras plats, when it had gone straight through the centres of Norrköping and Linköping. A long, long time ago it had even run the length of Götgatan in Södermalm. Now the E4 was nothing but a minor Autobahn. But after taking the Mjölby exit the country roads wound their way through the beautiful landscape as if in a fairy tale. Lakes, meadows, farmyards – and a cistern with a gigantic cheese painted on the side in Boxholm. Wasn't that the one there'd been all that fuss about? That creamy cheese? All because the new owners had wanted to move the Boxholm cheese factory away from Boxholm? Hmm. And the fur trading town of Tranås, where surely no one bought or sold furs any longer. Another twenty kilometres along the road, now back in Östergötland again, Sara pulled off route 131, in the direction of Torpa church. Bubbetorp. Peculiar name. A sign for Solviken. The occasional red house with white trim. A barn. A pond. And after a while a beautiful church on the right-hand side above a lake that her satnav told her was known as Sommen.

After the church there was a field rolling down and then back up again, like a hammock. Opposite the field was a row of older houses and then the red-painted vicarage situated behind a thick hedge.

The drive wasn't cordoned off, so Sara pulled into the front yard and came to a halt. She lingered for a couple of seconds, looking at the house. It appeared to be nineteenth century in origin, but perhaps it was far older than that. It was painted in the classic red paint of the Swedish countryside, with white sills; two storeys and two outbuildings, with an expanse of gravel in the middle.

The blue and white police tape probably lent the peaceful scene a hefty dose of drama in the eyes of most, unless you were Sara, who was completely desensitised. For her, the tape was nothing more than a marker of being at work.

She climbed out of the car, stopped and hesitated for a moment. Was she really going to do this? She could just get back in the car and go home – and nothing would come of it.

'Whatever it is will probably have to be put to the diocese.'

Sara turned around and saw two figures standing watching her from the gate: an elderly woman and a huge man with a long beard. It was the woman who had spoken, but the man took over in a mild, placatory tone.

'What Mother is trying to say is that the vicarage is out of bounds. The priest has departed. So any matters will probably have to be raised with the diocese in Linköping.'

'"Trying to say"?! That's what I said.'

'In Mother's own way.'

'Did you know Stiller?' Sara interrupted, taking a few steps towards them.

'Not very well. He did what he had to, said his goodbyes and left.'

'What Mother means is that he would come to the coffee morning at the local hall, but he didn't say much more than was demanded of him.'

'Thank you. I'm quite capable of explaining what I mean myself.'

Her towering son swept his arms in a gesture of 'be my guest'.

'What was he like as a person?' Sara asked. 'Was he unstable? Depressed?'

'German.'

'Oh?'

'Abrupt. Effective. Kept himself to himself. The wife too.'

'Mother's perception of Germans is her own, as you can tell.' Angry looks were exchanged between mother and son.

'Have you seen any strangers around here lately? Any cars you didn't recognise?'

'We can't see the front of the house from ours. We live on the other side of the river,' the woman explained.

'Which is actually a bay of the lake, as it happens. It's just become overgrown.' The son's hand fumbled around his chin and vanished into his beard.

'The outlet from the Boxholm mill is so rich in nitrogen that the reeds have run riot.'

'"The reeds have run riot"? Good grief. Talk some sense.'

Sara followed the ping-pong match between the two figures, realising that they might keep going for some time without achieving more than a draw, and decided to find information by herself.

'Thanks for your help. I need to get to work.'

'Are you a policewoman?' the bearded giant said. Sara flashed her police ID, wondering whether it was wise but discarding the thought.

'He played music,' said the bearded hulk. 'Lalle, who lives in the tenant farmer's cottage, passed on Friday night and said that he heard music coming from inside.' A nod towards the vicarage.

'Some sort of hard rock or opera, he said. But that's never been Stiller's style.'

'So far as we know,' said the elderly woman.

'So far as everyone knows,' the son countered.

'Yes, so far as everyone knows. We all know.'

Sara judged that she had got all she was going to get out of the two, so she thanked them and turned to head towards the house.

Unsurprisingly, the vicarage was locked, and Sara was unable to find a spare key in any of the usual spots.

But she had elbows.

She went round to the rear, checked the coast was clear, put her back to the back door and rammed her elbow through the pane of glass. The glass fell to the floor with a faint tinkle and Sara was then able to stick her hand through unimpeded and unlock the door from the inside. Nothing but a good old chamber lock with a knob on the inside. Once she had crossed the threshold, it was too late to go back.

The wide wooden floorboards creaked reproachfully. She tried to stick to the rag rugs, but it was basically impossible to move through the vicarage silently. She looked around. A violin on the wall triggered a guilty conscience at the thought of her own lack of playing, but judging by the dust on it, this violin was used no more frequently than her own had been before she had smashed it to pieces in a rage at the Bromans, who had given it to her. Embroidered tapestries hung on the walls with messages like 'Sunny outside, sunny inside, sunny in your heart, sunny in your disposition' and 'Early to bed, early to rise, makes a man healthy, wealthy and wise.' On one wall there were dozens of photos of brides and grooms with handwritten notes of thanks for their beautiful weddings. A living room with a rocking chair, a folded-down gateleg table and an old-fashioned sofa bed where you raised the lid and pulled out the base. It smelled damp and musty.

Room by room, Sara went through the house. No music player anywhere, she noted. An unassuming transistor radio – too small to be heard out on the road. Patches of blood on the upstairs landing, and there was still a knotted rope hooked to the ceiling in the kitchen with the stump of the cut-off rope still hanging there. Had they checked for fingerprints on the knot, or were they so sure it was suicide that they hadn't looked for any evidence at all? Cederqvist hadn't said anything about forensics. They must have done something, but they clearly hadn't found anything.

Apart from the fact that the bodies had been removed, nothing seemed to have been touched. The Bible was still lying on the kitchen table open to the twenty-seventh chapter of Matthew. Hedin had been right – it was too blatant. Almost as if the murderer wanted to test how stupid the investigating officers actually were.

She leafed through the Bible without knowing why. Like most people, she thought to herself. Of all places, it was surely here in the deceased's home that there would be something that would offer a clue as to why Stiller had been killed. But where?

Sara searched each room inch by inch. Did old vicarages like this have secret passages or hidden rooms? It seemed not. When it was almost half past ten, she had reached the priest's study, which had several shelves of books and scriptures. Theology and history, but nothing about politics, a number of notebooks and a diary written in German. After spending a half hour or so leafing through all the books without finding any mysterious notes or loose leaves, she settled down with Stiller's diary. Sara didn't remember all of her schoolgirl German, but she had enough to understand most of the contents. The notes seemed to relate primarily to daily routines and ecclesiastical tasks that fell to the leader of a flock with a small congregation.

In a cigar box hidden behind a copy of the *Swedish Biblical Reference Encyclopaedia* in the bookcase she found thousands of kronor in coins and notes, together with lists of names, dates and sums. Sara noted that all the dates were Sundays and that most of the name were recurrent – she guessed that Stiller had been keeping records of how much his congregation members had been donating to the weekly collection. And that he had kept the money for himself.

Sara continued to root through all the drawers of the desk, checked under the rug and heaved the bookcases forward without finding anything else.

Eventually, she stood in the doorway and surveyed the room.

She had checked it all. Well, other than the classic one, she realised: the bottoms of the desk drawers.

She went over to the desk and pulled the drawers out, and that was where she actually found something. There was a note stuck to the underside of the bottom drawer on the right-hand side, a handwritten note in red ink in ornate, pedantic handwriting, that read:

Messer 100

Axt 100

Faust 100

Lorelei 100

It was the only thing out of the ordinary that Sara had found, but the position of the note told her that it was important. What was more, a couple of the words were familiar to her.

Axt and Faust.

Weren't they?

Yes. Sara had seen them somewhere . . .

It didn't take her long to remember where.

Hedin's papers.

They were code names for Stasi collaborators.

Had one of them killed Stiller? Or were they mixed up in something that had led to his death? Was this yet another spy ring? And what did the numbers mean?

She called Hedin but went straight through to her voicemail. She left a message reading out the list of code names and numbers, firmly convinced that the information would pique the academic's interest too.

Sara looked around thoughtfully, but made up her mind that she had found what she was going to find. She found a roll of tape and a plastic bag in the kitchen, using them to cover the hole in the pane of glass she had left in the back door before exiting, then she stood there for a while surveying the view of the lake and church. A field of cows grazing down by the shoreline, a couple of boats out on the water and dark, dense pine forest on the other side. What a picturesque place for a spy to end up! Sara wondered whether it had been God's will for Stiller to live in such a beautiful setting, or whether it was only his final fate that God had determined.

At half past eleven, she got back behind the wheel again. She called Herman Cederqvist at the police in Linköping and explained that in connection with the murder of Stellan Broman she had come across several code names related to Stiller, which she had cause to believe were relevant to his death. She said nothing about where she was. Cederqvist noted the four names and on the off-chance, Sara asked him to check whether the priest's bank accounts showed any trace of unusual deposits or withdrawals. Sums in the hundreds of thousands – kronor or euros – were of particular interest. Or dollars, for that matter.

Cederqvist responded with a long-winded pontification that boiled down to a demand that if he told Sara what he found then Sara would share everything she knew with him, even if there wasn't much to be found in relation to a tragic suicide and the murder of a family member.

'Of course,' said Sara, without meaning it.

As she drove through the small village of Hestra, passing what must once have been a grocery store, she dialled the number for Brundin at Säpo. A modest bluff was worth a punt.

'Brundin.'

'Who killed Stiller?'

'Don't know what you're talking about.'

'Oh yes you do. Jürgen Stiller. Koch. Found hanged. Was supposed to look like suicide, but it's so textbook it's almost provocative. Who did it? Messer, Axt, Faust or Lorelei?'

'No comment.'

'You know I won't give in.'

Because it was true.

The very possibility that the two murders were somehow her fault was enough, she realised. If that was true, then the least she could do was find the murderer, if not for Stiller's sake then for his innocent wife's. She wasn't going to give up.

15

She had never taken the ferry from Slagsta before – a yellow car ferry sailing from Skärholmen to Ekerö. The boat slowly crossed the strait to the sound of gulls and lapping waves, as if it were in its own small bubble far from the big city and the hustle and bustle despite the E4 motorway and a string of concreted suburbs being in direct proximity.

It was almost three o'clock. Sara had left Torpa at half past eleven. By now she was a couple of hours late, but she hoped that her colleagues would think she had been out in the line of duty. And she had, in one sense. The crossing on the ferry only took ten minutes, but it felt as if time was standing still while the ship was out there on the water. Her arms and back were feeling the seven hours spent behind the wheel, but now she could at least let her brain rest a little. Reset for her actual job.

There were men fishing off the ferry pier on either side of the strait, men of all ages, most from immigrant backgrounds, residents from Fittja and Skärholmen and the other nearby suburbs, she assumed. Did they know what had almost been dumped in the lake they were fishing in? Perhaps there were corpses all over the place in Lake Mälaren. Perhaps the fish those men were reeling in lived on human bodies slowly disintegrating on the bottom of the lake. Would they have fished just as eagerly if they had known about it?

Sara thought about the notorious serial killer known as the Laser Man, who had been caught during her youth largely thanks to an angler reeling in a revolver that the Laser Man had thrown into the water off the Lidingöbron bridge. And sometimes it felt as if her own job worked in the same way: aimless fishing that very rarely and only with a big dose of luck ever led to the arrest of someone. But the whole business with the East German spy ring had actually proved the opposite to be true. In that case, it had been Sara's stubbornness and focus that had led to a solution.

These ferries might not exist soon, if and when the new tunnel bypass project came to fruition. The tunnels would emerge in the middle of beautiful, rural Ekerö. They were fully occupied blasting and digging and had been for several years, careless pillage taking place with the consent of the politicians, wounds being torn open in the idyllic landscape like the blow of an axe striking into the bark of a beautiful tree. The parties responsible would surely be remembered, but not in the way they thought. The worst thing was that the guilty would never be held accountable. It was inconceivable to Sara. She had spent her entire working life hunting down crooks and would happily have taken on those bad guys too.

Back to the present. Bielke, charged with leading the preliminary investigation, was out at Ekerö with the diving team. Residents in nearby Kolbotten had testified that the boat the dead men had been carrying keys for had been tied up there for at least six months and used occasionally by men who had driven in using the private road and parked their big SUVs on the patch of gravel. Someone had also seen the boat moored in one place on the water on one occasion, which was why Bielke was now supervising the dive searching for other bodies.

'You're late.'

Axel Bielke looked her right in the eyes, the way he always did when talking to someone. It was a firm, penetrating gaze from eyes that never seemed to blink. It was hard to guess his age. He was grey-haired with a furrowed face, but straight-backed and athletic, which made him seem more youthful than most of his subordinate younger colleagues. Nevertheless, he had to be in excess of sixty, Sara guessed. But he was handsome – still very much an alpha male. He was always elegantly turned out, regardless of whether he was wearing a suit or jeans and a polo and short-haired, fit, almost military in appearance. An active manager who was prepared to listen, but who demanded obedience when issuing orders. Sara contemplated whether he felt threatened by the younger personnel, challenged for his role as the lead male. But if he was, he didn't give that impression.

Sara tried to produce an apologetic smile, but it felt more akin to a grimace.

'Yes, sorry about that. I had to sort something out.'

Bielke suddenly scrutinised her with even greater intensity.

'I hope you weren't getting involved in another case.'

'No.' Sara grew worried. Did Bielke know something? Would he continue this line of inquiry? But it didn't seem that he did. 'Why would there be?'

'I've heard about the business with Stellan Broman. And I don't want other cases to take you away from your job.'

'They won't, I promise.'

Bielke's gaze lingered on Sara for a second, as if he was debating whether or not to believe her.

'Good,' he said in conclusion, before switching straight to the case in hand. 'Poles. Jozef Koson and Adam Wiernik. Good old central European gangsters, according to Interpol. They started out as football hooligans in some of the violent groups of ultras and from there they were drawn into right-wing extremist groups and convicted repeatedly for acts of violence. These particular gentlemen had Wisla Krakow tattoos all over their bodies – it's a club known for its violent fans and right-wing tendencies – they openly display Nazi imagery. Presumably in their old age they grew tired of drinking lager and fighting in the streets, and their rap sheet made them perfect recruitment material for some criminal gang that was looking for hitmen and foot soldiers.'

'But Interpol didn't know anything about that?'

'No, the two dead men don't seem to have drawn any attention in recent years. Perhaps because they're no longer involved in visible acts of violence.'

'What were they doing here?'

'Unclear. Drugs? Unpaid debts? Market-related turf wars? Or just a paid job. Sometimes the gangs bring in outsiders to cover their tracks. Perhaps they've advanced to using professional contract killers. We'll just have to hope it doesn't mean there's a new gangland war brewing.'

Sara squeezed her car key with her hand and it suddenly hit her.

'Why didn't they take the ferry?'

'What?'

'Why didn't they take the ferry? Bekas lived more or less round the corner from the pier on the far side. The quickest way to get here would have been on the ferry.'

'The ferry?'

'From Slagsta. Norsborg. They drove via Bromma.'

'Well, either they didn't know where they were going to begin with, or they didn't drive from his home address.'

'But he was hiding out there – in the neighbourhood where he had friends he could hide with. What would have persuaded him to leave there? Alone, without his mates?'

'Yes, that's a good question.'

'Have the divers found anything?'

'It's a big area to search. I don't think we should set our hopes too high.'

'Well, what do we do next then?' Sara asked.

'Wait for the call logs from Bekas's mobile over the last twenty-four hours, check the phone records for the other gang members, ask his pals about Polish contacts, keep an eye on rival gangs. I'm trying to get extra manpower for surveillance work. And I think we need to talk to everyone again. These aren't the sorts of people who usually talk to us, but perhaps we can find some small crack in the façade somewhere.'

'OK, which one am I taking?'

'Bielke.'

Sara hadn't heard a ringtone or even a soft vibration, but his phone must have rung because Bielke was now speaking into his mobile. His eyes narrowed increasingly as the call continued.

'We're on our way,' he said eventually, before hanging up. 'Come on!' he said to Sara without looking at her, running towards his car.

'What is it?'

'They've shot the leader of a rival gang.'

'I'll take my car.'

'Not the ferry. Take Essingeleden. And make sure you use your blue lights.'

Sara tucked in behind Bielke doing one hundred and fifty kilometres an hour on Ekerövägen heading back towards the city, and they hit one hundred and sixty on Essingeleden heading south towards Alby.

The shot man was one George 'Jojje' Taylor Jr., twenty-six years of age. He hailed from Botkyrka, his father a South African and his mother from Kungsör. He was one hundred and ninety centimetres tall and strikingly big, weighing in at almost one hundred kilos, of which only a few grams were fat. He had dazzlingly white teeth, dark brown eyes and hair done in cornrows. He had been hit three times by a shooter who had been sitting on the back of a souped-up moped. Jojje had been as lucky as his attackers had been unlucky. None of the three bullets had damaged any vital organs, so he was conscious when Sara and Bielke arrived on the scene. The attackers, on the other hand, had come crashing down when they hit a traffic island. The shooter had been knocked out cold and had managed to fire a shot into the back of his driver. Given that things were more critical for the moped driver than Jojje, the first ambulance had prioritised him, while the first officers arriving on the scene had been able to arrest the shooter.

The officer in command of the first patrol to have arrived was able to inform Bielke and Sara that George Taylor Jr was the leader of a rival gang and that the shooter was the fifteen-year-old younger brother of murder victim Cesar Bekas.

'Did your organisation kill Bekas?' was Bielke's first, highly direct question to Jojje. They didn't have long before the next ambulance arrived. Gunshot wounds naturally took priority over police questioning.

'"Organisation"? There's no need to big us up,' Jojje said, grinning.

'Did you?' Bielke said, ignoring the quip.

'Look mate, why the hell would we?'

'Why else would someone want to shoot you?'

'Maybe it was some AIK nutjob? I'm a Hammarby man, innit.' Jojje smiled again – a broad, self-confident smirk. Sara recognised the attitude from other alpha males in his world. The important thing wasn't to be funny – it was to be cocksure.

'What's the quarrel over? Drugs? A girl? Divvying up the spoils?'

'You've been watching too much *Snabba Cash*, mate. We're not criminals, we're businessmen. Look.'

Jojje pointed and Sara and Bielke followed his finger with their eyes.

'Pizzeria St Tropez. That's mine. And I've got another three. And a dry cleaner's. And a convenience store. You hungry? Pop in for a pizza. Best in town. On me. Tell them I sent you. Have a "King of the World", best bloody pizza in the whole fucking world. All the toppings. All of them. But don't forget to tip.'

'And why does a fifteen-year-old take three shots at a pizzeria owner?'

'Maybe we wouldn't sell him beer? You know how it is, we always card people.'

Jojje pressed his hand against the dressing applied to one of the gunshot wounds and grimaced with pain.

'He's just a kid,' said Bielke.

'He shoots like a kid,' said Jojje, glancing down at his wounds and laughing.

'The last thing we want is a new gang war,' Bielke continued.

'Don't start one then.' Jojje shrugged.

'You know what I mean.'

'Hey, I ain't starting no war.'

'But you get your own back if you're attacked?'

'Wouldn't you?'

'I'd talk to the police.'

'You'd talk to yourself? Creepy!'

Bielke looked Taylor Jr right in the eyes.

'Don't seek out revenge,' he said with emphasis.

Jojje raised his eyebrows.

'What have I got to take revenge for? Them driving like little bitches? Look, seriously, it was no fifteen-year-old that shot me.'

'No?'

'No. It was a white boy in a suit. Looked like he worked in a branch of fucking Nordea. You know how it is – loads of them suit monkeys coming down here and causing a fuss. They try to launder their Baltic cash through our pizzerias. You bring the Nordea management team in for an identity parade and I reckon I'll be able to pick him out. Or do you protect criminals?'

Bielke turned on his heel and left without saying a word. Jojje switched his attention to Sara.

'What's your name?'

'Beyoncé.'

Jojje grinned.

'Beautiful name. What's your number?'

'Go fuck yourself.'

'You don't want me to call you?'

'No.'

'What if I remember something?' the gangster persisted.

'I thought you didn't talk to the cops?'

'"You"? Which you mean? Niggas?'

'Crooks,' Sara said curtly.

'I told you I ain't no crook. I'm a businessman. I have a company and everything. I always help the police if I can. I'm a mother-in-law's dream. What's your number?'

'No date.'

'No, no, I swear. I'll only call if I hear something, mate.'

Sara gave Jojje her number and wondered whether it was flattering or insulting to be referred to as mate by him.

'Or if you ever want to try out my pizzeria some time?' he said, looking deep into Sara's eyes with a meaningful smile.

'Listen, Mr Horndog. I'm twenty years older than you.'

'Twenty? Pfft. Why so focused on numbers? You an accountant or something?'

'No, and I wasn't born yesterday either.'

'The fact that you ain't no bimbo with no clue about what she wants turns me on. I've had hundreds of them, innit. "Is this what I should do?" "How do you want me?" Boring.'

'And you're boring to me.'

The second ambulance arrived and two paramedics got out and unfolded a trolley that they helped George Taylor Jr onto. But before they rolled him away, he raised a hand to stop them and he smiled at Sara again.

'You have no idea what a kick I'd get outta pulling you. Like trapping a lion.'

'Is that how you see me? As quarry?'

'Yes. You like it?'

'Not one fucking bit. Lucky for you that you didn't say "catching a whopper of a pike" at least.'

Sara turned around and left. The paramedics lifted the stretcher into the ambulance while George watched Sara departing, his expression confused.

'What's a pike?'

16

'My contact in Berlin has got back to me.'

Hedin had neither introduced herself nor offered a greeting – she had got straight to the point, too focused for formalities. Sara had apparently guessed correctly that Stiller's list of names would get her going.

'Yes?'

'There's actually information about those code names you gave me.'

'There is? Good. What?'

Sara pulled into a petrol station by IKEA to find some paper and a pen to take notes.

'Not on the phone,' said Hedin. 'Are you good at drawing?'

'What? No. How do you mean?'

Sara looked suspiciously at the dried-out felt-tip pen she had managed to find, emblazoned with the words 'You could become a blood donor too'.

'Then you'll have to find a picture in a newspaper or something. Something you'd be willing to get a tattoo of, a flower or a dolphin.'

'I would never get a tattoo.'

'No? Well, you'll just have to imagine that you would. Take that picture to Black Rebel Tattoo at 142 Folkungagatan. Go in and show them the photo and tell them you want it to say "For Eva" on it.'

'What? Are you kidding?'

'Why would I do that?'

Hedin hung up.

A tattoo?

Sara had no intention of getting one, but otherwise she decided to do as Hedin said, if nothing else, to see what happened next.

She looked around and spotted the desolate-looking petrol station shop. She popped inside and grabbed a magazine at random, paid and went back outside. She leafed hastily through the pages. Personal finance, health, culture. Not much in the way of tattoo inspiration. A home interior section had pictures of an old set of Rörstrand china made by Swedish Grace. That would have to do. Why not get a soup bowl tattooed on your shoulder?

Then she pulled back out onto the E4 and headed for Södermalm.

Black Rebel Tattoo was at the end of Folkungagatan, just before the hill down to the London Viaduct and the ferry terminal for boats to Finland. The shop window displayed several dozen photographs of tattoos, presumably ones inked right here. Everything from gossamer butterflies to horned monsters with bloodied tusks. Demons, skulls and flames were somewhat over-represented. Sara peered at her torn-out magazine page, smiled at her piece of china and then stepped into the tattoo parlour. A small bell sounded as the door opened and then closed again.

Inside the premises it was dark. The large show window facing the street was blocked off and the walls were covered in black velvet, skulls and satanic symbols. In the centre of the floor there was a large, elevated couch beside a tattoo machine and a couple of switched-off lights. The only light source comprised an artificial torch on the wall with plastic flames emanating from it. A black veil was suddenly drawn aside and a small, thin girl in her twenties appeared. Her skin was chalky white, her raven-black hair reached down to her waist, and she must have broken a record for wearing the most mascara around her eyes. There were a dozen rings in her nose and her entire body was covered in tattoos. Crucifix, the sign of ankh, aum symbols and various characters from *A Nightmare Before Christmas*.

'Yes?'

Sara held up her magazine page. The girl looked at it.

'We don't sell plates.'

'I want a tattoo like that. The soup bowl. And it should say "For Eva".'

The girl looked at Sara.

'"For Eva"? Why didn't you say? Here.'

The girl drew the black veil to one side and Sara followed her into a small kitchenette with a window onto the rear courtyard. Surprisingly, the room was pink and white with small Hello Kitty dolls everywhere. The heavily made-up woman opened the window and pointed.

'Between the buildings over there and across the yard. Then you'll see her kitchen window. Lower ground.'

Sara hesitated for a second. Was she serious? Was Hedin, the goddess of the night, joshing with her? But she decided to play along and squeezed through the window into the back courtyard. The girl shut the window behind her, probably relieved to be able to return her full focus to death.

On the other side of the large courtyard Sara managed to locate Hedin's kitchen window thanks to the blue hallway on the far side of the room which she remembered from her previous visit. She went up to it and tapped on the pane, and after a while Hedin appeared and opened it. She invited Sara in with a sweeping gesture. Sara looked at the window which was well above waist height.

'What? Should I . . .?'

Then she shrugged and heaved herself up onto the windowsill, leaned forward and allowed herself to tumble into Hedin's flat. What was it about Hedin and climbing through windows?

On the far side of the small flat, Sara saw that the curtains were drawn, shutting out the street. The dark contributed to the lugubrious atmosphere. Something was afoot – she could feel it.

'OK, I demand an explanation. What's with having to cross the river of Hades to get here?'

Hedin didn't look at all amused, but looked at Sara gravely.

'You're on the trail of something very dangerous.'

Sara wanted to protest. She wasn't on the trail of anything. All she wanted to do was give Hedin information so that the researcher could continue her work. Sara had a job to do. And a family to think of.

'Surely it can't be dangerous enough that I have to crawl in through your kitchen window?' she said eventually.

Hedin switched on a small portable radio and turned the volume up.

'The code names you gave me aren't for regular informants or spies,' the old woman said.

'OK . . .'

'You've probably heard of the Baader-Meinhof Group – they referred to themselves as the Red Army Faction. But there were several groups like that. Violent terrorists prepared to die for their beliefs.'

Sara pictured long-haired men with walrus moustaches, angry women with automatic weapons, and kidnapped executives with slogans slung around their necks, not entirely dissimilar to the videos IS had broadcast showing their victims. Young Germans taking up arms against the police and authorities in their own country to fight capitalism, uncompromising rebels who had terrified all of Europe in the seventies.

'And these names were in those circles?' said Sara.

'They seem to have been put together in a cell to operate here.'

'Why Sweden?'

'It was easy to hide here. No wanted posters, no police actively looking for them. And when the occupation of the West German embassy went wrong and Sweden deported the people they'd arrested to West Germany, Sweden became an arch-enemy because a couple of the terrorists died of their injuries. Their thesis was that Swedish politicians had blood on their hands – above all Anna-Greta Leijon. They got it into their heads that she had made the decision to deport the wounded, which wasn't actually true.'

'I remember that. Operation Leo. They built a cage for her, didn't they? In a basement somewhere here in Södermalm?'

'On Katarina Bangata. The people's prison was what they called it. Half a dozen fanatics who claimed to speak for the masses. It all boiled down to the idea that West German society was still riddled with old Nazis at every level who had never been held accountable. They wanted to deal with the fascists. Then, when they were arrested, they were replaced by others who tried to get their idols released. And they were arrested, and new supporters carried out new acts of terror to get them all released. And so on. It was a huge spiral of completely senseless violence.'

'And you're saying that they still pose a threat to society? Wasn't this in the seventies?'

Hedin set down two cups of tea that smelled herbal, and proffered a plastic tub to Sara.

'Garlic capsule?' she said. Sara shook her head. Hedin placed two capsules on her tongue and leafed through her notes, made on the back of various cut-up milk cartons and cereal boxes.

'It began in 1967 and culminated in the seventies and eighties. Continued into the nineties. People nowadays think terrorism is something new, that it all started with al-Qaida, but they've forgotten about the IRA, PFLP, RAF, ETA and all the others that menaced us for decades, detonating bombs in London, Madrid and Paris – and right here in Stockholm in 1986. The Red Army Faction didn't give up until 1998 and various IRA factions remain active to this day, despite the ceasefire in Northern Ireland.'

'You mean that these four people may still be active?'

'Many of the people arrested showed no regret whatsoever. They never distanced themselves from armed struggle.'

'So what did they do? Wasn't it mostly just talk, like everything in the progressive wave?'

'It wasn't just talk,' said Hedin in a tone that made Sara feel ashamed, as if she were disappointing a strict schoolmistress. 'The

Red Army Faction bombed, kidnapped and murdered completely indiscriminately. Here in Sweden, they shot two attachés in cold blood during the occupation of the embassy, and they were set on executing the rest of the staff if their predecessors in the RAF weren't released from jail in West Germany.'

'How did they end up so militant?'

'They went to training camps in the Middle East, learned hand-to-hand combat and how to build their own bombs and use automatic weapons. And they received help from their Palestinian and Arab friends. On one of those occasions when PFLP hijacked a plane, they shot the pilot and were prepared to blow up the entire plane just to get Andreas Baader – leader of Baader-Meinhof – released. As I said, some have never regretted their ways and still consider lethal violence to be justified. And above all, there are many who have never been uncovered or brought to justice.'

'Just like they thought that the former Nazis had never been punished,' Sara commented.

'Exactly.'

'And these terrorists are connected to the murder of Stiller?'

'That's who was on the list you found.'

Sara looked at Hedin, taking in the intense fervour in her eyes.

'I didn't think you were interested in Stiller's murder,' she said.

'I'm not.'

'No?' said Sara, smiling meaningfully.

'No. But I am interested in Lotta Broman.'

'A trade?'

Hedin shrugged, but she continued staring at her.

Sara paused for a moment's thought. What could she say? It didn't feel right to lie to the old woman who had helped her so much, but Sara knew that it was impossible to know what Hedin would do the information. As a researcher, the pursuit of the truth came before all else. It was more important than any possible consequences for Malin and her family, for Sara or even for Hedin herself.

'What is it you want to know?'

'Where is Lotta? Why is she missing? What's her connection to Geiger? Does she know anything about Geiger's espionage? They wouldn't have concocted a cover story like that if it hadn't been important to them. But why is *she* important?'

Hedin was on the trail of the truth. Sara couldn't deceive her indefinitely, but she might be able to buy some time.

'I can find out more from Säpo.'

'How?'

'I've got a hold on them.'

Hedin seemed satisfied with that.

'All right. Let's give you some names.'

Hedin bent down to the small fridge on the floor. She opened the door and then popped open the freezer box. From it she removed an archival folder and passed it to Sara.

'The freezer?'

'Who looks there?' said Hedin.

Sara looked at the file.

'And this is . . . ?'

'Messer, Axt, Faust and Lorelei, the core of an overseas terrorist cell. Country, Sweden, judging by what you've found. The Stasi supported lots of terrorists throughout Western Europe. This seems to have been one such group.'

Sara opened the file.

Hans Gerlach, Stefan Kremp, Otto Rau, Marita Werner.

'Is that . . . ?' said Sara.

Hedin nodded in confirmation.

'The real names of the people on the list you found. There's no trace of them in Sweden though. It's quite possible they're called something else entirely today.'

Sara went through the various documents in the folder: copies of old files, so it seemed. Cover names, real names, code names for operations, reliability assessments, ties to other members. Sara checked the key words using Google Translate. The woman was described as 'Ideologically reliable'. The men were 'Dedicated', 'Uncertain' and 'Boundless' respectively.

German terrorists, active in Sweden, with Stasi backing. It definitely sounded like it might be connected to Stiller. Might any of the four old terrorists lead Sara to the murderer? Or was one of them the murderer? She looked at the names again.

Gerlach, Kremp, Rau and Werner. At least one of them would know something.

The problem was that she couldn't pursue this. Bielke wouldn't be best pleased if she continued rummaging around in this case, plus it might be dangerous. Hedin had been very clear. And someone had evidently murdered Stiller.

But it didn't matter. It was her mess to clear up, Sara decided. She would just have to be careful.

'If you find out where they live, I promise to try and find out the truth about Lotta,' said Sara. 'Säpo owe me a favour.' A big favour, she thought to herself. And her thoughts once again went back to the odd incident at Bromma Airport.

Sara had threatened to go to the media and tell them everything about Abu Rasil and Geiger's true identity. Brundin had made a call and then she had taken Sara with her from the Södersjukhuset hospital to Bromma Airport and an isolated room with a door opening straight onto the apron. After twenty minutes, a small private jet had landed outside the glass doors, a Gulfstream 5 bearing the livery of Vanguard Executive.

But no one had got out.

Then the vehicle carrying Lotta Broman had arrived. Six members of the police task force had led the detainee into the room in handcuffs and shackles with a hood over her head.

Seven men in unmarked black uniforms had emerged from the jet, their faces covered in balaclavas. None of them had spoken. Two of them had quietly slipped to one side and taken up a watch on the hallway. They had clutched automatic weapons while the others had led Lotta to the waiting aircraft, still in complete silence.

Just as Sara and Brundin had turned to leave, another plane had landed outside the glass doors, and a stretcher with a whole team of medics surrounding it had been rapidly rolled through the departures hall and out onto the apron. Lying on the stretcher had been a thin figure connected to a drip and various other machines. Someone with short, grey hair. Sara had looked at Brundin, who had met her gaze.

'She doesn't have long left. We have to get what she knows out of her.'

'Where are they taking her?'

'Neither you nor I will ever find out.'

17

The big apartment was empty when Sara got home. At any rate, it felt that way. She heard music coming from Olle's room, but his door was shut and compared with just a few years ago, when both Olle and Ebba had spread their possessions throughout the flat and had loads of friends round constantly – a daughter who had moved out and a son who constantly shut himself away in his bedroom made for a rather desolate existence.

She went into the kitchen and poured herself a glass of water, then thought for a moment before taking her water into the living room. The parquet creaked as she crossed the expansive floor. Unlike Martin, she didn't usually turn the lights and TV on the second she got in, she liked to sit in peace and quiet for a while after she returned home. To listen to the silence.

Sara knew that Martin was out preparing for Uncle Scam's visit. The megastar had been booked into the Grand Hôtel, but would actually be staying in another hotel amidst the greatest secrecy. According to Martin it was for security reasons, but Sara suspected it was more about self-assertion. Martin was the only one who knew where Scam was staying since he was the boss, and he had to go there to check in person that the secret accommodation lived up to the fussy rapper's standards. Sara had asked to see Scam's list of demands – his contractual riders – but Martin had refused. He probably realised that Sara would call him and his company morons if she saw what they had agreed to in order to bring the star to Sweden. He knew exactly how annoyed she got about the police having to provide so many officers for events like gigs and football matches. It was money that could be better spent elsewhere. Sara thought that Go Live ought to pay for all security around its events itself and she let Martin know she thought that every time major concerts requiring a police presence took place.

In the solemn silence that reigned within the huge living room, Nadia's battered face appeared in her mind's eye. Jenna had seemed oblivious, despite the fact that Nadia had assumed she would understand the warning.

What peepshow was it Nadia had been involved in?

The word moved her thoughts on to old men in small dark booths with glass partitions looking towards a stage where a girl was undressing. Old, stale and degrading for all involved. Nadia must have been part of a peepshow that had gone off the rails. Perhaps she didn't want to go as far as the clients did, and they had assaulted her? Or the organiser had beaten her instead of paying her? No, she'd had loads of cash in her handbag. Whoever had hurt Nadia, Sara wanted to catch them.

She picked up her laptop from the coffee table and searched online. The word 'peepshow' mostly turned up hits for some British sitcom. She tried 'peepshow Stockholm' which gave her hits relating to Reeperbahn's old record and a couple of doll's houses up for auction. Not much to go on.

As the different cases merged into one in her head, it occurred to Sara that the whole of East Germany had, in one way or another, been one big peepshow in which tens of thousands of Stasi employees had monitored and bugged their fellow Germans. And it was really the same today, with the NSA and GCHQ, FRA and especially China's i surveillance apparatus. They could find out everything, about everyone. Everywhere. Who you mixed with, what you said, what you read. Millions of people all over the world busy watching other people. It was a peculiar thought.

But right now it was Nadia and the peepshow that mattered.

Sara decided to get in touch with David again, apply some pressure. Coming from Olle's room, she heard the pounding bass of some Uncle Scam song but she didn't want to fall out with the only child she still had living at home with her, so she went up to the top of the tower to make her call. Above Slussen, a late summer evening was sinking into the warm darkness that characterised a good August.

David didn't pick up, so Sara left him a message and called her other old colleagues. Neither Pål nor Jenny had heard anything about a peepshow going on, but they promised to ask around.

Why didn't anyone know anything? It was usually impossible to do anything without tongues wagging all over town. New prostitutes, new sex clubs, new sex drugs. Police operations. Everyone knew everything about everything. But no one knew anything about the peepshow.

Since it was Nadia who had mentioned it, Sara reflected that other sex workers might also be aware of the peepshow. Would any of them talk to a cop? The girls were generally way too scared of being punished by their traffickers or pimps.

But there was one.

Eva, the woman who had told her about Stellan's abuse of young girls. She had been on the streets for many years and ought to know. She was her own woman and didn't seem afraid of anyone. Mostly because she no longer had anything to lose. Sara called her.

'Peepshow?!' said Eva, with a hoarse, cigarette-inflected chuckle. 'You kidding or what? That was the seventies! Blokes in hats trying to hide their stiffies. Not even *I* have worked a peepshow.'

'There's nothing like that now?'

'Absolutely not. Who the hell would cough up to watch a girl stripping when there's unlimited free porn online? Although it's a pity. Peepshows aren't that bad. You don't have to get too close to the johns. Hi there, you looking for some fun?'

The last bit wasn't for her benefit but for someone she had just seen, Sara assumed. And given that Eva abruptly cut the call, it suggested someone had been looking for some fun. But how 'fun' it would be for Eva was uncertain for Sara.

She remained sitting there for a while, letting the darkness grow beyond the windows before she finally went back downstairs.

Just as Sara switched on the TV for some braindead entertainment, her phone rang.

'Hi, it's Christian here. Lotta's husband. Lotta Broman.'

'Hi,' said Sara, trying to make these pieces of information fit together in her head. Christian. Lotta's husband. He was calling . . . OK. 'How are you doing?' she added, remembering that the mother and wife was supposedly on a sabbatical.

'Yeah, fine.'

'How's Lotta?'

'Good, I think. We get the occasional email with some photos. It's beautiful there.'

'Where was it she went?'

'Mauritius.'

'Why didn't you go too?'

'She needed peace and quiet. You know how much rest you get with two hyperactive kids around.'

'Yeah, of course.'

'Er, look. I'm calling about something else,' Christian continued. 'Well, actually, I suppose it's connected. Your mother left her umbrella behind.'

'My mother?'

'Yes. She stopped in to see how we were doing, but when she went she left her umbrella behind.'

Sara couldn't make it add up. Firstly, Jane would never accidentally leave anything anywhere. No chance. And secondly, why on earth had she gone round to Lotta's family home?

'My mother? You're absolutely certain?'

'Completely. I can't get hold of her, so I thought you might be able to let her know. Or if you're passing you could pick it up. You're in town, aren't you? And she's still out in the sticks, isn't she?'

'Vällingby.'

'Yeah, exactly,' Christian said with a nod. Well, it felt as if he were nodding.

'I'll pop by first thing tomorrow.'

Sara ended the call and rang her mother, but the call went straight to voicemail.

'Lotta's husband Christian called. You left your umbrella at theirs. Why? I know you didn't forget it. What exactly were you doing there?'

Sara hung up and stopped by one of the windows looking over Kornhamnstorg and the water. Right now, there was no one working on the building site at Slussen – they had all gone home. Or perhaps to the barracks that the construction workers from Poland and elsewhere lived in when they were here working. Darkness had descended on Stockholm but the lights of the city were doing what they could to extend the day for its inhabitants. Lifting her gaze, she tracked a metro train crossing the bridge from the old town towards Slussen. The rush hour had ended long ago and the carriages were almost empty – just a few individuals, a handful of couples and the odd group. Who were the people on that train? Where were they going? What was waiting for them when they arrived? She would never find out.

She stared beyond the Hilton and up towards the heights of Södermalm. Bastugatan, Laurinska huset, Monteliusvägen. There were lights shining from many windows, some of them safe and cosy homes, others sad and depressing flats, and some probably dangerous and frightening accommodation. The view ought to have been soothing, but Sara couldn't escape an aching sense of worry in her body.

Jane didn't usually turn off her mobile. Had something happened? Why had she been round to Lotta's?

Her mother was up to something. The only question was what.

18

Time seemed to have had no impact on the place.

She hadn't been here in more than thirty years, but it all looked just the same.

The white house, its design inspired by functionalism, the garden running down to a jetty and Lake Mälaren, the small guest chalet by the jetty that had been their home for so many years. The only difference was that the garden shed had burned down.

And now here she was – the victor.

The one still standing at the end of the bout.

Now she could finally move freely around the house. No one could stop her.

The spare key was still at the back of the house under the pot from Waldemarsudde, just as it always had been.

Jane took the key and went inside. She needed to get on with it before they finished drawing up the estate inventory, before the house was sold or taken over by one of the daughters: a new generation of evil in the house of horrors.

She stopped for a moment in the spacious hallway and listened. Small, imperceptible creaks in the walls. The ticking of a clock in the living room. If she shut her eyes, she could hear the voices of the past. From all those parties and events that she had served at, from the children playing and causing a nuisance, Agneta telling her what to do.

The living room with the shabby Pernilla reading chair in which Stellan had met his maker. The Josef Frank sofa with Aralia upholstery that she had been under orders to keep spotless, Falsterbo Stripe wallpaper from Boråstapeter on the walls and souvenir plates from all sorts of places around Europe.

On so many occasions she had been lectured by Stellan and Agneta about what everything was called and how much it had all cost, so that she would understand how carefully she had to look after their beautiful home. For the home was undeniably beautiful, unlike the people who had lived in it.

But what she was looking for was probably upstairs, she thought, as she slowly climbed the stairs.

19

They emerged from the impersonal but flashy apartment at 8B Eastmansvägen at 07.56, harried and late for school and work. Christian, Leo and Sixten, Lotta's husband and children.

What did they know about Lotta's fate? What did they think? Were they worried?

What was it like living without her? Sara was convinced that it had been Lotta who called all the shots in the family, and now she was gone. How had they reacted to that? Were they lost and anxious, or happy with their new-found freedom? No, a mother was always a mother, Sara thought to herself, realising that she was attempting to convince herself of that too, in part.

Had Lotta been able to make contact with her family before she was taken away? If so, what had she said? 'Mum has to go away for a while . . .'?

The emails they were receiving were probably written by someone else entirely; how would they react if they ever found out the truth about their wife and mother?

Sara felt a prickle of guilty conscience about the fact that the trio were being forced to live without Lotta, but reflected that an absent mother was still a far better alternative than hundreds of thousands dead.

She honked. Christian looked up and around, spotted Sara and came over to her car to pass her the umbrella.

'Everything good?'

'Definitely. You?'

'Definitely.'

The usual pleasantries were dealt with quickly and then Sara sat there, staring at her mother's umbrella.

She still didn't believe for one moment that Jane had forgotten it. She had left it there on purpose. But why?

So that she could come back, of course.

If she needed to.

But why?

Sara started the engine, drove around the back of Sabbatsberg and onto the Barnhusbron bridge, along Fleminggatan onto the Klarastrandleden and then to Solna. But she wasn't going to work quite yet. She had half an hour to spare, so instead she went around the big, empty roundabout, past Tomteboda and up a steep hill. At the top loomed the colossal headquarters of the Swedish Security Service, the Olympus of law enforcement, with uninterrupted views and a giant, cloudless sky above it, like an eagle's nest, a medieval fortress. For the Bavarian dukes, inaccessibility had streamlined fortress defences just as much as it had impeded opportunities for escape – but who would want to escape from a place like that?

Yellow and red signage posted on the building's façade declared photography to be strictly prohibited, in addition to banning any drawings or attempts to document the building. Its shape and size did not appear in any mapping application but the address was a matter of public record. Strange logic, hiding in plain sight. Or to draw a parallel with the water in the nearby Saltsjön bay: it was a brackish transparency. And it was in those waters she intended to trawl.

Sara parked her car in one of the spaces on the opposite side of the street from the entrance and looked up at the newly built grey façade. On so many occasions she had sat inside and been questioned in the months since Geiger and Abu Rasil had attempted to detonate the bombs in Germany.

She saw that the guard by the door was keeping his eye on her – just as he was supposed to. Everyone who approached the building was kept under close observation. But Sara was in no hurry to show her police credentials.

First she pulled out her phone and made a call.

'Brundin.'

Still just her last name. Unusual for a woman, Sara thought. And she was quite certain that Brundin had saved her number so she knew who was calling. Sara got straight to the point – a habit she had picked up from Hedin.

'Messer, Axt, Faust and Lorelei were the Stasi code names for a group of West German terrorists. One of them – or all of them – murdered Stiller, the priest. I know their real names now. Tell me what happened to Lotta and I'll tell you what I know.'

Silence for a few seconds. Complete silence, as if Brundin had hit 'mute' – possibly to consult with someone. Then she returned, brusque as ever.

'Come in.'

Sara got out of the car and went over to the door, where the guard had just received instructions in his earpiece. Sara flashed her police ID, the guard scanned it and admitted her into the security complex. In the background, she heard the sound of a train on its way somewhere.

Just as she was entering, Sara's mobile rang. Anna. It would have to wait. She rejected the call and switched onto silent.

Brundin came to meet her by the lifts without offering a word of greeting. Today she was wearing a blazer and sequined T-shirt teamed with a pair of high-waisted jeans. The intelligence operative piloted the ordinary detective through a number of locked doors and past a series of cameras mounted in every corridor and room they passed.

Their walk ended in a small meeting room with sandy-coloured walls, white floral curtains and a meeting table made from blond pine. On the table was a tray containing napkins, coffee mugs and single tetrapak portions of milk. But no coffee.

Sara sat down and Brundin sat down opposite her. Lying on the table was a beige folder with the words 'SEKR AVT' and Sara's personal identification number on it. The Säpo officer put her hand on the folder, and Sara pondered whether it was because Brundin wanted to shield the contents or because she intended to whip them out.

'Since you let me in, I assume you're interested in what I know about the four terrorists,' said Sara.

Brundin didn't answer – she merely raised her eyebrows in a gesture that might have been interpreted as, 'And that is?'

'First I want to know everything about Lotta,' Sara said. 'Where is she and why has it all gone quiet? There hasn't been so much as a whisper that Europe was seconds from a devastating attack.'

'That's down to the EU. Not us.'

'But you know why.'

Brundin merely looked at Sara without her expression even flickering.

'Where was she flown to? Who took her? And Agneta? Did you get what you wanted from her? She can't have lived long.'

'This concerns a matter pertaining to international terrorism and multi-state cooperation on issues of security. You will never have a full view of what occurred and why. This is well above both your and my pay grades. Lotta and Agneta Broman were processed by intelligence officials from Sweden and the EU – that's all you need to know. But as you are aware, you are not permitted to tell anybody this in accordance with the non-disclosure agreement you signed,' Brundin said and tapped her index finger on the skin-toned folder on the table.

'When I was in hospital with gunshot wounds and burns, zonked out on painkillers.'

'Just accept the facts.'

'Can I take a look at that agreement?' said Sara, reaching out for it with her hand. But Brundin quickly withdrew the folder without saying a word. She stared fixedly at Sara, one hand resting heavily on the folder containing the agreement.

'Lotta has supposedly taken a sabbatical, and Agneta was supposedly found dead, shot by the same burglars who killed Stellan,' Sara said, glowering at the Säpo woman.

'That's correct.'

'Why are you protecting Lotta?'

'No one is protecting Lotta. We're protecting the people of the European Union.'

'Or perhaps you're protecting the powers that be in the EU? By keeping it quiet that the union almost suffered a huge terrorist attack, and that a Swedish director general involved with a German intelligence operative was the brain behind it all.'

'Nothing but speculation. Everything is to protect the people.'

'I also think that Eva Hedin should be told the truth.'

Brundin assumed an irritated, almost disgusted expression when Sara mentioned Hedin's name. Perhaps it was because Hedin had prevailed over the Security Service in the Supreme Court. Or perhaps she simply thought Hedin was an idiot.

'About both Lotta and Geiger,' Sara added.

'That won't be happening. And don't get it into your head to say anything.'

This time, Brundin picked up the folder containing the NDA and waved it around in a way that made Sara think about the old photos of Britain's Neville Chamberlain declaring 'peace for our time' in 1938.

Sara fell silent and stared at Brundin for a while. The other woman was immobile, with an expression that it was impossible to interpret. It was neither irritable nor anxious, nor even confident. It was completely blank. What a perfect talent for a spook.

'What about the code names, then?' Sara said by way of persuasion. 'You promised you'd explain.'

'Only about Lotta Broman. And you promised to tell me everything you knew about the murder of Stiller. The police in Östergötland reported it as suicide. After he killed his wife in some marital dispute.'

'But none of us believe that.'

'What do you know about the people you mentioned?'

'What do *you* know about them?'

'That wasn't the deal.' Brundin was still implacable and Sara found herself giving in.

'Messer, Axt, Faust and Lorelei were actually called Hans Gerlach, Stefan Kremp, Otto Rau and Marita Werner. But those names aren't in any current records. They're presumably living under new identities. The question is what they're called today, whether they're involved, and why Stiller was killed? Was it because something is happening? Something connected to what Geiger was preparing for? Or was it simply to protect their identities?

Sara fell silent.

'Are you finished?' said Brundin.

'Yes.'

'OK.'

They sat in silence.

'So which is it?' Sara said at last.

'Which?'

'Why was he murdered? Who are these four people?'

'No comment.'

'Why aren't you interested in what I've told you?'

'I'm unable to offer any comment on anything. Not as to whether we know who you are talking about, nor whether any of them are subjects of interest to us or other intelligence agencies. All I can do is advise you to leave it well alone. Don't you have a job to be doing? Three dead in Ekerö, aren't there?'

'So you're keeping tabs on me?'

'No comment.' Sara discerned an ever-so-subtle smile at the corner of Brundin's mouth. The sly fox.

'Stiller was murdered. Do more people have to die just because you're protecting former terrorists?'

'No one is protecting any terrorists.'

'I won't leave until you've given me some information about these four. Do they have new names? Do you know where they are? Who are they today?'

'No comment.'

'OK. Should I call the papers? About Lotta and Abu Rasil and these four people?'

Sara pulled out her mobile to emphasise the threat, at which point she saw she had five missed calls from Anna and another from Bielke, in addition to a text message from Anna that read: 'Where the fuck are you? Gang war! Come now!'

20

Once she had escorted Nowak out, Brundin returned along the corridors and knocked on the door of Nyman's office. She hoped he wasn't dissatisfied with her efforts.

'Come in!' Nyman called through the door.

He still had his eyes glued to the screen showing the room where Brundin and Nowak had just been. He was leaning forward with his hands clasped together.

Brundin knew that her colleagues regarded her boss as a paper pusher. In their eyes, Quintus Nyman was a lawyer rather than a proper law enforcement official – having served out a career as a bureaucrat, unlike most people in the building who had spent the best parts of their working lives doing fieldwork. Had it been possible to rhyme anything with Quintus, she was sure there would have been many sobriquets applied to him.

A bald crown, grey-speckled beard, a ring of silver hair around his skull and a narrow, pointy nose that propped up a pair of steel-rimmed spectacles. He could have worn plain clothes, but he always wore a uniform to work – despite the fact that, or perhaps because, he had not been a police officer from the beginning. And true to form, he had a meticulously tidy desk and perfectly arranged folders in the bookcase behind him. No passwords on Post-its stuck to the keyboard here, no dirty coffee mugs, umbrella and wellies standing by, in case it should rain at home time.

Nyman looked up from the computer screen and only then did Brundin settle down into one of the armchairs provided for visitors.

'Where on earth did she get those names from?' said Quintus Nyman.

'Hedin, I should think.'

Damned Hedin was what she wanted to say. But Nyman didn't swear. So Brundin didn't either.

'Otto Rau,' said Nyman, mostly to himself, as he looked up at the ceiling. Then he fixed his gaze on Brundin again. 'She won't give in, will she?'

Brundin shook her head.

'Do you think she can find them?'

Reluctantly, Brundin realised she was proud that Nyman was consulting her for advice. It showed that he trusted her and appreciated her expertise. But that ought to be a matter of course after thirty-five years in the Security Service, rather than something that she reacted to like a schoolgirl. Pull yourself together, she urged herself.

'She found Geiger,' she said. 'And unmasked Abu Rasil.'

Nyman took off his glasses and pinched the bridge of his nose, closing his eyes.

'And she was close to ruining the whole set-up with the Germans,' he said. Then he put his glasses back on again, took a deep breath and exhaled audibly.

'Should we take her into custody?' said Brundin.

Nyman nodded thoughtfully. Then he shook his head slowly, mostly for his own sake, it seemed.

'No,' he said at last. 'She'll keep.'

That wasn't the answer Brundin had been hoping for, but she trusted that Nyman knew what he was doing.

'I'll notify our German friends,' said Nyman.

'Should we stand by for the time being?'

'No,' said Nyman. 'Definitely not. Stick to her. I want to know everything she does. All of it. She might actually find them. Keep me in the loop at all times. OK?'

'OK,' said Brundin, standing up. 'Should I note the case as being linked to her, or those terrorists?'

Nyman checked himself.

'Neither. There is no case. This is strictly off the books. Don't leave a trace anywhere. Got it?'

That answer surprised Brundin, but she trusted Nyman.

'Absolutely.'

21

Sara was in Slagsta for the second day in a row. This time she pulled into the car park of the Max hamburger chain immediately after the exit from the E4. It was cordoned off. There were police cars with flashing lights, blue and white tape and uniformed officers on full alert. A few were standing guard, others were redirecting traffic and yet others were speaking to patrons and staff in the burger joint. There was also a heavily armed unit from the task force in their dark garb. Today's gang had been heavily armed and hadn't been shy about opening fire. The risk of a cop getting in the way of a stray bullet wasn't something that made them back down. Quite the contrary.

The forces of nature were engaged in their own war as the late summer sun offered warmth and the autumn breeze cooling, meaning that anyone to windward was freezing while anyone out of the gusts was sweating. On the asphalt beside the climbing frame outside the restaurant were two bodies lying under bright yellow blankets. Their heads were covered – a clear indication that they were dead.

Bielke was talking to someone that Sara assumed was the task force leader. When her boss spotted Sara, he left the other officer and approached her with rapid footsteps.

'Where the hell have you been? Hall got a call from Säpo to say you'd been there asking questions about that priest in Småland.'

Superintendent Tom Hall, that spineless climber of the career ladder who was open to being used by anyone so long as he thought it would serve his own ends. Now Brundin had called him to cause trouble for Sara.

'And Anna says you rejected her call while you were on duty!'

'Technically, I hadn't yet come on duty. Where is Anna?'

'At Ekerö. They've found more bodies in Mälaren. But don't change the subject. She called you fifteen minutes before you were due to start. There's not much chance you'd make it to work in that amount of time. You must always be contactable – you know that!' Bielke stared at her, his expression more intense than usual. For several seconds he said nothing at all but didn't drop his gaze. They were standing close together and it almost felt as if he were going to touch her. It was almost embarrassing. Sara decided it was best to get out of this and move on.

'Sorry.'

Sara wondered how her boss could have such a firm grasp of her shifts. Did the same apply to all his subordinates?

'Now you have a choice to make,' Bielke said. 'Drop that priest business, or put in for a transfer. Although I don't know who is willing to take you – lost property up in the Arctic circle, perhaps.'

'Who are the victims?' Sara chose to ignore the last bit.

'Hakan Ulc and Moses Sserangi. Two guys from Bekas's gang. I assume it's revenge for the shooting of Jojje Taylor.'

'Both dead,' said Sara. 'Any other victims? Any witnesses?'

'The whole restaurant. But no one saw anything.'

'Cameras?'

'Oh yes. But the shooters were masked up and the car was stolen. It's probably on fire somewhere as we speak. Automatic weapons, children present and right next to a petrol station. Utter madness.'

Sara couldn't disagree.

'Nowak,' said Bielke, turning to her.

'Yes?'

'You get that I just want you to do your job, right?'

'Yes, of course.'

'I'm sorry if I was harsh just now.'

'I don't think you were. I would have been much angrier in your shoes.'

142

Bielke looked at her for a second with an expression verging on amusement. Sara met his gaze. She realised she liked Bielke. He had a reputation as something of a square, but he was a good boss. And handsome. He was of an age where you could say that about him without anyone thinking it meant anything. The silence between them extended without either of them averting their gaze.

'What do we do now?' Sara said at last.

Bielke seemed almost thrown by this straightforward question. It took a while for him to find his footing.

'Let's talk to George Taylor Jr and Bekas's gang. As far as we're concerned, we want to understand the reasons behind all three shootings, and for the sake of our colleagues out here it's about making sure that others don't seek revenge for the revenge. They're going to have their hands full keeping an eye on all the factions.'

Sara pulled out her mobile and rang the number Taylor had given her. No answer. Hardly surprising.

She hung up and shook her head at Bielke.

'Keep trying to get hold of him. Söderort are looking for members of Bekas's gang to stop them from doing anything else. But they're obviously lying low.'

'This might really go tits up,' said Sara.

'You can say that again.'

Bielke looked at the two bodies on the ground.

Sara knew she was up to her ears in work, that she really should drop Stiller, at least for now. She didn't want to draw any more of Bielke's ire – she had realised she actually wanted to stay in Västerort.

The only question was whether she would be able to stay away from the priest's murder.

No matter how hard she tried, she couldn't escape the feeling that it was her fault that he had died. And what was worse, that his wife had been murdered. She felt a responsibility to at least try and find out who had killed them and why. But if she waited too long, the murderer would have time to clean up their tracks.

And she believed the key to the murders lay in the present-day identities of the four terrorists.

22

Schönberg was still in a good mood as he strolled past the internet café and Conny's Container, puffing away on his pipe. As a reflex, he scanned the people he encountered on the busy pavement, as well as the people who had got off the tram at Marienburger Straße and were now crossing Prenzlauer Allee. Mothers with prams. Students clutching lattes and laptop bags, white AirPods in their ears. White-haired, furrowed men in black, struggling with the heat, holding rosaries and walking sticks. It was necessary to keep an eye on them all equally. When he reached the pedestrian crossing and turned around and was unable to spot anyone who seemed to be following him, he smiled as he did so often at the genius of picking premises next door to Deutsche Post. Given that DP were blurred out on Google Street View for security reasons, FADO's door was too, without any suspicions being raised. In practice, FADO was in far greater need of secrecy than Deutsche Post.

FADO stood for Frisch aus dem Orient, and it was a company that imported all sorts of foodstuffs from the Middle East for wholesale to restaurants across Germany. Julius Arnold Schönberg had been appointed managing director just a month earlier at the venerable age of seventy-two, and he still loved the scents that welcomed him as he stepped into the premises. Cinnamon sticks, chilis, garlic, figs, pistachios, mint, cardamom, coriander. Cornucopias in the form of large woven baskets filled with oriental treats. His diet had changed radically in the last month, since the company had vast quantities of goods such as dates, falafel, feta, bulgur, sambal oelek, lamb sausages and couscous that would only go to waste if he didn't take them home with him.

After the Abu Rasil disaster, Schönberg was simply relieved that he hadn't been sacked. If he hadn't known the right people and had so little time left until retirement, he would almost certainly have gone on that day. It was undeniably advantageous that all the people involved in determining his fate were people he had hired, so instead of leaving he had requested and been granted a transfer to a completely different part of the BND – a front company that traded in oriental foods and was thus able to engage in intelligence gathering via its branches in Lebanon, Syria, Jordan, Egypt, Saudi Arabia and Iraq. They also did a modest trade in providing restaurants in the Middle East with German foods such as sauerkraut, maultaschen, spätzle and German sausages made using beef, chicken or turkey rather than pork. The official business was actually run in the black, which was more than could be said for the other fronts that Schönberg had worked for previously. But above all, FADO was enabling him to bring to fruition the plan he had been working on for so many years and that had almost hit the buffers when Abu Rasil had been unmasked in Sweden. He probably only had one chance left, one final opportunity to end his career in a spectacular fashion. He wouldn't just hang up his hat and discreetly leave by a back door to be quickly forgotten – he would be remembered forever. He might even become an industry legend.

Schönberg nodded amiably at Samir and Leila, the young employees who managed contacts with the branches overseas, receiving and cataloguing information while also scrutinising every unfamiliar face that entered the premises. These unexpected guests could be everything from lost tourists and hungry Berliners who had mistaken the wholesaler for a regular shop, to spies dispatched there by foreign intelligence agencies. Samir and Leila always greeted people with a friendly Salam aleikum – Leila in her headscarf, Samir with his long beard, which hopefully gave the impression of orthodoxy. Of course, the two of them were actually BND officers with security clearance.

Schönberg grabbed an orange as he went by, stepped through the drapes at the rear of the unit into the small office with all the folders and sales records and the smell of incense. He went straight to the toilet and locked the door behind him. By undoing a catch behind the tap, he was able to push aside a wall in the shower cubicle. Behind this was a door made from armoured steel with a palm scanner and a separate iris scanner, just as he had for his safe room at home. Once his hand and eye had been checked, he was able to pass through the door and close the shower cubicle wall behind him.

He turned on the lights, put the orange on the desk and switched on the computer.

A flash. Something important had happened.

He read it.

Damn it!

Stiller was apparently incapable of even dying without causing trouble.

A message from Sweden. Sara Nowak had been going through everything and had somehow stumbled across the names Gerlach, Kremp, Rau and Werner. This was worrying in itself. But if he knew her, she wouldn't give up until she had dug up the whole truth, which would cost many lives. Including most likely her own.

That Swedish bigwig Nyman had requested all the information the BND had on the four terrorists. Well, he could forget about that.

Schönberg bit into the orange without having peeled it, and quickly spat out the equally unexpected and unwelcome pieces of peel onto the desk. He began to pack tobacco into his pipe to bring a better taste to his mouth.

So she had found the old leftist command. This was not good news. He really had thought Stiller's death would pass for a suicide.

What different times they had been! The Red Army Faction, the revolutionary cells and the 2 June Movement. And all the groups that had followed in their footsteps. It had all started in 1967 after a student, Benno Ohnesorg, had been shot dead by a police officer at a demonstration against the state visit of the Shah of Iran – on the second of June of that year. A fatal shooting that had shaken the entire radical world and triggered a tidal wave of terrorism, although it had transpired much later on that it had been perpetrated by a Stasi agent working as a West German police officer. Double-dealing and triple-dealing. If he ever wrote his memoirs, that would be a good title. He made a mental note.

The world was different now. In a way, it would be a relief to retire, but he couldn't escape the gnawing anxiety about what might happen when he was no longer there to keep an eye on the bad guys. What sort of mischief would they get up to then?

And what would happen to everything he knew? He would never be able to set all his knowledge down on paper. How could you digitise practised instinct?

Schönberg had increasingly begun to think about how much knowledge vanished with each person who died. And not just the knowledge itself, but above all, the intuition, the gut feel for what was right, what might correlate, the sudden impulses where the ability to identify almost invisible connections that a computer would never manage came to the fore.

But that was how it was. And no one would ever find out which threats he had helped to neutralise, no one would ever find out how the world would have been if he hadn't given his life to the nation's security. His war on the invisible front would remain unknown. No one would remember his name.

What would his legacy be? Of course, he could influence that himself. As a fellow human being, he really ought to warn Sara Nowak – but as a representative of the BND, he refrained from doing do.

Rau would surely tidy things up now that he had disrupted the splendid order that had been established following the Cold War.

It was that order which the BND cared about, all that mattered in this case.

Admittedly, Nowak was a pity, but this was the only way, given what was at stake.

Rau was necessary, if the others were to be drawn in and that meant they couldn't take any risks with Swedish detectives pursuing their own initiatives.

Schönberg logged on to the intranet and wrote a message to the top brass.

'Problems with our good lady friend in Sweden. Request free hand to remedy.'

The reply came in less than a minute.

'Granted.'

23

A sense of calm had pervaded the room. Which was odd given the brutal events that had brought them all there. Perhaps the dead had found peace? That, at any rate, was Anna's theory. Sara chose not to comment.

White tiles surrounded them and strong lighting shone down on the stainless steel benches that held the naked bodies. Had any of the deceased imagined that they would end up lying here today, cut up, their organs removed, examined as objects? No longer people, simply evidence in the investigation of a crime. Had they sensed what awaited them?

The four corpses were all badly wounded, two of them very seriously.

The divers were continuing their work in Lake Mälaren, but the four bodies that had been found to date were those of two men and two women with crushing injuries, burns, stab wounds and other penetrative injuries. One man's throat had been cut. Both women had been subjected to serious sexual violence. They were young, naked and seemingly of non-Scandinavian origin. They had tattoos and cheap jewellery in the form of rings, ear-rings and ankle bracelets. One of them had long, manicured fake nails, while the other's nails were worn and bitten short. One man was middle-aged, of northern European appearance and slightly overweight, wearing a Brioni suit and Johnston & Murphy shoes. He had cufflinks but no wristwatch. The other man was around sixty-five at a guess, tall with blue eyes and white hair around a bald crown. He appeared to have been in good physical shape, with the exception of a scar left by a presumed heart operation. What connected the four? More than the fact that they had met with a violent death before being dumped in a lake in close proximity to each other . . .

'Not typical victims of gang conflict,' Sara noted, taking a step back. It was almost as if the contrast between the gleaming surfaces and the dead bodies reinforced the smell of decomposition. Odd.

'What the hell is it all about in that case?' said Anna.

'Not a clue. Someone murdering people at random?'

'Almost looks that way. I'll check reported missing persons matching these descriptions.'

'Fifty kronor says no one has reported the girls missing,' said Sara.

'I won't take that bet. Will you do dental photos?'

The forensics staff confirmed they would take photos and email them as soon as possible. Sara and Anna checked the belongings of the dead, which in this case were comprised solely of rings and jewellery, double hearing aids for the older man and a Dupont cigarette case from the besuited man's inside pocket. No wallets and no money, but robbery was hardly the cause of these murders.

When Sara's mobile rang, she went into the corridor to answer, whether out of respect for the deceased or to avoid disturbing the forensics team she wasn't sure.

'Sara Nowak.'

'Hi, it's Herman Cederqvist, Linköping police. Look, those names you gave us, and the thing about the money . . .'

'Yes?'

'We checked up on the priest's accounts. And the bank were very cooperative. I'm not sure that the clerk was really allowed to give us the information – maybe she likes cops. You get to find after a while that there are some people who really want to help, and then there are those who totally refuse. Wouldn't talk to the police if their own mother was on fire. Well, what am I saying? I mean, if their—'

'What did the bank say?' Sara interrupted a little brusquely, hoping that Cederqvist wouldn't be offended.

'Well, it was quite interesting, actually. Stiller had recently received three deposits of exactly one hundred thousand apiece. From three different depositors.'

'Three? Not four?'

'No, so I suppose it might not add up, or perhaps one of the four didn't pay, because he didn't have time or didn't want to.'

Sara wondered whether to share Hedin's theory that Stiller had been murdered with Cederqvist, but she decided to keep that to herself. While they hadn't yet launched a murder inquiry down there, she was technically in the clear when it came to not getting involved in someone else's investigation if she kept digging. And after all, she didn't think the murderer was still in Östergötland. Cederqvist cleared his throat following what was, for him, an unusual silence.

'So, as I said, we've got three names—'

'Let me guess? Three out of these four: Hans Gerlach, Stefan Kremp, Otto Rau, Marita Werner?'

'No, not at all. Well, not and not. The three names the bank gave us were Bo Enberg, Günther Dorch and Marita Leander. So at least one of those first names was right: Marita.'

'Günther Dorch?' Sara repeated. The name was familiar. Where did she recognise it from? 'And these three people paid a hundred thousand each?' she continued.

'Exactly.'

'And the bank clerk was sure about the names?'

'Oh yes. Whether she was really allowed to help us I don't know, but it was the savings bank down in Ydre, and my wife's parents are from Asby, so they know who I am around there and perhaps they're up for helping people they know. And what with one of their customers dying in such tragic circumstances, well, I don't know—'

'Did you get addresses for the trio?'

'No, she wasn't able to see that information. But she was able to determine which bank accounts the funds had come from. I think there were two in Stockholm and one in Gävle.'

He gave Sara the details, and she thanked him for the information and hung up. She promised herself that if she found anything that had a direct impact on Stiller's death, she would pass it on to Cederqvist.

There was only one Bo Enberg in Gävle the same age as Stiller. There was only one Günther Dorch in Stockholm, and the same applied to Marita Leander, so Sara assumed they were the right people. None of them had a police criminal record, and using Google, LinkedIn and the online phone book, she was able to determine that all of them appeared to be retired. Bo Enberg had previously been a lecturer in political science and had headed up a number of major inquiries on behalf of parliament. Marita Leander had been a journalist at Radio Sweden, as well as both of the broadsheets, and now had a column on balcony gardening published in a pensioners' magazine. Günther Dorch had worked for many years at Saab and had been an active trade unionist.

And now she remembered where she had seen Günther Dorch's name before. It had been amongst those who had been affected by Geiger's reports to the Stasi about East German refugees. He hadn't wanted to talk about it when Sara had called, which she had interpreted to mean the memories were too painful. But there was perhaps an altogether different explanation. Why would a dissident pay money to a spy, or an informal collaborator – an IM as they were known? She couldn't figure out the logic as far as Dorch went, but she thought paying him a visit might help set her on the right track. She found mobile numbers for all three of them online, but resolved to speak with Hedin first.

'I've got three names,' she said, when the old woman answered. 'Are you at home?'

'No, I'm out for a walk. And I don't need any names from you. You've got some names from me, that's more than enough.'

'I need to brainstorm with you. Where are you?'

'Ringvägen.'

'Where exactly?'

'The crossroads with Södermannagatan, but I'm on the move.'

'Just keep going on Ringvägen and I'll find you.'

Sara drove across to Södermalm through the tunnel and took a right to the end of Ringvägen, where she did a U-turn before slowly driving along the street, keeping a lookout for Hedin.

She caught sight of the familiar figure outside the Ringen shopping centre and pulled over by the kerb, despite the fact that it was a bus stop. Hedin threw something in a bin and turned around when Sara honked at her. She waved to Hedin to jump in but it took the academic a while to understand what Sara meant and in the meantime a bus pulled up behind her car and honked at the moron who had stopped at the bus stop. Shrugging, Sara switched on her blue lights. Then she wound down the passenger-side window and shouted to Hedin:

'Get in!'

Hedin looked at Sara, turned around and stared into the bin before sauntering over and getting into the car. Her plastic carrier bag rattled as she got in: the sound of empty cans.

'You off to return your empties?' said Sara.

'Yes, once I've collected enough.'

Sara digested her answer for a moment.

'You're collecting empty cans?'

'Yes, you wouldn't believe what people throw away. Money in can form.'

'But I . . .' Sara didn't know what to say. She had seen people who had seemed to be neither beggars nor homeless collecting cans, but had assumed they were a mixture of weirdos and poverty-stricken pensioners. Hedin was perhaps a bit of both.

'What were those names you wanted to tell me about? Is this to do with Stellan Broman?'

'Yes. Because it's to do with Jürgen Stiller.'

'And?'

Hedin kept her gaze fixed on the pavement as they drove down Ringvägen past Tanto and towards Zinkensdamm, probably keeping an eye out for more deposit cans. Like a buzzard on the hunt for field voles, thought Sara.

'Bo Enberg, Günther Dorch and Marita Leander,' said Sara.

'Who are they?'

'Three people who paid money to Stiller. One hundred thousand each. So I assume those are the former terrorists' new names. But if they're false identities then it should be easy to unmask them.'

'Drive back to Tanto,' said Hedin when they reached Hornsgatan. Sara did a U-turn when the lights turned green and three other motorists honked at her. But she wanted to stay in Hedin's good books.

'Drive down towards the youth hostel. Along Zinkens väg.'

Sara indicated right and turned down the narrow road that ran down towards the large open expanse of the Tantolunden park.

'Haven't you read my books?' Hedin asked when she stopped at the end of the road.

'Yes . . .' Sara said slowly. 'Well, skimmed them. I was kind of busy for a while, if you remember.'

'You only have to read the tabloids, if you feel more comfortable with that. *Aftonbladet* picked up on stuff from my books about the priest, Stiller, and how he had been involved in the production of fake IDs for spies and illegals from the eastern bloc. Given them new identities.'

Agneta Broman too, Sara remembered. What a fool she had been not to think of that connection sooner.

'What? So Gerlach and the others . . .'

Instead of answering, the academic opened the car door and began to stroll towards the grassy expanse. Sara folded down the sun shade so that the police emblem on the back was visible. She left the car in the turning circle and hurried after Hedin, who was peering in bins and at the ground.

'So Gerlach and the others have completely watertight new names?' said Sara when she had caught up.

'Can I have this?' Hedin said to a family picnicking on a tartan blanket, pointing to an empty beer can lying on the ground beside them. The father, a bearded wannabe hipster, made a waving gesture that she clearly regarded as affirmative.

After a few minutes, Hedin noticed that Sara was following her, so she stopped for a brief moment before continuing to plough across the grass.

'Not just new names. New identities. The anti-terrorism legislation introduced in 1973 meant that foreign citizens who were considered to pose a risk to national security could be deported without being suspected of any crime.'

'But as Swedish citizens they were protected from that?'

'Exactly. With a little help from a priest and an absolutely genuine birth certificate, they were home and dry – impossible to trace. They could live quite openly in Swedish society without any risk of being discovered. This was back before the Tax Agency took over the population register. No one ever doubted church-issued papers, and if they had done so then Stiller would have been able to personally testify that they were genuine.'

'Why did they come to Sweden in particular then? Was it to do something here, or just to keep out of the way?'

Hedin shrugged, seemingly uninterested by the question. Sara thought for a moment.

'And given that they paid using Swedish bank accounts, they must still be in the country. But why?'

'Perhaps they haven't dared go home. Out of fear of being recognised. Their crimes aren't subject to statutes of limitations, and with facial recognition technology these days they're probably worried. Either that or the comfort factor.'

'Comfort?'

'Yes, they may simply have made new lives for themselves here that they're happy with. Married, had children. Found their dream home. My God, how stupid!'

Hedin had come to a halt. She fished a crumpled energy drink can off the ground and tried to smooth it out.

'So the money they paid to Stiller . . . ?'

'Well, who knows? Funding for a new operation years and years after the fact? Maybe as revenge for Geiger's plans being stopped?'

'Or extortion?'

'Yes. Stiller undeniably knew some serious details about them all. But on the other hand, they knew something about him too.'

'But you had already blown his identity.'

'Yes. True. Anything is possible, I suppose,' said the researcher, looking at the now-smoothed-out can with satisfaction.

'Do you really think that one of them killed him? They must all be over seventy by now.'

'Former terrorists schooled by the Stasi, trained by the PFLP, with blood on their hands and everything to lose – yes, I think it was one of them. Or someone they reported to.'

'Stasi?'

'Yes, they were decidedly active sponsors of western terrorism.'

Sara took all of this in. It might add up. But how to determine which cover name belonged to which terrorist?

'The one with the woman's name is presumably a match,' said Hedin when Sara asked. 'And at a guess, Marita Werner is Lorelei. The Stasi sometimes gave their operatives code names that were from a different gender, but usually not. But it's hard to know who's who out of the others.'

'And who the fourth one is – the one that hasn't paid.'

'I suppose you'll have to ask them.'

24

The Marita Leander who had deposited one hundred thousand kronor into Jürgen Stiller's bank account just days before his death lived on Sjöbjörnsvägen in Gröndal. Which, it transpired, was the address of the renowned Stjärnhus buildings – a sort of post-functionalist style of architecture that had reputedly been copied the world over. Sara would have liked to live here, were it not for the noise of traffic from the Essingeleden motorway. But they were charming buildings in a fantastic location and with incredible views.

Sara parked the car by the motorcycle bays and pulled down the shade to show the police emblem. The buildings facing the street were a warm yellow, but the façades facing inwards were green or white. She entered the leafy inner courtyard where the main door for number 52 was located, tapped in the police door code and opened it.

Leander lived on the northern side of the Stjärnhus buildings, with views of Lilla Essingen and Marieberg. After showing her police ID, Sara was admitted to the flat, albeit with some reluctance, she thought. While Leander carefully locked the door behind her, Sara noted a comfy armchair outside on the balcony beside a small table on which she saw a teacup and a book about cultural profiles. There were pots filled with plants and flowers of every kind. Sara had never seen such a verdant balcony. Inside the flat, the counters and windowsills were filled with small pots and milk cartons cut in half and filled with soil and small, sprouting shoots and saplings. Hoya, spotted begonia, aloe, Christmas cacti, cyclamen, hortensia, she was told.

Sara scrutinised the owner of the flat. Marita Leander was a white-haired woman with a long plait and round glasses, Gudrun

Sjödén attire and an open smile. Just as expected, Sara thought, almost a little disappointed.

Leander gestured to indicate that Sara should sit down on the sofa in the living room. It was a neat sofa, with two armchairs from the forties recovered in mismatching upholstery with patterned blankets on top. A real festival of colour.

'Look out for the cats,' the Gudrun Sjödén lady said.

Lying on the sofa were two sleek, grey pedigree cats, glowering at her with disinterested green eyes.

'Aren't they beautiful?' said Sara. If there was one thing she had learned in her years as a police officer, it was that it always paid to praise people's children and pets.

'Korats,' said Leander. 'They're called Palle and Stina. As in Palestine. Inventive, right?'

Sara smiled politely.

'We also have a cat,' she said. 'Walter.'

'Named after the pistol?'

'No.'

'Would you like tea?' Leander added.

'No thanks. I've just got a few quick questions to ask you. About Jürgen Stiller.'

Sara stopped speaking to interpret Leander's reaction. All she noticed was mild annoyance.

'You deposited one hundred thousand kronor into his bank account a few days ago.'

'Where did you get that from?'

'Isn't it true?' Sara asked.

'I thought banking transactions were a private matter in this country.'

'Jürgen Stiller is dead. Murdered, but made to look like a suicide.'

Silence.

'Did you know him?'

Marita Leander took a deep breath.

'I-I bumped into him a couple of times. Many years ago. I don't suppose I need deny that. But it was a long time ago.'

'In what context?'

'Through our mutual commitment to the Third World and global justice.'

'When you were a member of the Red Army Faction?'

Leander snorted.

'I've never been that.'

'The Stasi even had a code name for you: Lorelei. And they helped you secure a new Swedish identity. Marita Werner to Marita Leander.'

'Stasi? That wasn't the Stasi. That was because I got married to Lennart Leander, the author. Don't you have Wikipedia down at the station?'

'But Stiller gave you a birth certificate with another identity.'

Leander smiled again. She seemed almost amused about explaining.

'Yes, that was how it worked back in the day. Everything was so flipping secretive. Although I was a Swede, I needed a different Swedish identity, even though I was only on the fringes.'

'On the fringes of what?'

'Well, these political groups. In the struggle against American imperialism and the police state in West Germany and here. Neither country had dealt with the legacy of guilt that remained from Hitler's Germany. In West Germany, much of the state apparatus remained under the control of former Nazis, and here in Sweden no one talked about the transits of German troops through the country or our export of iron ore to Hitler's factories of war. We wanted to break that silence.'

Leander leaned forward slightly, as if she were a lecturer seeking to emphasise her message for the audience.

'And replace democracy with a communist dictatorship?' said Sara.

'It was only a democracy in name,' said Leander, raising a critical finger. 'Brutal imperialism hidden behind a genial Santa mask.

A Coca Cola Santa, spreading material gifts around with one hand and taking our freedom with the other. We wanted to tear the mask off the face of capitalism.'

'And then what? What did you want to achieve?'

'A better world. We wanted to draw attention to the abuses in Vietnam and Palestine which were being ignored by all the so-called democracies.'

'And that justified armed resistance? Killing people?'

Leander looked almost hurt.

'I've never killed anyone.'

'Perhaps not you personally.'

'No, quite. Now I'm afraid it's time for you leave. I need to play with the cats.' Leander stood up quickly from her armchair but stopped for a moment and looked at Sara. 'It's for the cats' sake, you see. They get ill if they don't move.'

She grabbed a cat toy in the form of a long stick with a string on the end and began to run the string along the floor in front of the cats on the sofa. Palle and Stina looked passably interested. And Sara pointedly remained in her armchair. Leander turned towards her, but she was still running the string along the floor.

'You see, they don't dare play when there's someone here.'

'You were happy to tell me about your commitment until I asked about the killing. Is that something you're ashamed of?'

Leander stopped trying to tempt the cats to play and turned to Sara.

'I've got absolutely nothing to be ashamed of. I can tell you everything.'

'Do that.'

Leander took a seat, still clutching the trailing cat toy. She looked out of the open balcony door towards the waters of Lake Mälaren where a white steamer was passing by.

'I still think what we were fighting for was important. What do you actually know about that time?'

'A bit.'

'Not enough, I fear. All we wanted was to end war and killing the brutal bombings of civilian populations, massacres of children. It all began peacefully, but was met with violence. Like in Italy during the demonstrations against Nixon's visit. All we did was express our views, and for that we were beaten down – with terrible brutality. They set dogs on us and trampled peaceful demonstrators with their horses, at Hötorget here in Stockholm, and down in Båstad – at all the demonstrations. And we were so shocked, so angry. They really wanted to hurt us. And eventually some people had had enough, wanted to hit back. That's not so strange. We started out as pacifists, but were beaten into realists – that's what we used to say.'

'The police have to maintain law and order.'

Leander took a sip of tea and put her cup down on the table. Then she smiled at Sara.

'Exactly. The law and order of the powerful. And that includes napalming children in Vietnam and massacring refugees in Lebanon. And it wasn't just then. Look at the riots in Gothenburg in 2001, when that police officer shot a demonstrator in the back but was cleared. The demonstrators, on the other hand, got stiff sentences. All because the President of the United States visited. Just think if the bootlickers in the Swedish government had been shown up in front of Bush.'

'Did you ever attend a training camp in the Middle East?'

Leander was quiet for a while.

'I've never hurt anyone.'

'What did you do more specifically then?'

'Well, at first it was very innocent. Demonstrations. Selling the *Vietnam Bulletin*. Stencilling flyers. Collections. That was how most people got into the movement.'

'Then you became a militant? How? Something happened?' Sara said.

'I was working as a journalist and a German lawyer invited me to a meeting at the school in Åsö, where he told me about the awful conditions they were subjecting members of the Red Army Faction to in prison. I wanted to know more and he put me in touch with a German living in Stockholm, Dieter. Or Joachim, that was his real name. A gardener. We shared an interest in plants.'

'And he radicalised you?'

'You make it sound so dramatic,' Leander said. 'You think we were out and about all day shooting at people and running around, but it was mostly the daily grind and just waiting. Watching people. Getting hold of cars and flats.'

'Were you at the embassy for the stand-off? When they executed the two diplomats and shot at the police?'

'I wasn't inside the embassy.'

'But during the preparations?' Sara said, probing.

Leander shrugged.

'I showed Stefan – the seventh member – around town so that he knew where all the news agencies had their offices. So that he could drop off their communiqué about the operation.'

'You tell it like any other memory. It sounds as though you have no regrets.'

Sara thought about Stellan Broman and felt a sudden disgust towards the woman she was talking to. Stellan had also never regretted his actions, never confessed, never apologised. Sara wondered whether she was like that herself – or could end up like that. Was it possible to inherit such negative personality traits? Was it nature or nurture? Stellan had concealed his dark side from the world. Well, from everyone except the young girls whom he'd raped. And then there was Lotta, who had exploited her father's perversions for political ends. Sara didn't know which one of them was worse.

'It wasn't meant to go wrong like that,' said Leander, bringing Sara back to the present. 'The interesting thing is that when the Croatian fascists hijacked SAS flight 130 and took hostages, their demands were met and the prisoners were released, but when the communists took hostages, no one was let go. Palme and Geijer preferred to let two hostages die.'

Although it was possible Leander had a point, Sara realised she was in no mood to try and understand. She could tell she wasn't going to get much more out of this conversation. Time to get to the point.

'Why did you transfer the money to Jürgen Stiller?'

'It was a loan.'

'For what?'

'I don't know. I didn't ask.'

'When were you last in touch? Before he needed the money, I mean.'

Marita Leander was silent. She stared out towards the verdant balcony and after a while she leaned back and sighed deeply. Then she sat up again.

'OK. He wanted money from me to keep his mouth shut.'

Sara nodded, as if to show that this was no surprise.

'And I paid,' Leander said. 'But you still found me. So it was a waste of money. Do you think I can get my money back?'

'Are you serious?'

'It was every penny I had, and I'd like to get an allotment.'

Sara looked at Leander and wondered whether the woman was messing with her, but she appeared to be deadly serious. She was even smiling slightly, as if thinking about how wonderful it would be to have her own allotment.

'Aren't you afraid?'

'Of what?'

'That something might happen to you. That the person who killed Stiller will come for you.'

'Why would he do that? I haven't done anything.'

'Do you want police protection?'

'Most certainly not.'

Without standing up from the armchair, Leander made an attempt to engage the cats, but without any success.

'What do you know about the other people that Stiller was black-mailing?' said Sara.

'Nothing. I didn't know there were others. Who were they?'

'Hans Gerlach, Stefan Kremp and Otto Rau. Two of them are now called Bo Enberg and Günther Dorch.'

'I remember Stefan well. We actually had an affair. Incredibly charismatic. He was from some godforsaken place in Germany . . . Osnabrück. But he had real vision. The struggle was everything. I've no idea where he is these days.'

'What about the others?'

'Otto was an old fighter. Always wanted to pull off spectacular operations, shake up the bourgeoisie. I admired his fighting spirit, but he was a little frightening. Completely focused. Almost obsessed. I barely remember what Hans looked like. He was mostly one of those people along for the ride. A bit timid. You usually ended up ganging up with the people you worked best with – forming into rock-solid units where everyone was ready to die for the others.'

'Like all terrorist groups.'

'We weren't terrorists. That was the name the police and the authorities gave us.'

'What were you then?'

'Freedom fighters.'

'That was your name for yourselves.'

25

She had to turn up with something, Jenna thought to herself. But she'd only thought of it at the last minute, so she was a bit ashamed when she handed over the presents: a bouquet of flowers from the supermarket featuring marigolds and oxeye daisies, and a small cuddly toy from a souvenir shop, a little grey mouse with big front teeth and wide eyes. But it was the thought that counted. Nadia smiled when Jenna proffered the gifts, bending forward to embrace her. Then Jenna straightened her back and looked at her friend.

She looked dreadful. Her black eyes were a shade of purple, blood had seeped through the big gauze dressings, the teeth that had been knocked out hadn't been replaced and her eyes were still bloodshot. Judging by her grimaces when she shifted position in the hospital bed, she was in terrible pain.

'Did that cop find you?' said Nadia. 'That woman?'

'Yes. But I pretended not to understand.'

'Why?'

Jenna didn't answer.

'Are you still going to do it?' said Nadia.

'Why not?'

'Look at me.'

Nadia splayed her arms as if to show her full self. Jenna looked her friend in the eyes.

'I've had worse,' said Jenna. 'Without getting paid.'

'It's not the same thing.'

'No, exactly. I'm getting paid.'

'It was awful.'

'Did you get the money?' said Jenna after a short pause.

'Yes.'

'Show me.'

Nadia retrieved her handbag from under the duvet and showed the wad of cash to Jenna. The sight of the money seemed to satisfy her. When Nadia saw the resolve in her friend's eyes, she regretted not lying and saying she'd never been paid. Why hadn't she thought of that? It would have been that simple.

'They've promised me two hundred and fifty thousand,' said Jenna, her voice uncertain.

Nadia looked at her for a long time.

'Then it's going to be worse than this. Take a look at what they did for a hundred thousand.'

'Or I'm worth more.'

Nadia realised that Jenna didn't want to give it any thought – the idea that she too would soon be in hospital, perhaps even more badly injured. Perhaps so badly that she would never heal. Once they had got started, they had struggled to stop themselves.

'In what way?' said Nadia. 'They only pay more if they get to do worse stuff. What did they say?'

Jenna didn't answer.

'Jenna, what did they say? Tell me!'

'OK. It's three guys.'

'No!'

'But I've done it before. For a few hundred extra.'

'Jenna, don't do it. Look at me. They will hurt you.'

'Two hundred and fifty thousand is enough for me to quit. Go home, buy a house for my parents, see my sisters. And they'll let me. I can't carry on. They've promised to leave my family alone.'

'My God, Elena, you need to listen to me!'

Hearing her real name made Jenna start. It was as if Nadia had opened a door to her old life. A big, heavy door that she had locked and thrown away the key for, in order to keep the men here out of the only thing she knew that was beautiful: memories of her mother and sisters.

'It always looks worse than it is,' she said to Nadia. 'You're free now, right? You can go home and take the money with you.'

'But I regret doing it.'

'Or you're just jealous because I'm getting much more than you.'

'Jenna, I'll share my money with you. You can have half. Just don't do it.'

'You're forgetting one thing. I can't go home like you. I've got to stay, otherwise they'll take my sisters.'

'But they said you could go home in a year.'

'They said that a year ago too. I want to go home *now*.'

'Jenna . . .'

Jenna forced a smile.

'The worst thing that can happen is that I end up here with you. And then we can lie here planning our lives together. Which cafés to visit, where to live. Do you think it's like it was before back home?'

Nadia didn't reply. She didn't know what to say.

26

Günther Dorch wasn't answering the phone, so when Bo Enberg said he was at home and would be happy to see Sara, she headed off to Gävle instead. Her satnav said it would take one hour and forty-seven minutes, but Sara did it in an hour and a half. It was stupid, but she wasn't thinking about the time it took. She just didn't want to be overtaken, which meant she had to put her foot down.

Enberg lived at 2 Lilla Brunnsgatan in an incredibly charming and picturesque little wooden house in a neighbourhood filled with similar cottages. Apparently this was what had survived the great fire of 1869 in the town. Perhaps that was why there was an air of calm and assurance in the area, a feeling that no misfortunes could befall you here.

Sara knocked on the door even though there was a doorbell. Knocking felt more fitting, somehow, more dignified. Enberg opened up almost immediately. He was a strikingly short man, with the kind of exaggerated upright posture that many short men had, completely bald, clean-shaven with small, rimless glasses. Sara couldn't stop herself from noticing a lot of hair in his ears. He wore a pale blue shirt neatly tucked into a pair of beige chinos, and a belt with a large buckle at the waist. On his feet were a pair of clogs.

'Sara Nowak. Hello.'

'Bo Enberg. Come in.'

Enberg led her into the kitchen of the small house where they sat down at the table. A woman in her seventies with purple hair, wearing heavy mascara, set a pot of coffee down on the table.

'My wife, Annica,' said Enberg. The woman nodded, turned and left them alone.

'So how can I be of assistance to the police?' said Bo Enberg, smiling.

'Tell me about your relationship with Jürgen Stiller.'

'Who?'

'Jürgen Stiller. A priest in Torpa in Östergötland. A Stasi agent code named Koch. The same priest who provided you with the birth certificate that made you Bo Enberg.'

Enberg's gaze wandered.

'I don't know what you're talking about,' he said at last.

'Last week you transferred a hundred thousand kronor to Jürgen Stiller, as did several other people he was blackmailing. And on Friday morning he was murdered – perhaps by one of you.'

'He's dead?'

'Stiller? Yes. So you knew him?'

'An old acquaintance. I had considered asking him to marry me and Annica, but then . . . it didn't work out that way.'

'Why did you give him a hundred grand?'

'I didn't.'

'We've verified the payment.'

'It was a donation. To his church. I think church buildings are both beautiful and culturally significant,' said Enberg, puffing out his chest.

'So you donated one hundred thousand kronor to a church that's more than five hundred kilometres away?'

'Yes.'

'How many other churches have you given money to?' Sara took a sip of her coffee and looked at him calmly.

'Er . . . Just that one so far. But the church in Oslättfors is a strong candidate.'

'Come on! Stiller was blackmailing you because he knew your new identities. That you were actually Gerlach, Kremp, Rau and Werner. And that you did things you'd rather didn't become known.'

'That's not true. You've got completely the wrong idea about the course of events.'

'Does your wife know your true identity?'

Bo Enberg stared at Sara, taken by surprise.

'Surely you're not going to say anything?'

'Don't know. Tell me more about yourself. I don't hear an accent, but surely you're all Germans – at least, you men.'

'Yes – I thought it was idiotic to change my name and get a Swedish identity but speak with a German accent. So I practised hard. I even consulted a speech therapist to get my pronunciation right. And I've lived here for almost fifty years now.'

'Who was who amongst you? Axt, Messer and Faust?'

'I was Messer. I don't actually know the others. It was supposed to be secret so that we couldn't snitch on anyone else.'

'What did you do?'

Enberg looked at her uncomprehendingly.

'That was worth a hundred grand to keep quiet about,' Sara clarified.

'Nothing! But being associated with Baader-Meinhof and Siegfried Hausner and Holger Meins isn't desirable today. It's the victors who write history, and it was the other side that won. In their eyes, we were terrorists – a danger to society.'

'But you robbed banks and carried out other operations too.'

'Yes, it was mad, to be honest. You completely lost perspective. We really did discuss kidnapping ministers, triggering an armed coup, awakening the working masses.' Enberg snorted. 'I guess we all knew that we didn't have the working classes with us. But if we had said that aloud there would have been a trial.'

Sara looked at him quizzically. He chuckled to himself and shook his head.

'You know we had trials, right? Internally. To try our orthodoxy. "Criticism and self-criticism", it was called. You had to confess your petty bourgeois inclinations and revisionist tendencies and criticise those of others. Several of us reported ourselves for deviations and demanded punishment.'

'And you were involved in all of this?'

'Yes. You end up a little . . . it can be hard to slow down.'

'What were Kremp and Rau like?'

'Kremp was the ideologue. Rau was the steam engine, the one who drove things forward. Violent. He wanted to provoke the police state into showing its true face. But I don't know, maybe he was just projecting his own inner chaos onto society. He was pretty paranoid too – never appeared in pictures. But he was the one who maintained contact with our friends and got us our money.'

'Which friends? East Germany? The Stasi?' said Sara. The retired academic nodded. 'Are you proud of those friends? Of what they did to their citizens?'

Enberg was silent for a long time, then he removed his glasses and buried his face in his hands.

'We did so many stupid things . . . It – it was . . . awful. Inconceivable. It was as if we were hypnotised. Stefan droned on and Otto agitated. Anyone who hesitated in the slightest was told off, threatened. They said they would get rid of anyone who betrayed them. We . . . A couple of times they carried out mock executions.'

'Of someone in the group?'

'Yes. For the sake of discipline.'

'Of you?'

Enberg looked at Sara for a long time before answering.

'Yes.'

'How?'

'They put a noose around my neck and put me on a stool. They even filmed me when I broke down and forced me to watch the tape over and over.'

He put a hand to his throat, as if he could still feel the noose.

'Was Marita involved?'

'Oh yes. She added fuel to the fire, played us off against each other.'

'And Stiller issued you all with new identities?'

'At first it was merely out of practical necessity, to ensure we weren't deported. But later on it felt pretty great, as if no one could get to you. Having a secret life was like a superpower. Especially when the other Germans were deported after the embassy drama and we flew under the radar. But the new identities needed refining, so we got jobs, started studying, made new friends, perhaps found love, and eventually the new identities took over. I must say that I never think of myself as Hans Gerlach any longer. I am Bo Enberg. My political engagement gave me the chance to create the person I wanted to be. A better person.'

'After you helped to kidnap and murder innocent people.'

Before Sara set off home, she Googled Dorch again and realised that he hadn't worked for Saab building cars – he had worked for the armaments manufacturing part. Rather different – especially as the individual in question had been part of a terrorist cell.

She continued trying to reach Dorch while driving and as she was passing Uppsala she got an answer. The two towers of the cathedral across the plain appeared on the horizon at the very moment he picked up.

'Dorch.'

'Sara Nowak. I called you a while back in connection with your past as an East German refugee. And you told me that your family had been punished after a spy had passed on information about you.'

'Yes, it was awful. But I don't want to discuss it.'

Dorch hadn't managed to lose his accent.

'It's just that someone you know has been murdered, and there's cause to believe that the murderer comes from your former circles.'

'Who?' said Dorch, surprised.

'Jürgen Stiller.'

'Don't know him.'

'Yet you transferred one hundred thousand kronor to him.'

'Where did you get that from?'

'The bank.'

Everyone was driving so slowly today, Sara thought to herself. Instead of constantly changing lanes, she decided to stay in the outside lane.

'If I transferred money to anyone, then that's my private business,' said Dorch. 'Who knows, perhaps I made a mistake. Wrote the wrong numbers.'

'Who were you? Axt or Faust?'

'I don't know what you're talking about.'

His reply came a little too quickly, as if he had decided to deny everything without any further thought. And there was only one explanation for that: he knew exactly what Sara was talking about. Now she knew how dogs who had caught a scent must feel. The focus, the drive. She had to continue.

'Bo Enberg told me everything,' she said. 'Well, Hans Gerlach, as you knew him. About everything your little terrorist cell did.'

'I've never been in a terrorist cell. I don't even know what one is.'

'You managed to deceive both the authorities and your employer. Saab would never have hired you if they had known the truth. But an anti-communist who fled oppression was fine. Did you spy on your employer?'

'I've got nothing to do with espionage or terrorism, and I'm going to hang up now.'

'Your real name is Rau or Kremp. If you don't confess, I can simply ask the German police for photos of you.'

Bloody hell. She was doing one hundred and sixty kilometres an hour. She had become completely absorbed by the call. Sara slowed down while Dorch switched gears.

'But where is this all coming from?' he said with irritation in his voice. 'Listen to me, if you've found old papers depicting me as a former terrorist supported by the DDR, then you should remember that disinformation was the biggest feature of the Cold War. The DDR spread false information about everyone who managed to escape the dictatorship. So use some judgement and consider the fact that spreading rumours like that can ruin people's lives.'

'Were you Axt or Faust?'

'I was nothing.'

'Your life may be in danger. The person who killed Stiller may be after the rest of you too.'

'No one is after me. Goodbye.'

Dorch hung up.

27

The first roundhouse kick missed, but Anna performed a lightning quick spin and planted the second kick onto her temple.

Sara cursed the fact that she had stayed on the spot like a beginner, even if it had only been half a second.

She had allowed herself to be hit.

Instead of backing away and opening herself up to another blow, she stepped forward, cutting off Anna's room for manoeuvre. She executed a quick, hard blow straight to the solar plexus while Anna was still open after her high kick. She twisted her hip to add extra power.

And she saw how Anna was winded.

Sara exploited this to use her fists to thunder down onto her friend's head in a furious series of pummels. Anna got up her guard, but she was now on the defensive.

Sara paused to seek out a weak point, which Anna took advantage of immediately. She threw her arms around Sara's neck, locking her hands while dragging Sara's head and upper body down. Then she began to apply hard knees to her midriff.

It was extremely painful, but Sara was never one to tap out because of a little pain. She had made up her mind. Something would bloody well have to break before that happened. Instead, she wrapped her arms around Anna's waist and squeezed for all she was worth. With this grip, she could also have bitten her opponent's face. If she had spat out her mouthguard first, and if her opponent hadn't been Anna.

Her friend whimpered in pain.

Sara saw the panic associated with being unable to breathe in growing in her eyes and Anna tapped out.

Three short, rapid taps on the ground or on any part of the opponent that could be reached showed that you were giving up. At which point the other person let go immediately. Just as Sara did now. It was an important reflex for all practitioners of martial arts. Especially important when training in sports with throttling and breaks. Even a delay of a second or two could have lethal consequences.

'Idiot!' said Anna, after catching her breath and slapping Sara on the shoulder. Neither of them liked losing.

Both of them lay on the foam training mat panting, sweat pouring off them. It was one of the advantages of having a three hundred square metre apartment – you could have a dedicated training room. Martin, who as always had to take it a bit too far, had kitted out the old dining room with thick training mats on the floor and walls so that Sara could spar in there as much as she liked.

'Tell me everything,' said Anna once they were standing under the adjacent showers in the large bathroom.

'I was born in 1975 at the general maternity hospital . . .'

'Ha,' said Anna, her voice dripping with irony. 'About that priest.'

What Sara had said about her birth was a secret that she hadn't known about until recently. She had always thought she had been born in Poland and that her father had been a Pole. But she hadn't told anyone else about her discovery about Uncle Stellan, and now that she had stumbled she was glad that Anna merely took it as a joke.

'Remember Eva Hedin, the researcher? Well, she claims that it's a typical old Stasi method to get rid of people and make it look like suicide. But in this case it was almost a bit blatant, with the Bible opened to Judas' death. And I found a list of code names—'

'Back up a moment. You were there?'

Sara was quiet for a second, realised that she had just admitted to a serious infraction: she had visited a crime scene where she had nothing to do with the investigation. But good God, this was Anna. What harm could it do?

'Yes. I went down there. I couldn't help myself.'

'Sara!'

'But it was lucky that I did. I don't think the police down there would have found the list of names. Above all, they wouldn't have known what it meant.'

'What were the names?'

'Code names. Messer, Axt, Faust and Lorelei.'

'Aren't they the seven dwarves?'

Sara smiled. She stepped out of the shower and reached for a towel.

'No, I think it's Agnetha, Anni-Frid, Björn and Benny?'

'Ah yes, you're quite right,' said Anna, rummaging in her toiletries bag. 'My God, double sinks are good.'

That had been Sara's only demand for the apartment: a double vanity unit with mirrors to match in the big bathroom. And she had been grateful for it almost every day since. All those times when Martin needed to brush his teeth at the same time as she was applying or removing makeup, not to mention when Ebba had become a teenager and refused to use the small bathroom because the light was so much better in Mum and Dad's. Before blocking one of the sinks for hours at a time.

Sara glanced over at Anna's weapons of choice as they got ready. Dr Hauschka and Biotherm. Sara used YSL and Helena Rubinstein. That was surely the very point of makeup – to find the brands and products that suited your face and your face alone.

'You hurting?' said Anna.

'Hell yes. You landed some really good blows.'

It was important not to be a bad winner but to remain humble in success. But what Sara wanted to hoot more than anything was: 'I won! I won!'

'Fun to train together again,' said Anna. 'And that you're back.'

'Or whatever you call it.'

'What do you mean?'

'I don't know whether I'm back, or whether I'm actually someone else now.'

Anna appeared to be thinking over what Sara had just said.

'It's not like you not to pick up the phone.'

'No,' said Sara. 'I don't know why I . . .'

'I don't know whether you want to be left alone, if you don't want me to call. When it's about work though, I have to.'

Sara turned and looked Anna straight in the eyes.

'I'm very happy that you've kept calling.'

Anna smiled briefly at Sara, but quickly resumed her serious expression.

'How did it actually feel?' she said. 'To come so close to death?'

Sara was silent for a long time.

'I'm focusing more on the fact that I survived,' she said at last.

'Yes, and thank God for that.'

'It wasn't thanks to God. Now let's change the subject.'

'OK. Your spies,' said Anna, producing a mascara brush and leaning closer to the mirror.

'They weren't spies. They were terrorists. You know, Baader-Meinhof and all that. There were all sorts of Commands, X, Y, and Z during the seventies that were aiming to crush imperialism and try to release each other from prison. And there were four members of one of those commands that the priest issued birth certificates to, with new identities. And now he seems to have been blackmailing them. Three of them had paid.'

'But not all of them?'

'Perhaps it was the fourth one who killed him. Or the murderer is one of the ones who paid, to avoid suspicion in case anyone discovered the racket.'

'From Baader-Meinhof? So they were Germans?'

'Three of them. The woman is Swedish. But they all live in Sweden now. Well, the three of them I've met, at any rate.'

'You've *met* them?'

What the hell was wrong with her? Had she let down her guard completely? With a sigh, Sara put her toiletries to one side and met Anna's suspicious look.

'I wanted to know why they had paid,' she said, after a pause.

'Did they explain?'

'No. Only that they didn't want their true identities to be revealed. But I think it's about what they did back then. They were pretty hardcore.'

'You'll be careful, right?' Anna looked at her anxiously.

'Oh yes.'

Sara turned her gaze to the mirror and examined her face. She contemplated the scars from the fire. She had thought she was being careful then too.

Made-up and dressed, they went into the kitchen and picked out one of Martin's eye-wateringly expensive bottles of wine. They selected two wine glasses that were almost certainly intended for another grape and climbed the stairs to the tower room. Before they reached it, they heard the front door open and Martin call out:

'Darling? Are you at home?'

'You go up,' Sara said to Anna, passing her the bottle and glasses before going to meet her husband.

A hasty kiss, as always whenever they met or parted. As if to prove to both the world and themselves that they belonged together. It could be easily forgotten otherwise after more than twenty years together.

'He might be coming here!' Martin said in agitation as soon as their lips parted.

'Who? Our master? I suppose we'll have to get things in order.'

'Scam!'

'Surely not here!'

Sara looked around. It was chaos, as usual. Clothes everywhere. Books and magazines, Martin's latest gadgets and the boxes they had come in . . .

'Yes. He's a bloody Yank – apparently they invite each other round to their homes. He's expecting it.'

'But this place is a tip!'

'Tip' was obviously relative, but it was perhaps sub-optimal to have heaps of clothes and dustballs all over the place when a senior executive was hosting a megastar.

'I know,' said Martin. 'I'll find a cleaning company.'

'Not on my life!'

Her childhood taunts to her own mother still rang in her ears, Malin and Lotta's cry that she would always regret having chimed in with: 'Cleaning woman, cleaning woman!' Poor Jane. No woman should have to take care of another woman's crap to survive. That was Sara's absolute understanding, and wrapped up in it was the retroactive shame of having tormented the person who had birthed her.

'It's your turn,' said Sara. 'You'll have to clean.'

'Don't have time. Things are crazy right now. Do you get how big he is?'

'No bigger than this fucking flat I bet.'

'Much bigger.'

'No cleaners! Apart from that, do what you like. Clean or host him in chaos.'

Sara turned and left. Martin was silent for a couple of seconds, then his mobile rang.

'Martin.' His name was followed by intense humming and hawing. 'I'm on my way!'

Then the front door opened and closed again while Sara climbed the stairs to the tower room.

'I'll call back,' said Anna, ending her call when Sara appeared. 'A date,' she explained.

'OK. Was it Lina?'

'What?'

'The waitress.'

'Er, yeah. It was.'

Anna even blushed, Sara noted. Perhaps this might be going somewhere.

'Oh yes,' said Anna. 'On the subject of Lina. Would you give this to Martin?'

Anna pulled a flash drive out of her pocket and proffered it to Sara.

'What is it?'

'Some songs. She's one hell of a singer. I thought Martin might like to hear them.'

Anna noted Sara's sceptical expression and began to defend herself.

'No, it's not how you think. That's not why she . . . It was me who . . . Ack, forget about it.'

'Thanks.'

Anna put the flash drive away again, then they each took a big gulp of wine and the flash drive was history.

'Crazy that you don't have the bedroom up here,' said Anna, looking out towards Kornhamnstorg and Södermalm. 'What with this view.'

'You mean the building site?'

'It should be done in a few years.'

'We'll move up here then. More wine?'

Sara poured generously from the expensive bottle into the almost certainly unsuitable glasses.

'What did Martin want?'

'To bring in a cleaning company.'

'OK.'

'Not on my life. But he's completely nuts about that Uncle Scam guy and wants to invite him round when he's in Sweden.'

'Here? For real? Oh my God, that's cool.'

'Not if it involves cleaners.'

'Did you see the article in *Aftonbladet*? About how much he spends at the club? Hundreds of thousands of kronor in a night. Thirty thousand just in tips.'

'Pay me that tip and I'll be more than happy to clean,' Sara said with a shrug.

'But it's kind of funny that he's visiting the home of a police officer. Our dear colleagues will probably have him under surveillance given his reputation – Practically half his songs are about drugs.'

'So now I'm going to be flagged too, because I'm mixing with a known junkie.'

'Yes, we'll have to keep you under surveillance too,' Anna laughed.

'Anyway, I've told Martin he can't go near drugs. I'd quite like to ask him to video the whole thing so we have evidence, but that might be pushing it.'

'And there's no way of knowing how much of it is image and bragging. What's his real name again? Cornelius something? Not quite the same cachet as Uncle Scam. But what will you do about Ebba?'

'How do you mean?'

'If he's coming here. Surely you've read about it – he's crazy about young girls . . .'

'What, Ebba? Give over.'

'I'm just saying.'

'She can't come here. No way.' Sara shook her head and made a mental note to tell Martin and Olle not to mention anything about the visit to Ebba. At the same time, she knew that if Ebba found out that Sara had tried to stop her from meeting Scam, she would be furious with her mother and do everything in her power to meet the star. Raising children was a high stakes game. A little like poker, it involved bluffing just the right amount, betting the house when you had to and hoping you wouldn't be seen. Well, perhaps the similarity wasn't that close, Sara reflected.

'Doesn't Martin ever get jealous of all the artists he meets?' said Anna, taking another sip of wine. 'I mean, he's still doing a lot with his own band, isn't he?'

'I can't help wondering whether he still thinks he can get his big break.' Sara looked across the rooftops of Stockholm's old town, wondering what that said about her husband.

'It's almost cute. I guess there's a diva in all of us.'

'Mine is properly locked up in some small cage. Might even be dead. Martin, however, is constantly feeding his. Not to be cruel, but I think it's more about a desire to be seen rather than to entertain.'

'Nice tactic,' Anna said thoughtfully. '"Not to be cruel", before saying something really cruel.'

'But I *didn't want* to be cruel!'

'Not to be cruel, but you're the ugliest person on the planet.' Anna grinned at her.

'Look, it's like this. Martin was really keen on the stage even back at school. And it's never stopped. He always has to perform at the company's parties, and his poor employees never dare say no. And just last June he tried to play at Ebba's graduation party, but she refused.'

Sara smiled, but the smile faded when she thought about the days around Ebba's party, the days before her showdown with Abu Rasil, the final days before her 'normal' life that she had thought she would always live had ended. The life she would never be able to return to.

'My God, these glasses must have holes in them,' said Anna. 'They're already empty.'

Sara refilled them and Anna raised her glass in a toast. First to Sara, and then a couple of times in mid-air in various directions. Sara looked at her friend sceptically. Anna met her gaze.

'Surely you feel it too?' she said.

'What?'

'There's someone here.' Anna looked around the tower room. 'Perhaps it's those Nazis? There's no harmonious energy in this room.'

Sara had once told her the old rumours that a former owner of the apartment had hidden Nazis on the run from Germany at the end of the war.

'It's probably the rats. Cheers.'

At that moment, her mobile beeped. Martin, Sara assumed. But it was from Hedin.

Going to Berlin. Will tell you more later.

Berlin? Why was she going there?

Sara hoped it wasn't her fault and that she hadn't sent Hedin off on some dangerous wild goose chase.

Anna raised her glass again, but suddenly all Sara could think about was a murdered priest.

28

Sara woke up at around seven, her head heavy following the two or three bottles of wine she had shared with Anna the evening before. Good grief, there had even been hugs, confessions and 'I love yous' while drunk. Downright amateurism at a relatively low level of intoxication. She didn't know whether to be ashamed of herself or proud.

Martin was already up even though he had got home at two o'clock. She got up, visited the bathroom, did her press-ups and went to find her husband in the kitchen. Her husband, who despite all the stress and expectation ahead of the big star's visit, had taken the time to make her a cup of tea. She gave him a kiss as thanks. And since the day was technically classified as a hangover day, she skipped her morning porridge and spread soft garlic cheese onto half a baguette instead. Heavenly.

Then Walter wanted feeding by way of thanks for guarding the kitchen against rats overnight. Luckily, he hadn't caught any. It was always up to Sara to deal with the bodies, since Martin's rat phobia extended to dead rats. Sara considered a parallel with her job – it was up to her to deal with the rats of society too. But being philosophical didn't help. Bloodied rat corpses were just as disgusting either way.

Martin vanished carrying his cup of coffee. There were cordons and guest lists and press accreditations to review. Ahead of these particular two concerts, Martin wasn't trusting anyone else, or so it seemed. When she heard the front door close, she wondered how many coffee cups Martin had taken to work and never returned with. At least a dozen.

She checked the news online. There was nothing about a priest in Östergötland, nothing about a missing former director of a government agency, nothing about former West German terrorists. But there was plenty about Uncle Scam. Lists of his best songs, the biggest scandals, his career highs and lows, competitions to win tickets. On Martin's preferred radio station, they were wittering away about the gigs – two sold-out nights at the Friends Arena. And it was rumoured that Scam was going to do a top secret club appearance – the only question was where. Sara switched over to P2. The Brandenburg Concerto No. 3 in G major. She thought about her violin which she had smashed to pieces in a fury. Was that carnage the end of her violin playing days? The thought of it was both sad and liberating at once. Like finishing school.

In the middle of her baguette, Jane called back – bright-eyed as ever at this early hour. Sara got straight to the point. Just like Jane always did.

'Did you visit Lotta's family?'

'Yes.'

'Why?'

'In case they needed anything.'

'Did you say anything about Stellan?'

'No.'

'Or me?'

'Why would I do that?'

'Why did you leave your umbrella there?'

'I forgot it.'

'You never forget anything. You wanted a reason to go back.'

'Why not? I'd be happy to visit them again.'

'Come on, Mum. You're up to something.'

'Yes, I'm watching the television.'

She got no further. Jane switched to talking about how dull the morning news programme she watched had become, at which point Sara said she had to go. Her mother was up to something, but Sara couldn't work out what it was and Jane was apparently not going to confess. The worst thing was that she was certain that her mother was keeping it secret precisely because she knew that Sara wouldn't like it. Just as Sara would have done herself, she realised.

After a long hot shower she got dressed and stepped outside into Kornhamnstorg. Unfortunately, the ice cream parlour wasn't open. Bomonti, which was in the same building as her apartment, did the best lemon sorbet in Stockholm – possibly in Sweden. It was the only lemon sorbet Sara had ever eaten that didn't leave a bitter aftertaste. Lemon sorbet didn't need to have that – there were more than enough things to deal with in life. But it still did. After the events in Bromma, she had promised herself to get better at enjoying life. Eating lemon sorbet was part of that, but there were also other, more important things. She had around an hour left until she needed to be at work, and she had an idea about what she should do with that hour.

'Sara,' said a voice beside her. When she turned around she saw C.M. – Carl Magnus something-or-other, the Bromans' neighbour.

'How are you?' he said with sympathy in his voice. How much did he know about what had happened? Perhaps the police had been obliged to explain what his shotgun had been used for. Although how much did the police really know?

'I'm fine. How are you?'

'Oh, I'm well. I was passing and thought I'd take a look at this spectacle,' he said, gesturing towards the eternal building site immediately outside Sara's front door. The scandal that was Slussen. 'I don't think they're going to finish before I shuffle off this mortal coil.'

Sara wondered how C.M. actually felt after having been held prisoner in his own home with the risk of not being found. He had told the police that he and Agneta had had an affair in the past, but that he had never guessed who she really was. Now he was one of very few people who knew the truth about Agneta Broman. Or at least part of the truth. That she had been some kind of secret agent, but not that she had been a Soviet illegal living under a false identity for all those years while monitoring the Stasi's spy, Geiger, on behalf of the KGB. Sara had also realised that Agneta had forsaken her ideology and done all she could so that her beloved grandchildren would not have to grow up in the shadow of Cold War intrigues and false loyalties. But given what she knew about Agneta's duplicity, Sara wondered why the old woman had had an affair with C.M. Perhaps it had been nothing more than the ordinary human requirement for closeness? Perhaps spies needed body contact too? And she had presumably had little in the way of married life with Stellan, given his awful secrets. At any rate, Sara would always be grateful that in her childhood she had learned that C.M. had a very expensive shotgun made by Fabbri. It had saved her life – as well as many others in Europe.

She waved goodbye to C.M. and strolled up to Östermalm via the Skeppsbron bridge and Nybroplan.

There, through a large glass door on the corner of Torstenssongatan and Riddargatan, she saw her first-born standing behind a large reception desk in a suit, her hair up, smiling at staff arriving for work.

Friendly and charming, with a cheery word offered to all who passed. Although Sara would have loved to benefit from this side of Ebba, she was glad to see it being expressed in the company of others. Her daughter wasn't always angry. This Ebba was also the result of predispositions inherited from Sara and Martin, as well as their efforts to raise her.

To be perfectly honest, it hurt a little that Ebba was so happy to work with her grandfather, but that was temporary. A first job on the way to her own career and her own life. And Sara hoped she would play a greater role in that respect than she had done during Ebba's teenage years. That was what she had always looked forward to, standing by her daughter's side as she created her own life.

Sara put her hand on the brass door handle and pushed it open. Ebba turned towards the entrance with a smile, but as soon as she spotted her mother her face contorted into a grimace.

'Mum, I'm working!' she almost hissed.

Sara looked around. Carpeted floor, Arne Jacobsen Egg arm-chairs, Noguchi tables and the company's logo in two metres of brass on the wall. 'Titus & Partners'. Ebba smiled and greeted passing colleagues, but glowered at her mother in the intervals between them.

'What do you want?'

'To see how you're getting on,' Sara said to her daughter.

'I'm great. They're so incredibly nice to me here.'

'Yes, of course. When your grandfather owns the company.'

'God, you're rotten. That's not the reason at all.'

No, it had been a stupid thing to say. Sara regretted it. Why couldn't Ebba be allowed to think that people were pleasant with-out any ulterior motives? Why shouldn't she be allowed to think the world was beautiful? She would realise what it was like in due course, but she had to learn it herself. The hard way.

'Good morning, Ebba.'

The deep voice made Ebba not only smile but also straighten her back and raise her eyebrows.

'Good morning! I hope you're well?'

'Absolutely splendid.'

Sara turned towards the voice and saw a handsome man in his forties in an elegant suit, without a tie but with a handkerchief in his breast pocket, or a pouchette as she knew it was called. Green eyes and thick brown hair combed back and curling into his neck. He looked at Sara and reached out with his hand.

'I don't think we've had the pleasure. Tom Burén, Executive Vice President. Are you new?'

'No, I'm Ebba's mother. Sara.'

'You'll forgive the cliché, but how is that possible? You look more like sisters.'

Sara flashed a wry smile at him.

'With a twenty-five year interval.'

'Well then, all I can do is thank you,' said Burén.

'For . . . ?'

'Giving the world such a talented daughter. A real asset to the firm.'

Ebba blushed where she stood behind the reception desk. Sara realised that Tom Burén had built a career on his gift of the gab, but she still couldn't help feeling some maternal pride.

'It's all to her credit,' said Sara. 'She's never listened to her parents.'

'What's all this then? Just hanging around? You'd think you were working for the council.'

Eric Titus smiled at them from just inside the main door.

'I've just met Ebba's mother,' said Tom.

'Go easy, she's packing heat,' said Eric, and his deputy laughed.

'But I only shoot if you touch my daughter,' said Sara.

'Don't you worry,' said Tom, showing his ring finger, which bore a large gold band.

'Have you ever been in before?' Eric asked, turning to Sara. 'I don't think you have?'

Sara realised it was true – she had never visited Eric's office. Even though she had spent a quarter of a century with his son.

'Come on in,' Eric said, pointing to some pictures on the wall by the lifts. 'Projects in Asia, America, Africa. And Europe, of course.'

'You construct buildings?'

Eric laughed.

'You know a little. Yes, we build buildings – or so you might say.' He tapped in a code and the lift door closed. 'Construction is one of our pillars, major projects characterised by Swedish quality all over the world. Communications, energy and logistics are our other three pillars. But I don't want to bore you. Here's my office.'

The lift let out a discreet ding and Eric led Sara into what was clearly his own part of the building. A pretty young girl was standing by a desk outside a smoked glass partition wall with large doors leading into a corner office with a magnificent desk, a separate meeting table and a group of Swan armchairs.

'This is Sanna, my assistant,' said Eric, pointing to the girl by the standing desk. 'Sanna, this is my daughter-in-law, Sara. Mother to Ebba, down in reception.'

'Pleasure to meet you,' said Sanna, smiling kindly.

The fact that Eric had introduced his assistant made an agreeable impression, Sara thought, hoping that it was his natural behaviour rather than something he was only doing because he thought it would be appreciated by Sara. Nevertheless, it was typical that it was a young woman rather than a young man standing there. Or a middle-aged man. With dandruff.

Sara went over to the windows and looked down towards the Nybroviken bay and the island of Skeppsholmen on the other side. The water glittered as a white archipelago ferry cut through the small waves on its way out to sea.

'Coffee?' Eric went over to a small, wholly automatic Jura machine on the other side of his big office. 'Latte? Cappucino? Black?'

'I'll try a latte, please. It's always the best indicator of a machine's quality.'

Eric pressed a button, handed Sara a latte and then chose an espresso for himself.

'Take a seat,' he said.

'Do you have time for me?'

'I've got all the time in the world. That's the wonderful thing about growing old. I can do what I like. The company runs by itself. And I've ensured that I have only hired competent people, so I would say the company runs better the less I get involved. But it's still rather pleasant to come here and feel important.'

Eric smiled again. Self-awareness. A good trait.

'Well, would you like to hear the sales pitch? Turnover, how many countries we're active in, the new sectors we've entered? Or perhaps you'd just like to chat?'

'Chatting sounds good.'

'Fifty-six billion kronor, thirty-four countries, telecommunications, superconductors and green energy. Oops, I said it anyway.'

'Good coffee,' was Sara's judgment.

'Like I said, I surround myself with the best.'

'Like Ebba?'

'She really is doing a splendid job. Always on time, remembers everyone's names, always knows which bookings are coming up and where people are. You've got a girl there who's going to go far.'

The thought struck Sara again. Did other people see things in her daughter that she didn't herself? Or was Ebba different with her grandfather? Well, she was clearly different with everyone who wasn't her mother.

'Go far? Well, I suppose if that's what's most important.'

'You can't live in your big flat or sit here in my office with that nice cup of coffee and say that there aren't advantages to success,' said Eric, raising his eyebrows.

'Have I succeeded? How does a police officer fit into the formula for success? You definitely don't get rich doing it.'

'Social good. That's the most important purpose of all. I'm incredibly impressed by the important job you do. Which means I think the least your family can do is make an effort to provide you with a tolerable existence, given that society doesn't reward its most important workers to an adequate extent.'

Sara meditated on this for a while. Did she really buy the reasoning? Eric had never shown any interest in anything other than business and empire building so far as Sara could remember. But perhaps she had been a little too quick to judge him. He might really think that. And it didn't really matter whether they were values he had always had or ones that he had acquired in order to appreciate Martin's choice of partner. Why wouldn't a business executive have sides to him other than the desire to focus on his career? Sara thought to herself. Simply because she didn't? She

193

smiled slightly at her self-criticism. At least they shared a love of family – that much was definitely true. And it was more important than anything else.

'It's really lovely to see that there are grown-ups that Ebba isn't angry with. Gives me hope that it might spread to us too one fine day.'

Eric looked at Sara for a second and then sat down with his espresso cup.

'Sara, it's not my intent to come between you and Ebba. I mean, with all the presents and the driving lessons and so on. I suppose it's a parent's duty to practise driving with their child.'

'I'm just relieved I don't have to. We would kill each other.'

'And I recognise that in one way I am buying her devotion with all the expensive presents, but I'm just so incredibly fond of my grandchildren. I want to give them everything in the whole wide world. I'm afraid I've never managed to get close to Martin in that way. It feels as if on the one hand he has to prove something to me and on the other he kicks up a fuss and goes his own way. You don't have to be a psychologist to understand that his need to be on stage is a desperate attempt to get his father's attention. But even if Martin and I have a bit of a ramshackle relationship, it's been light years better than the one I had with my own father. You just have to regard it as a gradual development – generation by generation.'

'So what was your father like?' Sara asked, thinking that she was pleased that Martin and Olle were on such good terms. They were almost more like friends than father and son, but that was better than having nothing in common.

Eric laughed and shook his head.

'Old school. Didn't you meet him?'

'Oh yes, but only the once. A very impressive man.'

'Then you know what I mean. I was over forty before I felt that he accepted me, when this company began to grow. Then we enjoyed a good relationship in his final years, which pleases me a lot.'

He sat in silence for a while, looking down at the desk. It was unusually introverted for Eric – a faint smile playing on his lips. Then he looked up at Sara with a slightly scrutinising gaze, as if he were thinking about something.

'I wanted to be an artist too. I don't think I've ever told anyone that. But my father wouldn't let me. I was to join the military or business life.'

'So you didn't pursue your own path?'

'It wasn't even on the map. Society was completely different back then. A different world. And I honestly think he might have killed me if I'd tried. Rather than have a juggler for a son.'

'So what did you want to do?'

'Become an actor. I sang and performed for my mother and young siblings, but when I was ten years old my father caught me at it and locked me in the wardrobe and I wasn't allowed out until I promised to stop my childish behaviour.'

Eric looked rather sad, so Sara reached out and placed a hand on his. Her father-in-law gave her a look of gratitude.

'So that was why I actually encouraged Martin to become an artist. In those brief spells we had together as he grew up, I wanted to see him perform. All I insisted was that he become the best at whatever he did. Otherwise there wasn't much point in it.'

'And he may not have become the best.' Sara thought about Martin's beloved part-time band with amusement.

'No, he was decidedly more talented at organising, so I suppose I indirectly contributed to his success.' Eric smiled, almost a little surprised. As if he had never considered this angle before. He even nodded to himself before continuing. 'If I hadn't encouraged him to perform, he wouldn't have put so much into it, and he would never have discovered his talent. And you would be living in a one-bed rented flat in Hökarängen.'

'You'd never let your grandchildren live in such cramped quarters.'

'You know me far too well.'

'Perhaps I'm getting to know you.'

A light tap on the glass wall made both Sara and Eric look up. Sanna was standing on the other side with a bundle of papers in one hand and an elegant pen in the other, her eyebrows raised in a quizzical expression. Eric waved dismissively at her with his hand and then turned towards Sara.

'You know something? You can feel sorry for yourself about what you didn't get to do, dreams that were never fulfilled. But you learn a lot from not getting to do what you dream of. It might not help you, but it can help you to help others.'

'I don't think we've ever talked this much,' said Sara. 'I like it.'

'Sara, I . . . I don't exactly know what happened to you around midsummer, but I gather from Martin that you've gone through something traumatic. And I can see it on your face, if I may be so vulgar as to mention your exterior.'

'You may.'

Sara remembered the first time she had seen her reflection in the mirror at the hospital. The nurse had thought she ought to wait, but Sara had demanded to see it when they had been redressing it. She had decided beforehand that she would be horrified, but wouldn't panic that her face was ruined. Perhaps that was why she had been completely calm when she had seen the burnt, scarred skin. She had expected it to be worse, she had been promised that it would heal more and above all she had decided to accept life as it came. There was no reason to feel bad about something she couldn't change. Better to put her energy into changing things that were wrong and that she was capable of influencing.

'I'm glad you survived,' said Eric. 'And it was a reminder that life is fragile. We could all go at any time, and I don't want to depart this present life without having got to know my daughter-in-law a bit better.'

'That's a very beautiful thing to say. I completely agree.'

'There's one more thing.' Eric paused for a longer time, and then he conjured up his winning smile again. 'I want to offer Ebba a trainee position here. With the long-term aim of her working her way up to the executive team. My dream is for someone in the family to want to take over the business. Martin is neither interested in nor suited to it, but Ebba is just the right kind of person. If she applies to the School of Economics, she can study at the same time as working here, and then work her way through all our subsidiaries and various divisions. She could be ready to take over in ten years' time.'

'Take over?'

'Yes.'

'I'm sure she would be flattered by the offer, but I think she wants to do her own thing.'

'If I say that I would like her to take over, I think that will be the path she wants to follow.'

Sara didn't know whether it was protecting her daughter's free will or whether it was quite simply envy that someone wanted to build a future for Ebba, but the proposal made her recoil instinctively.

'She has to make her own mind up.'

'She doesn't need to take over Martin's company – it's already been sold.'

'But perhaps she wants to do something else entirely.'

Sara had imagined that Ebba might become a human rights lawyer or perhaps travel the world with Médecins Sans Frontières, saving lives. Not become the up-and-coming young woman in her grandfather's company.

'Don't confuse what she wants with why she wants it,' said Eric. 'There's something very satisfying about building up to a goal.'

'Building up, yes. But you just want her to be the custodian of what you've already built.'

'It's not finished yet. Not by a long shot. Ebba would be the perfect person to lead an ecommerce venture, for instance.'

Little Ebba 'Lead an ecommerce venture.' She'd only just got out of nappies.

'Eric,' said Sara. 'I don't honestly know how I feel about this.'

'What is there to feel, except that it's a fantastic opportunity?'

Sara had no arguments to offer against this, but she still couldn't accept the idea off the bat. She was infinitely grateful when her mobile rang and interrupted their conversation.

Eva Hedin.

'I need money.'

'OK. Do you use Swish? How much do you need?'

'Ten thousand euros.'

'Well, I don't have that in my account. What do you need it for?'

'To pay a source.'

'And he needs ten thousand euros? Are you sure he knows anything?'

'Do you need money?' Eric asked.

'Not me. My . . . friend.'

'Sanna!' Eric barked into the intercom, and the assistant from the standing desk outside hurried into the office.

'I need you to transfer ten thousand euros – the person my daughter-in-law is speaking to can provide you with the account details.'

'OK,' said Sanna, stretching out her hand towards Sara, who hesitated for a few moments. But eventually she handed her mobile to Eric's assistant, who quickly left the room.

'Hello, Sanna speaking. Do you have an account number for me?'

Sanna shut the door behind her and Eric looked at Sara with a satisfied expression.

'Sometimes it's good to have plenty of money. Don't you agree?'

29

'We now know a bit more about the bodies we fished out,' said Axel Bielke, taping printed photos of the deceased to the white-board. 'The girls are sex workers from Ghana and Romania respectively. Obviously we're having trouble getting hold of their real names, but in Sweden they called themselves Lola and Angel. The men found with them in Mälaren were Swedish – Juha Kallio and Jan-Olov Åkerman. Kallio was an advertising executive at Sky Limit Group, while Åkerman was a pensioner and lived in the suburbs in Mälarhöjden. Both were single. According to his former colleagues, Kallio was a frequent patron of the city's more elegant bars, and his consumption of both alcohol and so-called party drugs was reportedly high. He was living it up, with both a Ferrari F430 and a Bentley Bentayga in the garage, as well as a three-bed apartment in Östermalm with an eight-million-kronor mortgage secured against it. And his most recent tax return shows an annual income of seven hundred and forty-five thousand a year. Åkerman didn't have any relatives so far as we know and is described by his neighbours as, and I'm quoting here, "a bit of a misery", "a moron", and "fucking Hitler".' Bielke surveyed the gathered detectives and paused before continuing. 'Find the common denominator for this bunch. There's a hundred kronor for whoever cracks it.'

'Were the men customers of the girls?' said burly Ergün.

'Possibly. But it doesn't explain why they were all tortured to death. And they died at different times. We're talking about a period of around six months.'

'Hardly drug dealers,' said Anna.

'No, "fucking Hitler" didn't exactly look like some street pusher,' said Sara. 'More like a retired teacher.'

'Assuming he didn't start selling to the kids in the class-room?' said Peter, who regarded himself as the funny one in the group.

'Well, what does a teacher's pension add up to?' asked Peter's sidekick Carro. 'Maybe he needed to supplement his income?'

'Come on people, focus,' Bielke interjected. 'Tell me more about what type of group this is. Åkerman was, for the record, a retired corporate lawyer.'

'Perhaps they were killed at random?' said Ergün. 'Someone killing for pleasure?'

'Serial killers don't hire hitmen to dump the bodies. Is there a criminal connection?'

'Might Åkerman have seen something he shouldn't?' said Anna. 'Like the hunters at Ekerö. Except he didn't have a rifle handy.'

'Quite possibly. The other three seem easier to join together.'

'I bet Kallio owed some drug lord a ton of cash.'

'What about the girls?'

'Threatened to go the police?' said Ergün.

'OK, at least we've got a few ideas,' said Bielke, turning to the whiteboard and making notes. 'We've also found a text message of interest on Cesar Bekas's mobile phone. It's from his girlfriend, Abeba Idris. She keeps it short and sweet: "At 8 behind the church?" and Bekas replies: "OK. Kisses." Those are the final messages he sends and receives.'

'Just before the murder?'

'Were they going to pray together?' said Peter. 'Was Bekas born again?'

'He had started going to church with the family, Abeba's father said, but that wasn't a secret.'

'Behind the church, she said? Not *in* the church.'

'OK, a meet-up. But behind which church? Theirs? Weren't they members of some free church? The girl's family, I mean.'

'The Holy Church of the Divine Resurrection and Ascension of Jesus,' said Anna. 'But it's in the city centre at Norra Bantorget in a regular building.'

'OK, so another church then. Are there any churches nearby?' Sara pulled out her mobile to check. 'There's one right by where the girlfriend lives. St Botvid's Catholic church. And there are woods behind it, or so it appears.'

'Then it was probably there. But why didn't she say anything to us about it?'

'Her parents were there,' said Carro. 'The girl probably didn't want to mention she was meeting her gangster kingpin in secret. Didn't you say they were Jehovah's Witnesses?'

'Dude, I said it was the Church of the Ascension,' Anna said with a sigh.

'What's that?' said Ergün. 'I've never heard of it.'

'All you have to do is Google. Ten million members around the world – mostly in South America and Africa. Around fifteen hundred members in Sweden. They focus on the sanctification of Jesus, I think they say. Very devout it seems.'

'OK, but she must have deleted the message from her phone then?' said Sara. 'Did the girlfriend lure him into a trap?'

'And was it conscious or unconscious?'

'Unconscious?' said Ergün. 'How do you lure someone unconsciously?'

'Well, if she really did agree to meet him, but that meant the hitmen could get to him.'

'I suppose we'll have to ask her.'

*

'What were you and Cesar messaging about? On Friday at 20:34?' Sara and Anna were once again seated on the sofa in the Idris family home. There were no biscuits this time, but Abeba appeared to have recovered a little.

'I wasn't. I was watching TV at that time.'

'Can we see?'

'The TV?'

'Your mobile.'

'Sure.'

'I'll get it,' said her father, Ndeme. 'Don't get up.' He stood up with great effort like all older fathers and left the room.

'More tea?' said Abeba, and her mother Rosa topped them up from the gold-rimmed teapot before they could reply.

'Thank you,' Sara managed to say.

The father returned with the mobile and handed it to his daughter. She pulled up her text message thread with Cesar and passed it to Sara. There was no message sent by Abeba on Friday evening.

Sara quickly checked the call log too, but saw nothing there from Friday night. Four numbers appeared more frequently, and there were a few numbers that appeared to be for companies or public bodies judging by the numbers. Lots of zeroes. Perhaps the daughter handled contact with the authorities on behalf of her parents. That wasn't particularly unusual. However, a few of the calls were from earlier on during Friday. That might mean something.

'We need to take this with us,' said Sara.

Abeba looked up at her father, who nodded.

'That's fine,' said Abeba.

'What's the PIN?'

'There isn't one.'

'Was there anywhere you usually met?'

'No. He came here.'

'Not behind the church?'

'No. Just here.'

'He was so nice,' said Rosa. 'He always brought small gifts and flowers. For me, too.'

'He was a good boy,' Ndeme agreed.

'OK, we'll return the mobile to you when we're done with it.'

Sara and Anna thanked them for the tea, got up and headed for the door. As they were heading down the front door steps, Abeba called out from behind them.

'Wait!'

There was something harried about her voice that made Sara and Anna come to a halt. Sara realised that she even had her hand at her holster out of pure reflex. Abeba came running from inside the house with something in her hand.

'The charger!' she called out.

'We've got those at the station,' said Anna.

'But take it anyway. Just to be sure,' said Abeba. She came out to them and passed over the charger. As Sara took it, Abeba leaned forward and whispered:

'We met at his too, but Mum and Dad don't know that. I always tell them I'm with friends. Please don't tell my parents!'

'We promise.'

Abeba disappeared inside and Sara and Anna looked at each other.

'OK, so apparently there are a few secrets here . . .' said Anna.

30

'You just made a call and got given money?'

Landau had checked with his bank and received confirmation that a deposit of ten thousand euros had been made to his account. Strangely, it would be a couple of days before he could spend them even though everything was digital these days. But he knew for sure they were en route.

'I can't get any more,' said Hedin, who had seen in Landau's eyes what he was thinking. 'So you'll have to tell me now.'

Manifestly stout, Uwe Landau stubbed out his unfiltered Roth-Händle and lit a new one. He kept coughing, sounding like an old, worn-out lorry engine that wouldn't start. White stubble covered his soft, flabby cheeks and his white hair was cut into some kind of hedgehog style with all the short strands standing right on end. He was wearing a tracksuit that was the worse for wear with an emblem on the breast where the words 'FC Carl Zeiss Jena' were just about legible under a layer of cigarette ash. At his feet there was a blue bag with the word 'Interflug' on it.

'It's not about the money,' said Landau. 'The only reason I've agreed to meet you is because my old friend Rabe asked me to.'

'Everything's about contacts,' said Hedin. 'It was ever thus.'

The choice of meeting place struck a discordant note with Landau's threadbare appearance. Glücks Café was a modern, trendy little place. It had concrete walls and a large window facing the street opening onto outdoor seating where the duo were sitting. The menu featured ambitious soups, salads and small plates inspired by the Mediterranean, the Middle East and South America. Hedin wondered whether Landau even knew what quinoa was. But she realised it was the location itself that had been the deciding factor.

On the opposite side of the street – the lively Chausseestraße – was the newly-completed, gigantic complex that housed the Bundesnachrichtendienst. The BND had moved from Pullach – probably for practical reasons, but it was also a symbolic break from the old. The facility that had overseen national security since the days of the Third Reich and had been taken over by the Waffen-SS. Now it was as if they were saying: 'Forget the old, we're living in a different world these days.' Or at least that was what they wanted people to believe.

Perhaps the sight of the building meant the former Stasi officer felt at home here. Or he wanted to torment himself by sitting in the shadow of the proud fortress of the victorious. Or perhaps he just wanted to remember a time when he had been respected and feared by all those working inside the security complex. Even if most of the people working there today hadn't been born when their side had emerged victorious from battle.

Now he got to feel important all over again because what he knew was worth something. These days nearly everything was about right-wing extremism and Islamism. Tedious doctrines, lacking in history. Socialism against capitalism was another matter entirely. The struggle for a just world using all means available. Here, he was on his home ground. Here, he was the indispensable pathfinder. Before the disaster, he'd had a house in Waldsiedlung Wandlitz, with the woods, lake and all the big villas belonging to the Stasi chiefs nearby. The head of state security, Erich Mielke, had lived in villa number 8. Everyone ranked major or higher had access to holiday homes in wonderful rural settings, free weekends at one of the Stasi's twenty-four spas, not to mention the shops filled with western goods.

Everything had been, well, *the best*.

Before the Wall fell.

Now he was worth less than the empty bottles that everyone worked so hard to recycle. Who wanted to recycle him? Hedin was the only person who had ever taken an interest in what he had achieved. She seemed almost fixated on the Stasi and its personnel.

'Messer, Axt, Faust and Lorelei,' said Landau. 'Kommando 719. Named after Andreas Baader's cell number, naturally. Messer and Axt came from the 2 June Movement and RAZ – the revolutionary cells – and Lorelei admired the Red Army Faction. Even though they were so useless that they all went down, the lot of them. And they put a Heckler & Koch in their emblem instead of a Kalashnikov, which was what every liberation movement in the Third World used.'

Landau managed to rattle off a malicious laugh.

'What do you know about them? What were they like? What were Axt and Faust like?'

'Faust wasn't much of an ideologue, if you ask me. More of a fighter who wanted to stir up trouble. He wanted to hurt for the sake of hurting. What they all had in common was a desire to make the West show its true face by provoking the repressive police state. And we were more than happy to assist in that regard.'

'You trained terrorists in East Germany?'

'West Germans, Arabs, Africans, Latin Americans. We provided anyone who wanted to cause a revolution with the skills to do so.'

'And the weapons.'

'And the cash.' Landau snorted. 'And what difference did it make? An atom bomb over Bonn is nothing compared to a dagger in the back.'

'And you provided them with protection?'

'Carlos the Jackal, Abu Nidal, Abu Daoud, the Red Army Faction, the PFLP, Black September. We were very international.'

'And Kommando 719.'

'I helped to train them myself. Close combat, believe it or not.'

Landau gestured at his own shabby figure, as if to emphasise what poor shape he was in.

'Lorelei was called Werner and Messer was called Gerlach, so we gather. But which out of the other two was Axt and which was Faust?'

'Rau was Faust. The devil himself.'

'And what is he called today? What was his new name?'

'No idea. We weren't allowed to know. This was some of the most secret stuff we were involved in. Communist cells in the West taking up arms. Subversive operations. If our enemies had been able to prove that we supported this, then there would have been a war.'

'But Rau was the driving force, you said?'

'Definitely. He was the engine of that group. He wanted things to happen, to see blood.'

Landau laughed, which set off yet another earthquake-like coughing fit. This time the attack lasted a little longer and he concluded the outburst by spitting a large quantity of matter into some napkins. Hedin turned her head away.

'What happened to Faust?' she said, in an attempt to get back to the subject.

Landau shrugged.

'Given his fervour, I doubt he gave up. But he may have found new ways to fight on.'

'You don't think he just hid under a false name?'

'Well, you can count on the false name. But he won't just have hidden. Someone like him would struggle to live a normal life. He's probably in this world in one way or another. He simply disappeared after the Wall fell. Everyone who could hide did back then.'

Hedin could tell that Landau didn't count himself as one of this cowardly band. She knew that he had always stood by his work for the East German security services and surveillance state. He had been charged but freed after a trial in which accusations and censure had been cast at him. He argued that his activities had been completely legal in the system that applied in the country at the time – in no way different from what they were engaged in across the street in the present day.

'But perhaps he was useful to someone else,' said Landau.

'Who?'

The former Stasi major shrugged.

'The Palestinians, the Israelis, the West? Who knows?'

'Is it possible to find out his new name? The one he got in Sweden?'

Landau shook his head.

'It's not documented anywhere. It was only in his handler's head, and he's long dead. Just as I will be soon.'

'Not even in the files they're putting together using computers now?'

'Some details were too secret to be recorded – even for the Stasi. The idea with the new identities was that they wouldn't be traceable. In that regard, comrade Koch did a magnificent job. Only he knew.'

And he tried to exploit it, Hedin thought to herself.

'What else do you know about Rau?' she said.

'He knew Sweden well – he'd visited quite a bit and worked up a network of contacts. I think he had a Swedish mother. So yes, he led operations there. He was good. Merciless.'

'Would he kill someone threatening to unmask him?'

'Without even a second's hesitation,' said Landau, before adding: 'And he'd enjoy it.'

Hedin looked up towards the gargantuan building across the street. The world's biggest intelligence service headquarters. A grey concrete colossus with completely straight lines that looked more like an East German prison than a grand fortress for the defenders of freedom. Was there an agenda in building something so grim? She allowed her gaze to wander across the anonymous façade.

She suddenly had the feeling that someone was looking down at her from one of the windows. She squinted up towards the building, but of course she could see nothing.

In the meantime, Landau's body shook with a new attack of coughing. He spat into a new wad of napkins, but his coughing continued.

'I've only got three months left,' he said between coughs and without looking up. 'I'm going to spend my final days living like a king on that money.'

'Then you can tell me what the purpose of Kommando 719 was. They were preparing for something specific.'

'You don't want to know.'

Landau looked around for more napkins.

'Yes I do,' said Hedin. 'And I've paid for it. You wouldn't have spent so much money on them if they hadn't had something very special brewing.'

'Many millions,' said Landau with a wry smile.

'Exactly. So tell me.'

A new round of coughing, and Hedin saw him put a hand to his ribs. The powerful convulsions were probably painful. Eventually, Landau looked up at Hedin with bloodshot eyes.

'If you open that door then there is no going back.'

'OK.'

Landau took a deep drag from his cigarette.

'Do you understand what kind of man you're looking for?'

Hedin didn't reply.

'Do you really want to find him?'

'Yes. Tell me now,' Hedin said impatiently. 'What was the purpose of the group?'

The ungainly man looked at her with something verging on sympathy.

'You don't want to know,' he repeated.

'Yes I do,' she said again. 'What have you got to lose? You've got three months left to live.'

'That may be longer than you have.'

31

The floodlights blinded him. They cast an intense white light, as if he had got too close to the sun.

He shut his eyes, turned his head and tried to make out his old friend in the darkness behind the light. When he squinted he could make out small windows with the curtains drawn at the back of the room. The walls were painted black and his nostrils were filled with a sweet scent – of sweat and something else, something unpleasant.

Leather straps held him to a bunk with a mattress on it – they were cutting into his wrists. And the bunk wouldn't budge. It seemed bolted to the floor.

'Otto?'

No reply.

'Otto? Let me go. Message received. I won't say anything. I promise.'

'Message? I have no message.'

'Warning, then. Call it what you like.'

'Warning?'

The voice now came from behind Bo Enberg, but he could only turn his head a little and the rest of the room was in darkness.

'The people's court is convened in the trial of the traitor Hans Gerlach under his revisionist alias of Bo Enberg. Deliberations shall commence. Where did you call?'

Rau's voice was now directly by his right ear.

'I haven't called,' said Enberg, while turning his head as far as he could.

'Your first lie! The accused has called the police. The tool of the oppressor. What was the purpose of your call?'

Enberg sighed. Rau had apparently been bugging his phone. He might as well show his hand.

'I called Säpo. But it wasn't to tell them about you. Only me. I promise.'

'What were you going to tell them about yourself?'

'What we did. What *I* did, I mean. Nothing about anyone else.'

'And why were you going to tell them that?'

'Because I can't carry this burden any longer.'

'You shouldn't have to do that.'

'Otto! I would never say anything about you.'

'What would you be able to say?'

Bo Enberg paused for thought. What did he actually know about Rau? What they had done back in the day . . . But now? Nothing.

'Nothing. I don't know anything about you. What you do, where you live, what you're called.'

'Do you want to know that?'

'No! And I can take responsibility for what we did.'

'You're going to claim the credit?'

'No, the punishment.'

'You're not proud?'

'Of what we did? No.'

'Of our struggle for a better world. What did you tell Sara Nowak?'

'Who?'

A sharp pain at his cheek followed by the taste of blood. He shuddered and felt a long thin metal object against his tongue, stuck into his mouth from the side. It was so sharp that when he grazed it with his tongue, he cut himself. Blood poured from his mouth and down his front. He hadn't even noticed that Rau was close to him.

'Otto!'

'What did you tell Sara Nowak?'

'Nothing! I promise! Otto, I'm bleeding.'

'Tell me what you said.'

'Nothing!'

A shadow flashed past and then a quick cut to his throat. He felt the blood pouring out, down onto his clothes.

'Otto, stop before it's too late. I haven't said anything. You have to believe me. I know full well what you would do to me if I talked.'

'This is exactly what I would do.'

'Otto . . .'

'Did you mention Wahasha?'

'No! Absolutely not!'

'Why not? You wanted to unburden your mind,' said Rau, sounding quizzical.

'That was completely separate from the other things we did. No one can know!'

'You're right about that. Hans?'

'Yes?'

'Do you swear that you haven't told Sara Nowak anything else?'

'Yes.'

'Then I'm going to free you.'

The immediate relief that Bo Enberg felt was immediately replaced by chilling horror when he realised what Rau really meant.

'No! Please . . .' Enberg pleaded.

But he got no answer.

He knew Rau.

'OK,' he said with a sob. 'Get it over with.'

'There's no rush. Is there anyone you'd like me to send the video to?'

'What?'

Enberg's voice was thick with terror.

'I'm just joking. It's private.'

Otto Rau turned on the music. 'Open the Gates' by Dark Funeral – thundering hell music as far as he was concerned, something he would never otherwise listen to. But it was a good fit for this. A very good fit. He cranked up the volume. He checked the frame, adjusted the camera slightly and when he was satisfied he started recording.

Then he went over to the small adjacent table, opened the hard plastic container and pulled out his Makita HR2630J – a drill that could go through concrete without any trouble. And it went through soft objects even more easily.

Before long, Bo Enberg was drowning out 'Dark Funeral'.

32

Abeba's text message to Cesar was occupying Sara's thoughts as she climbed the stairs to the apartment. Everyday fitness, they called it, and an opportunity to summarise the issues they were grappling with, so that she could let go of work when she got home.

They would soon know the truth about Abeba's text message. Had she sent it or not? Perhaps she had simply deleted it and then denied sending it so that her parents wouldn't find out? It might have nothing to do with Cesar's death at all.

Sara wondered how it felt to live a double life like that. One life for her parents and one of her own, which had to be kept secret.

Two floors to go. Her final questions before she switched off her work brain for the evening.

Alternative theories: might Abeba have consciously lured her boyfriend to an encounter with his enemies? If so, had she known they were his enemies? And why would she have done that? Was it really possible? Her grief had seemed genuine.

Sara stopped. Had they checked whether the mobile they had been given by Abeba was the same as the one Cesar had received the text message from? In a world of constantly changing phones, it wouldn't have been strange if Abeba had used the same tactic too. But Sara hadn't thought to check that. Stupid! She wrote a reminder to herself to check in the morning.

Then she was at her destination. She unlocked the front door and went inside. Ebba's shoes were in the hall and Sara perked up. Perhaps the prodigal daughter was missing her family after all?

'Ebba?' Sara called out.

'She's in here,' Jane replied. Sara turned around and checked the hall floor again. Indeed, there were Jane's shoes too, neatly inserted into the shoe rack rather than abandoned in the middle of the floor like Ebba's.

Sara entered the living room to greet her mother and daughter, and also spotted her husband and son. All of them with strange expressions on their faces – and that was putting it mildly. Martin looked astonished. Ebba angry. Olle sulky.

'Hello?' said Sara.

'Jane has told us about Stellan,' said Martin, which made Sara's stomach do a somersault.

'What about Stellan?' she said, looking from her husband to her mother. Jane looked her directly in the eyes.

'No more secrets,' she said.

'Surely you haven't . . .' was all Sara managed to say.

'Yes, I have.'

'Are you out of your mind?! I said I didn't want to!'

'They need to know what their background is.'

'Why?'

'Was he my grandfather?' said Ebba. 'Uncle Stellan?'

'Why didn't you say something?' said Martin, looking more sympathetic than upset.

'There's nothing to say.'

'Yes there is, that he was your dad,' said Ebba.

The anger welled up inside Sara. Both in respect of her mother's betrayal and her father's very being.

'He wasn't my father. I have no father!' Sara picked up one of the white Series 7 chairs positioned around the dining table and threw it at the wall. Then she swiped at the vase of white roses, so that it fell to the floor and smashed, the roses raining through the air. Martin looked frightened, but Jane and Ebba were the picture of calm. Olle mostly looked sulky. 'I don't want to hear another word about it, OK?' said Sara. 'And above all else, I don't want a fucking thing from him!'

The last comment was directed at Jane.

'OK, I don't care who my granddad was,' said Olle. 'Can I go back to my room?'

'Yes, go. But you can never tell anyone about this.'

'No, why would I? "Hello there, have you heard the news? A dude I never met was my granddad"? Big deal.'

Olle snorted. An Uncle Scam song was seeping out from the AirPods in his ears as he strode away.

'Does that mean we have to go to his funeral?' said Ebba, her voice worried. 'I mean, I hate funerals.'

'No, you're not going to a funeral. I'm going for Agneta's sake – if I think I can keep myself from spitting on his coffin.'

'My God, Mum, what the hell's wrong with you? Why are you so angry? You were there tonnes when you were little, weren't you? I've heard about all those wonderful summers in Bromma like a thousand times.'

'I don't want to talk about it. And I definitely don't want any of you to talk about it. To anyone.'

'He was my granddad. Not everything is about you.'

'Yes, it's actually the kids' roots that we're talking about here,' said Martin.

'You've got a father and his two parents – your grandfather and grandmother. And you've got a mother and her mother – your other grandmother. That's it. OK?' snapped Sara.

'No, it's not,' said Ebba. 'Most importantly, you don't decide what I feel. Uncle Stellan was my granddad. It's important to me.'

'My God, you want me to tell the truth about him?'

'Or you can just accept the truth about yourself?'

'Go to hell – all of you!'

Sara turned and headed for the door.

'Good – that's what a proper mum says!' Ebba called after her. Sara couldn't help turning around again.

'A proper mum has a family that listens to her!'

'Sorry . . .'

Sara turned around towards an unfamiliar voice with a heavy accent. A young woman in tracksuits bottoms, a sweatshirt and yellow rubber gloves was standing behind her.

'I'm done now, but I did find one thing . . .'

'Who is this?' said Sara, looking at her husband.

'I was going to have a bit of an after-party with Scam after the gig, so I wanted everything to be spick and span.'

'So you brought in a cleaner?!'

'Well, neither of us has any ti—'

'Idiot! You know what I think about that!'

'Yes, but maybe I have some views too.'

'There's not going to be any bloody after-party here! And you . . .' Sara turned to the cleaner. 'You can go. I'm sorry my pig of a husband tricked you into coming here. We don't have servants in this household.'

'Yes, yes, I'm going. I'm done. But I found something.'

'Martin's brain?'

'This. A weird . . . microphone? It was under the coffee table.'

A little electronic gadget rested in the girl's gloved hand. Sara bent forward to examine it. It undeniably looked like a microphone. A little home-made unit featuring a mic, transmitter and battery. What was it doing here? Who had put it there? And why?

In her home. With her family.

As if in a trance, she picked up the little microphone and shouted for all she was worth into it:

'Who the hell has bugged my home?! Go to hell, you fucking moron!'

Then she threw the little microphone against the wall, smashing it to pieces.

'What was that?' said Martin, looking at the fragmented remains. 'A microphone? Who put it there?'

'Don't know. Maybe the paparazzi? Your band is going great guns.'

217

'No, but seriously. Was it crooks?'

Sara took a deep breath and looked her husband in the eyes.

'Not now, Martin. Not now.'

*

Sara sat in the tower room for a long time watching darkness fall. She saw the city illuminated and life continuing outside, ordinary people coming home from their ordinary jobs to their ordinary families. Martin and Olle went to the concert and Jane went home to Vällingby. And here she was.

Bugged.

In her own home.

Unless it was some fanatical Uncle Scam fan trying to listen in to the planned after-party. But she didn't believe that far-fetched explanation.

So what *was* the explanation? And how long had the bug been there? Might it have been Breuer who put it there when they were searching for the old spy ring? The German spook had been engaged in some sophisticated double-dealing. Perhaps . . . It was the most probable explanation. Or the only possible explanation that wasn't extremely worrying.

She would have liked to have someone with her now. She just didn't know who.

Sara stayed up in the tower room until she heard the front door open at half past midnight. She went downstairs to find Olle accompanied by a girl in her twenties.

'Will you be OK now?' Sara heard the girl say.

'Yeah, absolutely,' said Olle. 'Thanks, Tindra. You didn't need to drive me. I could have got the tube.'

'Hi,' said Sara. 'How was the concert?'

'Totally sick,' said Olle happily. 'I was right at the front and got to meet Scam backstage afterwards. Look!'

Olle pulled out his mobile and produced a selfie of him together with a thin white guy in a cap, with loads of tattoos.

'Who's that?'

'Scam,' said Olle, as if his mother had completely lost her senses.

'Is he white?'

'What did you think? That all rappers have to be black? That's old-school racism. Or whatever it's called. Inverse racism. That's what he sings about. "*You don't know where I've been, you only see the color of my skin.*"'

Olle looked at Tindra, seeking support in the generational war, and perhaps continued contact with the young girl.

'Yes, yes. I didn't know,' said Sara. 'Good that you had fun anyway. But where's your father? Weren't they having an after-party here?'

Sara looked at the lined up bottles of spirits and champagne on the dining table, which had been moved into the living room. Cognac, grappa, calvados, vodka, gin. Dozens of bottles of Cristal.

'No, you said he wasn't allowed, so they went to the club.'

'"Wasn't allowed"?' Sara glanced at the young girl and realised that the nonsense you said often only seemed like nonsense if an outsider heard it. 'But he sent you home on your own?'

'No, Tindra gave me a lift. But I could have taken the underground. I'm used to it.'

'You most definitely are not,' said Sara, oblivious of her son's desire to impress a good-looking older girl. 'And who are you then?' she said to the girl.

'Tindra. I work at Go Live.' Tindra proffered the laminated backstage pass that was slung around her neck as if to certify her truth-telling. The pass said 'GoLive', 'Uncle Scam – Scamerican World Tour' and 'Backstage pass, access all areas'.

'How sweet of you to run Olle home. Are you OK to drive home yourself? You're not too tired?'

'I'm not going home. I'm going back to work.'

'Tonight?'

'All night. And from seven tomorrow.' Tindra squeezed out a smile. 'People think the music industry is so flipping glamorous, but it's actually quite a lot of work.'

Sara didn't think the music industry was one bit glamorous, and she wished she could have forced Tindra to go home and get some rest, but it would only have caused trouble for the poor girl.

Tindra bade them goodnight and just about managed to contain a huge yawn until the door closed.

'Bedtime,' said Sara, speaking on behalf of both her son and herself.

Olle obediently headed towards his room and Sara went to the living room to turn off the lights. She saw the devastation – just as she'd left it.

Well, she had broken the vase – no one else. Nevertheless, it bothered her that no one had taken the time to sweep up the pieces and pick up the roses. It would have felt like the other members of the family had acknowledged her right to be upset if they had cleaned up after her outburst. Now she would have to do it herself, and it felt as if no one had understood her, hadn't even wanted to understand her. As if it didn't matter that Sara's father was the most disgusting human being she had ever encountered and that he had even come close to abusing his own daughter. Did they really not understand that Sara refused to have anything to do with him? She refused to give him even a millimetre of her life.

She swept up the pieces of glass, mopped up the water and then vacuumed and wiped to catch the smallest shards. The roses might have been saved but she simply chucked them onto the dining table. They might as well stay there as a reminder of Sara's feelings about her father.

When she pressed the button to retract the cord on the vacuum cleaner, her eye was caught by something else on the floor. A small piece of metal. She bent down and picked it up.

The battery from the bug.

What did the planted microphone really mean?

The fact that it had been there meant that someone had been into their home and planted it which meant there was someone listening to her . . . watching her?

But who – and why? And what would happen if Sara did something that the unknown watcher didn't like?

What would happen if she had already done so?

Somewhere in the shadows dark forces were lurking with plans for Sara, and she had no idea what they might be.

And what you don't know you can't guard against.

33

The bedroom reeked of booze and Martin was snoring so loudly that the walls were vibrating. He had tumbled into bed at around half past five in the morning. Sara had tried to fall back to sleep but after half an hour she had got up to stake her hopes on breakfast instead.

She hoped Martin had had fun, and she thought about Tindra, the assistant, who had probably got to bed just as late, but had to get up again soon and keep working on the second gig. Online there were stories about the 'Superstar's night of wild partying' illustrated with photos from various hip bars' VIP sections with Uncle Scam and various local celebrities. Martin could be glimpsed in a couple of the photos. It was lucky that the newspapers reported on this, Sara thought. If you couldn't party with superstars, then at least you could look at photos of other people doing so.

Sara put her used coffee cup and yoghurt bowl in the dishwasher and headed for the shower.

When she emerged into the hall, there were two bangs in quick succession followed by the sound of breaking glass and a big smash.

She looked towards the crash first and saw a framed lithograph had had its glass smashed and had fallen to the floor.

Where the piece had been hanging there were two small holes in the wall.

She quickly looked towards the window. Two matching holes.

Sara didn't want to understand what this meant, but it ate away at her nonetheless.

Someone had shot into her apartment.

Had tried to hit her.

And had been centimetres away.

Her knees gave way and she fell to the floor.

Was that another shot? No, it was her body hitting the parquet.

She couldn't think clearly. Had it really happened? She looked up towards the window. Yes, there were two holes. And the same went for the wall.

Panic spread through her body. The trauma from the Bromans' shed washed over her again, just as powerful now as then. Someone wanted to kill her and one little bullet could tear her body to shreds so that she couldn't be saved.

She wasn't even safe at home.

This was what she had been afraid of, but she had tried not to think about it. And now it had happened.

She began breathing heavily. But she still felt that she couldn't get enough air. She couldn't move.

It became warm. It felt as though there was a fire again. She couldn't move her head, could only glance to either side. Was there a fire? No, but it still seemed as if the flames in the shed were licking at her body, stinging her. She had the clear feeling that they were going to take the rest now – what they hadn't managed to destroy last time.

What was she going to do? Shoot back? Call for help? Call the police? Shout to her family to take cover? Yes, she had to. And it was urgent. But she couldn't do anything.

Now she wasn't able to take in any air at all. She lay there desperately gasping for air. She felt tears begin to flow. Was life going to end now? And she couldn't do anything about it. Couldn't even move.

'What's going on?'

Olle, sleepy-eyed, was staring at his mother.

The sight of her son in the firing line yanked Sara out of her paralysis.

'Down!' Sara shouted, tugging Olle to the floor beside her. Good God, what if they had shot again? What if Olle had been hit? Her hands trembled as they rested on her son's arms.

Olle looked at her, still drunk on sleep and completely uncomprehending.

'Why?' he said.

'It's from the building site,' Sara said, thinking she needed to bloody well pull herself together. Get a grip. 'Flying stones. They're doing blasting work. Stay away from the windows – you hear me?'

'Yes.'

'Good. Now go back to bed!'

Olle began to stand up, but Sara brusquely pulled him down again.

'Crawl!'

'Yes, yes . . .'

Olle obediently crawled back towards his room. Her son and husband would surely sleep for another few hours. That gave Sara some time.

She wriggled forward and drew the curtains across the bullet-holed window, before quickly crawling around and closing the blinds and curtains in all windows facing Slussen. She dressed and retrieved the broken lithograph then put it in a cupboard and fetched a painting from the living room that she hung up in place of the damaged picture, so that the bullet holes weren't visible. Neither Martin nor Olle would notice the change.

She swept up the shards of glass for the cat's sake. Then she fetched one of Walter's cat toys – a long stick with a string attached to it. She pried the curtains open a notch, put one end of the stick to the bullet hole in the wall and the other towards the bullet hole in the window. That gave her a bullet trajectory to enable her to see where the shot had been fired from. And her likely trajectory ended by the Hilton hotel at Slussen, in a small opening between the big buildings there.

For safety's sake, she wrote a note in case Martin – against all probability - woke before Olle: *Stay away from the windows! They're doing blasting work for the building site and there are flying stones.*

And then she ran.

She shoved early-to-rise pedestrians and electric scooter riders out of her way. And after passing the hotel on the way up towards Bastugatan and the Söder heights, she found the spot she had seen from her shot-up window. An open, cobbled area with the rather fancy name of Guldfjärdsterrassen. She had never been here before.

It was completely deserted but afforded incredible views of the railway tracks, the water and the old town.

And Sara's home.

The shooter must have stood here. And they must have been a good shot, equipped with a telescopic sight in order to see Sara's figure as she passed the window.

She probably shouldn't have shouted into the bug, probably shouldn't have shown that she had found it, and above all she shouldn't have challenged whoever had planted it. She had put her entire family in danger. But now she could at least be certain that it hadn't been Breuer who had bugged her. Someone was after her.

The bastards, Sara thought. They might have hit Olle. And that would have been Sara's fault, completely down to her.

A blend of rampant guilty conscience and a growing hatred of the person who had put her family in mortal danger consumed her. The anger she felt towards herself was in turn directed to the person who had shot at her. He wouldn't get away with this. Not a chance!

Sara turned around and looked up towards the hotel windows and office buildings around her. No police, no sound of approaching sirens.

No one had reacted.

Had a man with a rifle really passed completely unnoticed?

But all she saw were inanimate façades and further away the portal into the Söder Tunnel. No people – even though she was in the middle of the city. She retraced her steps a short distance and looked down towards the entrance of the hotel. It was empty except for two taxis waiting for fares.

One driver was asleep behind the wheel of his car and said he hadn't seen anything in the last half hour, while the other, standing outside his car smoking, said a rather odd car had just left. And that he had spoken to the driver.

'Well, I saw him getting a rifle out from his wheels which got me curious. I didn't think he was no robber or anything, so I wasn't scared. Just curious. You're born that way, aren't you? A bit *nysgerrig* as the Danes say. But it said "game warden" on his car and he explained that this is what the city do. They shoot lots of animals in town – rabbits and geese and pigeons – and they do it in the mornings so that there aren't as many people around.'

'What did he look like?'

'What did he look like? Who the hell was thinking about that? Bit older. Accent. Not like some Arab – German or French or something. I was thinking more about the gun than what he looked like. It was one hell of a rifle.'

34

Going against all standard procedure, Sara did not report the gun-shots to anyone. A particularly dim view was taken of attacks on the homes of police officers, and they were supposed to be reported in all circumstances. But Sara wanted to understand what was going on first. It was too big to become just another police case, or so she felt. But she realised her logic was poor.

But logic wasn't everything. Especially not in this instance.

She phoned the Hägersten glaziers and explained the situation. The official version was that they needed bulletproof glass at home because they were due a visit from the global superstar, Uncle Scam – and there was a threat against him. This meant that absolute discretion and maximum urgency were key. No problem, they said, and they were on the scene within half an hour and started work to replace all the windows with Hammerglass. Sara left a note for Martin and Olle saying that the glazing was being replaced for Scam's sake and coolly calculated that they would buy her excuse. But she decided to wait a little before getting out the filler and paint, instead leaving the moved painting as cover for the holes in the wall for the time being. She searched online for CCTV firms and sent a message to a company saying she wanted them to get in touch to arrange an installation at her home.

Then she called the City of Stockholm and was put through to the municipal game warden. No one had been at Slussen that morning and none of their vehicles had been stolen.

Finally, she went to work.

She told no one about the gunshots, not even Anna. Her friend was a police officer and would act like one, no matter what Sara said. And the gunshots were something she needed to get to the bottom of herself. Hedin was the only person she knew who knew anything about the world from which Sara was convinced the threats were emanating. Sara could tell her. Maybe . . .

Right now she had to focus on the job at hand. Her real job.

Sara surveyed the small team overseeing the Ekerö case. Her colleagues. Friends, she might almost have said. Even though the topic of conversation was grim murders, the morning meeting felt safe and familiar. Or perhaps it was because of that.

'We've got a couple of new pieces of information that are of interest,' said Bielke. 'Jan-Olov Åkerman, the oldest victim, had recently appealed against planning permission given for an extension to his neighbour's house and the appeal had been upheld. This reportedly led to aggressive confrontations. Perhaps Peter and Carro could look into this further?'

'Torturing a neighbour to death because you can't extend your pad? Right,' said Peter with a wry smile. 'We'll look into it.'

'Even more interesting is that the text message to Cesar Bekas was recovered by our forensics team from Abeba Idris' mobile phone,' said Bielke. 'She had deleted it and the reply from Bekas.'

'OK,' said Anna. 'So she has something to hide. No calls to another guy? Maybe she fell in love with someone else but didn't dare break up?'

'And instead she had him murdered?' said Sara. 'Is that what you do when you break up with someone?'

'We're all different.'

'Remember that her parents are Christians,' said Carro. 'Maybe she knew they wouldn't agree to her changing boyfriends? But with Bekas dead, she's good to go.'

'What exactly is your perception of Christians?' Sara asked.

'Pretty realistic, I reckon.'

'Or not.'

'I was raised in the Pentecostal Philadelphia Church right here in town. What about you?'

Sara didn't answer.

'No other erased text messages or calls?'

Bielke shook his head.

'And no other calls that we can connect to gangs. But we obviously don't know whether she has more phones – it's not altogether uncommon in such circles. At any rate, we've got her under surveillance in case she meets anyone. She sneaked out of the house this morning and we thought something was going on because she kept looking around. But in the end she just went to the newsagents to buy a newspaper. Anyway, we're keeping eyes on her.'

There was something at the back of Sara's mind, but she couldn't think what it was. Something about the mobile and text message. Annoying. She could tell it was an important reflection. She just couldn't find it in her head even though she racked her brains.

'We're still working to build a full timeline of Bekas's final hours,' said Bielke, handing out folders with different assignments. 'Where was he, who did he meet, what did they say? Talk to his homies, ask the staff at his usual haunts, people out and about. Which cars did he have access to, are there other mobile numbers we can connect to him? See whether you can get anyone in his gang to give you the numbers they had for him. After all, he's dead now.'

Midi, Maxi and Efti's old hit 'Bad, bad boys' screeched from Sara's pocket. It was the song she had chosen as the ringtone for all her contacts in the world of crime. It was probably silly, but it tickled Sara.

She pulled her mobile out and saw that 'Jojje' was trying to reach her. Hardly awe-inspiring. But appearances could be deceptive. George Taylor Jr was, in spite of his cute nickname, the leader of his own gang – one of the most violent in the county. And it was he who had been shot by Cesar's little brother and had probably ordered the subsequent revenge attack.

Sara stepped aside to answer.

'What the fuck were you playing at, opening fire at a hamburger restaurant?' was the first thing she said. She knew that everyone in

Jojje's gang had been questioned and declared themselves innocent and ignorant. But she also knew they were guilty, and she knew they knew she knew. 'And next to a petrol station! What if a bullet had hit a fuel tank?'

'Sweetheart, you know I'm innocent. That's not what I'm calling about.'

'I don't give a fuck why you're calling if it's not to confess.'

'Listen, I just want to help you out.'

'By confessing. Come on, be a man. Take responsibility for your actions.'

'I'm a man. Want me to show you?'

'You're a little boy.'

'You'd like that, yeah?'

'Come on, pull yourself together. What did you want?'

'I know what they did with Bekas,' he said, which made Sara pay attention. 'He did a peepshow.'

35

George Taylor Jr hadn't been able to explain exactly what he meant by saying that Cesar Bekas 'did a peepshow'. All he knew was that it was something very unpleasant that people threatened their enemies with.

Obviously, it might relate to something different, but Nadia had mentioned a peepshow too, and Sara had a feeling that it was no coincidence. They had been found the same day.

She was looking for the leader of Bekas's gang, but neither he nor anyone else in the gang was picking up. She requested a uniformed patrol to stop by and look for them, but she didn't have any great hopes of success.

Were there any other ways in?

Sara made her own deductions. Peepshows were normally part of the sex trade, an old-fashioned way of peeking, but Jojje and Cesar belonged to a completely different world. The heavily armed, extremely violent criminal world. If you combined those two worlds, Sara thought to herself, you ended up at SIN, the semi-legal strip club in Vasastan.

Officially, this was home to nothing more than striptease and 'exotic dancing', but Sara had seen all the small rooms in the basement with beds and stacks of towels. She harboured no doubts whatsoever about which services were offered down there. If the police raided the place, there was plenty of time for the male patrons to pull on their clothes and pretend to be enjoying a private dance while the police made their way down the steep staircase and into the narrow, winding corridors.

SIN was owned by a man called Peter Wäbel, a grotesquely toned former bodyguard who had suddenly – as he himself put it – 'taken over' the club from his boss. And after the boss had tried to get it back, he had been found shot inside his car round the back of Bromma Airport. Since then, SIN had been wholly Wäbel's.

'Sara Nowak,' she said when he answered the phone. 'I've got a question.'

Sara knew that Peter Wäbel could be just as frightening and obstinate when his own interests were threatened as he was pleasant and cooperative with the police and authorities when not under pressure. But Sara wasn't after him – not this time.

'Go for it,' said Wäbel.

'Peepshow,' said Sara.

'Watching or participating?'

'Just information. I've heard rumours about a peepshow – is there anything like that in town?'

'You mean a proper old-fashioned classic peepshow? Otherwise our club is a bit like a peepshow. "Look but don't touch" and all that, you know.'

Sara didn't know that at all – on the contrary she was convinced that all it was about was payment at a certain level to gain access to other services.

'Otherwise there's something like that in Södermalm,' Wäbel added. 'Real low-class stuff, not the kind of thing we do. We're not competing for the same clientele.'

If they had been, then the other place would have been blown up or taken down in a hail of bullets – Sara was sure of it.

'Whereabouts in Södermalm?'

'At the end of Bondegatan, in a basement next to the Co-op. We had to check it out to see whether we were competitors. Turns out we weren't.'

'How fortunate,' Sara said with feigned sincerity.

'It's called Studio Clasper.' Wäbel laughed. 'Have you ever heard a less sexy name? It's some kind of seedy wanking club for pis-sheads and other specials.'

Sara thanked him and hung up. Now she owed a pretty dodgy person a favour, but it had to be worth that.

Studio Clasper was online. It had a decidedly ugly website but it did include a phone number and the man who picked up agreed to meet Sara. But not at the studio he said, because they were filming.

'It's just a little low-budget thing,' the voice on the phone said with a snuffle. Cold, sad or cokehead, Sara thought to herself. 'It's called *Squirty Dancing*,' the voice continued with enthusiasm. 'You get it? Instead of *Dirty Dancing*.'

'I get it.'

Sara and the man from Clasper met at Kajas, the outdoor park café at Vitabergsparken. Which, it transpired, was a real oasis in the desert of the big city. Trees and undulating hillocks, a patch of gravel with round tables and parasols, colourful pennants fluttering in the gentle breeze and a whole family – mother and daughters – working behind the counter. The sight of the snuffling sex-club owner was quite a contrast to the surroundings.

'Klas,' he said offering his hand immediately after wiping his nose. Sara shook his hand anyway. 'But they call me Bass Klas,' he added in a tone that indicated he was pleased with the nickname. Sara assumed the epithet was the result of playing the bass, which his appearance suggested was the case. Long hair, skull rings on all his fingers, and a tatty denim waistcoat covered with Judas Priest, Motörhead and Slayer badges even though he was surely over sixty years old.

'It's just allergies – nothing to worry about, no illegal substances.'

Klas laughed at the joke before turning away to sneeze.

Sara looked around. The place was indescribably charming. It was somewhat overshadowed by the Sofia Church. She would never have found it if Bass Klas hadn't told her about it. Sara thought to herself that she ought to come here with Anna some time. Then she wondered why her first impulse hadn't been to come here with

Martin. Unclear. But she decided right away that it was naturally her husband she should come here with. For a beer. When had she last got drunk outdoors? That had its own charm.

'You have a peepshow,' said Sara when Bass Klas had drunk the first gulp of his beer.

'Yes,' said Klas, nodding as if to show that he was proud of it. 'Since '84, actually. Shit, time flies. Twenty-five years. Well, twenty-six. No, bloody hell. It's been thirty-six!'

He looked a bit taken aback.

'I was on the prostitution task force for many years. I didn't actually know about Studio Clasper.'

'No, well, it's not prostitution. And it's not a big place in itself. It barely stays afloat. But what the hell, we toil on in this mercenary society.'

'What do you do? What happens at Clasper?'

'Oh, y'know. Some blokes get to look at some naked girls. Or girls getting naked. Well, girls and girls. They're not exactly spring chickens.'

'No?'

Bass Klas laughed.

'No, Sonja's been with us from the beginning, and Rita for at least fifteen years. She's even a grandmother these days. Drives the grandkids to football at the weekends.'

'Are they the only ones who work there?'

'Yes. But I'm sure we've got room for one more.'

Klas smiled meaningfully, but it was such a kind smile that Sara couldn't feel aggravated by the invitation.

'Never anyone else?'

'No.'

'Not a girl called Nadia?'

'No, sadly not. Pretty name. Would look good on a poster.' He chuckled. 'Classy for Klas.'

'Cesar Bekas?'

234

'Caesar? Shit – an emperor!' He assumed a serious expression and raised his hand in a salute before laughing. 'No, but seriously. We don't know what the customers are called. Except for the regulars. But they're more like friends. We often grab a beer once the clubs closes. And some of the others that come in occasionally we call stuff like "horn dog", "sticky fingers" or "Skåne". But I don't know what they're called. Er, on another subject entirely . . .'

'Yes?'

'Could I get another beer?'

Sara went and bought a beer for the faded strip-club owner. Personally, she hadn't even touched her mineral water even though she was sweating in the late summer heat. But she would have preferred a beer.

'Is hitting the girls part of it?' said Sara when she set down the beer on the table in front of Klas.

'Which ones?' he said in confusion, clearly distracted by the ice-cold bottle.

'At the peepshow.'

'What, if they don't do as they're told? Like a pimp in some ghetto joint? "Shut up, bitch"?'

'I don't know. Like a part of the show?'

'No. Jesus Christ, that's shabby – it'd ruin the number.'

'Nadia was seriously assaulted.

'I've actually heard about a place that does that, lets people really have a go at the girls. Really dodgy.'

'What's it called? The place I mean?'

'Don't know. Don't think it has a name. And I don't know where it is. You know it's here, you hear rumours. Someone who knows someone who knows someone who says he went there.'

'Not much to go on.'

'Nope, but I know a girl who picks up girls for them – Vanessa. I think Rita knows her. I can try and get her number for you.'

'Just to be nice?'

'As a thank you for the beer.' Bass Klas raised the empty bottles. 'And because they take it too far. It's not the done thing. Not violence. They're ruining the fucking industry.'

36

'Wahasha. Operation Wahasha.'

Just as Sara had almost reached the station in Solna, Hedin called to say she was back, forcing Sara to return to the neighbourhood of Södermalm that she had just left. But instead of using the route through the tattoo parlour, she followed Hedin's instructions and entered a café on Erstagatan called Spuntino, asked for a latte to go and then said she was there to see Eva. Hedin wanted to support this pleasant little café, hence the coffee order. With a paper cup containing her latte in her hand, Sara was let out the back and was once again able to cross the large courtyard to Hedin's kitchen window.

The fact that more or less all the business owners on the block seemed to know about Hedin and her secrecy made Sara wonder how effective her cautious measures really were. But, as ever, curiosity overcame her scepticism.

'Wahasha? What does that mean?' she said once she was seated in Hedin's kitchen with the curtains drawn and the radio switched on to add an obstacle to anyone listening in.

'Beast,' said Hedin. 'Or monster.'

'In?'

'Arabic.'

'And Rau was Faust?'

'So says my contact.'

Slowly, the person Sara was searching for began to take shape. Now she at least knew who was who.

'And this Operation Beast was something that Rau was involved in?' said Sara.

'In the eighties. And it was so secret that my contact didn't even want to say the name at first, despite the fact that he didn't know what the operation was. But it was apparently meant to be something quite extraordinary.'

'Is it still live?'

'No. Not according to him.'

'Then how can it still be so important that Rau is prepared to kill to keep it secret? What awful things did they do back then? Are there any unsolved terrorist attacks?'

'Perhaps it was what he did to prepare for it?' said Hedin. 'There are still a lot of secrets from that time that would shake the world if they became known. Both sides did things they'd rather didn't come out.'

'Why an Arabic name?' Sara said, thinking aloud.

'They were very pro-Palestinian.'

'And now Palestine is back under discussion,' said Sara. 'With Israel beginning to warm up relations with some Arab states. That means the Palestinians lose influence. Might that be what's triggered all this?'

'Who knows? The bombs that Geiger was trying to help detonate were looked after by Palestinian interests at one point.'

'Have you Googled it? Wahasha?'

'Yes, it's a character in some computer game if I've understood correctly and lots of youngsters are using it as their handles on social media. But there's no connection to terrorist acts or the eighties so far as I can see.'

They sat in silence, each thinking. They didn't seem to have got much further.

Sara wondered whether she should say something or not, but eventually she told Hedin about the gunshots in the apartment and insisted that she didn't tell anybody anything about it. As usual, Hedin said: 'Who would I tell?'

But she took the threat of the gunshots with the utmost seriousness. She urged Sara to take all the security precautions she could. Close the curtains, never come and go at the same times, don't take the same route to work, preferably stay somewhere else for a while, and above all get her family out of there.

'If they had wanted to kill me, they surely would have done it already,' Sara countered, realising that she was trying more than anything to persuade herself. 'They probably wanted to scare me – but it just made me really angry. Otherwise I might have let all this go, but now I don't intend to give in. They could have hurt my family – Olle was at home. So I'm going to put away the person who did this. No matter what it bloody costs.'

The doorbell rang and Sara was interrupted in the middle of her fiery speech.

'Are you armed?' said Hedin, looking her in the eye.

'Yes,' Sara said gravely.

'I'm joking,' said Hedin. 'It's probably just the postman.'

The old woman went to open the door and Sara pricked up her ears in the direction of the hall, feeling a little on edge.

'Hi, Sofia – I'm the chair of the tenant-owners association,' said a chirpy woman's voice in the echoing stairwell.

'Hello.'

'Er, we've tried emailing you. A lot. You haven't paid the service charge. For several months, as it happens.'

'I've been away.'

'Oh, right, but the lights have been on in your windows.'

'I've been in Berlin.'

'OK. But now you're home. And I don't know if you're having problems with your online banking or what, but you do need to pay your rent.'

'I will.'

'Today.'

'I can't do that.'

'Then . . .' The chirpy voice lowered a few octaves. 'Then you might actually get evicted. Even if you're an owner in a tenant co-op, you can be evicted if you don't pay the service charge. And no one wants that. But you do have to do the right thing. It's about respect for your neighbours. If no one paid their service charge we wouldn't be able to look after the building. The association would go bankrupt.'

Sara was surprised by this trait suddenly exposed in her seemingly prim retired professor. She looked around the kitchen and couldn't help noticing a heap of envelopes on the kitchen table.

Bill, bill, debt collector, debt collector, debt collector.

A little shaken, Sara was still clutching the envelopes when Hedin returned.

'My apologies. People lose their minds when places turn co-op.'

'Sorry for prying, but what's this?' said Sara, holding up the heap of envelopes.

'Bills. They'll have to wait. It's not as if Telia, Fortum and Visa are exactly impoverished.'

'But why haven't you paid?'

'I needed money for my trip to Berlin. Flights and accommodation.'

'Why don't you have any money?'

Sara heard how stupid the question sounded, but Hedin didn't seem to react.

'I don't have grants any longer, so I have to underwrite my own research.'

'Don't you have a pension?'

'It doesn't go far. I have to remunerate my sources. Some of them charge handsomely. And I have to travel. There's nothing left. If my computer dies then I'm done for.'

'But . . .' Sara was completely dumbfounded. Then she made a decision. It was really a very easy decision. 'Is the service charge here too?' she said, flicking through the pile. There were three bills marked as service charges.

'I'll take these,' she said.

'Then I won't be able to pay them,' Hedin objected.

'I'll pay. And I'll take the others too.'

'Not on my life.'

'As payment for your work.'

'I don't work on commission.'

'OK, then you can pay me back when you can. If you like. But you can't be evicted.'

Sara put the envelopes in her bag to indicate that the matter was closed. Hedin shrugged.

'If they want to evict me then let them. If I'm to believe my source in Berlin, we have far worse things to worry about than unpaid service charges.'

37

Midnight.

That was all the text message said.

Jenna already knew she would be picked up by someone and that everything happened at a secret location.

Nadia had told her about how it worked before she went home to Romania, and then Micha had told her the same thing before it was Jenna's turn. Jenna took comfort in that – their accounts agreed. That meant there were rules of some kind.

She examined her face in the mirror.

What would she look like afterwards?

Would there be scars that never went away?

She had always feared losing her teeth; she'd had nightmares about it and had brushed them diligently twice a day her entire adult life, ensuring she flossed and gargled with her mouthwash. And now she might lose a few of them, just like Nadia had.

Although it wasn't guaranteed. She might do better. You never knew.

And the only thing that mattered was the money. She just had to get through this awful bit.

One day very soon, everything would have healed and she would be at home with her fortune.

A brand-new life.

She didn't quite dare to believe it, but Nadia had shown her own cash.

One hundred thousand to Jenna's two hundred and fifty thousand. She converted it to leu. It was an incredible sum of money.

Now she had to make herself beautiful so that they wouldn't change their minds.

Tonight, she wanted to be tastefully made-up instead of using the vulgar, bright stuff she used for her usual clients, the ones who wanted a real whore – someone to detest.

The people paying the bill tonight were men with plenty of money who struggled to live without satisfying their personal impulses. And who didn't have the odd impulse?

It felt better when she thought about it like that. Almost as if they were men with afflictions that she was going to help. Like redressing a wound they had.

She pulled Mikki Mouse out of her handbag – the pink cuddly rat that was her mascot. There was no need for it to come with her for this. 'Wait at home, Mikki,' she told the soft toy. 'And don't be afraid the next time you see me.'

She took out her gold-coloured lighter, lit the small candle in front of the sacred Madonna and made the sign of the cross. She asked for forgiveness in advance and reflected that as long as she had the Virgin Mary with her, nothing really awful could happen.

But the feeling of discomfort would not let up.

Jenna stopped and stared her reflection in the eyes.

What was she playing at?

She felt nauseous – she was on the verge of being sick.

A peepshow was what they had said.

That was as far as it would go, they said.

She had seen how far it could go in the shape of Nadia.

But soon it would be over. Nothing but a distant memory.

If she compared what had awaited her with all the men she had been forced to fuck, maybe this was like being with all of them at once. Dreadful, but in a way that brought it to an end. Once and for all.

It would soon be over.

Only . . . she wondered how she would feel then.

38

Sara was sitting in her car on Erstagatan, paying Hedin's bills on her mobile. Then she called the companies that had sent the debt collection notices and explained that she was Eva Hedin's daughter. She said her mother had been very sick and unable to pay her bills. She was now on the road to recovery – thank goodness – and all the bills had been paid. Might they possibly be prepared to draw a line under these late payments? Yes, they were.

Just as she started the car, the strip-club owner Bass Klas called. He had a number for Vanessa. And he had apparently had another couple of beers, given that he dared to ask whether Sara would like to see him sometime. Sara politely declined. Even though Bass Klas added that he didn't have a problem with the fact that half her face was covered in burns – he could look at the other half.

Sara called Vanessa and introduced herself, but the woman merely hung up. She apparently had no desire whatsoever to speak to the police.

Sara thought for a while and then she pulled out the unregistered pay-as-you-go mobile that she kept for occasions just like this. She sent a text message.

Need 2 girls for a special thing. Well paid. Vlad

The name was prejudiciously chosen and the entire message was sent on the wild off-chance, but it seemed to hit the mark.

Colour, size, age? Vanessa replied.
Doesn't matter, up for anything, you got pics?
Not got them yet ☺
OK you want money up front.

Always.
Where are you?
Swish me.
Cash.
OK. Teahouse in Kungsan in an hour.
OK.
Kungsträdgården.
OK.

*

She was tall, slender and blonde with unnaturally large breasts and pouting lips. But there was something self-assured about her gaze that contradicted the bimbo look, a trouser suit that was more business than sex, and a tablet with a spreadsheet open on it that emphasised the businesslike aspect. But Sara didn't hesitate for a moment in picking out Vanessa. The rest of the patrons were typical tourists in pairs, with cameras, bumbags and hiking shoes. They were peering at maps, reading guide books or taking photos of the opera house, the palace and each other. Vanessa was the only one in heels, the only one clock-watching. And the only one not obliged to wave off the sparrows and gulls from her table, as she didn't have anything to eat. Sara strode across the crunchy gravel. The smell of the sea in the middle of Stockholm had always charmed her.

'You have two options,' Sara said after sitting down at Vanessa's table. 'Either you answer a couple of questions and then I leave you alone, or you refuse and I ruin your operation. And believe me, I can do that.'

Vanessa looked at Sara first with surprise and then annoyance.

'I'm waiting for someone.'

'Yes, and the messages you sent are enough to put you away for human trafficking, together with the witness statements we have.'

Obviously there were no witness statements at all, but Sara had to play this for high stakes and sometimes she took useful advantage of the Swedish police force's reputation for honesty. No one expected a Swedish cop to bluff as brazenly as Sara did so sometimes it paid dividends.

'Do you know who I work for?'

'No, but feel free to tell me and we'll bring them in too. It's good that you're willing to give up your co-conspirators.'

Vanessa contemplated Sara like a poker player inspecting her opponent after they had just gone all in. Trying to read her, find signs that might give her away, disclose which cards were in her hand. But Sara was unreadable.

'I'm only going to say this one more time. Answer a couple of questions and I'll leave you alone, or keep your mouth shut and I'll do everything in my power to ruin things for you and your clients. And I'll make it my business to be very clear that it's all thanks to you.'

Vanessa's eyes were now radiating something more akin to contempt than anger.

And she didn't even know that Sara had no intention of letting her carry on trading vulnerable girls. But first Sara wanted to know more about this new type of peepshow.

'What questions?' Vanessa said finally.

Sara smiled.

'Why don't we have a cup of coffee? They do a good cardamom cake here.'

No answer.

Sara had been to the teahouse a lot as a teenager when it had been hot. All the Södermalm popstars who later went to hang out in Nytorget had been here. Popsicle, David Shutrick, Just D, Bo Kaspers, the Schultz sisters. And when foreign stars visited Stockholm it was here they came. She had stood behind John Malkovich in the queue, and had Bono's arse in her face when he had once been standing in the midst of the tables looking for a spot. She had difficulty visiting the teahouse without enjoying a slice of their cardamom cake, but the concern that Vanessa would simply leave meant she refrained on this occasion.

'Peepshow,' Sara said instead.

Vanessa looked at her expressionlessly. Almost defiantly.

'What do you know about peepshows?' said Sara. 'The quicker you answer, the quicker you'll be rid of me.'

Vanessa sighed.

'I've helped to find girls for a peepshow,' she said.

'Where they hit the girls?'

'I don't know anything about that. I find the girls, and they enter into an agreement with the club. I don't get involved in that.'

'You know what happens there.'

'Yes, fine, I guess things get a little wild sometimes. I mean, in the beginning it was group sex in front of an audience. Later on there were customers who wanted things a little rougher. More like group rape. Live. Where they could control it all from their booths.'

'And you helped with that?'

'The girls are in on it. And they get well paid. A lot of them are actually happy when I ask them about the peepshow. It's a lot of money. So much that they can start a new life. Just think. They get away from their pimps, no longer have to be worried that something could happen to their families, and they get a fuck ton of money. Far more than they could ever earn otherwise. So it's a pretty good deal.'

'That's truly generous of you,' Sara said. 'And if a crook ends up in your peepshow? A guy, I mean.'

Vanessa thought about this for a long time before replying. Eventually she said curtly:

'Then he's in the shit.'

'But what happens? Surely he doesn't get gang-banged?'

'If you've fallen out with the wrong people you can end up in a peepshow as a guy. Then there are lots of blokes sitting in the booths watching as well, but it's not sex they're paying to see.'

'Paying?'

'Yes, what the fuck did you expect?'

'Who watches?'

'Anyone. Regular joes, gangsters, accounts monkeys, pervs. People who've heard about it and want to see it. And can afford it. Some of the motorbike gangs do peepshows on people who end up in bad standing with them. All the members sit in the booths watching.'

'And no one reports it?'

'The people watching like it, and the ones who end up there, don't want to come back.'

'What is it they do?'

'With the ones sitting there?'

'Yes. Are they tied up?'

'Bound and terrified. Screaming and crying.' Vanessa laughed. 'It's actually pretty funny to see big tough gangsters suddenly turning into little cry-babies, begging for their lives., pissing themselves. Most people who end up in that hot seat usually leave town afterwards.'

'So it's some kind of internal settlement between gangsters?'

'No, anyone can end up there. Someone who did someone over in business. Someone who's done someone else's wife. People who need punishing or warning. But it can also be some tramp who's just been unlucky if there's a lot of demand from the customers but no one has ordered a peepshow for anyone.'

'And what do they do to them more precisely?'

'Give them a beating. One hell of a beating. It's drawn out, excruciating. The people watching want to see suffering. They hit, slice, burn. Maybe even cut something off. The patrons control that.'

'Do people die?'

Vanessa fell silent again. She scrutinised Sara with watchful eyes.

'Not that I've seen,' she said after a pause.

Sara's stomach turned at the hesitant tone. She tried to determine what was beneath Vanessa's words.

'And anyway, I don't find girls for that,' she said. 'Just regular sex with a bit of rough stuff.'

'How can you be sure about that?'

'Before I agreed to supply them I checked it all out.'

'You were there?'

'Yes.'

'Where is it?'

'Don't know. I was blindfolded.'

'But you watched?'

'Yes.'

'And you didn't have a problem with that?'

'On the contrary. It was cool. Sexy.'

'Them hitting people for payment?'

'Seeing some idiots take a beating. And a bit of gang-banging with a firm hand. I liked it. You should try it.'

'Why don't you?' said Sara.

Vanessa seemed to think about it for a moment, then she unbuttoned her blouse and pulled it open. There, on her breast just above her shiny purple bra, Sara saw three streaks. Old, faded scars that seemed to go down right across her stomach.

'And I wasn't even paid,' she said.

39

Kornhamnstorg was cordoned off. There were riot barriers, police officers and vans with flashing blue lights. Hundreds of young people were pressed up against the barriers. They were pouring into the street, making cars and buses hit their brakes while drivers honked. There were cries and shouts and loud police voices through megaphones.

At first, Sara was alarmed. Had the shooter returned? Was someone in her family hurt? Or dead?

'What's happened?' she asked an officer when she reached the fence. She showed her police ID and at the same moment noticed a Lamborghini, a Ferrari and two Rolls-Royces parked outside her own building.

'Uncle Scam's here,' the officer said wearily. 'God knows how all these kids got wind of it.'

'OK. He's probably at mine,' said Sara. 'I'll climb over.'

She made to jump onto the riot barrier, but the policeman took a step forward and raised a hand to ward her off.

'Sealed off. We can't let anyone in.'

'But I live here. That Scam guy's in my apartment. My husband brought him here.'

'Sorry, it's sealed off.'

'Are you kidding?'

'Do you get how big a deal this is? There are more cops out here than there would be for a state visit.'

'But why the hell are the police handling this? Surely they can hire security?'

'Didn't you say your husband brought him here?'

'Yes.'

'Well, tell him that. It makes no difference to me. With a little luck, I might get a selfie with Scam. I've got one with Obama and one with Katy Perry,' the policeman said with satisfaction.

'Who's in charge here? Of the cordon?'

'No idea. The record company?'

Sara pulled her mobile out from her pocket and called Martin while screaming youths pushed from behind, jostling her up to the barrier.

'Get back!' she shouted over her shoulder. It was no use.

No answer.

Then Olle called back.

'Mum, guess who's here?' said Olle, who sounded like he was bursting with pride.

'I know,' said Sara. 'Guess who can't get into her own home? Give the phone to Dad.'

'He's with Scam.'

'And I'm here with a thousand screaming teenagers. Give Dad the phone!'

'Yes?' Martin's voice was audible on Olle's phone. 'Is it important? I'm a little busy.'

'Yes, it's important! I can't get in. They've sealed off the whole square for the sake of your little popstar. Tell them to let me in!'

'Show them your police ID.'

'It's not helping. They say it's the record company calling the shots. Fix it. NOW!'

'Yes, yes.'

Three minutes later, the young assistant – Tindra – emerged from the main door with her laminated backstage pass on a lanyard around her neck, a clipboard with lots of sheets attached to it and three mobiles clutched in her hand. She looked around, found Sara and went to the closest police officer – the one hoping for a selfie.

'She's OK,' said Tindra, pointing to Sara.

The policeman waved to Sara that she should climb over, and then had to quickly run forward to stop the teenagers trying to emulate her.

'Thanks,' said Sara. 'Did you get any sleep last night?'

'Half an hour,' said Tindra, flashing a feeble smile.

'Look, could you do me a favour?'

'Of course.' There wasn't even the slightest hint of hesitation even though she must have had a thousand things to do.

'Can you make sure that guy doesn't get to take a selfie with Uncle Scam,' Sara said, pointing to the policeman who had prevented her from climbing over the barrier.

'OK,' said Tindra, making a note on her clipboard.

The bass was audible from three floors down. And when the lift reached the fifth floor, the music was pounding from inside the apartment. Sara followed Tindra into the hall, then she went into the living room and turned down the volume.

An elated, tipsy Martin turned his gaze towards her. The person he had been talking to, a skinny little guy in a vest and with tattoos all over his body, took a drag on a very fat cigarette. Uncle Scam, she presumed.

The sofa and armchairs were occupied by half a dozen other young men with caps and bandanas on their heads and trainers on their feet. But wearing three-piece suits, which surprised Sara. Apparently she wasn't keeping up with hip-hop fashion.

'Hi, darling,' said Martin. 'Did you get in all right?'

'Yes. Thanks for helping out,' said Sara with irony that did not transmit.

'We're just loading up for tonight. This is Scam.' Switching to English, he added: 'Scam, this is my wife, Sara.'

'The cop?' said the skinny man in amusement, raising his hand to fist bump. Sara opted to do likewise but felt incredibly ridiculous.

Uncle Scam was barely one hundred and seventy centimetres tall, thin and pale, but with tattoos that reached all the way up to his throat and parts of his face.

'You coming tonight?' Scam said politely.

'No, sorry, working,' said Sara. She reverted to Swedish, addressing Martin: 'There are several thousand youths down in the square,' she told him, while Scam turned away to his besuited entourage.

'Yes, this secret was meant to be secret. We even sent the lookalike for a ride in the limo, but it leaked that Scam was coming here. I actually think it was Olle's fault – kind of. He told people at school that Scam was coming round to ours today and then it spread. You know how it is with social media. But apparently he was king of the school.'

This time it was Martin almost bursting with pride, but as far as Sara was concerned it wasn't really worth it. Hanging out with stars in exchange for being unable to get into her own home.

'Can you promise me that this is the last time you bring some bloody megastar here?'

'Definitely. I don't think we'll ever get another star this big to come here. But now we have bulletproof windows – so we can bring basically anyone here. I told Scam – he was into it.'

'Good,' said Sara. 'We want him to feel safe.'

'Absolutely,' said Martin. 'Thanks for helping.' Then he looked a little uncertainly at Sara for a moment before continuing. 'Can I . . .' He twisted his hand in a gesture mimicking the turning up of the volume dial.

'Yes, yes,' said Sara, heading for the kitchen.

There was presumably no prospect of dinner with the family tonight, what with father and son bewitched by an American boy idol. She took a vegetarian lasagne from the freezer and while waiting for the microwave she Googled the big star she'd just had the honour of fist bumping.

[Wiki] Cornelius Crane Jr, better known by his professional name Uncle Scam, born 18 June 1996 in Manhattan, New York, is an American rapper, songwriter and actor. Uncle Scam is the most-streamed artist of the 2020s to date, with almost one billion streams of his big hit "Colour of my skin". Uncle Scam grew up in Manhattan's Upper East Side, where his mother was an attorney and his father a Wall Street hedge fund manager. Uncle Scam has been the subject of criticism for pretending early on in his career that he had a tough childhood, but he has dismissed this, arguing that where you grow up does not say everything about who you are.

'Did you talk to him?'

Olle came into the kitchen wearing his Uncle Scam top and headphones that were pumping out the very man's music.

'I said hello,' said Sara. 'Uncle Sam or whatever he was called.'

'They picked me up from school. Did you see the cars? That was one fucking sick line of cars.'

The kids weren't allowed to swear, but Sara had never seen her son so exhilarated. She only hoped that he didn't know what his idol was smoking in their living room right now. But she knew she probably oughtn't to harbour any illusions.

'Mum,' said Olle, sitting down at the kitchen table, 'I'm a teenager now.'

'Yes,' Sara said, steeling herself. Something big was coming. But she had absolutely no intention of buying booze on his behalf.

'And being a teenager, that means you're not a kid any more. You want to show who you are, right? And things are different now to how they were when you were young.'

When you were young. He wasn't selling it well so far, whatever it was.

'What do you want?' said Sara.

'Nothing.'

'There must be something. I know you.'

'But I don't want anything. I want to *do* something.'

'OK . . .'

'Look, Mum. Think about it. Look around town. Everyone's got a tattoo. It's not unusual.'

Get a tattoo? Little Olle?

'Olle, when you turn eighteen you'll be legally an adult. And then you'll be able to make your own decisions. That is, provided you are getting by on your own, rather than living at home or off your parents. If you're providing for yourself at eighteen then you can get as many tattoos as you like. But consider this: a tattoo is for life. And you can end up being stigmatised if you're tattooed.'

'Maybe it was like that for your generation. Back then it was only sailors and hobos who got tattoos. But now it's almost weirder not to get a tattoo. And you don't want people to think I'm weird, do you?'

'No tattoos. End of.'

'You're so fucking boring!'

Sara's mobile rang. It was Tore Thörnell, the retired colonel who had served with NATO in West Germany during the Cold War and who had helped her with information about the bombs that Abu Rasil and Geiger had been trying to detonate.

'Thörnell,' Sara said. 'How nice to hear from you.'

'You need to put a stop to that,' Thörnell said on the other end of the line.

'Answering the phone?'

'Saying people's names on the phone.'

Yet another lesson about the workings of the shady world that Thörnell had been in.

'OK,' Sara said, if nothing else to placate the old military man.

'I've got something I need to discuss with you.'

'Would you like to confess to a crime?'

Thörnell paid no heed to the attempt at a joke.

'When can you come here? And what on earth is that noise?'

'Right away,' Sara said as the bass rattled the kitchen windows. 'So I can escape this racket.'

'Good. Oh, and by the way – don't tell anyone you're coming here.'

40

The façade almost looked as if it were glowing in the golden shimmer of the evening sunlight. The sky above was cornflower blue, a warm breeze rippled through the treetops in the cemetery of Kungsholm Church and a squirrel ran across the deserted street. The place was, as always, remarkably peaceful given how close to the city centre it was. Number 16 Bergsgatan looked like a small castle. Or fortress – an impenetrable one, to which Sara had the magic key. The door code – 1814, the last time Sweden had been at war. Officially, at least.

Thörnell opened his door and admitted Sara into his imposing apartment, which had once been the headquarters of the secret resistance network known as Stay-Behind. From here, they had planned the resistance against any occupying power. It was so secret that not even everyone in the government knew about it – let alone the Swedish population. Thörnell had shown her the secret door behind the large hall mirror. A door that led into the beating heart of the movement, a room where all the desks and typewriters were still to be found – a reminder that the past never really leaves. It was a large, beautiful apartment with a fascinating history that was known to almost no one but her.

'Coffee? Water? Wine?'

'A glass of water would be great.'

'Sorry. It'll have to be coffee.'

Thörnell ushered her into the drawing room, where there was already a tray with cups and a coffee pot on it. Outside the window the treetops in the cemetery were visible, while far in the distance was Södermalm and the Högalid Church. Thörnell's view was no worse than Sara's.

She shifted her gaze from Södermalm to Thörnell. A grey slip-over, well-ironed shirt and tie, polished black shoes and dark blue trousers with sharply-pressed folds. His white hair was perfectly combed. He looked Sara straight in the eyes, presumably as he did with everyone he spoke to.

'I see that you bear traces of what happened following our last encounter.'

'This? This is nothing compared to the scars left by the bullets.'

Sara touched the rough skin on her cheek. Typical of Thörnell to get straight to the point. There was no embarrassed silence or misdirected goodwill. And he continued in the same fashion.

'You're looking for someone called Faust.'

Sara was startled and met his gaze.

'Hedin called,' he said by way of explanation.

That probably shouldn't have been a surprise. After all, it had been Hedin who had originally put her in touch with Thörnell. But why had she told him about Faust?

'What do you know about him?' said Sara.

'Enough to advise you to refrain from pursuing this further.'

'Why would I do that?'

'Tell me what you know first and then I shall try to explain.'

'His real name is Otto Rau; the priest Jürgen Stiller gave him a birth certificate with a Swedish identity. It's unclear what. He was the driving force in a communist cell that comprised mainly German terrorists with the Stasi as financial backers. Kommando 719. They were preparing something spectacular. The others in the cell are now called Bo Enberg, Marita Leander and Günther Dorch, and they all live in Sweden. They're well-established and sufficiently keen to keep their past a secret that they paid one hundred thousand kronor each when Stiller blackmailed them. Except for Rau, which is why I suspect he was the one who murdered the priest.'

'And that's all you know? No further clues?'

'Someone said that he was probably still active in that world – ergo, espionage and intelligence.'

Sara paused while waiting for a reply. But it took a while.

'You might say that,' Thörnell said eventually.

Sara nodded. She was a step closer to identifying Faust. She scrutinised Thörnell and had the strong feeling that he was hiding something. But what?

'You know something about him,' she said at the moment the realisation hit her. Perhaps she should have kept it to herself and been more tactical, but sometimes taking people by surprise worked too. 'You know who he is.'

'I know what kind of person he is, at any rate.'

'So you can help me to find him?'

'The reverse, actually. Given that I know what he's like, I want to help you to *not* find him.'

'He fired shots into my apartment. While my son was at home.'

'Was anyone hit?'

'No.'

'Then he was just sending a warning. And I must say that you should probably heed that warning.'

'Isn't it your duty as a former NATO officer to unmask him?' said Sara. 'We're dealing with a former terrorist backed by the Stasi.'

'The Stasi no longer exists.'

'But Rau exists.'

'Since the end of the Cold War, the world is no longer quite so black and white,' Thörnell said, leaning back in his armchair. 'There are many shades of grey. It's hard to make out anything, to be honest. To an outsider like you, it may look simple enough on paper. But it is anything but simple. It was difficult to comprehend back then, but it is ten times more difficult now.'

'Try.'

Thörnell adjusted an already perfect crease on his trouser leg, brushed an imaginary piece of dust from his lap and then raised his gaze and became lost somewhere in the distance.

'This was its own world, that existed in parallel with yours. Its own dimension. We saw you, but you didn't see us. While you went to work at the factory, did your grocery shopping and ate your oven-baked sausage slices, we were reconnoitring secrets, standing guard against invisible enemies. And if we hadn't done so, then the world would look different today. At that time, there were two sides – you were either on one or the other – but today loyalties criss-cross in every imaginable direction. You have no idea where tomorrow's enemy might appear from, and which of your old contacts might come in handy then.'

'Then let me make it simple for you,' Sara said. 'I'll summarise it into one single question: why do you want to protect a terrorist? Just because you and your friends might have a use for him in future?'

'It's not him I want to protect. It's you.'

'Haven't I proven that I can manage pretty well on my own?'

'You have to understand – these were no ordinary sympathisers out demonstrating and holding out their collection tins outside Systembolaget on a Saturday. Kommando 719 were highly focused and they were violent.'

'I know. They robbed banks and went to training camps in the Middle East. And they were well-armed. But then so are most gangsters nowadays.'

'Have you heard about urban guerrillas?'

Sara shook her head.

'It's a concept that emerged from the dictatorships of South America, where revolutionary groups were fighting against the police and military in urban environments. The name comes from Brazil, but the tactic was quickly adopted by the Tupamaros in Uruguay, and then by the Red Army Faction in West Germany. And for them it really was a war. They killed without the slightest hesitation, carried out contained, rapid attacks against key points in the police state, and just like the guerrillas of the jungle they were almost impossible to find and stamp out.'

'Sweden is hardly Brazil or Uruguay,' Sara objected.

'Our Swedish groups were also reinforced by hardened terrorists from West Germany,' Thörnell said, taking a sip from his coffee. 'And South Americans with their own experiences of urban guerrilla warfare. And a few really violent fanatics from Italy, Japan and France. "The Internationale" put into practice. All with the support of the Stasi – with the utmost secrecy. Would you like to see something interesting?'

Thörnell stood up and held out his hand as if to entice Sara. She followed her host through a large room with Gustavian dining furniture and into a room accessed directly from the last one in this gigantic apartment. The innermost room, it turned out, was Thörnell's study. The walls were covered in bookcases filled with volumes on history and security policy, while in the centre of the room there was a large desk made from dark wood with brass fixtures. Sara thought it might be British in style, with desk drawers both under the desk itself and along the sides. There were probably a couple of secret compartments too. Thörnell picked up a small gold-coloured badge from the desk and handed it to Sara. It bore a hand with a rifle, the East German flag, the number 40 and the words 'Ministerium für Staatssicherheit'.

'A souvenir badge to mark the fortieth anniversary of the Stasi,' Thörnell said. 'Which they never had time to hand out because the Wall fell.'

'But they managed to make them?'

'Yes. And when I look at it I am reminded that you never know what might happen and that existence can change very quickly. But above all, it is evidence that we achieved something incredible. If it hadn't been for us, the Stasi would have celebrated their fortieth anniversary uninterrupted. And perhaps their fiftieth and sixtieth too.'

'Why are you showing this to me?'

'Because it's fascinating. Don't you agree? And perhaps because I hope that you will show a little trust in those working in secret today too. The badge proves that we know what we're doing, if you ask me.'

'At any rate, it shows that you knew what you were doing, but it's no guarantee that you do now.'

'Touché,' said Thörnell with a smile. 'Come, let's return.'

He proffered his hand, retrieved the badge and returned to the drawing room via the three elegant rooms situated above the treetops.

'Now, where were we?' said Thörnell once he had retaken his seat. 'Oh yes, terrorists. By the way, would you like anything else? A biscuit? A glass of wine? Water?'

'No thanks.'

'Good. Don't lose focus. Anyway – after the initial groups there came new and passionate souls, sympathisers who became activists. When Baader and Meinhof were imprisoned, Kommando Siegfried Hausner, Kommando Ulrike Meinhof, Kommando Andreas Baader and so on followed in their wake. Various successors to the original Red Army Faction. And the focus shifted from the struggle against imperialism to a struggle to get their idols out of prison, through murder, kidnap and hijacking. Lufthansa flight 181, Hanns Martin Schleyer, Jürgen Ponto. Etcetera. And these groups became increasingly brutal. People have forgotten quite how much of a threat terrorism posed.'

'Here too?'

'Most certainly. In Denmark they had the so-called Blekingegade Gang who spent fifteen years robbing banks and sending money to the PFLP in Palestine. They had adopted the so-called parasitic state theory. They didn't believe it was possible to enlighten the working

262

classes about the necessity of revolution. The workers in the West had been bought by capitalists with high wages and welfare. So the revolution had to come from the Third World. They managed to piece together a total of thirty million kronor from their heists. The Blekingegade Gang bankrolled many acts of terrorism.'

'Did Kommando 719 send money to the PFLP too?'

'No. Not that we know. However, it seems that they spent a vast sum of money. They were preparing something big.'

'Operation Wahasha.'

A slight raise of the eyebrows revealed that the ever-discreet Thörnell had been taken very much by surprise.

'Where did you hear that name?'

'First tell me what you know about it.'

'Nothing. It's a name that appears in the papers, but it's not known what it refers to.'

'But it was Kommando 719 and Rau that were preparing for it?' Sara insisted.

'So they say.'

Sara scrutinised Thörnell and pondered what he had said.

'Why do I get the feeling that you know more than you're saying?' she said.

'I don't know. I was stationed in West Germany; I had no direct oversight of what the Stasi or their terrorist cells were occupied with here in Sweden.'

'But you knew about Wahasha.'

'It was talked about. And based on what I've heard about Rau, I would say he's a man that everyone should keep their distance from.'

'Why haven't the Germans done anything about Rau's group?' Sara leaned forward and fixed her gaze on the old colonel.

'The Germans had quite a lot on their plate when the Wall came down, given the thousands of spies and informants that were unmasked. The whole state apparatus was infiltrated, or so it transpired when they unsealed the archives. The ones that hadn't been destroyed, that is.'

'So they forgot about these former terrorists?'

'Hmm, well, it would also appear that the Kommando's new identities worked rather well. It probably hasn't been possible to trace them. And I would think our good friend Faust is more than keen to preserve his anonymity.'

Sara contemplated what Thörnell had told her. She had undeniably been able to rely on him in relation to Geiger and the bombs. So should she trust him now too?

'So you think I should just drop this? Not give a shit about Rau . . .'

'With the exception of your choice of words, that's exactly what I would counsel you to do.'

'Yes, yes . . .' Sara sighed.

'You don't really have any reason to chase some forgotten old terrorist from the past.'

'Yes I do. It's my fault that Stiller is dead. And his wife. He called me and wanted to warn me about a dangerous man. I think that was Rau.'

'Does that mean you won't give up?'

Sara thought about the gunshots into the apartment. As long as Rau was at large, she was in danger.

'Not now,' she said. 'He's gone too far.'

'I really would like to plead with you one last time.'

'Sorry.'

They contemplated each other in silence. From the corner of her eye, she saw a seagull fly past right outside the window. That was what it was like when the shoreline at Norr Mälarstrand was round the corner. Sara remembered a bird once flying into the window in Vällingby. She wondered whether the seagulls around here ever did the same thing. It was an unpleasant thought. When it had happened at home, Sara had been in her angriest phase of teendom and had mostly wondered how any single being on earth could possibly want to get into their sad flat.

The sound of a door carefully closing made her start and return to the present.

'Is there someone else here?'

'No.' Thörnell looked at her impassively.

Sara looked towards the wall that faced the secret room. She stood up and hurried into the hallway. She inserted a couple of fingers behind the frame of the large mirror and pressed. There was a click and the mirror swung open, allowing Sara to step into the secret room. On the wall adjoining the living room there was a painting that had been taken down to reveal a one-way mirror and a small speaker. Anyone in here could see and hear everything being said in the living room.

She turned on her heel and rushed towards the door.

She skipped the lift and ran down the stairs, emerged into the street and stood in the middle of the road looking in every direction.

There was a black car that had pulled away from the kerb down by Wijnjas the cheesemonger, a food delivery on the other side of the street, and a few people sauntering along. There was no one who appeared to be fleeing or in a hurry.

But there had been someone. Sara was certain of it.

She went back up to Thörnell and fixed her gaze on him.

'Who was it?'

'Not who you think,' said the old colonel.

'Rau.'

'I can neither confirm nor deny that. You know that.'

'You helped him to find out what I know.'

'I helped you to protect yourself. Trust me, you really should refrain from taking this further.'

'I probably should. The problem is that I never do as I'm told.'

41

She hoped the blindfold hadn't smudged her makeup. It probably wouldn't be all that visible in the dark room anyway, but she liked to feel like she was good-looking and in control of her own appearance. A piece of spinach caught in her teeth was about the most embarrassing thing she could imagine or a stain on her dress that she had missed.

Just as they took the blindfold off her, they switched on a spotlight so that she had to screw up her eyes not to be dazzled.

She slowly opened them and squinted towards the small stage in the centre of the room. There was a table with a mattress on it and leather straps. There were spotlights illuminating it so that no one would miss a thing. The walls of the room were painted black and it smelled faintly of bodily fluids and a couple of suffocatingly sweet odours that she didn't want to know any more about. The walls contained a series of windows forming a circle around the stage. Well, an octagon. All the windows had steel blinds drawn down in front of them and a red light next to them.

Three muscular guys in nothing but underpants were snorting lines of a white substance and popping small blue pills which they washed down with neat vodka while looking at Jenna without greeting her.

'Do you want to shower first?'

A burly man with a shaved head and leather jacket asked the question in heavily accented English.

'I showered at home,' said Jenna.

'Where do you want this?'

An equally well-toned but somewhat younger man came in carrying a first-aid kit, and the shaven-headed one waved towards the corner beyond the spotlights.

Jenna looked anxiously at the first-aid kit and then at the shaven-headed man, who met her gaze.

'It's going to be rough. But we've got a doctor here. And when it's over you'll be rich.'

'What's the safe word?'

He stared at her.

'That's not how it works here.'

42

Sara emerged from the door of Thörnell's building and lingered on the pavement, staring into space. She couldn't understand what had happened.

Thörnell had betrayed her.

He had let someone listen in while Sara told him what she knew and hadn't been able to deny that it was Rau.

Could Thörnell really be on Rau's side? Had he been deceiving Sara all along? Although if so, wouldn't the former terrorist have killed her right away?

Perhaps Rau had tricked Thörnell? Or had it been someone else hiding in the secret room? Sara had regarded Thörnell as an ally, but now it was hard for her to tell what his intentions were. Perhaps he might be able to influence Rau? Perhaps what had happened might be in her interests? She had difficulty believing that could be the case.

Sara shivered despite the late summer heat. Too much death. Too many threats. Too much ancient history overflowing and taking over the present.

Near the church, she saw a mother helping two small children over the wall into the cemetery. The mother continued along the pavement while the children ran across the tombstone-studded grass before they were reunited at the gates. Two happy little girls of perhaps four and five years of age who thought it was fun to take their own path and then meet up with their mother again. They had small backpacks which looked huge on them and were clutching colourful drawings. Sara thought about her own children and her husband. She was once again letting the so-called big world win out over the little one, she realised. And she didn't want that.

She made up her mind.

It was time to take back her life. Her family. Her husband.

Once that fucker Scam was out of the country, Martin would be hers again.

One more night.

It was time to start preparing for the recapture.

On the way home from Thörnell's, she stopped in at Wijnjas where she bought a couple of packs of saltines and sea-salted crackers, and some amazing cheeses: Gruyère, Délice de Bourgogne, Baskeriu and Saint Albray. They already had enough wine in to last for centuries.

Despite the recent unpleasant surprise, life felt rather splendid as she crossed the Vasabron bridge, carrying her small bag. The decision to focus on her family told her she was on the right track. To what, she didn't know, but she had a good gut feeling. Not even the electric scooter riders could rile her up. She was convinced that they were doing the best job they could over at the government offices in Rosenbad, in parliament and in the House of Nobility. It felt good to be positive, and she thought her life might just depend on it. Stora Nygatan was – as usual – full of people just loitering, stopping without warning to take photos or check maps. The kind of things she usually hated. But now that she had decided to recapture her life, it was nothing but pleasant. She reflected that these people had travelled here from other countries and parts of the world just to see her neighbourhood. How nice of them!

She passed the old town bookshop. It really was high time she stopped in. Why not right away? For Sara, reading books was a strong indicator that her life was in balance and that she was feeling good. And they had to be good old proper physical books. The bookshop was shut, but she spotted her next purchase in the window. The final parts of two different trilogies: one by a female author and the other by a male. She had started reading one of the trilogies in her youth, while she had spent her summer on the other.

There were no screaming teenagers, no cops or cordons when she returned home this time. However, there was a long white limousine parked outside the door and a flabby man in uniform pushing the buzzer.

'Do you live here?' said the man when Sara slipped past and tapped in the code.

'Yes.'

'I'm here to pick up Olle Titus and his guests. For the Friends Arena. Do you know whether that's the right name? There's no answer when I buzz.'

'He might be asleep. I'll tell him. If he's home.'

'Thanks.'

Then it occurred to Sara that she had just told Thörnell that she was going to continue her pursuit of Faust, and someone had heard her say it. Had the person eavesdropping left the apartment in such a hurry because of that? Because stupid, stubborn Sara Nowak refused to give in?

Faust had already shot into the apartment once.

Now that the windows were bulletproof, perhaps he'd made his way into the apartment . . .

'He might be asleep,' she had said about her son. But what if that wasn't true? What if something was wrong?

Surely they hadn't done anything to Olle?

Why wasn't he answering when the driver buzzed?

The lift had never been as slow as it was right now.

Sara pressed the button urgently, determined to make the lift go faster. She pulled out her keys and made ready and as soon as it stopped, she ran to the front door, unlocked it and tumbled inside.

'Olle?'

No reply, but she heard pounding music from his room.

Hadn't there been music when the priest had been killed too?

She pictured Olle bound in his bedroom, beaten, shot, anything. Or dangling from the ceiling.

Her stomach somersaulted.

But to her great relief, when she yanked open Olle's door she was met by the sight of Olle and his friend Gabriel staring at a video of Uncle Scam playing at top volume. They were mimicking his moves and sipping fizzy drinks through straws. If Sara knew her son, then it was almost certain that some of Martin's huge bar stocks had made their way into the cans, but she was far too relieved to start banging on about a bit of covert teenage drinking.

Olle and Gabriel both turned towards Sara, who had practically fallen into the room. Her face probably looked weird too. Frightened and scarred and relieved and fuck knew what else.

Then Sara saw what was going on onscreen. Uncle Scam and his entourage with a bunch of bare-chested women simulating oral sex while the men waved automatic weapons around and dived into heaps of white powder.

'What the hell is that?' Sara was unable to prevent herself from saying. She realised the huge piles of powder weren't real cocaine, but did the boys?

'Scam's VIP section,' Olle said proudly. 'Scam gave me the login.'

Sara looked at the screen again. What kind of signal was that piece of trash sending to the millions of young boys who admired him? What impact would it have on Olle?

'It's dreadful,' she said. 'Turn it off.'

'What did you want?' said Olle, closing his laptop without leaving the web page.

'There's a limo outside waiting for you. The guy's been buzzing you for a while now without any answer.'

'Shit. What time is it?'

'After that video, I'm not sure whether I'm going to let you go.'

'Chill out. Not funny. Come on, Gabe, let's head.'

Gabriel drained the last of his fizzy drink while Olle opened the bottom drawer of his desk and removed a small brown envelope.

'What's that?' said Sara.

'It's Scam's.'

'OK, but what is it?'

'Dunno. But the fuzz are always checking him out. His stuff is never left alone,' her son said indignantly. 'The bloody cops just hassle him.'

'Bloody cops?'

'All cops are bastards,' Gabriel interjected, fortified by his secret cocktail.

Sara looked at her son's friend ironically. Just a few years ago they had spent their days playing cops and robbers. Now they hated the fuzz.

'Well, yes, technically speaking I am a bastard,' said Sara. 'Show me.'

Sara took the envelope from Olle's hands.

'No!'

Olle tried to take it back, but Sara turned her back on him.

'It's Scam's!' her son protested.

'That's why I want to take a look,' said Sara.

She tore off the tape that sealed the brown, well-stuffed envelope. Inside there was a bag filled with white powder. Sara was no drug expert, but under no circumstances could Olle take this with him.

'Mum!' Olle yelped.

She really ought to hand this bag to her colleagues on the drug squad but where was she supposed to tell them she'd found it? That Scam had left it in their apartment? That her son had kept it? Maybe she'd be better off flushing the lot? To make sure Olle didn't end up in trouble, given he'd been in possession. His fingerprints and DNA were probably all over the envelope.

'It's Scam's!' Gabriel piped up. Both boys seemed completely crestfallen.

'I promise I won't keep it for myself,' said Sara. 'But I'm not letting two fourteen-year-olds wander off with this.'

'He'll be totally fucked off.'

'That's nothing compared with what I am. And you're both staying at home.'

'No way!'

Olle ran out of the room with Gabriel hot on his heels. Sara didn't know what to do. She was conscious that Olle would never forgive her if he didn't get to go to the concert and hang out backstage with his new friend, Scam. And it was bad enough that she had taken Scam's envelope. She had to get it tested. Perhaps the big star just wanted to mess around with Olle, or impress him – to live up to the myth. But even then it was unacceptable. Or totally not OK, as the kids were saying these days.

Sara knew how busy Martin was ahead of the concert, so to be sure she sent him a text message before calling. 'Answer when I call!' And then she called, whereupon Martin actually picked up.

'Have you been calling?' he said. 'It hasn't got through.'

'No, I just wanted to make sure you would pick up.'

'OK. What's up? I'm with Scam.'

'Martin, he gave drugs to Olle. Our son – a child – was storing drugs for your awful friend. I have to report him.'

'No! You mustn't do that. How can you even be sure it's drugs? Scam knows Olle's a minor – it was probably just a joke or something.'

'Come home,' said Sara. 'We have to talk about this.'

'Can't. The gig's starting. And then Scam wants to go out.'

'It's your job or your children.'

'My children. And Olle loves Scam. He's coming here. I can talk to him then.'

Sara knew how much use that would be.

'Come home.'

'Yes. Later.'

And then her husband hung up.

Sara was alone.

No Ebba, no Olle, no Martin.

What was she supposed to do?

Well, if her family weren't prioritising her, then she didn't need to prioritise her family.

Not right now, anyway.

She just wanted to forget all the business with Uncle Scam for a while.

It would be mean to carry on watching a series that she and Martin were following together. She would have liked to listen to some music, but Martin's latest stereo acquisition had shut her out of the system. She could live with massive speakers and a beefy amplifier, but he had gone and bought a DA converter – a Chord Hugo 2. And while he claimed that it sounded much better, Sara didn't have the energy to learn how it worked. It was just a bunch of different coloured lights and she had no idea what they meant. She had wanted to listen to Grace Jones at top volume, but it would have to keep.

Instead, she could read up on terrorism. Had there really been that many attacks and threats in the 1980s?

She read online about ETA's bombs and assassinations of police officers in Spain. About IRA bombs in England that claimed dozens of lives, and how close they had come to killing Prime Minister Margaret Thatcher. Photos of hostages Aldo Moro and Hanns Martin Schleyer, who were both later executed. Carlos the Jackal, who kidnapped all the leaders of OPEC in Vienna. Black September, who murdered eleven Israeli athletes at the Olympic Games in Munich. The bombings of police stations, shops and cinemas in Paris.

And now she remembered the long queues at the French embassy that the Broman sisters had told her about when they needed visas to go there on their family holidays. The terrorist attacks had increased security and people had had to stand around waiting for hours. Hadn't it been the same the time that Camilla went to Paris with Stellan and Lotta? The trip that Sara had missed, which had saved her from being sexually exploited by her wretch of a father.

It surprised her that the German terrorists came from such bourgeois and well-established families. Gudrun Ensslin was the daughter of a pastor and a regular churchgoer in her youth, and she had played the violin just like Sara. And Lotta. Ulrike Meinhof's foster mother had been a professor and Andreas Baader had been raised by a mother, aunt and grandmother who spoiled him. No broken homes, no poverty. But they all took up arms.

The ties between the Red Army Faction and the Stasi were stronger than Sara had previously understood. Not only had East Germany armed and trained the West German terrorists; the ones who had wanted to withdraw from the RAF had been given new identities in the DDR along with regular jobs and a big dowry to help start their new lives.

Sara had completely lost herself in the violence of the eighties when a harsh buzz from the intercom cut through the flat and a voice bellowed:

'What the hell have you done?! Are you out of your mind?'

Sara got up from the computer and went over to the intercom.

'Who is it?'

'Malin! Who the fuck do you think it is? Let me in!'

Sara didn't think she had heard Malin swear before. Something serious must have happened. She pressed the button to open up, and then she went to the front door and opened it so that Malin could come straight in.

A minute later, her old childhood friend was in the apartment. She came straight up to Sara and gave her a resounding slap.

'Idiot!' she shouted.

Sara's reflex after all her years of Krav Maga training was to strike back without thinking, but she managed to stop her hand mid-movement. Which was lucky for the other woman's chin. Malin looked at the clenched fist with contempt in her eyes.

'You going to hit me too?'

'You hit me,' said Sara. 'Why?'

'What do you think?' said Malin, thrusting a piece of paper into her face.

Sara took a step back, prised the paper free and looked at it.

An application for a DNA paternity test. Signed by Sara Nowak.

Sara looked dumbly at Malin.

'What is this?'

'Your application! To make Dad your dad!'

Sara looked at the signature. It wasn't at all like hers.

'He wasn't your dad!' Malin roared. 'He was *our* dad. Stop fantasising. It was embarrassing enough at school, and it's a lot more fucking embarrassing now!'

At school? That rang a faint bell in Sara's head. Fragments of memory about how she had impressed the other pupils by telling them that the famous TV star Stellan Broman was her father. Or had she dreamt it? No, she remembered it. She had even stolen things from him and shown them to her classmates to prove her claim. A pocket diary with his name in gold lettering, a pipe, a pair of reading glasses.

'It wasn't me,' was all Sara could say.

'No,' said Malin ironically. 'No, no, it must be the other Sara Now—'

'Malin! It's not me. I promise.'

'Well, who the fuck is it then?'

'Don't know.'

But she knew full well.

'It's your name and your signature,' said Malin, her eyes wild. 'And it's so embarrassing that you should kill yourself. My dad has been murdered and now you're trying to make him your dad – taking your chance now that he's dead and can't deny it. Are you just insane, or are you after his money? What do you think Lotta will say?'

'Malin, I'll put a stop to this. Because believe me, it wasn't me who did this, I promise.' Sara gritted her teeth.

'You seem to be completely obsessed with him. First you try to portray him as a rapist, then a spy, and when none of that works you try to make him your dad. You're sick. Truly. A mental case. You need help.'

'Malin, I'll fix this.'

Malin gave her a long, burning stare, tore the paper into two pieces with a protracted ripping sound and then turned around and strode out of the apartment.

Sara bent down to pick up the pieces of paper.

DNA testing.

Now she had gone too far.

Sara was on the verge of running to the car and heading out to Vällingby, but she settled for picking up the phone.

'Are you insane? Forging my signature?!'

'Did you get an answer?'

'No, but Malin just came round. She was off the scale angry and I can understand why. She hit me.'

'Yes, they're mad. The lot of them.'

'Mum, this is the most stupid thing you've ever done.'

'Not at all. I've got DNA from every member of the family and I've sent it in to an independent lab for testing.'

'How did you get their DNA? Lotta's I can understand – you went round to their house. But the others?'

'I went to Bromma. Strands of hair.'

'You broke in?'

'I unlocked the door. Like you.'

Sara sighed. Her mother had a point.

'But burglary and forgery! It's madness.'

'Where do you think you got your stubbornness from? Life is a war – everything's allowed.'

Jane was apparently tougher than Sara had thought. But still.

'Why did you do it? I don't want anyone to know that I'm his daughter! I don't want to inherit anything from him either.'

'And I want everyone to know what he did. What's more, it's your money. It's only right.'

'Mum, do you need money?'

'No.'

'Do you think *I* need money?' Sara gestured at the gigantic apartment she lived in, despite the fact that her mother couldn't see the flat or her hand. But it didn't matter in relation to this argument.

'Money schmoney,' said Jane. 'Things should be made right.'

'I'm going to withdraw the application.'

'Then I'll say it was me who forged your signature. Do you want to see your mother go to prison?'

'You won't go to prison,' Sara sighed.

'You've no idea what else I'll confess to.'

'Confess all you like.'

'I'll send in a new application!' Jane threatened.

'Stay the hell out of my life!'

'It's my life too!'

And that floored Sara.

Jane's life too?

Well, she supposed it was. Just like Ebba's life was also Sara's. But Ebba would never have agreed with that. She would have been just as angry with her mother as Sara was with Jane.

All the anger drained out of Sara.

'Please, Mum, let me withdraw the application.'

'No.'

Whether it was because she had survived the trauma of the Bromans or that she had just got a little older and wiser, she didn't know. But for what she believed to be the first time, Sara felt she should do as Jane told her, even though she completely disagreed. If she was to succeed in having a good relationship with her family, she had to give them some space and let go of her own need for control. Compromise or live alone. Perhaps that attitude could help her with Olle and Ebba too, she thought to herself when they had both been silent for a while.

'How did you feel when I moved out?' Sara said at last.

'That it was good for you.'

'But how did it feel for you?'

'The child is the important thing. All mothers get upset, but that's part of the package. You can't lock up your children in a box their whole lives.'

What was more, Jane had been completely alone when Sara had left. Sara had Martin, and would get to keep Olle for another few years in a soft transition to the role of distant observer of her children's lives.

The only question was what she should say to Malin if she didn't withdraw the application. That she had lied when she said she hadn't been the one who had submitted it? That she really wanted to be acknowledged as Stellan's daughter? And that she was looking forward to cosy dinners with her new sisters' families?

Sara pushed that decision into the future, bade her mother goodnight and began to turn off the lights in the apartment. She left a lamp on in the hall for Martin – who knew when he'd get in? Personally, she really needed to get some sleep.

She brushed her teeth, removed her makeup and inspected her face in the bathroom mirror. Beauty that she hadn't asked for, which she had hated in her youth, but which she had already started to miss now that it seemed to be leaving her. Why couldn't you be allowed to wander around being beautiful without everyone thinking they were entitled to you?

Just as she had crawled into bed and was about to turn off the lights, the doorbell rang.

Had Martin sent Olle home early again? No, Olle had keys. Maybe it was poor Tindra, sent to fetch something for her boss?

Sara wrapped her lime-blossom green silk dressing gown around her body and went to open the door.

There was something blocking the front door outside.

Sara had to really push.

The heavy object on the other side moved very reluctantly, sliding slowly across the stone floor.

When the door was a quarter open, the obstacle fell to the side and a pair of feet appeared in Sara's line of vision.

There was a body in the way.

Sara pressed herself through the crack to see who it was. A drunkard? A neighbour who'd had a heart attack?

Neither.

It wasn't easy to tell, since the body was covered in dried blood from the many holes in the body and head.

But after a short time, she recognised Bo Enberg.

The former terrorist who had once been known as Hans Gerlach.

And the man who had known the most about Faust.

43

Ebba really did have the art of wrapping her grandfather round her little finger down pat – Eric was well aware of that. But as it happened, he had nothing against that.

This time Olle hadn't wanted to go home after a concert and Martin had been busy with the artist, so Martin had called Ebba and asked her to pick up her brother.

And Ebba had called Granddad.

Who was now smiling wryly at the thought that he could have been at home with a good book and a Cognac instead of trying to wind his way through the building site that was Slussen.

Eric Titus pulled his Maserati onto Kornhamnstorg but was unable to park in front of the main door as he usually did. Instead, there were three police cars there. The aggressively flashing blue lights illuminated the Stockholm night and the pale faces of the officers. Eric pulled over to the kerb and stopped outside the bureau de change – far too close to the pedestrian crossing.

'Wait here,' he said to Olle, going over to the police.

'It's cordoned off,' said one of them even as Eric was still approaching.

'My son lives here with his family, and I've got my grandson in the car. What's happened?'

The officer looked at Eric and seemed to be thinking over what to say. The family ties and Eric's sharp suit decided matters.

'A dead body has been found in the stairwell. Where does your son live?'

'Top floor.'

'Then it was probably his wife who found it.'

'Where is she?'

'Don't know. Up there, I suppose.'

'Can she come out?'

'As soon as they're done.'

Eric called Sara, who explained to the police that she was going down to see her son in the square outside, and then she emerged from the door around a minute later. Eric's face radiated anxiety as she came towards him.

'Where's Olle?' said Sara.

'In the car,' said Eric, pointing to it.

'Is he angry?'

'That probably depends on whether you reported that popstar to the police or not.'

'Something else came up.'

'It was very shocking to see the blue lights outside your door and be told they'd found a dead body.'

'Yes, it's awful,' Sara sighed. 'And now there's a full crime scene investigation going on up there.'

'Can you stay here tonight? Otherwise we've got lots of space.'

'We'll see.'

'What's happened? Is Scam there again?'

A group of inebriated youths had stopped next to Sara and Eric and were pointing at the patrol cars.

'No,' said Sara, who was almost tempted to satisfy the curiosity of these passing strangers.

'Come on, let's go and ask them,' said one of the guys.

'For fuck's sake, no. I've been smoking – they might frisk us,' his friend replied.

'For asking whether Scam is there? Seriously?' said one of the girls in the group.

'Let's head to Wirströms instead!'

'Why isn't Martin here?' said Eric when the partygoers had disappeared into the distance.

'He's not picking up his mobile – he's out with a superstar so his family can't disturb him.'

'Have you texted?'

'Oh yes. I said "Answer!". But it's not like he'd be able to do much if he actually came.'

'He'd support you. How are you feeling?'

'Good. Angry as hell,' Sara said curtly.

'You found a dead body.'

'Outside our bloody door.'

'Who was it?'

Sara shrugged.

'Is it a neighbour?' Eric continued. 'Or some junkie who died of an overdose? If you found the body in the stairwell, that is.'

'It was a man I met the other day.'

'What? Someone you knew?' Her father-in-law sounded shocked.

'A former German terrorist who's been living here under a false identity for decades.'

'What was he doing here? How did he die?'

'Tortured to death.'

Eric stood there in silence for a long time, just looking at Sara.

'Tortured to death,' he said at last. 'And someone left him outside your front door?'

'Yes.'

'Sara, what is all this?'

'What's what?'

'Someone you just met is murdered and dumped outside your door. What if it's you next time. Or your family? Olle?'

A pang of guilty conscience. Eric didn't know anything about the gunshots into the apartment. If he had done, he would presumably have reported her to social services. The impulse to protect the family was almost greater in him than in Sara – which made her feel like a very bad mother.

There were lots of types of bad mothers. Self-absorbed mothers, angry mothers and tired mothers. But mothers who exposed their children to mortal danger probably numbered just one. Sara.

'It's just a warning,' she said, and she heard how hollow that sounded.

'"Just a warning"? Sara, your son can stay the night with us. And then you need to review your security here. And drop whatever it is you're doing. Do you know who's responsible for this?'

'A former terrorist who wants to conceal their identity.'

'How on earth have you managed to get dragged into this?'

'I think it's connected to Uncle Stellan and the spy accusations against him.'

'You've never said exactly what happened at the Bromans' that night.'

'There's nothing to tell.'

'Those burns tell a different story,' Eric objected.

'They come with the territory.'

'This isn't the Sara I know, the Sara that Martin married.'

'It's the Sara he's married to now.'

'I'm just thinking of the kids.'

Sara knew that. The grandchildren. The progeny. The ones who would continue Eric Titus' name and life's work for all eternity. No, perhaps that was unfair. If nothing else, caring about his life's work meant that he also cared about his family. Sara knew that Eric would do anything for Olle and Ebba. It didn't matter if his true motivation was to propagate his genes.

'Martin isn't answering my calls either. I'll take Olle home.'

Judging by his tone, the matter was settled.

Sara went over to the car and tapped on the window. Behind the glass a very sulky Olle was glowering at his mother. Sara opened the door.

'Olle, do you want to go to Granddad's? Something has happened in our building, and it's going to be a few hours before the police are done.'

'Have you reported Scam?' said Olle.

'No. Not yet. What did he say about the envelope?'

'Dad talked to him.'

'Good.'

'But he could have been really pissed off. Do you get what you might have messed up for me?' Olle exclaimed resentfully.

'It wasn't me who asked a fourteen-year-old to look after my drugs.'

'If you report him then I'm never coming home again.'

Sara let out a deep sigh. Being a police officer and the mother of a teenager was no easy combination.

'OK,' she said.

Eric came over to the car. Instead of a hug, he looked sternly at Sara before getting into the driver's seat and starting the engine, as if to emphasise his previous exhortations. Sara closed the passenger-side door and Olle turned towards his grandfather. The Maserati sounded like a tiger on steroids as it roared into life. Of all the grown-up toys men played with, a car that sounded like that was one of the few things she could wrap her head around.

Sara watched Eric's car as it pulled away from the kerbside and the red tail lights disappeared into the distance. Then she turned back to her own building and saw the blue lights from the police cars shimmering across the façade.

Right there and then, she couldn't help but wonder what she was playing at.

44

It would soon be over. That was the thought sustaining her now. She had no idea how long they'd been at it. It had felt like hours. But they had finally stopped.

She had made it.

Now she just had to get to a hospital as quickly as possible.

If she could walk. It didn't feel like it.

They hadn't spared a single part of her body.

All the years of violence and degradation had been compressed into one single night that had almost cost her life.

She realised she would have scars. She would never be as beautiful again.

But she would be away from this.

From male strangers who got to do what they wanted with her.

She had her whole life to heal. She was going to have a proper family, or at least have children, she'd decided. That was the thought that had kept her going and had saved her from the hell of that night. And she was going to shield her children from this world. She would teach her sons what a real man should be like. No, no sons actually. Not after this. But she would warn her daughters and teach them to defend themselves.

They would move far into the countryside and keep out of the way. They would grow their own food and enjoy the tranquillity. Preferably by a lake or with a small river passing the house. Fruit and vegetables from their own garden, home-grown potatoes and freshly baked bread. They would pick flowers from their own flowerbeds and make beautiful bouquets to put on the kitchen table. She and her daughters.

She looked at the dark windows enclosing the room. Almost all of them had their blinds raised. That meant there were men sitting behind them watching, men who had paid to see her raped and assaulted, who had wanted to see her hurt, who had heard her screams and seen her bleed.

What kind of people were they?

Did they have their own daughters? Wives, sisters, mothers?

If she ever got rich or acquired any power, she would find out who the people who paid for things like this were and expose them all so that everyone knew.

'Look at what your husband is up to.' 'You didn't know that about your son.'

She would get her revenge. Her redress.

A red light came on by one of the windows.

One of the armed guards went over and listened to the small speaker beside it. He nodded and then he came back to the masked, naked men standing around Jenna. Men whose bodies were completely covered in blood and who still had erections thanks to the Viagra.

'A little change,' said the guard. 'Number 8 pay for snuff.'

The blinds were lowered over the other windows. Only the window with the illuminated red light remained uncovered.

Snuff, Jenna thought. What was that? Wasn't it . . . ?

The guard pulled a big roll of duct tape from his jacket pocket, pulled a few inches out, bit it off and covered Jenna's mouth with it.

Then the guard went to the table by the wall and picked up three long knives that he brought over to the naked men.

The armed men, still sporting erections, approached her slowly.

Jenna screamed behind the tape. She screamed and screamed and screamed.

45

The police had vacated Kornhamnstorg at half past three, and Martin had got home at five, blind drunk. He had collapsed in the hall and started snoring like a cracked diesel engine, but he had woken up after a while to run in a panic to the toilet where he had vomited in cascades. Fortunately he'd picked the guest toilet. She could simply shut the door on that and he would have to clean up the next day, Sara thought to herself.

Between the bouts of vomiting, she tried to tell him what had happened, but he wasn't entirely receptive. Eventually, he grasped that they had found a body on the stairs.

'Who?' he managed to say followed by an unfathomable sob.

'A former terrorist.'

'Anyone we knew?' he said, wiping his mouth.

'No.'

'Good,' he said, spitting into the toilet.

And with that, Sara had led him to bed.

She usually put out aspirin and Berocca for him, but he was so drunk right now that nothing would alleviate his hangover.

'Jesus Christ,' he said when Sara led him into their bedroom.

'Time to sleep.'

'I wuuuuuuvvvvvv . . .'

He hugged Sara tightly and tried to kiss her, but the stench of vomit disgusted her.

'Go to sleep.'

'Where's Walter?'

Martin was looking around.

'What?' said Sara.

'Walter,' said Martin, slightly annoyed. 'He's a cat. Where is he?'

'Why?'

'For the rats.'

'I'll fetch him. But there aren't usually any rats in bed.'

Martin was placated by this promise, and before Sara had made it out of the room he was already snoring. She gave up on the cat.

Instead she went to lie down on the sofa to try and get another couple of hours of sleep. But at around six she was woken by her mobile.

'A body outside the front door?' said Bielke as soon as Sara picked up.

Sara groaned.

'Who? How? Why?' said Bielke. The words were like slaps to her temples. He sounded both angry and disappointed in her, and that was definitely not what Sara wanted. She had far too much respect for him.

'OK,' said Sara, steeling herself. 'It's one of the left-wing terrorists that Stiller was blackmailing so that he wouldn't tell anyone he gave them birth certificates so they could get new identities.'

'Wait, wait. He was blackmailing people? New identities? Exactly how much involvement have you had in this? And what do Lidköping have to say about it?'

'*Lin*köping. And I'm not getting involved in anyone else's investigation, because they don't believe it was murder.' Sara thought it was important to emphasise that.

'But you do?'

'Yes.'

'So you're carrying out your own investigation? Have you agreed this with anyone? Because you certainly haven't run it by me.'

'I know what you're thinking. But listen—'

'It's not about what I'm *thinking*! It's about regulations. How we carry out police work!' Bielke thundered.

'Yes, it is. You're right. But I wanted to see whether there was anything in it before I triggered something bigger. That's what we all do. We review a case first in order to assess whether there is anything to pursue further.'

'So what's your plan now?'

'Now there's demonstrably been a murder so we have to investigate it,' said Sara.

'Not "we"! It's a case for Södermalm. You're on the Ekerö case.'

'Yes, but I know things that—'

'Sara, you're working on Ekerö. If you spend another minute on that priest or anything to do with him, you're suspended.' Bielke almost growled the last bit.

'OK,' said Sara. 'There's nothing for you to worry about.'

'I hope so.'

'For sure. See you later – I'm going to Stellan and Agneta Broman's funeral today, so I'll be a bit late. But that's just a personal matter. It hasn't got anything to do with any case, OK?'

A brief silence.

'OK.'

Sara hung up and processed Bielke's warning. She really didn't want to clash with him or betray his trust, but at the same time she felt a responsibility for what she had started off. If she hadn't gone to Bo Enberg's, he would probably still have been alive. She only seemed to be making things worse, so the best thing would probably be to step back. But first she had to minimise the damage. Several lives might be in danger.

She scrolled through her call log and redialled Marita Leander. She apologised for calling so early but said she needed to see her as soon as possible. Leander said she couldn't until later in the day because she had to take the cats to the vet. Sara tried to dissuade her in the strongest terms, but Leander stuck to her guns. Sara told her that she should exercise extreme caution. Another of her old compatriots had been murdered. But Leander said she had no reason to be afraid, she didn't have as much on her conscience as they did.

Günther Dorch didn't pick up when Sara called, so she left a message in which she explained that his life might be in danger, and that he should call her as soon as possible.

Then she was unable to fall back to sleep. Instead, she lay there thinking over what she knew.

Rau was still in the shady world that had formed him – as a spy, terrorist or agent. Why did both Säpo and Thörnell seem to be protecting Otto Rau? Surely not just because he was dangerous? She felt there were parts of the puzzle that she was missing.

She got up, showered, and dressed. Then she went to 285 Vantörsvägen in Hägersten – the address that Dorch was registered as living at.

No one opened the door when she rang the bell, and when she tried his mobile she couldn't hear it ringing inside the flat. Even though it was barely eight o'clock, she rang the doorbells of his neighbours on the same floor. A family with young children were in the middle of their stressful morning routine and an elderly couple had already reached their morning coffee break. Neither had seen Dorch for a couple of days, but the old woman had seen him leave with a suitcase. He had been in such a rush that he hadn't even said hello. Very rude. And Sara had to agree.

So Dorch was gone.

Why?

Even if Sara knew the truth about him, he wasn't risking punishment just for having been a member of the cell. If he and Rau were guilty of something for which the statutes of limitations hadn't expired, then it must have been very serious.

Or was he fleeing from Rau?

Like Bo Enberg should have done.

Then it hit Sara. Perhaps he wasn't fleeing from Rau at all?

Maybe he was hiding precisely because he *was* Rau.

46

Bromma Church was one of the oldest buildings in Stockholm – over eight hundred and fifty years old, almost from the Viking Age, the victor that remained standing while the heathen temples fell victim, one by one, to the inexorable advance of Christianity.

Back in the day, the church had been in a completely rural setting and had dominated the landscape, but now it was itself dominated by the constant sound of take-offs and landings at the adjacent airport. A different kind of heavenly ascent was more appealing to present-day Swedes than the one being intoned from the pulpit. These days no one was forced by the powers that be to attend church, so it was no longer as well visited. Nevertheless, it was beautiful.

The clouds were high in the sky when Sara climbed out of the taxi and the sun was shining on the several hundred black-clad funeral-goers. There were more people than she had been expecting. There were broadcast vehicles for both radio and TV, as well as many journalists taking photographs of the assembled celebrities and trying to get decent vox-pops. Some of the guests appeared to prefer to be left alone, while others seemed eager to be pictured and heard commenting on what Stellan had meant to them.

The funeral had been delayed for a long time while awaiting the autopsy and murder inquiry, but now it was finally time for everyone in celebrity Sweden to turn up and pay their respects to the dead legend. Some had Stellan Broman to thank for their careers, while others had merely grown up in Uncle Stellan's Sweden and were now being given the opportunity to mark the definitive end of an era. Some of those present were perhaps wondering who was next in line. Better to grieve and miss than to be grieved for and missed.

Sara surveyed the gathered celebrities. Television presenters, singers, actors, sports reporters, news readers, authors, directors, celebrity chefs. Everyone was there.

Given the tragic circumstances, the family had announced that there would be no wake afterwards. Perhaps Malin didn't want to draw any attention to the fact that Lotta wasn't in attendance – to avoid unnecessary questions.

Her sister was reported to have taken a timeout for personal reasons, but a timeout was surely something anyone would interrupt for their own parents' funeral. At any rate, that was what Sara assumed people would think.

Nevertheless, Lotta's husband and sons were standing together with Malin and her family outside the church, speaking to the Bromans' neighbour, C.M., whose surname Sara still couldn't remember.

While waiting for the guests to be allowed into the church, Sara wanted to stay out of the way, so she strolled around reading the tombstones, comparing them for size and scale of ambition. Competitive and seeking out status, even in death. She thought about La Recoleta, the fascinating cemetery in Buenos Aires that was like a small city for the dead, with their own houses and monuments. It was such a long time since she had been there. That trip had meant so much to her. It had been revenge on the Broman sisters, who had always been able to travel. Thanks to the money from her modelling, Sara had been able to travel around the world to the USA, South America and Asia, alone and without any inkling of what awaited her. It had been a quarter of a century ago – and how different her life was today. But the graves in Buenos Aires still looked exactly the same as before, ready for new backpacking twenty-year-olds to discover them and take their selfies in front of them. And perhaps to remember them twenty-five years later when their own mortality had become more tangible.

'Sara Nowak!'

Sara turned around but was caught in a tight embrace and kissed on the cheeks three times before she was able to free herself and see who was so pleased to see her.

The man in question was Boris Kozlov, the former Soviet ambassador who had stayed on in Stockholm for all these years as a pensioner, and the one who had told Sara about the illegal known as Desirée – Agneta Broman's true identity. Kozlov was dressed in black and even had a black armband over his jacket sleeve. He grasped Sara's chin between his thumb and forefinger and turned her head first one way and then the other while inspecting her face with an apologetic expression.

'Did you get them?'

'Who?'

'The people who did this?'

'Yes.'

'Good. Otherwise I would have arranged it on your behalf.'

Then he let go of her chin and smiled at her.

'Still just as beautiful. I am sorry for your loss. You were close to them.' Kozlov waved towards the church.

'Agneta, not Stellan,' said Sara.

'It's a pity it ended the way it did. She was fantastic.'

Kozlov had been very fond of Agneta, or rather the illegal Desirée, who had been posted to Sweden with a false identity and had helped Kozlov rise to the rank of foreign minister for a brief period during the final phase of the Soviet Union. It had been an inconceivable success for him that he was still deeply grateful for, so he had explained.

'It was awful,' said Sara, realising that the loss she felt didn't relate to either Agneta or anyone else in the Broman family. Nor was it her own childhood that she missed. It had been entirely false – that much she had realised as a result of the events of the early summer – but it had been a source of joy to her. Now her childhood was nothing but woeful from start to finish. She missed believing that she had been happy as a child and regretted being unable to grieve at her own father's funeral.

'They're going inside.'

Kozlov kissed Sara's hand and returned to a couple of stocky men waiting outside the door to the church. They wore expensive suits and had what Sara considered to be a typical Slavic appearance with high cheekbones and grim expressions. Or was she just prejudiced? Kozlov had been a resident of Sweden for decades and surely had Swedish friends? The trio joined the flood of people entering the church and Sara slowly followed. Inside the church, she noted that they were sitting at the very back. She opted for the middle.

And then the ceremony itself. Celebrity chefs and TV presenters gave eulogies about the significance of Stellan Broman, both to them personally and to the country. Everyone sang 'Day by Day' and 'Children of the Heavenly Father' together. A famous musical star sang a hymn. The priest gave a sermon about the happiness of a life as long as that enjoyed by the departed and the incomprehensibility of his brutal end. In his eyes, both the light and dark were evidence of God's greatness. Sara didn't entirely agree. On the other hand, she was moved by the atmosphere in the church and the palpable nature of seeing the two coffins at the front. Two of the most important people in Sara's life had been boxed up for their journey into the next life or to be recycled, depending on your life perspective.

Following the funeral ceremony, those who wanted to file past the coffins to place flowers were permitted to do so. Almost everyone did. White and red roses, lilies, carnations, a single sunflower. Sara was at the back of the queue and the whole process took almost an hour. A small mountain of flowers took shape on top of Stellan's coffin, while Agneta's received just a few. Sara placed her flowers solely on Agneta's coffin, leaving nothing for Stellan. Her awful father might have received more flowers, but on Agneta's coffin there was a medal. A gold star with a red, white and blue ribbon.

The medal was attached to a bunch of red roses with a simple white card and the name 'Yuri' on it. Sara looked around for Kozlov, but he and his friends were gone.

After the funeral there followed the burial. Twelve pallbearers carried out the two coffins on their shoulders. Sara couldn't help but notice that Agneta's coffin appeared to weigh far less than Stellan's.

Once both coffins were in the ground and the closest mourners had cast earth onto them, the crowd began to disperse and Sara headed for the exit. She was searching on her phone for Russian medals since the ribbon attached to the star had been in the Russian colours. She found the 'Hero of the Russian Federation Medal', which was what someone had left on Agneta's coffin. Was it hers? Odd for a Soviet spy to receive a Russian Federation medal.

'Sara,' said a voice in the hubbub. She turned around. Adnan Westin, *Aftonbladet*'s reporter on the crime beat, was coming towards her. He was always friendly, always faultlessly turned out. His head was shaven and he was wearing a jacket with a handkerchief in the breast pocket along with dark blue jeans. 'Do you have a moment?'

'No.'

'Just one question. We have reason to believe that you uncovered that Stellan Broman assaulted young girls.'

'Oh?'

'Yes. And that he forced them to have sex with loads of men so that he could later blackmail those men,' the reporter added.

'I said no. Didn't you hear me?'

'But is it true?'

'No comment.'

'I'll take that as a yes.'

'Is it really necessary to bring this up here at his funeral? My God, his daughter is standing over there. Her father was murdered,' said Sara, glowering at Westin.

'Do you think it's connected to the rapes?'

'Not my investigation.'

'We've obtained stills from these films that you supposedly found.'

'From who?'

Sara had left the films exactly where she had found them and she was pretty certain no one else had found them. But Westin had said he'd obtained stills and that was exactly what Sara had sent to Eva Hedin. Sara was pretty sure about where he'd got his pictures from, even if he didn't answer her question.

'Would you be able to share the films?' said Westin.

'Why the hell would I do that?'

'We think it's highly newsworthy.'

Click-chasing hyenas. How was she going to put a stop to this? Not that she felt sorry for Stellan – he might as well be hung out to dry. But it wasn't fair on his family. Stellan was dead and wouldn't be hurt by the publicity, but his grandchildren might suffer. And Malin would be incensed with Sara.

'Please, don't write about this. It won't benefit anyone.'

'You know what my answer is going to be. Public interest, consequence-neutral reporting, blah blah blah.'

'He hasn't been on the telly for thirty years!'

'He's current right now. Look at all the people who are here. And there have been countless tribute shows. And supplements. You name it.'

'Just let it go. Leave it alone, I'm begging you.'

'If you give me the films then I can make a decision based on that.'

'Forget it,' said Sara.

'OK. The names of the girls then. You're said to have found several of them.'

'Never.'

'Malin!'

Westin had spotted Malin passing by and hurried over to her. At the same moment, she turned around to see the reporter on his way over from Sara. Sara realised that it wouldn't look good when she heard his questions, and she hurried after him.

'Adnan Westin, *Aftonbladet*. We've obtained stills from several films in which your father is having sex with very young girls who were reportedly coerced into it.'

Malin looked straight at Sara.

'You gave the films to the papers?' she said with hatred in her eyes.

'So you've seen these films?' said Westin, a hint of victory in his voice. 'How did that feel?'

'Malin, don't say anything,' said Sara. She turned to Westin. 'We're at her parents' funeral. This is a bit heavy-handed.'

'The pictures say it all,' said the reporter. 'Uncle Stellan, a rapist. A straight-up paedophile. Malin, do you have any comment to make?'

Malin turned to Sara again.

'What pictures have you given them?'

'None,' said Sara, spotting out of the corner of her eye Westin holding out his mobile to show one of the stills that Sara had sent to Hedin. It depicted a very young girl looking terrified while a middle-aged man raped her.

'That's not my father,' said Malin.

'But he's in other films, so we gather. Ones that are far worse.'

Malin's eyes glowed with contempt.

'At Dad's funeral?'

'Believe me, I didn't—'

'Leave.'

'Malin . . .'

'LEAVE!'

Malin seemed to be close to breaking point. C.M. had realised this and approached to put a protective arm around her.

'What's going on?'

'Sara gave some sick films of Dad to the papers.'

Sara looked at C.M. with pleading eyes, as if he were a judge or a strict teacher tasked with determining guilt.

'No, it wasn't me. I promise!' she said.

'Was it Eva Hedin again?' said C.M.

'I think so,' said Sara. 'What do you mean by "again"?'

'Please would you leave?' C.M. said to Westin, approaching him with his arms spread as if to shoo away a dim-witted cow.

Whether it was C.M.'s authority or because Westin realised Malin was in the middle of a breakdown was unclear, but at any rate he did as C.M. said.

'What are you doing here?' Malin said to Sara when both men left. 'He wasn't your dad. No matter what you say.'

'I don't want him to be my father either.'

After a while, C.M. returned.

'What did you mean by "again"?' said Sara.

'That this isn't the first time. She wrote those books trying to sully Stellan's reputation and tried to get the papers to write about it.'

'But she had some evidence, didn't she?'

'Eva Hedin has been obsessed with Stellan since she made a fool of herself on his show when she was young. Are you OK?'

The last question was to Malin, who shook her head while looking angrily at Sara.

'What show?' said Sara.

'A Thousand Answers, I think it was. In the sixties.'

Sara hadn't even been born then, but like all other Swedes she had heard the theme tune hundreds of times. 'A thousand questions, a thousand answers, let's see whether you've got what it takes.' A quiz with twelve questions. Participants often became celebrities, at least if they got through all twelve questions or had entertaining personalities. 'Chef' Lundström, Little Harry Bolin and Margit Obré were more or less public idols after their appearances.

'She was on that?'

'Her specialist subject was Clark Gable, I think, but she got some basic question wrong. Said she hadn't heard it or something, but that didn't make any difference. So she went out on the first question. And Stellan was pretty brazen in his teasing of her. I think he even called it "doing an Eva" when people went out on the first question after that.'

'She hasn't mentioned anything about that.'

'Tell her to go.' Malin now sounded more contrite than angry.

C.M. took Sara by the shoulders and led her towards the gates.

'Come on.'

Sara allowed herself to be steered without protesting. Outside the church gates, C.M. came to a halt.

'Where's Lotta?' he said. 'I don't believe one word of this sabbatical thing.'

Sara didn't reply.

'Agneta held me prisoner in my own home and left me there, tied up. What made her do that? The shed burned down. They removed multiple bodies, according to the neighbours. And I still haven't got my shotgun back from the police, so it must have been used for something. By whom?'

Sara didn't reply. She didn't explain that she was the one who had taken C.M.'s expensive Fabbri gun and shot a legendary terrorist dead with it.

'What exactly happened that night?' C.M. persisted.

'I'm afraid I can't say. Sorry.'

C.M. looked at her for a long time.

'Is it over? Whatever it is. You look tense.'

'As I said, I can't say anything about it. Sorry.'

But C.M. asking like that made Sara realise that she was well aware it wasn't over. Far from it.

47

'In an hour,' was what Marita Leander said when Sara called her again.

'No, now,' said Sara. She had no desire to wait. Dorch hadn't called back and it was becoming more and more urgent to find Rau.

But a short while later when Sara rang Leander's doorbell, she didn't open up and she wasn't answering her mobile either.

Another one missing. Another who had wanted to postpone the meeting to buy time? Or who was merely hiding inside the flat? Perhaps she'd been planning to flee but hadn't got away because Sara had arrived so quickly.

This wasn't Sara's case, and Leander wasn't suspected of anything, so she couldn't summon a locksmith to gain entry to the flat and she still had no intention of giving in. She went down to the car again, opened the boot and pulled out a crowbar. She was going inside.

On the way back to the door into the building she noticed a purple figure slowly ambling back and forth across the grass with her arms outstretched. After a couple of seconds, she recognised Leander. She was out taking her cats for a walk. On leads.

'I said I needed an hour,' said Leander. 'You can't stress Palle and Stina – if you do then they can't do their business.'

'But why aren't you answering your mobile phone?'

'It's on silent. The cats don't like mobile ringtones when they're out. They get nervous. Isn't that right?' Leander's last comment was addressed to the cats in a prattling baby voice.

'You shouldn't go out like this.' Sara looked around. Leander was completely unprotected here. Sara realised that she was too.

'I'm not afraid,' said Leander.

'You ought to be. And I can't arrange police protection for you.'

Leander laughed.

'Police protection? You think a former Red Army Faction member would agree to police protection?'

'You really could do with it.'

'Why do you have a crowbar?' Leander said suddenly.

'Would you look at that! So I do,' said Sara. She had learned that when you had no good explanation to offer it was always better to offer nothing. 'Dorch is missing,' she said instead. 'Why? Is he afraid or was he Faust?'

'Don't know. Dorch is his new identity – I've no idea whether it was Kremp's or Rau's. We weren't supposed to know each other's new names.'

Sara couldn't fathom how they had managed to keep track of all the layers of made-up names and false identities. But the point had presumably been just that – it was hard to identify them.

'What was it you were planning? What could be so secret that people have to die today – thirty years later?'

'No idea.'

'I can tell you're lying.'

Leander stopped.

'I can't tell you. You have to accept that.'

'Do you trust him? Rau? He's killed two of you. Perhaps three. What makes you think that you're not next in line?'

'The fact that I'm not talking.'

'How does he know that? He seems to know about my every move, and right now I'm talking to you. He's presumably some-where watching us right now.'

Sara looked around. Lots of tall buildings and countless win-dows and roofs. The Dagens Nyheter Tower, the Sweco building, the Russian embassy. The hill with Fyrverkarbacken on it. Faust could be just about anywhere without being seen.

'And he doesn't know *what* we're talking about,' said Sara. 'And if I know him, the very suspicion that you've told me something will be enough for him to kill you. Are you prepared to take that risk?'

Leander didn't reply. She kept her gaze glued to her cats.

'Do you want to die too?' said Sara.

More silence.

'What was Operation Wahasha?'

Leander looked at Sara.

'You know about that?'

'Yes. I know it was something big. What was it?'

No answer.

'Tell me. Or would you prefer me to arrest you? I can hold you for seventy-two hours. How would your cats cope with that?'

Sara was telling a barefaced lie. But it didn't seem to be enough. Leander merely looked at her, unaffected.

'I can make Rau believe that it was you who told me about Wahasha.'

An ice-cold bluff and highly dubious in moral terms. But it worked. Leander looked at Sara as if she wanted to be certain that she was serious about her threat. Once she had seemingly decided that she was, she cast quick, frightened glances around, and after a period of silence she said in a low voice:

'. . . the king.'

'What about the king?' Sara leaned towards the purple-clad figure.

'The 1990 state visit. The Israeli president Chaim Herzog was scheduled to come to Sweden for a state visit. To see our king.'

'And?'

'Well, the king was a symbol of the oppressor state and Herzog of the war to exterminate the Palestinians. A former general who had fought in both the army and Haganah – that's the terrorist group that became the army when Israel was founded.'

'You were going to kill the king?'

Sara could barely believe her ears.

'You have to understand – it was a different time. We were just responding to the violence. The bombing of civilians in Vietnam, the women and children massacred in refugee camps in Lebanon, the reckless violence directed by the police towards peaceful protestors here in Europe. Now they want us to join NATO, so that we have even less say. What do you think will happen to freedom of expression then? How do you think it'll go for the Syrians, the Palestinians, the people in developing countries that are persecuted for the sake of oil? It's still the same struggle today.'

'The same struggle today? So you're still prepared to kill the king?' Sara said in astonishment.

'Not me personally. But I would understand it if others wanted to, if it helped the struggle. The Palestinians are still in their camps. Imagine if you and your family had seen your home stolen and then you were banished to another country where no one wanted you. If your children and grandchildren had to grow up in tent camps. If they never had the chance of a dignified life. If no one did.'

'How close did you come to realising Wahasha?'

Marita Leander stared across the waters of Mälaren before turning to Sara.

'Is it still punishable? Can I be charged if I tell you?'

'Definitely not. I just want to get to Rau. Tell me.'

Leander had to think a little longer before making her mind up. She looked around, looked at her cats and then finally at Sara. And then she lowered her voice again as she spoke.

'We had spent months preparing. We'd reccied escape routes, suitable locations to attack the motorcade, had written a manifesto we were going to disseminate afterwards. We were going to strike in three places simultaneously – that was the idea. The motorcade with the king and Herzog; the American embassy; the police headquarters on Kungsholmen. It would be revenge for the failures during the embassy drama and Operation Leo. And for the decimation of East Germany. We wanted to show the fascists that they hadn't been victorious in the slightest, that the battle was far from over.'

'How were you planning to pull off an attack on the American embassy? Surely it was heavily armed even back then?'

'Rau had got hold of some anti-tank grenade launchers. The Carl Gustaf ones that Sweden sold to various dictatorships and warmongers. We thought it was a form of poetic justice – turning those weapons on their makers. We planned to get close to the embassy by pretending to be two women with their prams out for a stroll around Gärdet. And once we were close enough, we would pull out a grenade launcher each from the prams and fire at the embassy. We knew where the ambassador's office was, so we were going to aim for that.'

'And you were one of the women?'

Leander paused for a long time before replying.

'Yes.'

'But you never executed Operation Wahasha?'

'No.'

'Why not?' Sara asked.

'Don't know. Perhaps because the Wall had fallen. It was very expensive to run an operation like this and after the Wall came down there was no more money coming in.'

'So you gave it all up? Having worked towards it for months?'

'Several years, actually.'

'Several years?'

'Yes. Our preparations were very thorough. We were waiting for the right target. And when we heard about Herzog it all fell into place,' said Leander.

'And Rau wouldn't want this to come out?'

'No. But above all, he was wanted in West Germany.'

'Hasn't the statute of limitations timed that out?'

'He was wanted for murder. Multiple murders. Or that was how the police state described it anyway.'

'And he might still think he's killing for a good cause?'

'The world hasn't got better, has it?' said Leander, raising an eyebrow. 'There's still a lot to do.'

'Do you really believe that terror makes the world a better place?'

'Terror is the oppressors' name for what we did. If you're surgically removing a cancerous tumour you also have to remove healthy tissue. That's just how it is. No matter how unpleasant it may seem, you have to sacrifice a small part to save the whole. Strike one to educate one hundred, as the Red Brigades used to say.'

'How did Stiller contact you when he wanted to blackmail you?'

'By letter. Good old-fashioned snail mail. I suppose the intelligence agencies are focused on the digital world these days – no one cares about regular letters.' Leander looked down at the cats, which were glowering with hatred at the leads fettering them to their mistress.

'Can I see it?'

'I burnt it after I had paid. Never leave any trace – it's in my bones.'

'What did he write in the letter?'

'It was very formal – rather old-fashioned. Something like "Dear Marita, if you do not pay one hundred thousand kronor into the account below then your current name, your cover name of Lorelei and your true name of Marita Werner will be brought to the attention of the BND. They are most interested in your group following the recent removal of the spy ring around Geiger." And then an account number at the bottom.'

Sara's mobile buzzed and she pulled it out to see what it was. She didn't want to miss anything work-related and irritate Bielke further.

But it wasn't work. It was a text message from Ebba.

I hate you.

48

Ebba wasn't answering her calls or text messages, so Sara went to Titus & Partners, double parked outside, folded down the visor to show the police emblem and ran inside.

The professional smile on Ebba's face as she stood in reception vanished as soon as her mother appeared.

'Leave,' she said staring pointedly down at the desk. 'Otherwise I'll call security.'

'Do that – I'm armed,' said Sara. 'What is it?'

'"What is it?"' said Ebba, with an expression on her face as if Sara had run over her firstborn and was wondering why she was so worked up.

'Well, what is it? Why do you hate me this time?'

Without a word, Ebba turned the screen of her reception desk computer towards Sara. On it was the *Aftonbladet* website with the leading headline 'Uncle Stellan the sex offender'. Adnan Westin had apparently not refrained from writing his story. Sara saw the subheading too. 'Assaulted minors.'

'So now everyone knows that my granddad was a paedophile!' said Ebba, looking furiously at her mother. 'Thanks for giving me that grandfather!'

'Firstly, I didn't choose him. One of his victims was your grand-mother. And secondly, it wasn't me who told you that he was my father. I wanted absolutely no one to know. I wanted to spare you exactly this kind of thing.' Sara pointed to the display.

'So you're blaming Grandma like normal?'

'What do you mean "like normal"?'

'Apparently everything is her fault. Everything that's bad in your life.'

Sara made an effort not to offer an immediate retort – she wanted to pause for a moment's consideration first.

'I did feel that way before, but I don't any longer. But perhaps you recognise the feeling? That everything is Mum's fault?'

'It is. You and Grandma aren't at all alike.'

'And your daughter will think everything is your fault and that you're stupid for thinking it's all my fault.'

'If you ever tell anyone that he's my grandfather then I'll never forgive you. I promise I'll never speak to you again. I'll never come home. It'll be over.'

'Ebba, I think it's awful too. Dreadful. But it's not actually my fault that things are the way they are.'

'Don't you get it? I'll never be able to get a good job if people find out that I'm related to that . . . pervert!'

'I don't think your grandfather would mind too much about that, actually,' Sara said with a smile.

'Oh yes he would. He puts his company first. This isn't good PR. They have a set of values.'

'OK. But perhaps the worst thing isn't offending against the values of Titus & Partners, but all those girls whose lives Stellan ruined. Be happy that you're not one of them.'

'But thanks to them I'll probably be stuck in reception my whole life. I want a career!'

Sara left before Eric walked by, wondering what she was doing here. She couldn't repair the relationship with Ebba right now. At least, not without help.

Outside Hotel Diplomat she got into a waiting taxi and gave her mother's address in Vällingby.

*

'Ebba hates me.'

The words had a marginal impact on the hater's grandmother.

'If you're going to come here every time she says that then you'd best move in.'

Jane opened the door wide to let in her daughter. The flat was just as meticulously clean as always, and as usual her mother had moved the furniture around and changed the paintings and posters on the walls since Sara's last visit. The only constant was the framed portrait of the old pope.

'This time it's for real,' said Sara, following her mother into the kitchen where a statute book and a yellow highlighter divulged what Jane had been in the middle of doing. Sara noticed that the beautiful medium blue brick was open at the laws of inheritance, but she was too preoccupied with her daughter's emotions to deal with her own.

'What is it now then?' said Jane, ignoring Sara's gaze taking in the legal text.

'She's found out the truth about Stellan.'

Jane filled a glass with water and gave it to her daughter.

'The problem isn't that she's found out,' said Jane. 'The problem is that that monster is part of my child and my grandchildren. The worst and the best parts of my life are merged into one.'

'That monster is part of my child.' The words shook Sara. She put down the glass and tried to digest what her mother had said. She felt something against her cheek and pulled back her head. Only then did she realise that it had been herself unconsciously fiddling with her scars.

Why did her subconscious connect Stellan with the injuries? Was the burnt half of her face the monstrous part? The external proof that Stellan had become part of her? Was she like him? No, she wasn't. And no one was going to be allowed to think that either. The scars were the result of her stopping evil – not her becoming part of it.

Sara put her hands together in a pleading gesture.

'Please, won't you withdraw the application? For the sake of my children?'

Jane snorted at the question.

'They can look after themselves.'

'They're *children*.'

'Ebba is an adult now. And she has no right to take your father away from you. What she thinks isn't important. He's your father. You have a right to be acknowledged as a daughter.'

'But I don't *want* to be.'

'You don't understand. Listen to me – you're someone's child.'

'Yes. Yours.'

'And his. He was an evil man, and you're the person who can tell the truth about him. It has a lot more impact if you are his daughter. That's why Malin and Lotta don't want you to be his child. They want everyone to believe their version.'

'But do you have to prove it with DNA? Everything's in the papers now – isn't that enough?' Sara objected.

'They're just writing what he did. Not that he was your father.'

'Why is it so important? Isn't it enough that everyone knows what he did? Why do I and the kids have to be related to him too?'

'Because my father renounced me! It hurt. It still does. And I've never had the chance to prove the truth about myself,' said Jane, looking at her steadily.

'He renounced you? You've never mentioned that. You just said your parents were dead.'

'They are now. But he lived a long life and he was never held accountable. But my mother died far too soon – thanks to him.'

Jane had never opened up like this before. And Sara had never seen the vulnerability that was now visible in her mother's eyes.

'Mum, sit down,' said Sara, taking her mother's wrist and pulling her down onto one of the kitchen chairs, while she herself took the other. 'Tell me. I don't know anything about your parents.'

'There's nothing to tell.'

'Tell me. They're my grandmother and grandfather. Your mother and father.'

Jane looked out of the window, down at the statute book and then at her daughter.

'They were both members of the Communist Party,' she said. 'My father was a party official and my mother was a secretary at the party offices in Kraków. He seduced her, but when she found she was with child, he denied that it was his. That I was his. And Mum was sacked, excluded from the party and forced to work at the Nowa Huta steel mill instead. It turned out my father was already engaged to the daughter of a party bigwig in Warsaw and as a single mother stigmatised by the party, Mum could never meet anyone new or get another job. She worked herself to death.'

Sara placed a hand on her mother's and was silent for a long time.

'OK, I get what this means to you,' she said finally. 'But do you really want Olle and Ebba to be related to a monster? Stellan was even worse than your father. Ebba thinks it might ruin her career.'

'She's like you. Nothing's going to stop her.'

'Is that good or bad?' said Sara, unable to help smiling a little.

'It's good. Perhaps not always so much fun for the people around you both.'

'I think we take after you.'

'And my mother. Your grandmother. You never got to meet her. That was my fault.'

'Your fault?'

'I went home to see her before she died. 1987. In June. Then she died in July. She was only fifty.'

'Fifty? I'll be that soon.'

Jane nodded.

'You wanted to come with me, but had to stay with the Bromans. And you were so angry. I thought you'd never forgive me.'

'Do you know what, Mum, I had completely forgotten about that. I remember it now you say it, and of course I would have liked to meet my grandmother, but there are many who have it worse. The important thing for me is that my children have got to know *their* grandmother.'

'I was just so worried that the communists would arrest us,' said Jane. 'I would probably have coped in prison, but you were so little. And they might have taken you from me because I had fled, so I didn't dare.'

'But you didn't say that. You just let me be angry at you.'

'All children are angry at their parents. It's part of the package. But if you had known why you couldn't come with me, then you would have gone on your own. Just to defy me and the communist regime.'

'You might be right about that,' Sara admitted.

'So now you know. It feels good to have told you.'

'After thirty-five years?'

'Better late than never.'

Sara smiled at her mother, and then her gaze fell on the open statute book.

'But are you really sure you want to tie us to Stellan?' said Sara. 'Can't we forget about this DNA thing?'

'I've already told you: I want everyone to know what he did. *Everything* that he did.'

'How does it help? He's dead.'

'Sara, we're witnesses. It's our duty to tell others. Haven't you read about #MeToo? This is *my* #MeToo.'

Sara was silent. Now she understood her mother better. And she found it difficult to disagree with her.

'OK,' she said at last. 'Then we'll do it.'

49

At home she encountered the next family tragedy.

Martin was still asleep even though lunchtime had come and gone. A half-empty whisky bottle on the floor by the bed implied he had tried the hair of the dog. Quite a lot of hair, at that. Sara hadn't seen him this low in many years – possibly never, in fact. Just to be on the safe side, she asked him whether he needed to see to his beloved Uncle Scam before the man left the country, but Martin didn't answer. Instead, he merely slurred something inaudible and curled up under the duvet.

He would have to take responsibility for his American superstars himself, Sara thought to herself before leaving. She was working tonight, so he would have to grapple with his hungover angst by himself. Perhaps she ought to do her husband a little kindness and go and buy some crisps and fizzy drinks for his hangover munchies? They usually had everything necessary down in the Munkbrohallen grocery store.

Romantic dinners would have to wait for a while. Martin was going to be a wreck all day, Sara realised. The best-case scenario was that he would be back on track tomorrow, worst, it might take another couple of days. In the meantime, every manner of junk food was the best way for Sara to show her love for Martin.

Just as she put her hand on a bag of cheesy puffs down in the shop, her mobile emitted a beep: a new email. Given everything that had been going on over the last few months, Sara opened her inbox right away.

It was a video clip from Malin. An old black-and-white film that her childhood friend must have got some poor archive monkey to dig up and digitise. After all, Malin worked at SVT and had been accustomed to telling people what to do since the early days.

Not until the name appeared did Sara recognise the young girl the clip focused on.

The sequence was from an episode of the quiz show *A Thousand Answers*. And the contestant, according to the presenter, was Eva Hedin, aged just thirteen. Who got a question wrong about Clark Gable. The question was in which order Clark Gable had a) become a grandfather, b) had a son and c) died. The correct answer was that he had become a grandfather, died and then had a son. But young Eva Hedin had said that it was impossible to have children after having grandchildren, and answered b-a-c. When she found out she was wrong, she claimed, with desperation in her voice, that she had misunderstood the question. But the presenter, Stellan Broman, didn't offer her a second chance. She was obliged to leave the TV studio to the sound of cheery music played by the band. Meanwhile Stellan joked about her hasty retreat, making the audience roar with laughter.

It was admittedly true that she had been humiliated by Stellan, but was that what had driven Eva Hedin to unmask the TV star as a Stasi spy? The circumstantial evidence pointing to his guilt had been truly overwhelming, but Hedin still didn't know that Stellan had actually been innocent. He had been guilty of many atrocities against young girls and he had been very positively disposed towards East Germany, but he hadn't spied on their behalf. The spy, Geiger, had been someone else entirely.

The question was whether Sara should tell Hedin the truth.

And whether she dared to mention her involvement in *A Thousand Answers*.

But just as she was thinking about that, she received a text message. It was from Tore Thörnell.

Must speak to you urgently. Are you in a safe place? If not, make your way to safety immediately.

Sara looked around the shop. Surely there were no threats to speak of here?

Then suddenly everyone looked equally dangerous: the Japanese tourists, the old man with his walking frame, the young girl with a nose ring, the bloke in a suit whose trousers were too short and whose bare feet were slipped into loafers, the mother of the small child in a pushchair. They were all transformed before Sara's very eyes into disguised terrorists. Nothing was as it seemed – that was her new perspective on reality.

OK. Where? she replied to Thörnell.

He'd never done this before. It had to be about something important.

Where are you now?
By the Gamla stan metro station.
Lars Johansson.
What?

No answer.

OK. Lars Johansson?

It didn't mean anything to her. Why was Thörnell suddenly being so cryptic? Had Rau bugged her phone, and if so, did the colonel know about it? Had he decided to suddenly go against Rau? If he had wanted to lure Sara into a trap, he would hardly have messed it up, and he definitely wouldn't have warned her. She would have to go on gut feel. She had to solve the riddle.

She searched for 'Lars Johansson Stockholm' in the online phone book and got fifty-eight companies and eight hundred and thirty-six people in her hits. It was impossible to sift through them. Wikipedia gave her sixteen Lars Johanssons to choose from, ranging from several politicians to Joe Labero's real name.

Sara knew that Labero had performed at Berns, and that wasn't all that far away. But was a magician really the reference that Thörnell would choose?

Then she spotted the name Lasse Lucidor in the Wikipedia list. It sounded familiar. It transpired that Lasse Lucidor was a poet who had been killed in 1674, in a duel at the tavern known as Källaren Fimmelstång. According to Wikipedia, it had been located at 14 Kindstugatan three hundred and fifty years ago. But the address was still there, so Sara began to walk towards it.

She headed up Tyska brinken, past both Lilla Nygatan and Stora Nygatan.

She was constantly on tenterhooks, worried about Thörnell's warning.

It turned out to be well-founded.

In the crowd at the crossroads with Västerlånggatan she heard footsteps approaching quickly from behind her. And she felt someone very close to her.

She instinctively took a step to one side and saw the blade of a bayonet shoot past.

If she hadn't stepped aside, it would have gone into her body.

She looked at the man holding the bayonet. An older man with a shaven head, dark eyebrows and a pointed white beard. His green eyes stared at her wildly.

'Looking for me?' said the man, flashing a contorted smile. Sara recognised the voice from her calls to Günther Dorch. She hadn't found him, but he had found her.

Dorch drew his hand back to take another swing and Sara leapt away again.

Thoughts rushed through her head and she considered crying out for help, drawing attention from the people surrounding them, but she was afraid that someone might get hurt.

At the same time, Dorch grabbed hold of Sara's collar with his free hand to assume control of her and have an easier target.

'Stay still,' he said.

Sara twisted sideways as he took the next swing but she didn't manage to completely avoid it.

The bayonet pierced her fluttering jacket and scratched her abdomen.

The feel of the sharp edge set her adrenaline pumping. Sara pulled out her gun, smashed the barrel against Dorch's nose and then shot the bayonet out of his hand.

The gunshot rang between the old building walls. People nearby jumped.

For a few seconds, Günther Dorch looked at her in shock. Then he shouted loudly:

'Gun!'

As the tourists around them began to scream and run in different directions, he shoved Sara aside and vanished into the crowd.

Västerlånggatan quickly emptied of people and Sara decided to disappear too.

50

Brundin couldn't understand the fuss over the old customs house at the far end of Blasieholmen. What did it matter whether they knocked it down? It wasn't as if they needed it any longer. On the other hand, she couldn't understand the point of building a Nobel Centre either. As was so often the case, she thought both sides were wrong. She considered herself to be neutral in this matter. Or perhaps calm and balanced.

And it wasn't the customs house they were heading for, even if they parked right by it.

In all the years that Quintus Nyman had been her boss, they had only travelled together in a car on a couple of occasions, and he had never driven. But today he did. He parked at the far end of Blasieholmen with the waters of the Nybrokviken bay on one side, the island of Djurgården dead ahead of them and the rear of the Lydmar Hotel in the other direction. He adjusted the rear-view mirror so that he could see his own reflection and then he combed his grey mane with his fingers, smoothed his beard and slightly adjusted his glasses. Brundin had never thought of her boss as vain, but that trait was apparently present even in the greyest of bureaucrats.

They set off on foot along Hovslagargatan, but almost immediately, before they had reached the Lydmar, Nyman turned into a small, cobbled courtyard surrounded by green bushes. There was a three-storey red-brick building with a garage door and a brown door to its left – 4 Hovslagargatan. He hadn't said where they were going, but now she knew.

Nyman climbed the steps and rang the bell. FADO, it said on a small metal plaque by the bell, with the clarification underneath of 'Food from the Middle East Export & Import'. The lock buzzed and Nyman opened the door. When she stepped inside, Brundin noted the tiny camera lens in a crevice at the edge of the window by the door.

A pale man with a beard and wavy hair appeared to receive them, but he didn't greet them.

The building seemed to consist solely of long, winding corridors, at least on the lower floor. A staircase led to the upper floors but was protected by a locked gate with a palm scanner beside it.

Finally they reached a poorly lit meeting room with posters displaying various foods of the Middle East, a board table made from dark oak and a bulky black leather sofa suite. The tall windows were all darkly tinted and covered by curtains. Brundin assumed they were bulletproof.

They were directed to the sofa and the pale man vanished without asking whether they wanted coffee. They sat in silence as was their habit when unsure whether they were being bugged.

After ten minutes, an older man entered the room. He was wearing an elegant three-piece suit and bow tie, as well as reading glasses on a chain around his neck. An academic, Brundin thought to herself contemptuously.

Nyman stood up, smiled in recognition and shook the old man's hand.

'Brundin – Schönberg,' Nyman said, introducing them to each other. Then Schönberg offered them fruit from the company's range.

'Do you know much about the restaurant trade in Stockholm?' said Schönberg. 'We have far too few customers in the city. It's a miracle that we manage to stay in business here.'

Schönberg laughed at his own comment and Nyman joined in. Brundin managed to produce a smile, realising that Nyman thought it was part of the social game.

They warmed up with a little small talk. Was the family well? What a pity to hear about Schönberg's wife, condolences. Brundin's

German wasn't as good as Nyman's, but when she didn't understand something all it took was a quick glance to her boss and he translated.

Once personal matters had been attended to, it was time to talk shop and swap old war stories. Schönberg carefully filled a pipe and lit it without asking whether his guests minded. Then he leaned back and puffed away on it pleasurably. Smoking in the workplace. Definitely not OK, Brundin thought to herself, but she couldn't help taking a little enjoyment from someone so flagrantly disregarding the rules.

'I didn't actually know you had this place,' said Nyman, looking around.

'It's a different section. I've been on the move of late. It was considered desirable for me to step aside after the misfortune with Abu Rasil.'

'Yes, that didn't quite go according to plan.'

'We used to have the building next door,' Schönberg said in English, turning to Brundin, a new pair of ears to tell old stories to. 'But it came with a lot of history.'

When Brundin didn't react, a small wrinkle of irritation appeared on Schönberg's brow and he leaned forward to explain.

'During the Second World War, Germany's embassy was in the adjacent building – at number 2 – which is now a hotel. And there were spies running around the place day in, day out. As the capital of a neutral country, Stockholm was a real spy centre – and a good transit between the conflicting sides. But after the War, we wanted to distance ourselves from Nazi Germany and the rather brutal activities that occurred in the embassy. So we got a new embassy. But since so few people knew that the intelligence services had this building at their disposal, we kept it. Well, I say we. It was before my time. Organisation Gehlen, as the agency was called to begin with. It's said that the real reason we kept this building was that the local bureau chief, who carried on after the War as if nothing had happened, was so fond of the food at the Grand Hôtel that he wanted to remain close by.'

Brundin made an effort not to reveal how uninteresting she found all this. At the same time, she didn't want to look so interested that he would continue. A curt nod was her compromise.

Nyman had forewarned Brundin that there was always some small talk up front with the Germans before they got to the point. But this wasn't small talk, it was an entire lecture. One she had no use whatsoever for.

Finally, after more than half an hour's discussion of espionage back in the day, the best way to store fruit and cereals, and the issues around keeping up with technological advances, they got to the point.

'Sara Nowak.'

'We have eyes on her,' said Nyman.

'Don't,' said Schönberg.

Nyman and Brundin looked quizzically at the doyen of German intelligence.

'I beg your pardon?' said Nyman.

'Don't have your eyes on Nowak. Leave her alone. Occupy yourselves with other matters.'

There was a period of silence while his words sank in.

'May I ask why?' Nyman said.

Schönberg puffed on his pipe and looked out of the tall windows.

'She has managed to dig up the name of Otto Rau. That is most unfortunate.'

'Do you want us to stop her?' said Nyman.

'I don't think we can,' said Brundin. 'I don't think she'll give up.'

Nyman flashed an irritated glance at Brundin.

'Of course we can,' he said.

'It doesn't matter,' said Schönberg. 'Rau won't be satisfied with that. Sara Nowak must manage by herself in this matter. Do not attempt to rescue her.'

'Are you also after Rau?' said Nyman. 'We can help you to find him.'

'My dear Quintus, it is far more complicated than that. But in no circumstances should you get involved in what is about to pass.'

'You're using her to lure out Rau?' said Brundin, to Nyman's great annoyance. 'Just like with Abu Rasil?'

Schönberg shook his head.

'There's no point in guessing. Just keep out of the way.'

51

Sara ran.

It wouldn't be long before the old town was crawling with police. Even though she had only defended herself, she didn't want to expose herself any further. She could only hope that no one had managed to catch what had happened on video. But tourists generally had cameras and mobiles primed at all times.

The soles of her shoes thudded against the cobblestones as she reached Kindstugatan. As she approached number 14, she stopped and looked around.

Was anyone following her?

It seemed not.

The next problem:

Should she really enter a building where Thörnell was?

What if he was cooperating with Dorch? With the whole cell? No, hardly. Thörnell had warned her about Rau just now. And if it had been a trap then surely Dorch wouldn't have attacked in the middle of the street. He could just as well have been watching Sara's door himself and then followed her through the old town.

She decided to go with her instincts. If nothing else, to see whether she had correctly guessed that Lucidor was the clue.

On the door of number 14 there was a sign informing her that this was home to an accountancy firm. Through the large window, Sara saw a couple of men and a woman in front of computers. It all looked decidedly harmless, so she rang the bell and one of the men came and opened the door.

'Lars Johansson?' said Sara.

'Welcome. I'm Fredrik,' said the man with a smile as he offered his hand. He had a beard and thick-rimmed glasses framing a pair of kind eyes. He was palpably muscular, but built like a bear so that he seemed more cuddly than dangerous. 'This is Peter and Anna,' Fredrik continued, gesturing towards the other two, who looked up from their screens. Sara scrutinised the group a little more closely and noticed that all three seemed to be carrying pistols in shoulder holsters under their jacket, cardigan, and blazer respectively.

'Nicely done,' said a voice beside Sara, and when she turned around Tore Thörnell was suddenly standing there, closing the front door behind him. 'You'll have to excuse the secrecy, but I'm most reluctant to state names and addresses that are classified on the phone or by text message.'

'No problem,' said Sara.

'That's the exact spot where he died,' said Fredrik, pointing to the floor by the small kitchenette. 'By the steps down to the cellar.'

Sara realised he meant Lasse Lucidor, but there were no steps where he was pointing. But then Thörnell pressed a button under the draining board and part of the floor slid aside, revealing a spiral staircase leading down into the darkness. Thörnell led the way, Sara following, and the hatch slid smoothly shut behind them.

'*Voi ch'entrate,*' said Thörnell, flattering Sara by not translating.

The spiral staircase ended outside a locked iron door. Thörnell pulled out his mobile and placed it in a metal box on the wall, nodding to Sara that she should do the same. She couldn't help wondering how smart it was to abandon her means of contact with the outside world.

Oh well, she still had her gun.

Once Sara had put her mobile in the box, Thörnell entered a code into the door beside it and stepped through. Sara followed and discovered a cellar filled with computer screens and servers beneath a vaulted stone ceiling. The contrast between the fourteenth century and the twenty-first was undeniably startling. In the centre of the vault there loomed a long, rather shabby meeting table that looked as though it might have been there since the days of Lasse Lucidor. Thörnell sat down and Sara sat opposite him.

'I'm glad,' said the colonel, pouring them coffee from a cafetiere into IKEA mugs. Presumably not his choice, Sara assumed. 'That you've come to no harm, I mean. Because you are in far greater danger than you realise.'

'Yes, I don't seem to be able to trust anyone,' Sara countered, looking Thörnell straight in the eyes.

'That wasn't at all what you think it was,' he said. 'You must trust that I have your best interests at heart.'

'I was just attacked on Västerlånggatan,' said Sara, showing him the hole in her jacket and the cut on her stomach. 'By Günther Dorch. Is he Rau?'

Thörnell shook his head and almost looked amused.

'If it had been Rau then you wouldn't have survived. What happened to Dorch?'

'He got away.'

'Take it as a warning. Rau is far more dangerous.'

'Yes, you keep saying so.'

'For good reason,' said Thörnell, scrutinising Sara while she sipped her coffee.

So Dorch was Stefan Kremp, Sara thought to herself. That meant there were two former terrorists out to get her.

A thought occurred to her.

'Do we have an audience today?'

She went over to the medieval brick wall and searched around the room. There was no false mirror or anything else that looked like camera lens. For safety's sake, she checked Thörnell's jacket and breast pocket too, but found no bugs.

'It's just you and I,' said Thörnell. 'Believe me, what I am about to tell you is something I do not want anyone else to hear.'

'And what's that then?' said Sara, sitting back down.

'You found a body outside your front door yesterday,' said Thörnell. 'Hans Gerlach.'

'Alias Bo Enberg.'

'Badly knocked about, so I gather.'

'Tortured.'

'By Rau.'

'Who else?'

'And before that, he fired shots into your apartment.'

'Missing me by a few centimetres. And he's been bugging the apartment,' said Sara.

'Why do you think he took those shots? And why do you think he left the body outside your door?'

'Isn't it pretty obvious? To warn me.'

'And why did you not take those warnings?'

Sara thought about this for a moment before answering.

'Why did he only warn me? He killed the others without hesitation.' This was something Sara had been thinking about a great deal.

'Because you're a police officer.'

'A left-wing terrorist and killer who wants to spare the cops? Maybe not, eh?'

'You have the wrong impression of him. Rau is on your side.'

'On my side?' Sara snorted. 'Those aren't quite the signals I'm getting.'

Thörnell looked at Sara for a long time, and she stared sternly back.

'Do you remember our discussion about Stay-Behind?' he said.

'Yes. A kind of secret resistance movement with its headquarters in the hidden room in your apartment. What's that got to do with this?'

Sara had spent much of her summer convalescence reading. About the Cold War, NATO, the Warsaw Pact, the Stasi, the CIA, the KGB and Stay-Behind in various countries. A whole stack of books that had fundamentally changed her perspective on the world.

Thörnell cleared his throat slightly.

'I must remind you that it was a contradictory time. An enemy's enemy became one's friend, and it was perfectly common to share mutual friends with one's enemies. Which made alliances a quagmire. Nothing that anyone said was true, and before long the construction of false fronts had gone so far that no one knew who anyone was any longer. False names, invented memories, different versions for different players. The game took on a life of its own and it became impossible to stop it. And as they lost their grasp on reality, it became increasingly dangerous. A tightrope walk on a slack rope in absolute pitch darkness, in which you had no idea what was at either end, but you were still obliged to walk it. You had to move forward to avoid falling.'

'Poetic,' Sara said acidulously. 'But it's really just another way of saying that no one knew what they were doing. Paranoid warmongers on both sides set the agenda.'

'I don't agree with that. Remember the Iron Curtain which was drawn after the end of the Second World War – the entire eastern bloc became vassal states to the Soviet Union. It was a very real policy that affected millions for decades. There was no paranoid warmongering in the desire to prevent that development.'

'And they were as afraid as we were of being invaded,' Sara commented.

'Which made them dangerous.'

'I'm not saying it didn't.'

'Communism also spread to other parts of the world,' the old colonel continued. 'The whole doctrine was based on acting to deliver global revolution. In Europe, the communist parties were particularly powerful in France and Italy. And close to taking power in free elections. It was assessed that a development like that would lead to these countries affiliating themselves with the eastern bloc.'

'"Assessed"? You mean the results of wild guessing?'

'Not quite. We saw it happen in Czechoslovakia when the communist party became the biggest party and helped to form the government. It led to them taking power in the country and assimilating into the Soviet sphere.'

'Surely there was a difference between Czechoslovakia and Western Europe?' Sara objected.

'Not really. Support for communism was immensely widespread in many of our countries. If they had been able to unite, they would have taken over. But such a course of events had to be stopped at any cost.'

'So after the war, the CIA and MI6 established secret resistance movements in all NATO member states, if I've understood correctly,' Sara added. She had read about this in her hospital bed. 'As well as in neutral countries like Sweden, Finland, Austria and Switzerland. In Italy, it was called Gladio, in Denmark it was Absalon, in Norway it was the ROC and here you opted for Stay-Behind. But what does this have to do with Rau?'

She drained the last of her coffee and poured another cup for herself. She glanced at the many computers.

'To prevent the communists from growing too powerful, we needed a counter-strategy,' said Thörnell. 'Instead of just sitting around waiting for a fait accompli.'

'You're thinking of the terrorist acts perpetrated by Gladio in Europe?'

'Some went too far. I do agree in that respect.'

'*Too far*?!' Sara shook her head. 'Bombs at Italian railway stations, the Brabant massacres in Belgian supermarkets. All controlled by the CIA and NATO. Just to lay the blame on left-wing terrorists and scare people into demanding bigger police forces and armies.'

'"Destabilise in order to stabilise" was how they described it. A lot of stupid things were done at the time.'

'Stupid? Yes, I guess you might call it that. Are things better now then?' Sara snorted.

'Much better.'

'Given your hatred of communists, surely Rau ought to be mortal enemy number one for you. Why don't you want me to chase him down?'

Thörnell was quiet for a long time. For once, he looked down at the table instead of meeting her eye.

'Sara . . . What I'm about to tell you is something you can never tell anyone. I really ought to have you sign a non-disclosure agreement, but I'm not sure that would make any difference in your eyes. I'll just have to trust you.'

'Like I trusted you, until you let someone listen to our conversation from your secret room.'

Thörnell refrained from commenting.

'You have children, a family,' he said instead. 'Your whole life ahead of you. So please, listen to me. And repay my trust in you by not repeating it.'

'Repeating *what*?'

Thörnell paused and slowly spun his mug one hundred and eighty degrees before answering.

'Our good friend Rau was a double agent. He was inserted into Kommando 719 by the West German Stay-Behind network.'

'What are you saying? The person who fired into my apartment is under NATO control?'

Sara felt anger welling up inside her again.

'Let me finish,' Thörnell said calmly.

'Don't you bloody dare try and defend him!'

'No. But you have to—'

'Did you know about it? Did you know that he would take the shots?'

'Definitely not. But let me explain.'

'How the hell are you going to explain that he might have killed my son?' said Sara, who had to restrain herself from lunging at Thörnell.

'Wait! Listen. Rau's mission was to incite the terrorists and make them show their brutality to the people here, thus minimising sympathy for the communists.'

'So you work with Rau? Do you still?'

'No. And I never have done. As part of my posting to NATO, I had a certain level of oversight, but nothing more than that. I know that Rau attended training camps with both the Red Army Faction in Lebanon and with NATO's Gladio outfit in Sardinia. There aren't many who have been trained by both sides like that. A successful infiltration. He was provided with a considerable criminal record by the West German police and then began turning up at demonstrations, in cafés and at various collectives where he was always militant in discussion.'

'So you wanted to agitate the communists through him and make them more violent? That sounds insane. How could you be so terrified of these tiny little groups? Did people really think there might be a revolution in Sweden?' Sara said, with doubt in her voice.

'They didn't just think it,' said Thörnell. 'Haven't you read all the articles in the tabloids about the Soviet plans for an invasion of Sweden? A constant state of alert was the reality we lived in back then. We were always on the brink of war.'

A memory returned to Sara. A nuclear strike drill at school, their teacher showing them how to crawl under their desks. As if that would have helped, she thought to herself.

'And it wasn't just the communists who had militaristic plans. Do you remember the op-ed written by that group of naval officers in *Dagens Nyheter*, or are you too young for that? The one where they attacked Olof Palme. In 1985,' said Thörnell, looking at her searchingly.

'I know about it. They thought he posed a security risk.'

'Exactly. Said he wasn't protesting the submarine incursions into Swedish waters because he was in the pay of the Soviet Union. It is worth noting that in all countries where military chiefs have publicly distanced themselves from a leader elected by the people, this has been followed by a military coup. It's probably very fortunate that we never found out what would have happened had Palme actually gone to the USSR that spring. There were widespread reports that a large group of military officers and police had laid the ground for a coup to take place while Palme was in the Soviet Union. In the end it never happened, since he was gunned down.'

'Didn't some people think the Palme murder was the beginning of a coup?' said Sara.

'Yes. And some still think it was, but that it failed because some key players backed out of it on the night of the murder,' said the colonel.

'You mean to say that there was reason to believe those theories?'

'What most people don't know today is how many different scenarios were possible at the time. Anything could have happened. It's easy after the fact to believe that the Soviet Union and East Germany were predestined to fall, and that Sweden was secure in its neutrality. But many times we were just minutes or millimetres away from catastrophe or a complete about-turn. No one realises how completely inconceivable it was just a week before the fall of the Wall that it would be torn down, or that the Soviet Union would disintegrate. Just like no one could conceive of the idea that Sweden might become a communist dictatorship. Or a fascist one, for that matter.'

Three loud beeps were followed by the iron door opening and Fredrik entering with an iPad in his hand. He went over and showed the screen to Thörnell, who looked at it and nodded.

'Yevgeny. And his wife. This is what the modern KGB man looks like.'

He addressed the last bit to Sara while holding up the tablet to her. The display showed the street outside. A forbidding man with chiselled cheekbones and a woman in head-to-toe Gucci were strolling past. Sara thought the man looked familiar. But where could she have seen him?

'Are we busted?' Fredrik asked, cool as a cucumber.

'I think they're probably tourists for real,' said Thörnell. 'Otherwise he would have brought another woman. They never bring their real wives on assignment.'

'OK.'

'But keep an eye out. They may have changed the rules. Because they know we know.'

Fredrik left and Thörnell turned back to Sara.

'I thought you were retired,' she said.

'I am. But they might as well ask me, given I'm here. Where were we?'

'Fascist dictatorship.'

'Ah yes. That's where Rau came into the picture too. Operation Winter was to have taken place in the spring of '86 – a brutal attack in Stockholm's city centre by Kommando 719 while the Prime Minister was in the Soviet Union. Forcing the military to deploy and save the country. But when Palme was assassinated, they cancelled the operation and regrouped.'

'Was it the same with Operation Wahasha?'

'Operation Wahasha wasn't our plan – it was the Stasi's.'

'But if Rau was deployed by Stay-Behind and he was the one running Operation Wahasha, then NATO had agreed to its execution.'

Thörnell looked at Sara for a while before he said anything.

'The attitude in certain key parts of the major defence alliance was that the Swedes were far too naïve. We Swedes perceived Sweden as being so stable and safe that we didn't believe anything could happen here. Our communists were not only tolerated, but almost had the common touch. Lars Werner was popular well beyond his own party. No one took them seriously; no one thought they would be capable of driving through a revolution. At the same time, they were largely funded by the Soviet Union and completely loyal to them. They sided with them in all international conflicts and demonstrated against the USA and NATO.'

'But Wahasha was about the king.'

'The assessment was that something big was needed to discredit the communists. And in Sweden the king has always been beloved, even by the proletariat. An attack on him carried out by communist guerrillas backed by the DDR and Stasi would nudge Sweden in the right direction.'

'You would have let them kill him?'

The idea was far too shocking for Sara to quite digest.

'It might not have been necessary,' said the colonel. 'It would probably have had the same impact if he had survived an assassination attempt.'

'And why did you think that impact was needed? Hadn't glasnost and perestroika already begun to transform the eastern bloc?'

'Gorbachev's popularity made the demonisation of the Soviet Union increasingly difficult, but the hawks at NATO didn't think his politics would lead to any form of democratisation. And West Germany was already home to Willy Brandt's "Ostpolitik" – which was based on forging closer relations with the East Germans and USSR. "Change through rapprochement" as he called it. The Soviet Union with a human face might deceive even more people.'

Sara did her best to take in all this information. She leaned back and shut her eyes for a while to order her thoughts, then she perched her elbows on the table and looked at Thörnell.

'So to summarise: you have to protect Rau to ensure that your own secrets don't come to light? Which would be particularly unfortunate given the current campaign for Sweden to join NATO?'

'It's not the ideal time, no.'

'Does that mean that I have all of NATO against me? And the CIA?' The thought was dizzying.

'We've tried to keep this in-house. Well, the Germans know about it.'

'Is Operation Wahasha still live?' Sara asked.

'What's live today is something I'm most definitely unable to say. But it would probably be a very good idea if you kept quiet about Operation Wahasha.'

'For both me and you, I suppose.'

Sara smiled grimly at him and got up, as if to show that their discussion was over.

Thörnell followed Sara out. They went through the metal door and she stopped a couple of steps up the spiral staircase while he locked up. 'You have no protection and no assistance,' he told her.

'You're helping me.'

'Only with information. I have no say these days.'

'Then I suppose I'll have to manage by myself,' said Sara, nodding farewell to Thörnell. Then she turned around and continued up the stairs.

'Wait, don't forget your mobile.'

Sara turned around again and took the mobile that the colonel had retrieved from the metal box.

She stood there frozen to the spot for a few seconds staring at Thörnell's hand.

And then it hit her.

'The mobile!' she shouted. 'Abeba's mobile!'

She turned on her heel and ran up the stairs and into the street. On the way, she called Anna.

Thörnell watched her disappear into the distance. Then he pulled out his own mobile and dialled.

52

'It wasn't Abeba texting Cesar,' Sara practically shouted when Anna eventually answered. 'It was the father! And he was the one who deleted it afterwards!'

Sara was running as fast as she could, zig-zagging between sauntering tourists along Kindstugatan and Köpmanbrinken.

'How do you know that?' said Anna.

'It was the way he went to fetch the mobile for her. She didn't make the slightest effort to get it for herself. Her eyes didn't even search for it when we asked for it, because he looks after it for her. If anyone asks for my mobile, I have an impulse to get it out. She didn't.'

'OK. I buy that.'

'I'm in the old town. Where can you meet me? We need to bring them both in,' Sara panted.

'I'm at home. Is this something we need to do now?'

'Yes! Anna, think! The visit to the convenience store!'

'What about it?'

'Why would Abeba sneak off, if she was just going to buy a newspaper? What can you buy in a shop like that which you'd want to keep secret?'

'Condoms,' said Anna.

'On the right track,' said Sara. 'Try again.'

'Pregnancy tests!'

'Exactly.'

'She's pregnant!'

'Or at the very least, she had cause to check. I'll get the car and pick you up by the Ringen mall so that we can go together.'

Sara put her mobile away as she ran down Österlånggatan towards Slottsbacken, where she took a left, passed the pissoir and reached the way down to the underground car park which was embedded into the wall under Slottsbacken itself. While Sara was heading down to the car park and her Golf, Anna called back.

'I just spoke to the surveillance team. Abeba and her father just left, they say.'

'Where for?'

'No idea.'

'Tell them to follow,' Sara said, taking three steps at a time towards the basement level.

'What do you think they were going to do? Stick around and stare into space?'

'Sorry. I'll pick you up in five.'

Sara drove the car out of the car park, looped around the old town and then drove down into the tunnel on Hornsgatan. Anna lived on Tullgårdsgatan in the high rise shadow of Folksamhuset, but she had made her way to the Ringen shopping mall so that Sara could drive across the Skanstullsbron bridge to Årsta and onto the E20 motorway southbound. She was constantly switching lanes and flashing at cars that didn't pull in when she wanted to overtake.

'Don't kill us getting there,' said Anna, glowering at her.

'I just have a feeling that this is urgent.'

'I thought I was the one with premonitions.'

'Abeba and her father aren't dead. It's ghosts you talk to.'

'Only when it's a quarter to three and I'm in a bar,' her friend grinned.

Just as they reached the E4, Anna's mobile rang. She answered, listened for a couple of seconds and then turned towards Sara.

'She's thrown herself out of the car. In the middle of the motorway.'

53

'My daughter needs me!'

Ndeme was agitated. He slammed his fist against the table to emphasise each syllable. The grey and white acoustic boards on the ceiling of the small interview room didn't do much to absorb the sound.

'First we have a couple of questions,' said Sara. 'And there's nothing to worry about. She's getting plenty of help from the doctors.'

Ndeme had braked when Abeba had opened the door and thrown herself out, according to the surveillance team following them. This had, without doubt, saved her life, because there was a big difference between falling out of a car at thirty kilometres an hour and at eighty. But she had still taken a real beating on the asphalt and had been bleeding profusely from her many scratches.

The real question was what had made her risk her life like that. The officers in the car behind had been obliged to floor the brakes in a panic to avoid crashing into Ndeme's metallic red Seat. They had seen to Abeba and ensured an ambulance was on the scene in the space of just a few minutes, and then Sara and Anna had asked them to bring her father to the police station in Solna.

'Why did she throw herself out?' said Sara.

'She didn't, she fell. That door's been causing grief. I was going to take it to the garage, but you never get round to it, do you?'

'What did you think about Abeba being together with Cesar?'

'It was very good. Cesar was a good guy. It was terrible for it to end like that. He wanted to leave the gang but they wouldn't let him.'

'So you believe it was his own gang that killed him?' Sara asked.

'You know, you don't leave those gangs so easy. "You owe us this, you owe us that." They don't want to let you go.'

'What did you think about the fact that Abeba was having sex with Cesar?' Anna interjected.

'She wasn't having sex with him! Careful what you say!'

'She's pregnant. Has she told you that?'

Ndeme said nothing.

'Where were you going?' said Sara.

'To buy clothes. For the funeral.'

'Was it the thought of the funeral that made her throw herself out of the car? I don't think it was.'

'She didn't throw herself. It was the door.'

'Anyway, the baby survived,' Anna announced, while Sara studied his reaction.

'Which baby?'

'Hers and Cesar's.'

'She's not pregnant!'

'The doctors say otherwise.'

Ndeme looked furious, but he sat in silence.

'You're accusing my daught—' he said, but Sara interrupted him.

'What's the PIN on your mobile?' she said, holding up the phone they had confiscated from him.

'No PIN. I have nothing to hide,' he said, shaking his head in irritation. 'You interrupted me. I said: you're accusing my daughter of living an impure life!'

Sara pressed a button on the mobile and quite right, there was no PIN.

'You can't look at it,' said Ndeme, raising a hand to stop her. 'It's my mobile. Personal privacy.'

'My finger slipped,' said Sara, opening his text messages.

Ndeme lunged across the table, knocking over the bottle of mineral water, which fell to the floor. With one hand he grabbed Sara's top and with the other he reached for his mobile. Sara instinctively grasped the hand clutching her top and twisted it

339

while following up with her other hand against his elbow. Then she twisted him into an armlock.

'Violence against an officer,' Sara said, bending him down towards the floor and leaning on his back, still with his arm locked. Together with Anna she raised him into a sitting position and secured his hands to the table using handcuffs.

'Now I'm *very* curious,' Sara said, picking up his mobile again.

'This is harassment! Religious persecution.'

'In that case God will punish us,' she said, returning to his text messages.

Messages from the postal service and his voicemail and the City of Stockholm about parking. Sara noted the date was last Friday, the night Cesar had been murdered. And the message was to remind him that his parking ticket would expire at midnight that evening. The time of Cesar's death.

She quickly scrolled through the other senders and recipients, who were largely his wife, his children, the odd colleague and a couple of relatives, judging by the names.

And there was a number without a name to it.

Sara opened the most recent message from the number.

37 greve von essens väg, 8pm.

She went back and read from the beginning of the thread.

Got your number from Ramon Velasquez. I want to do a peepshow.
OK
How much?
Just watch or do yourself?
Do myself.
200.
And the body?
Disappears without trace.

When?
Friday?
OK.
Where should we pick up?
11 Postängsvägen behind the church. What time?
8pm?
OK.

'What's a peepshow?' said Sara, looking up from the mobile to Ndeme.

'Just a game.'

'I've seen what people look like after they've been to a peep-show. What do you mean by "do myself"? Was it you who tortured Cesar?'

'I didn't do anything! Give me my mobile.'

Why so eager? Sara wondered. She went to find the video folder. There were only about ten or fifteen videos, and the oldest ones appeared to be innocent films of the family and house, judging by the previews.

But the last videos showed something else entirely. Sara clicked on one of them and saw Cesar's pained, bloodied face accompanied by a terrible shriek. Downright mortal anguish. She saw an arm appear in shot with a knife in its hand – it stabbed over and over. Ruthlessly.

'You've ruined her!' a voice shouted – Sara recognised it as Ndeme's.

The next clip showed more of the brutal murder – the protracted suffering. The murder cut his victim again and again, making him scream loudly.

Sara lowered the mobile and looked at Ndeme.

'Just because he got your daughter pregnant?'

Ndeme shook his head.

'I didn't know that then.'

Sara let the words sink in. An uncomfortable, dark-as-night realisation dawned on her.

'When did you find that out?'

No answer.

'Where were you going just now? When she threw herself out?'

Still no answer. Sara checked the final messages.

I want to do a peepshow again. When OK?
Friday again.
200?
Discount 2nd time. 150.
thank you.
should we pick up? same address?
can't. we'll come.
37 greve von essens väg, 8pm.

Sara checked the map on her mobile and saw the address was at Gärdet, not far from where she'd found Nadia.

'Where is this peepshow?' she said to Ndeme. 'Is it in Frihamnen? At the Free Port?'

When he didn't answer, Sara lunged forward, grabbed him by the lapels and shook him for all she was worth.

'WHERE?'

Anna put her arm between them and tugged Sara away, carefully so that it wouldn't be clear whether she was distancing herself from the violence or keen to emphasise to Ndeme how close Sara was to going berserk. That tactic had worked before – presumably because it was based on a highly realistic possibility.

'What were you going to do with Abeba?' said Sara, but by now Ndeme had regained his composure and was looking at her with derision.

His phone beeped.

Sara checked the mobile.

The message was from the same number as the other peepshow texts.

Where are you?

It really was as bad as she'd thought. She looked at the man before her. A servant of God who was willing to kill his own child because she wanted to live her own life.

'You were going to take your daughter to the peepshow? You were going to murder her in front of other people?'

'She's disowned. She has no family any longer. It's better for her to go to God.'

Sara imagined herself locking Ndeme into a scissors position and slowly suffocating him to death. Then she looked at the mobile and thought for a moment.

'And it's tonight?' She got no answer. 'I asked you whether they're doing a peepshow now?'

Ndeme shrugged.

'Are there several victims each time?'

The same movement from Abeba's father.

'Where is it? Where do they do the peepshow?'

'I don't know. They blindfolded us and drove us.'

She checked the second to last message again. *37 greve von essens väg, 8pm.*

Sara turned to Anna.

'There might be others who are going to be tortured and murdered tonight. We have to stop it.'

'How? He doesn't know where it is.'

'There's only one way.'

Sara grabbed Ndeme's mobile again and typed:

Bit late, there in 20.

54

The building at 37 Greve von Essens väg turned out to be a small pink palace on a low hillock on the edge of the Gärdet park. It was ordinarily an idyllic, secluded spot – almost straight from the pages of a fairy tale. It was usually rented out for weddings and celebrations, but when it wasn't being used, it was a very out-of-the-way place, free from prying eyes. Right now, it felt far from idyllic.

They'd had to act fast. There had been no time to secure proper backup. Her colleague Sonja had lent Sara a headscarf to conceal her increasingly flame-red hair. She was counting on the people they encountered not being experts in the dress code of the Church of the Ascension. And it would presumably enhance the impression of an oppressed daughter. Roger Nordlund had agreed to play the angry father. He was a legend in the force who had always led the charge completely fearlessly whatever the context and had then been promoted to head up the flying squad and personal protection unit. Now, however, he had been promoted well past his comfort zone to the rank of superintendent and a working life filled with meetings and negotiations. He was over the moon to step into a tight spot. His big beard and shaved head were a good match with the image of a dominant patriarch in a free church. The fact that Roger was one hundred and fifty kilos of muscle who easily bench-pressed two hundred kilos didn't do any harm. As a police superintendent, he always had a suit and tie waiting in his office for entertaining, and these were put to good use now.

As they sped through the city at ninety kilometres an hour, Sara told Roger everything. About the bodies in Lake Mälaren, about Nadia and Cesar and what they knew about the peepshow. She gave him Abeba's father's mobile in case he had to prove his identity.

She called Anna, connected her wireless earbuds and attached them to her clothing so that Anna could hear everything that was happening. And she turned on 'Find My iPhone' so that she could see where they were. But the first order of business was to try and have a patrol car standing by close to Gärdet.

'Tell them Nordlund says hello,' Roger said cheerily to Anna, and Sara was convinced it would make all the difference. Now she felt safe.

Sara knew that if she had asked Bielke for permission to take Abeba's place, he would have refused. He would never have agreed to a police officer risking her life that way, not even if it was the only way to find the peepshow. But once Sara was at a location where lives were at stake, then he would naturally send backup.

The only weak point in the plan was that they couldn't be sure how quickly backup would be on the scene.

When they reached the small fairy-tale palace, they got out of the car that Sara had borrowed from the police motor pool – a highly anonymous Skoda. Roger grasped Sara's shoulder with his hand to give the impression of a man controlling his subordinate daughter.

They were met by two square-shouldered men with blank expressions and cheap leather jackets, one with a crew cut with a small spot of hair left on top, the other with his head completely shaved. Behind them was a black BMW X5 with the doors open and the engine running. The men each held up a black fabric bag and Roger bent his head forward and let them put the hood over it. Sara did the same and hoped they wouldn't decide to tie her up.

She guessed that the same men who met the peepshow participants then got rid of the bodies, in which case the two who had met Ndeme when he had brought them Cesar were dead – shot after trying to dump Cesar's body in Mälaren. The whole set-up depended on it.

But with a hood over her face, the fear that these men were the same ones who had met Ndeme and Cesar grew. It would mean that they knew Roger wasn't Ndeme, and that they would therefore drive them to a remote spot and execute them. With the hoods on, they wouldn't have a clue what was going on.

They were led into the waiting car, which then pulled away.

Sara wondered how it had worked when they had snatched Cesar. Ndeme would obviously never have got him to come here. Had Cesar seen Ndeme by the church and realised what was happening? Or had the goons taken him by surprise and beaten him unconscious? Had Cesar thought that it was Abeba who had lured him into the trap? It was quite possible. Perhaps he had died thinking she had helped her father.

If their destination was Frihamnen, then the two men who drove them felt no need to disorient them by taking the long way. After a journey of just a few minutes the car stopped. Sara heard the sound of a large iron gate gliding aside and then the car drove for another few seconds before stopping. The front doors opened, then the back doors, and Sara and Roger were led out.

Sara tried to visualise what she was hearing. A large door being opened, the sound of footsteps on concrete, sudden beeping and then strong hands running over her body.

'A gun!' exclaimed a voice in heavily accented English a few steps away from Sara.

There was the sound of rapid feet and bodies jostling about.

'It's for her!' Roger yelled at last.

'For her?'

'Yes. I want to use it on her!'

A good excuse from Roger, Sara thought to herself while waiting nervously to see how the lie was taken.

A brief pause and then a curt laugh.

'We give you gun.'

A metallic sound – probably Roger's pistol being thrown away.

Then they were led forward a few metres through what sounded – judging by the echoes – like a fairly narrow corridor with a concrete floor. And then they stopped and heard a heavy door closing behind them.

'Take off his,' said one of the voices.

'Thank you,' said Roger.

Someone grabbed Sara's hands.

'No, it's OK,' said Roger. 'No cuffs.'

'Yes,' said the voice, bringing Sara's hands together behind her back.

'Sara, let's go!' Roger shouted at the same time as the black hood was pulled off her head. She saw that it was Roger who had pulled it off, and then he turned quickly and floored the man next to him with a quick right hook. Sara tugged her hands free, turned around and grabbed the man behind her around the neck. She drove her knee into his diaphragm three times and then once into his face. He collapsed to the floor unconscious.

Roger frisked the men and took their guns, a Beretta 9000 and a Taurus 9mm, handing one to Sara. She looked around. They were standing in a small room of no more than six or seven square metres, with black walls, a door at one end and a window with a blind across it at the other.

'One of the booths,' Sara said.

'So this is where they sit and watch.'

Sara picked up a laminated sheet with a picture of a bound, naked girl on it. It outlined a menu of choices.

'Solo show SEK 3,000. Couple SEK 5,000. Gang bang SEK 10,000. Sadistic SEK 50,000. Brutal SEK 100,000. Snuff SEK 250,000. DIY SEK 200,000.'

A price list for assault, rape and murder.

Sara was close to throwing up.

'What do we do?'

'Wait for Anna and the cavalry to arrive,' said Roger. 'We've got no idea how many of them there are out there. Or how they're armed.'

'Can we raise this?' said Sara, going over to the covered window.

'Probably not if we don't pay.'

'Sara!' Anna's voice was just faintly audible now that Sara's earbud was down at her waist. 'Hello?!' she shouted again.

'Yes?' said Sara, putting the bud in her ear.

'Jesus, it's a relief to hear your voice. I thought something had happened.'

'All OK so far. But we could do with your help now.'

'Can't!' Anna's voice was almost panicky.

'What?'

'We can't. You're on international soil.'

'No, we're in the Frihamnen.'

'Yes, but it's some kind of customs-free zone for ships to other countries. You're in Warehouse 7, and that's international soil. We're not allowed in there!'

'For fuck's sake, two police officers are in danger! Not to mention the people who are going to be subjected to a peepshow.'

'We've called Customs, but they want assurances that the operation won't pose any danger to their staff.'

'Of course it bloody will! Everyone is armed to the teeth in this place.'

'Then they'll never go in. Can you stay out of the way until it's over?'

Sara and Roger looked around the small booth.

'Probably. If we put our small gorillas back to sleep every time they come round.'

A wild scream from the other side of the glass window interrupted them.

Sara looked Roger in the eye. She got a nod in response.

That was all it took. Roger quickly set one chair half a metre from the window, backed up a couple of metres and then ran towards the window, leapt up onto the chair and hurled his one hundred and fifty kilos straight through the blind. Smashed glass flew everywhere.

Roger was immediately on his feet on the other side, just as Sara jumped in after him.

It was a large room with black walls and a series of windows in an octagonal ring around them. Four of the windows had their blinds raised. In the centre there was a brightly lit table with straps and a bloodied body writhing in torment.

'Police!' Roger shouted.

'International area!' protested one of the men by the illuminated table.

'So what?'

Before anyone in the room had time to react to his spectacular entrance, Roger reached the two knife-wielding men by the table and punched one of them in the jaw before sweeping round and kicking the other in the temple.

Now the guards finally began to realise that something out of the ordinary was happening.

Sara saw them raise their automatic weapons and step towards Roger.

But by the time she had raised her own pistol to fire, Roger had felled both gorillas with a shot in the knee for each.

They fell, bellowing, to the floor, and Sara hurried over and tore their weapons from their hands.

She scanned the area but saw no one else.

Two down by the table, two shot on the floor, and the two they had taken out in their booth. It was entirely possible that six men might be the full complement.

Roger checked how the strapped-down man was doing.

'He'll make it,' he said. 'But it's not pretty.'

Only now did Sara's thoughts turn to the four booths that had their blinds up. The dark windows revealed nothing about who was behind them. She raised one of the automatic weapons and took aim at a window.

'Look out!' she shouted before firing straight through the glass.

The same with the next one, and the one after that, and the one after.

For each window that Sara shot to pieces, Roger jumped in and yanked the person sitting in there out. Two of the booths were empty. The peepers had fled from those. However her colleague was able to drag several surprised and frightened men out of the other two booths – they still didn't seem to entirely understand what was happening.

Sara stood guard while Roger rounded up all the conquered thugs. Then she took Ndeme's mobile and called the number he had been texting about the peepshow. The inside pocket of the man with the shaved head who had met them at Gärdet began to ring. Sara went over and took the phone. It probably contained all sorts of numbers that might come in useful.

Then Roger took over guard duty while Sara looked around the space and spoke to Anna again.

'Police officers attacked with automatic weapons,' she said. 'Who bloody cares whether this is an international area? Send in backup.'

'Sorry. Bielke's absolutely furious. You need to get out of there. And leave everyone behind.'

Sara looked at the poor man strapped to the table. He wasn't conscious, but Roger was probably right that they had intervened in the nick of time. Unfortunately, they hadn't been able to save Nadia or any of the girls whose suffering had entertained paying headcases.

The floor around the table was covered in dark stains and the air stank of a suffocating mixture of blood and semen.

Sara took a final lap of the room and found a black door between two of the windows. She opened it and found some kind of office with a big A4 calendar with notes on it about which victims and treatments the peepshow had to offer.

There was a computer on the desk, and when Sara tapped the space bar it was apparent it was password protected.

But the wallpaper showed something that shocked her deeply.

It was a selfie of several of the men they had just encountered, taken in one of the booths.

In the background, on the other side of the window, Sara was able to make out a naked woman's body strapped to the table in the peepshow – a brunette who very much resembled Jenna.

But what shook Sara to her core was the person standing between the guards grinning broadly.

Uncle Scam.

55

The blue lights pulsed across the façades and stacks of containers in the desolate corner of the port. Two of the vehicles were from the flying squad, with heavily armed police officers ready to storm in at a moment's notice. Beyond the inner circle of police cars were five ambulances and a couple of civilian cars that Bielke and Anna had arrived in.

Sara had found Jenna's body wrapped in a tarpaulin in a corridor, stabbed, beaten, bloody.

It felt as if she were dropping through a black hole. She was in free fall down a mineshaft – in slow motion.

If only she had managed to get Jenna to understand she might still have been alive, instead of lying here like a bag of rubbish waiting to be thrown out. Yet another life on Sara's conscience.

Her colleagues still didn't dare enter the warehouse building, given that it was international soil. Bielke had been stopped by the police lawyers, who had caught wind of what had happened. As a result, Sara's boss was now trying to obtain permission from someone in Customs or the company who owned the warehouse, but it seemed to be almost impossible to find anyone responsible. In the meantime, Sara and Roger had bound or shackled all the detainees inside the warehouse and then carried out the man who had been strapped down and tortured. The others didn't have life-threatening injuries.

'Stop! Desist!'

Sara recognised the man who had shouted. Conny Mårtensson, a defence attorney who often represented the most serious criminals. He emerged from his British racing green Rolls-Royce Cullinan and raised a warning hand while walking towards the police with long strides. Sara examined him at a distance. He was well over sixty, but still boasted a thick mane of hair combed back and curling down into his neck.

'I represent Stirner Shipping. This is an infringement of a customs zone. You must immediately return everybody and everything that you have removed.'

'They're hurt. There are several people inside with gunshot wounds.'

'Stirner Shipping will deal with that.'

'Not a chance. They're murder suspects.'

'Not on Swedish soil.'

'They can be convicted of murder in other countries too.'

'But you can't arrest them in there.'

'Are you protecting murderers?' Sara said, taking a threatening step closer to the lawyer.

'Sara, there's nothing we can do,' Bielke said, putting a calming hand on her shoulder.

'But he has to go to hospital,' said Sara, pointing to the tortured man. 'He's on Swedish soil and may be dying.'

'Did you carry him out of there?' said Mårtensson.

'No,' Sara lied.

'Well then,' said Bielke, signalling to a couple of paramedics, who placed the man onto a stretcher and carried him away.

'There are six wounded people in there,' Sara said to the attorney. 'Shot in self-defence. And at least one dead body. Plus several detainees.'

'The paramedics may enter to tend to the injured and I will establish whether they wish to file a police report for attempted murder.'

'Under whose laws?' said Sara. 'They weren't shot on Swedish soil.'

Mårtensson scrutinised her and apparently made up his mind that she was right, because he said no more about the matter. Conny Mårtensson never entered a battle he couldn't win.

'There are most certainly no detainees in there,' he said. 'Because there are no personnel with adequate authority here to carry out arrests.'

'Bielke,' Sara said, almost pleading.

Bielke thought for a while, but then he nodded briefly to the lawyer. Mårtensson smiled and entered through the gate leading to the warehouse, followed by the paramedics.

'Are you just going to let them go?' said Sara. 'Have you seen what they do to people in there?'

'I'll leave two cars here to watch the area. As soon as anyone comes out, we'll arrest them. This is the only exit. In the meantime, we need to talk about that artist in the photo – who clearly must have been here and witnessed one of the murders.'

'Uncle Scam,' said Sara. She had taken a photo of the computer screen and shown it to Bielke. 'If he's still in the country. The final gig was last night.'

'He's still here. His suite at the Grand Hôtel is booked for another night, and the hotel says he's there right now, checking out in the morning. So I sent a car over to pick him up.'

'Good. We've got this too.' Sara passed over the mobile she had confiscated inside the warehouse. 'One of those gorillas dropped it when he met us over at Gärdet. Definitely Swedish soil. And I think you'll find all sorts of messages on it from people who are guilty of instigating murder, or worse. "Watch" and "do yourself" are the key phrases. I promise you that Juha Kallio and Jan-Olov Åkerman will be mentioned in there.'

'Thanks,' said Bielke, taking the mobile. Either he believed Sara or he chose not to question her account.

'Now I want to talk to Uncle Scam,' she said.

56

One of the conditions to persuade the big artist to come to Stockholm had been the best hotel suite in town. Go Live had therefore booked the Princess Lilian Suite at the Grand Hôtel – three hundred and thirty square metres, including its own spa, dedicated cinema and two terraces overlooking Strömmen, at a nightly rate of ninety-five thousand kronor.

The American rapper hadn't objected to being brought in for questioning, but had requested to come in his own cars – the caravan of vehicles worth millions that Martin's company had organised for him while he was in the country. So behind a Lamborghini, a Ferrari and two Rolls-Royces was a Swedish police car containing two rather uncertain officers.

The convoy naturally had the effect of allowing all the fans staking out the hotel to see him leaving and to quickly track the cars down to the police station in Solna. They laid siege to it, awaiting what might be a final glimpse of the star before he left the country.

They thronged in the street outside the building and began to pour out onto Sundbybergsvägen too, making cars brake and honk. The police dispatched a couple of officers to direct traffic and prevent anyone being hit. At the same time, residents across the street began phoning in to complain about the racket.

A host of theories quickly spread as to what the small excursion was all about. Was Scam going to make a video with Swedish cops? Someone thought he liked to mock the pigs in every country he visited. One informed source on the *Aftonbladet* comments page declared that Scam's entourage had had a consignment of narcotics seized; they thought he was going to be held accountable for that, or that he was there to ask for the drugs back. Sara guessed this voice belonged to one of Olle's friends. There weren't many other people who knew anything about the seized drugs.

It surprised her somewhat that the rapper had agreed to come to the station, but it also made it far simpler. There was no need to arrest him, and if they wanted to hold him after questioning then he was already in their hands.

Sara hoped against her better judgement that Scam would have an alternative explanation for the photo on the computer. That it was fake, or a montage, or that he had never seen Jenna, had just stopped by the peepshow and greeted the gangsters. Rappers liked the romanticism of gangsters – wasn't that still the case? Or was Sara out of date? Above all, she hoped for Martin's sake that Scam hadn't participated in the peepshow. But also for her own. She wouldn't want anyone who had done something that awful to have visited her own home. Wouldn't want her kids to have been near to a man who had watched a woman be tortured to death.

'Hi,' said a voice, rousing Sara from her thoughts.

She looked up into an unfamiliar face.

'Hi,' she said absently, offering her hand. 'Are you a friend of Scam's?'

She hadn't seen this guy before, but he did seem to fit into Scam's posse. He was practically a copy of the rapper.

'It *is* Uncle Scam,' said Anna, who had come in with him. 'I thought you'd met?'

'This isn't Uncle Scam,' said Sara.

'What? Yes it is. Even I recognise him.'

'No, I'm telling you. Look!' Sara pulled out her mobile and showed her the photo of the wallpaper. 'This is Scam. Compare the tattoos. Look at the eyes. And the mouth.'

'What the hell . . .?' was all Anna managed to say.

'He has a lookalike. To trick his fans.' And then memory hit her. 'For Christ's sake, he's at another hotel!'

'Which one?'

'I don't know!'

'What about him?' said Anna, pointing to the fake Scam.

'Where's the real Scam staying?'

'I'm the real Scam.'

'No. Come on, tell us.'

The lookalike gave up at once. He probably thought he'd done his bit.

'I wouldn't know. Some hotel.'

'Which?'

The doppelganger shrugged. Then he smiled.

'So did you guys catch the show yesterday?'

'What?'

'Forget about him,' said Sara, pulling out her phone. 'Martin must know.'

It rang ten times. There was no answer. She sent a text to say she needed to reach him right away, but she didn't dare pin her hopes on that.

'Olle.'

She called her son. He wasn't answering either.

'Can you call Ebba?' she said to Anna, showing her daughter's number. 'I don't think she'll answer if I call.'

'Didn't you want to talk?' said the lookalike, as if the masquerade was still going on.

'Shut up!' Sara shouted. 'And sit down!'

Scam 2 looked uncertain but took a seat.

'Hi, this is Anna, your mother's colleague. Sara needs to speak to you – it's important. Please don't hang up,' Anna said, passing over her phone.

'Hello, Olle's not picking up when I call. I think he's angry at me. And your father isn't answering either. We need to know which hotel Scam is staying at. I don't mean the Grand Hôtel, where he's pretending to stay, but where he's actually been staying. Call Olle

357

and ask him if he knows. But don't say that it's me who wants to know. Say it's you. Tell him you want to send flowers or something.'

Ebba muttered something indistinct before hanging up, and Sara could only hope for the best. The three minutes that elapsed before her daughter called back felt like an hour.

'He's at home,' she said abruptly.

'What do you mean at home? He's already gone?'

'No, at Home. You know, the luxury hotel in Lärkstan called *Home*. It's super-exclusive. He's booked out the hotel in order to be left alone, apparently. It's at 2 Sköldungagatan.'

'OK. Thanks Ebba!'

Her daughter hung up without replying.

'OK, Lärkstan,' said Sara, looking at Anna. She quickly pulled up the website for the hotel and found their phone number.

'Hello, this is Sara Nowak from the Västerort police. We've got an important message for a guest staying with you – Cornelius Crane Jr. He is staying there, isn't he?'

'I'm afraid it's our policy not to answer any questions about our guests.'

'I'm calling from the police – didn't you hear?'

'Anyone could say that.'

'Call the police then. Call the switchboard and ask for Sara Nowak in Solna and they'll put you through.'

'I'm afraid we still can't answer any questions about our guests. It would be a violation of their privacy.'

'But it's important – it's about a watch stolen during the gig at the Friends Arena. It's a Rolex worth half a million kronor. We think we've found it, but he needs to identify it. Personally. He'll be very angry with you if he doesn't get the chance to do so. He might even sue.'

Those words did the trick. The girl on the line took a deep breath.

'OK. I can't say anything about who is staying at the hotel, but we only have one guest at present. Plus entourage.'

'That's him!'

'And they're about to check out.'

'No!'

'Yes. They're due to fly home. They were meant to be staying another night, but there was a change of plan.'

'Get him to stay there!' Sara said, gesticulating to Anna to come with her.

'We can't do that.'

'You have to. Tell him there's something up with his passport or payment or something. Delay him by half an hour.'

'That's impossible. But it'll probably take ten minutes before we're done. I can let him know you called.'

'No! Don't say anything! We're on the way!'

57

The Home hotel was a palatial building in the most secluded corner of the Östermalm district. It was a brick-built fortress with turrets and towers and a small courtyard behind a wall. When the neighbourhood had been built, the plan had been to impress and Lärkstan was now full of embassies that appreciated the splendid buildings and wide, empty streets. It was no coincidence that Opus Dei had established their Swedish headquarters here behind railings and tall walls. In this corner of town, discretion was a point of honour.

Nine minutes and forty-five seconds after ending her call, Sara screeched to a halt in front of the hotel. Darkness had begun to descend on the city and an almost grotesque limousine – a stretch Hummer of the kind owned by pornographers – was waiting outside the entrance. The doors of the luxury hotel opened and Uncle Scam emerged wearing big black sunglasses and flanked by two enormous bodyguards. They were well over one hundred and fifty kilos each, Sara thought to herself when she caught sight of the men. But they were more fat than muscle – they only looked dangerous. Or so she hoped.

Sara and Anna got out of the car and approached the trio.

'Uncle Scam,' said Sara, showing her police ID. 'Police. We'd like to talk to you.'

'No,' said one of the bodyguards, stepping in front of Scam to ward Sara off.

'Yes,' said Sara, continuing to deploy her best schoolgirl English. 'We believe you're a witness to a murder. We need you to come with us. We don't want to cause a scene.'

'No,' the bodyguard said again, shoving Sara aside with his gigantic hand.

'He assaulted a police officer,' Sara said to Anna, indicating that they could now arrest the men. Using her left hand, she produced handcuffs while with her right she grabbed the wrist of the man who had pushed her. The bodyguard stopped and threw Sara aside with such force that she hit the floor.

She lunged for his feet, wrapped her arms around his shins and wrapped her own legs around his upper body.

With his legs locked, she was easily able to pull him over and he hit the ground with a loud thud, as if an elephant had fallen off the roof of a garden shed.

Sara threw herself quickly onto him and applied the handcuffs to one of his hands but then he recovered and pushed her off.

The other bodyguard made as if to intervene, but Anna pulled out her pistol and took aim.

'Don't,' was all she said. And he stopped.

Sara jumped onto the back of her opponent, put her arm around his throat and forced him back down to the ground. With his throat in the crook of her arm, she squeezed as hard as she could, while applying pressure with her other arm at the same time.

'Police brutality!' someone shouted, and Sara glanced to the side, spreading her legs as wide as she could to ensure the man couldn't topple her. The person shouting was one of a small group of young lads on the pavement across the street, all with their mobiles pulled out.

'Get lost!' Sara shouted, but they ignored her. Fucking brats. And this fucking colossus was still standing his ground.

'OK, OK, OK,' the bodyguard managed to gurgle at last, tapping Sara on the arm. He was tapping out. The sign that he gave up. Sara loosened her grip and dragged his hands together so that she could attach the handcuffs to his other hand.

'What the fuck is your problem?' was all Scam had to say.

'I'm gonna take your gun,' Anna said to the other bodyguard, raising her gun but keeping it at a safe distance from him while reaching with her other arm.

'It's just a toy,' the bodyguard said, opening his jacket. 'You guys have shitty gun laws.'

Anna fished the pistol out of his waistband and glanced at it quickly.

'Airsoft gun,' she said to Sara, pocketing it.

Then they handcuffed the other bodyguard and Scam, put all three in the back seat of Anna's car and set off for Solna. But when they called Bielke, he was of an entirely different opinion.

'Don't bring him here,' her boss said on the phone. 'He's got several hundred fans outside here. There'll be a riot.'

'But they already think he's there.'

'Yes, we'll have to let the lookalike go. Otherwise they'll storm the building. There's already a bloody clip of us beating up his bodyguards online.'

'Are you kidding? It only happened a couple of minutes ago.'

'Yes, isn't it special what you can achieve with a mobile phone these days?'

So instead, they drove as fast as they could to the Kronoberg remand prison, where the three detainees would be assigned a cell each along with a prison uniform. The only question was whether they had clothes in big enough sizes for the bodyguards, Sara thought to herself.

While the three men were being booked in, Anna told her that the internet was awash with the news that Scam had been hiding at a different hotel, that he had been arrested by the police and that he had been taken to Kronoberg. *Aftonbladet* were particularly on the ball and wrote about both the dramatic arrest and about the 'rapper's secret luxury hotel' where he had been hiding out from his fans.

'Lucky there's a back exit in this place,' said Sara, thinking about all the furious fans who were soon going to hate them. Including her own son.

Sara's mobile began to buzz hysterically. She looked at the display to see that it was Westin from *Aftonbladet*, then Tillberg from

TV4. When she didn't answer, the text messages began to arrive in a deluge.

Adnan Westin here. Call me!!!
Why have you arrested Uncle Scam? Drugs?
Hi, this is Tillberg from TV4. What happened at the Free Port last night?
So you don't deny that it's drugs?
Just a couple of quick questions, OK?
Westin again. PLS ring me!!
We'll just say it's drugs?

Then Bielke called again.

'Don't be angry – but they're gone.'

'Who?'

'Everyone in Warehouse 7. When the company finally agreed to let us in, it was completely empty. We found the booths you mentioned, and the room with all the spotlights. But no bodies, no weapons, no blood. Well, nothing visible. I guess they've only rinsed the floor. We can't carry out a proper investigation – Conny Mårtensson straight up refused that.'

'But how did they get away? Weren't you going to leave two cars watching the gates?'

'I had four cars there! And dogs. And no one left the area through the gates. However, there was a ship that just sailed.'

'And you let it go? Surely it's Swedish *waters* in Frihamnen?'

'We boarded and searched the vessel before it departed, but there was no one there. Just the Filipino crew. And none of the people you saw were Filipinos, were they?'

'No.'

'But the ship was loading containers until the last minute. From the Stirner Shipping area of the dock.'

'Didn't you check them out?'

'Weren't allowed to. They all had customs seals on them. International treaties, trade deals, and so on. We were up against some bloody powerful interests.'

'So they loaded everyone into a container and left?'

'That's the only possible explanation. Unless you and Roger dreamt it all, that is.'

Sara swore out loud. Repeatedly.

'That means Uncle Scam is the only thing we have to go on. Cornelius Crane Jr from the Upper East Side.'

'And you're not likely to get much out of him.'

'Thanks for your vote of confidence,' said Sara, hanging up.

'Who's the bloke you just brought in?' The remand officer was looking at Sara and Anna in bafflement. 'The whole street's full of people shouting and screaming and with streamers and shit. And the TV and press are here.'

'Just one of the biggest artists in the world,' said Anna.

'Shit,' said the guard. 'Like Carola?'

'Yes, like her,' said Anna.

'OK, well they're changed and ready to go.' The remand officer's statement meant the three detainees had been searched, provided with uniforms and taken to their respective cells.

Anna asked the guard to escort Scam to the interview room where they would be waiting for him.

Just as they sat down, Sara's mobile rang. When she pulled it out to put it on airplane mode, she saw Hedin's name on the screen, as well as several missed calls from her.

'I can't talk right now,' said Sara.

'I've found a picture you have to see,' said Hedin.

'Of what?'

'I can't say on the phone.'

'I'll be there as soon as possible.'

'OK. But be careful. But say nothing to anybody. It's ... sensational. Lethal. Trust no one. No one, do you hear? Absolutely no one.'

'OK. I'll be careful.'

Sara ended the call just as the American superstar was led in.

'Aren't you Martin's wife?' was the first thing Scam said, apparently forgetting to sound like he was from the Bronx. Or perhaps he thought he'd receive better treatment behind bars with his dulcet Upper East Side tones. Sara didn't answer.

'Is he here too?' said Scam looking around, despite the fact that he was inside a cramped interview room.

'No.'

'Then send him my best. And thank him for yesterday.'

They didn't get any further than that. Uncle Scam smiled kindly and denied having been to any peepshow the night before, denied in the strongest of terms that he had seen anyone hurt or killed. And he cited Martin, who would be able to confirm that he had been in the club. He said that if they had no evidence they had to release him. The bodyguards had attacked Sara and Anna, so they were welcome to hang onto them. He hated men who harmed women.

Sara took out her mobile and showed him the picture of the wallpaper from the computer.

'That's you standing next to some of the murderers. And the girl in the background is dead now. Murdered.'

'She wasn't dead when that picture was taken. What happened to her afterwards isn't my responsibility. People take selfies with me all the time. Obviously some of them are bad guys. Gangsters love me.'

'You were at the murder scene. At the peepshow. Warehouse 7.'

'Nope. Just a night club. Martin probably knows the name. Maybe that girl went with the others to a peepshow later on.'

'We're getting nowhere,' Anna remarked in Swedish to ensure he couldn't understand.

Sara looked at the photo on her mobile and thought for a moment. Then she glanced at Scam's prison uniform.

'If you have any more questions then I want a lawyer. But you really should let me go now. No hard feelings. You're just doing your job.'

'Wait,' said Sara.

'Where are you going?' she heard as the door closed behind her.

She found the guards and asked them to show her Scam's possessions.

Of course. His mobile. An iPhone 12 Pro.

'You have to sign for that,' protested the officer when Sara took the phone.

'In a second,' she said, jogging back to the interview room with Scam's phone. In the meantime, she checked to see whether it was locked. It was.

She opened the door to the interview room, stepped over to Scam and held the mobile in front of his face. Then she hurried out again before the rapper was able to say more than, 'Hey!'

The facial recognition had worked and she was into the phone.

She stopped in the corridor and examined the mobile. There were messages to and from Martin and a series of girls. And to his mother and father, so it seemed. Mum was proud of her successful son, Dad was more distanced.

And then the photos.

The most recent ones were from the hotel, and before that the camera seemed to have been used to snap all sorts of junk food and fizzy drinks.

But the pictures before that were from the peepshow.

Photos and videos.

Of Jenna lying strapped to the table and being abused and raped by three men. It appeared to have been filmed from inside one of the booths.

So he *had* been there. And they could prove it.

Sara sent all the photos and videos to her own phone.

She continued to scroll through these disgusting things until she came across one of the earliest photos from the peepshow. Before it had begun.

When payment had taken place.

In that photo there was a drunken man smirking as he held up his black American Express Centurion to one of the peepshow guards.

It was obviously the man footing the bill.

For the murder of Jenna.

And it wasn't Uncle Scam.

It was her husband, Martin.

58

The bedroom stank of vomit, the drawn curtains shut out all daylight and all the lights were turned off.

Sara went to the bed, pulled the duvet off Martin, who was curled up underneath it, and began pummelling him. Everywhere she could get at him. As hard as she could. He said nothing. He just let her hit him, and wailed like a wounded animal.

'What have you done?!' Sara shouted. 'You killed her!'

'I didn't know!'

He looked up at her. In the light cast from the doorway she saw that his eyes were red-rimmed with tears.

'It was you who paid,' she said.

'I . . . I thought it was for a regular sex show.'

'Why didn't you stop them? Why didn't you call the police? Why didn't you say anything when you got home?!'

'I felt so terrible. Do you have any idea how awful it was?'

'That you killed her? Yes. And don't feel sorry for yourself. Of all the disgusting men who buy sex that I've ever met over the years, you're the most disgusting of all! Waving your fucking black Amex around and murdering a poor girl just to turn yourself on!'

'I didn't know. I promise. I had no idea,' her husband whimpered.

'Why didn't you stop it then?'

'They had weapons. Automatic weapons. And we were on international soil so I couldn't call the police.'

'But when you left?' Sara shouted in his face.

'I couldn't grass on our biggest star. Do you have any idea how much money he brings in for us? Billions. And it still wouldn't have saved the girl's life.'

'I don't want to hear your apologies! You're going to tell us everything. Every single detail. And then you'll take your punishment. I'll make sure you never see your children again.'

'I feel so fucking awful. I just sat there while someone was being tortured like that. And the others just kept pushing. Demanding more. I don't know how I'm going to live with it,' Martin said, crying so hard his face was covered in tears and snot.

'And how the fuck do you think this is going to affect Olle? That his father and his idol think it's OK to pay to watch a woman be tortured to death? What if it had been Ebba lying there?!'

'You can't tell him! Not a word to the kids. I'll take my punishment, but tell them . . . tell them I'm away. Or that I'm in prison for fraudulent accounting or something. They shouldn't have to suffer for what I've done. They shouldn't have to be stigmatised as the children of a swine.'

'Where did you find out about the peepshow?' Sara said, pacing back and forth across the bedroom. She was afraid of what she might do if she stopped and really thought about everything that was happening. What she might do to her husband.

'I didn't know that was what happened. I'd just heard it was some kind of sex show, for people who liked the really rough videos online – but you could watch live. And control the action.'

'And you thought that sounded good?'

'I heard that Scam liked that kind of thing. But I had no idea what was going to happen. And then Scam wanted to see more, wanted to go all the way.' He fell silent and looked up at Sara. 'What was her name?'

'Who?'

'The girl. Wh-who . . . died.'

'Jenna. That wasn't her real name, but in this bloody country she was called Jenna.'

59

'Eva Hedin.'

  'Otto Rau.'

  'Who?'

  'Don't try that. But Faust is fine, if you prefer.'

  'Why are you calling?'

  'I gather you're looking for me.'

  'We just had a few questions.'

  'About Jürgen Stiller?'

  'Yes.'

  'You can meet me.'

  'I'm afraid that's not possible. I'm not in town.'

  'You most certainly are.'

  'No, I'm not.'

  'Oh yes you are. I can see you through the kitchen window.'

60

Despite the fact that it was late in the evening, the street outside the Kronoberg remand prison – Bergsgatan – was filled with hundreds of young people. Many of them had home-made streamers and signs. 'Free Scam', 'ACAB', 'Scam is innocent'. Given the tangible risk that someone might recognise Sara from the video showing Scam's arrest, she and Martin entered from Kungsholmsgatan instead.

Martin's mobile had started to ring while they were in the taxi – it was head office in the USA – but Sara told him to turn it off. Sara's mobile continued to buzz almost incessantly with calls from reporters, so she set it to refuse all calls except those closest to her – her family and her colleagues.

Anna met them in the mint-green fluorescent-lit corridor and told them that the American embassy had been in touch with the police top brass, that Scam's mother – the lawyer – was threatening to sue, and that the arrest was big news in the USA and the rest of the world. It had emerged that the arrest related to a conspiracy to murder. How the journalists had found that out when not even Sara or Anna knew what the charges would be was unclear. Fans in many countries were urging the boycott of everything Swedish: Volvo, Spotify and misidentified Swiss cuckoo clocks.

Conny Mårtensson was now Scam's Swedish attorney and had explained that the rapper denied all accusations. He had never been in Frihamnen, and had definitely not been to any peepshow. Furthermore, he denied having any images or films of illegal acts in his possession. Mårtensson pointed out that it was illegal to search Scam's mobile without the owner's consent. Nothing found in such circumstances could be used as evidence against him. On the other hand, the misappropriation would be reported.

Sara asked Martin to go into an interview room and wait, and then she had to tell Anna that Martin had been with Scam at the peepshow and was there to be questioned. Her friend had as much difficulty as Sara had believing it was true. Sara saw the slightly indulgent goodwill that Anna had always felt towards Martin transition into pure disgust.

'Is there *no one* who can be trusted?' said Anna, looking towards the room where Martin was waiting. Then she turned to Sara and her anger was replaced with sympathy. 'Sweetheart, how do you feel? It must be completely fucking awful.'

'It is.'

Anna hugged Sara.

'*I* feel guilty,' said Sara. 'My husband, my fault.'

'That's not true.'

'I don't know. I really don't know.'

'Is there anything I can do for you?' said Anna.

'Yes. Don't terminate this friendship. I need someone on my side in all this.'

'You've got it. Always.'

'And can you find someone to question him? It probably shouldn't be done by either of us.'

While Anna went to call for assistance from impartial colleagues, Axel Bielke turned up. For once, he looked almost impressed.

'This is completely insane,' he said. 'I've never experienced anything like it. There must be at least a thousand people out there. How are we going to keep them calm if we keep this guy on remand?'

'Apparently it's world news,' said Sara.

'What do we actually have on him?'

Sara pulled out her mobile and showed her boss the picture from the computer wallpaper and Scam's own photos and videos of Jenna's murder. Bielke grimaced.

'And these videos are from . . . ?'

'His mobile. Filmed by him.'

'Surely these aren't the videos that Mårtensson says we acquired illegally?'

'Of course he says that.'

'And how did we acquire them?'

'We're allowed to check the phones of suspects.'

'The phones of people formally in custody. And the decision to hold them in custody has to be based on sufficient evidence. He hasn't been formally remanded yet, so I hope he handed over the phone of his own volition?'

Bielke's words sank in for Sara. She knew very well what the rules were, but in her eyes the outcome came ahead of following the letter of the law. It was only people like Conny Mårtensson who liked the rules because they could exploit minor, formal errors or technicalities in order to free criminals.

'If I hadn't checked his mobile then we wouldn't have known he had the videos. That would have meant we had no evidence.'

'And by checking his mobile, you've ensured that we can't use the videos,' Bielke said with a deep sigh.

'What about the photo of the computer screen? You can see he's in the place, and Jenna is in the background.'

'You took that photo while on international soil where you had no right to be. Don't tell anyone you have it, or any photos from his mobile, or we'll be finished. *We'll* end up in prison.'

'But Martin can testify. He was there. He saw everything!'

Sara pointed to the figure sitting and waiting in the interview room.

'Martin?' said Bielke.

'Yes, my husband.'

'And he was with Scam at the peepshow?'

'Yes.'

'Then surely he's an accessory? Right?'

'Yes,' Sara said, indicating clearly that she wasn't interested in any further discussion.

Bielke looked at her, thought for a while and then nodded.

'Then I'd say it all hinges on his testimony.' He was silent for a moment and then he made a decision. 'We won't release Uncle Scam. I'll request that he's kept in custody on the grounds of Martin's witness testimony – not because of any photos or videos. Is he Martin Nowak?'

'Martin Titus. Anna has called to get someone impartial down here to question him.'

'Good.' Bielke paused and looked at Sara. 'How are things going with that other business? The priest in Småland?'

'Östergötland.'

'Have you found Rau?'

Sara was startled.

'What do you know about Rau?'

'That he's some former terrorist, right? With a new identity.'

'Who told you that?' But there was only one person. 'Anna?'

'It doesn't matter.'

'Yes, it does bloody well matter – a lot! Anna!'

Sara turned and went over to her colleague, who was talking on her mobile.

'Did you tell Bielke about Rau?!'

'Wait a minute,' said Anna into the phone before turning to Sara. 'I can explain. Bielke just wanted me to keep an eye on you . . .'

'So you did? You spied on me?!'

'Not spied. I was just keeping an eye so that . . .'

'Go to hell!' said Sara, turning on her heel.

'Sara!' Bielke shouted after her, but she wasn't listening. She headed into the street, where she pushed through the crowd of hip-hop fans who were putting on a show of support for their perverted idol. Evidently someone recognised her because they shouted: 'Fucking pig! Let Scam go!' but Sara didn't notice. Not now.

What was going on?

Bielke knew all about Rau.

Her best friend had been spying on her.

On behalf of their boss.

Why the hell had she done that?

61

Sara walked all the way home. She passed through a late summer Stockholm that had long ago switched from early Friday evening drinks into loud drunkenness, from expectations and planning to the actual implementation. Now they were all mid-battle, which would end in a couple of hours in success or defeat, sex or drunk food.

Anna called and texted, but Sara didn't answer.

On Tegelbacken, she sat down on one of the benches overlooking Riddarfjärden. She just sat there, staring out towards the white boats and the shoreline at Södermälarstrand on the other side. And while the inhabitants of the capital pursued happiness in every way they could, Sara did what she could to master the anger and frustration that she felt. The shocks and betrayals were almost impossible to handle. She wanted to smash something to pieces. Or someone.

What was she supposed to do now? Where was she meant to go? What would her life be like? She had no idea.

Everything was just empty. Black.

And it hurt.

After an hour, she had calmed down enough that she was able to pick up the phone when Bielke called.

But she soon wished she hadn't.

She wished she'd never had to hear what he had called to tell her.

The good news was that they had found out the names of the people who had ordered the murders of Kallio and Åkerman from the mobile that Sara had taken. A motorbike gang that had lent money in the case of Kallio, and the neighbour involved in the planning dispute in the case of Åkerman. They couldn't use the messages from the mobile, but they could now direct their efforts towards the guilty parties.

The bad news was that Martin had spoken to his bosses while waiting to be questioned.

And then he had denied everything that Sara had related.

Pale and grim-faced, he had confirmed Uncle Scam's version of events, and denied that any of them had been to a peepshow or even in the vicinity of Frihamnen.

This meant they had no usable evidence whatsoever against Uncle Scam. Which meant that Bielke had decided they had to release him.

Less than an hour later, Uncle Scam's plane had taken off, and it was about to leave Swedish airspace for good.

Martin had also called, but Sara hadn't replied. Instead she texted.

Don't come home. I don't want to see you.

Martin tried to explain in a reply.

I couldn't testify against Scam. My contract says I can't finan-
    cially harm the company.
No matter what you do, don't come home.
Sara, forgive me.
No.

A beautiful white ship with a party taking place on board glided past on its way to the Västerbron bridge and Lake Mälaren, accompanied by the sound of music and happy voices. With Haddaway's 'What is love' in her ears, Sara decided not to let Uncle Scam get away with it.

She Googled 'gossip magazine USA' and found the *National Enquirer*, which was described as a publication eager to cause scandal. She found their email address and used one of the anonymous email accounts she used for work to send all the photos and videos she'd taken from Uncle Scam's mobile. She just hoped they were interested.

Then she sat there and let the darkness envelop her. Out on Riddarfjärden there was music and shouting from a small motorboat with an illuminated cabin. Infatuated couples strolled past, some young people had settled down on the steps leading down to the water beneath City Hall and the lights of Södermalm were reflected in the dark waters of Riddarfjärden. Behind her, tourists passed by, engaged in unobtrusive conversation in foreign languages. There was the sound of electric scooters whooshing past, the waves lapping against the quayside, church bells striking one in the distance.

Sara realised that it would be easy to trace the email she had just sent if the publication were so inclined. And if they did, then she might regret her actions. But she wouldn't have been able to live with herself if she hadn't done something.

Finally, she got up and carried on homeward. She crossed the Vasabron bridge to Stora Nygatan. There were even more people in all the outdoor bars, tourists and Stockholm natives. The atmosphere here was calmer than in the city centre; here, there were people who had nothing better to do than sit and enjoy their beers, Sara thought, feeling almost angry at all the people who didn't have to go through what she was suffering.

Standing in front of the door that led into her building was a Maserati parked with two wheels on the pavement. It was Eric's – Sara recognised the registration. Her father-in-law had presumably parked with such nonchalance in protest against the city's parking wardens. A parking ticket would have no material impact on his wallet. But what was he doing here? Had Martin asked him to mediate? Or perhaps he had driven Olle home again? In the case of the former, he had no chance, while in the case of the latter she would have to thank him profusely.

When she emerged from the lift and inserted the key into the front door, she noticed that it wasn't locked. For a brief moment she thought of Rau. And Kremp.

She pulled her pistol from her holster and prepared to shoot.

But as soon as she opened it, she heard that it was Ebba.

She put away her weapon and relaxed.

Happy voices and laughter from the kitchen, where she found Ebba and two of her friends with their arms filled with wine bottles, Martin's expensive wines. But it served him right, so Sara didn't protest at a group of tipsy nineteen-year-olds drinking three thousand kronor bottles of wine when they would have been just as happy with the bargain basement alternative.

'Olle's staying at mine,' Ebba said when she saw her mother. 'He hates you for putting Scam away.'

'Isn't he any happier now that they've let the swine go?'

'Don't think so. Where's Dad?'

'In a hotel. Or with some friend. I don't know. And I don't care.'

'What is it now? Surely he hasn't done anything to you.'

'You don't know anything about that. And you're not going to either.'

'My God, why are you always so angry? You've got no right to be angry all the time.'

'Shut your gob. You have no idea.'

Ebba stared at her mother.

'God, you're a mess. You're going to be so lonely.'

'I already am.'

'Come on, let's go,' Ebba said to her friends.

'Are you going back to yours?' said Sara. 'Olle won't be able to sleep.'

'No. Picnic out on Djurgården,' Ebba said, dangling a car key in front of Sara's eyes. Eric's Maserati.

'Is your grandfather here?'

'No. I've borrowed the car.'

'You don't have a driver's licence. And you're intoxicated.'

'One glass.'

'That's enough. And like I said, you haven't got a licence.'

'I will soon. And I *can* drive. Better than you.'

Sara grabbed the car key and yanked it from Ebba's hand.

'Forget about it.'

'Stop it! Give me the key. It was me who borrowed the car from Granddad. I'm responsible for it.'

'Yes, I saw that. Parked on the pavement. Nice job,' Sara said brusquely.

'We're leaving right away.'

'Not in that car.'

Ebba stared at her mother with fire in her eyes. She was breathing heavily but she said nothing. After a few seconds, she turned on her heel and left, carrying her four bottles in a firm grip.

'Come on,' she said to her friends. 'We'll take a limo instead.'

'Bye,' said one of them to Sara, dropping a curtsy. 'Thanks for the wine.'

'Have a nice weekend,' said the other to her, smiling politely.

At least they had manners.

Sara tossed the car key onto the kitchen table. She didn't feel up to re-parking the car right now. Eric could afford the parking tickets.

She went and threw herself onto the sofa in the living room.

And then she just lay there. All alone in the huge apartment.

Ebba was on a binge, angry with her mother. Olle was at Ebba's, angry with his mother. Martin had been banished to some hotel or anywhere but home because she was raging at him. She refused to speak to her best friend.

She was alone.

She had pushed away everyone around her.

Why did she do that?

But Martin had actually pushed himself away. He had killed their marriage in the most awful way Sara could imagine. He hadn't done a thing to save Jenna, and then he had lied under questioning. For financial gain. Because his bosses had told him to.

If she had known that Martin would do this, was even capable of doing something like that, she would never have married him, would never have got together with him, would never even have spoken to him.

Right?

He had been the most popular boy in school. And perhaps he would have been even more popular if everyone had known how successful he would be. There were probably a lot of people who straight up didn't care about a single girl from Romania, people who would have thought her life was worth very little compared with the well-being of Uncle Scam, one of the most famous artists in the world. And Sara had long ago realised that much of the love she felt for Martin had probably emerged from the fact that he had been the most desirable, fêted guy in school. And then in sixth form too – the sixth form that Sara had never got to go to, because Jane had fled Bromma with Sara to get away from Stellan and his glances at his own daughter.

No, she had to convince herself that she would never have picked him if she had known. She didn't want to be an accessory. Couldn't doubt herself.

But she wondered what it said about her that she was married to a man who could do something like that.

The distant hum of the busy capital city disrupted the peaceful silence. She didn't want to turn on the TV, didn't want to listen to music. Music always amplified the emotional state she was in, and the feelings she was grappling with right now were most definitely not ones she wished to intensify. So she didn't drink wine either. And she had never liked computer games.

So what was she supposed to do?

Of course. Hedin had wanted something. And she was hardly likely to be out on a Friday night binge, so Sara could call her. But the academic didn't pick up.

Well, it would have to be in the morning.

Instead, Sara sat quite still while the events of the last few days replayed in her mind's eye without her making any effort whatsoever to analyse or understand them. All she did was watch the inner images without reflecting on them. The bodies at Ekerö, Ebba's move, Martin's party, Nadia's beaten face, poor murdered Jenna, Uncle Scam, Tore Thörnell, the peepshow. But of all the dramatic things that had happened, it was something decidedly low-key that lingered in her mind – the image of a young, humiliated Eva Hedin in the TV studio. Sara would have liked to ask Hedin how it had felt, and whether she still carried it with her today, but she was afraid that it was far too private a question for the reserved former professor.

After a period of silent thought processing, Sara switched on the TV and went to the SVT Play app to search for one of Stellan Broman's old shows in the archives – *Tivoli* from the sixties. She slowly slumped deeper into the sofa while she watched Stellan via the medium of grainy black-and-white television, prancing about in his suit with his pomaded hair as he perpetuated daft pranks and talked to famous and non-famous guests. All before an audience that laughed at everything the presenter said.

The sight of Stellan reminded Sara that there was actually some-one she hadn't pushed away. Or rather, she had tried to push her away for many years, but she had still always been there for her. Sara rang her mother without paying any heed to the fact that it was the middle of the night.

'Yes?' If Jane had been asleep then she hid it well.

'Eva Hedin wanted revenge on Stellan. Just like us. That was why she unmasked him as a spy. She was humiliated on his show.'

Hedin would have to forgive her – Sara had to share it all with someone. Her mother, of all people, would understand Hedin. And a quiet late summer's night like this felt like a free zone, an exception from reality in which no ordinary rules applied. In the still of the night, it was as if everything were said in confidence and nothing would be remembered.

'I know,' said Jane. Then she took a couple of heavy, audible breaths, as if she were apologising in advance for something she felt obliged to do. 'That was why they used her. Because it was personal.'

Sara sat up on the sofa.

'What do you mean "used"? Which "they"?'

'Lotta. And someone else. They got me to pass the information to Säpo, the stuff Hedin later found in their archives – loads of papers that reinforced suspicions against Stellan.'

'*You* framed him?'

'I told Säpo about him. As his former housekeeper, I was credible. Just like that spy Wennerström. It was easy to believe I had seen things. Sometimes servants are useful.'

'But hang on? What are you saying? And why would Lotta frame her father?'

'When the Berlin Wall fell, lots of archives were opened up, and there was information to suggest there was a spy at their address. I assume it was Lotta and that she wanted to protect herself.'

'And you helped her to do that?' Sara could scarcely credit what her mother was telling her.

'Not willingly. I was eager to get my own back on Stellan, but not like that.'

'Then why did you do it?'

'My goodness, you ask a lot of questions. Why do you have to know everything? This was a long time ago. More than thirty years ago.'

'Mum, come on. Surely you understand that I need to know! Why did you do it?'

'Well, why do you think? Because they forced me,' Jane replied.

'Which *they*?'

'Lotta and someone else. I don't know who. Someone with a gun.'

'Someone you couldn't see? How do you know he had a gun?'

'Lotta came round once when you weren't at home, just after the Wall fell.'

'In Vällingby?' Sara had had no idea that Lotta had ever visited.

'Yes. She told me to hand over papers to the Security Service and tell them I had seen Stellan talking lots to his gardener and other people. She showed me pictures of the people I was supposed to say I recognised if Säpo asked.'

'And you did that?'

'Yes.'

'But how did she force you?' Thoughts were spinning around Sara's head. 'Did she just claim they had a gun?'

Jane strung out her answer – she seemed to be thinking about how to respond.

'She didn't threaten me,' she said at last. 'It was you. Lotta asked where you usually sat at the kitchen table, and when I pointed to your chair, a bullet came through the window and hit the chair. Someone was sitting up on a roof with a rifle.'

Sara was silent. She could picture the whole scenario, and no matter how unrealistic it sounded, she realised it was completely true. She knew enough about Lotta to know that.

'There was only one thing to be done,' her mother said. 'Obey her.'

A gunshot into her home. Jane's account opened up very fresh wounds inside Sara.

Yet another old memory cropped up and shook her.

'The bird,' she said, already knowing the answer. 'Was that the time you said a bird flew into the window?'

Jane sighed.

'It wasn't a bird.'

Of course it wasn't. But Jane had kept quiet about it, as always. She had protected Sara.

'And you don't know who took the shot?'

'No. I just did as Lotta told me and then I had her off my back. It didn't matter to me that Stellan fell under suspicion.'

Sara couldn't tell Jane that the same thing had happened to her. She simply couldn't. She had brought that danger on herself. But it had happened to her mother and she was completely blameless. There was a huge difference. But a well-taken shot through the windows of both their homes was surely no coincidence? Surely? Was it the same shooter?

'Sara,' said Jane, and something in her voice made Sara pay attention.

'Yes?'

'The thing that happened before. In June. Was that my fault? Was it because I never told you about this?'

'What? No.'

'But if you had known that it wasn't Stellan who was the spy . . .'

The alternative made Sara's head spin. What if none of what had happened had needed to happen? But that would have led to far worse outcomes, she realised.

'It was lucky,' she said to Jane. 'If I had known that Stellan wasn't a spy, I might not have got involved. And then something terrible would have happened.'

'But it did. Look what your face looks like.'

'Something much worse, Mum. Believe me. The fact that you hadn't told me actually saved a lot of lives.' That was how Sara understood it, but it was a lot for her to digest on top of everything else. 'Get yourself to bed – we'll talk more about this another time. Goodnight.'

'Goodnight.'

'And Mum?'

'Yes?'

'I love you.'

'You don't have to.'

And with those words, Jane hung up.

Sara lay for a long time staring at the stucco on the ceiling, avoiding thinking. Memories forced their way through, seeking attention, but she pushed them aside. She also kept the mental images of everything her mother had told her in check. She focused on the ceiling instead and realised that she had never before spared a single glance for the room's upper limits. She saw that the ornamentation on the ceiling extended beyond ribbons and flowers – there were lions and dragons too. It was very ambitious stucco. It wasn't the done thing any longer.

The doorbell rang. Sara sat up but hesitated.

Was it Martin trying to come home? Olle and Ebba had keys and would just have walked in, but Martin would almost certainly have rung the bell at this stage. Might it be Jane who had decided to come over and see her daughter? No, Sara thought. She wouldn't have made it here that quickly.

Was it Rau? Who else would be ringing the doorbell after two o'clock in the small hours of Saturday?

But would a murderer really ring the bell?

Well, perhaps they might, simply because it was unexpected.

If he had been watching the apartment then he knew that Sara was at home on her own.

She got up, and fetched her service weapon. Then she opened the door, concealing the pistol behind her back.

It was Bielke.

Sara noted that he had his hand behind his back too.

'Sorry to disturb you in the middle of the night. But I saw that the light was on. Are you alone?'

Sara's grasp on the butt of the pistol tightened.

'Yes.'

'I wanted to apologise,' Bielke said, bringing out the hand that he had been keeping behind his back.

386

He handed over a bunch of roses. Red roses.

'For spying on you,' he said. 'It wasn't my intention to distrust you. But I asked Anna to keep an eye on you and report back to me. That was my condition when I granted your request for a transfer to us.'

'Why?'

'I was worried about you. After that spy saga and everything that happened, there weren't many people who were willing to take you on. They thought you should be signed off sick for a while or even that you should go completely. But I know that it's sometimes best to get back to work again. And I thought that might be the case for you.'

'Come in,' Sara said, carefully putting down the pistol on the hall table. Then she quickly put a hat over it.

'Would you like a glass of wine?' she said, accepting the flowers.

When had she last received flowers? And from her boss?

And she had thought someone wanted to murder her . . .

Sara showed Bielke into the living room. He stopped on the threshold and looked around, then he turned to her.

'I'm going to be completely honest. I had other motives for allowing your transfer to Solna.' He paused. 'I wanted to be close to you. I shouldn't say this. I'm well aware of the age difference and that you're married, but I promise that it won't have an effect on our working situation, and if you prefer you can request a transfer. Or I can. But I finally realised that I couldn't keep working alongside you without saying anything. I'm in love with you, Sara. I think about you all the time, and I long for you. But that doesn't mean you have to do anything. It's my problem. Right, well, that's out in the open. If I've seemed a bit strange lately, well, you know why now. And I knew you were on your own, because your husband said he was going to stay at a hotel. Sorry to disturb you. I'll be off now.'

Sara dropped the roses on the floor and went and wrapped her arms around Bielke.

And kissed him.

She had never thought about her boss in that way, and perhaps she never would again. But right now she did. And now was all she had.

She thought about her husband Martin while she kissed Bielke and she thought about the gangster George Taylor Jr. She thought about Tom Burén at Ebba's new job and she thought about her boss Axel Bielke. Different men, different lives, different Saras. In her eyes, Bielke was a mentor, a teacher, a father. Someone who could make things right. What she was doing now was no worse than what Martin had done.

She pulled him down onto the sofa and carried on kissing him. Then she let him kiss her.

She had a right to what was happening with Bielke now. She had earned it. She needed it.

Martin was no longer her husband.

He had betrayed her. He had ruined what they had.

She had to free herself, and that was what she was doing now.

She was making herself completely free.

And alone.

62

Naturally he was gone when she woke, and he should never have been there.

A call from Martin reminded her of the tragic truth underpinning the sweet lies of the night before, but now Sara had even more reasons not to answer, enough reasons never to answer.

With a strong sense of unreality, she got up, drank a glass of juice, showered and dressed, moving like a robot. She completely consciously avoided making any decisions or even trying to get a grip on reality.

Everything was chaos. It was so strange that there could be such calm around her.

It felt as if she were sitting alone on a raft in the middle of the Atlantic and somewhere, far away, there was a ship sinking that she had escaped from. The other passengers were screaming and drowning, but she didn't notice that.

There was no rescue for Sara either, but she didn't need to think about that right now. Here on the raft all was calm.

OK, Martin out of her head, Bielke out of her head, Uncle Scam out of her head, Anna Torhall out of her head, Ebba and Olle out of her head.

What did that leave?

Sara Nowak. And she wasn't at all interested in thinking about herself.

Hedin.

She had called and had wanted something. A picture. One that was so secret she didn't want to say on the phone what it depicted.

And she needed to re-park Eric's car. Then she was going to tell him not to let Ebba borrow it any more. But she didn't have much hope that he would listen to her. Ebba was his now, Sara thought to herself.

The car key was still lying on the kitchen table. And the pistol was under the hat on the hall table. She grabbed them both, went down to the car, picked off the yellow strip securing the parking ticket under the windscreen wiper and then drove towards Åsögatan.

Martin called, but Sara definitely didn't want to talk to him. Ever again.

If the picture was so secret, perhaps Hedin would be angry with Sara if she didn't take the window route in. She found a spot on Erstagatan just outside the Spuntino café and took it as a sign that she should use that entrance.

'I'm going to see Eva,' she said, smiling to the girl behind the counter.

'Then you can take her coffee. She hasn't been in to collect it.'

'Yes, yes, sure.'

The girl poured a black coffee into a small takeaway cup.

'And tell her she's welcome to settle her bill. I mean, there's no rush, but it's been a few months since she got up to date.'

'I can pay for it.'

To transfer ten thousand euros to a former Stasi officer, she needed Martin's or Eric's money, but Hedin's café tab was something she could definitely pay with her own wages.

'Can I add some credit too?' she asked.

'If you like,' the girl said, smiling.

Sara 'deposited' five hundred kronor into Hedin's virtual account. Then she took her coffee and was let out into the courtyard behind.

While crossing to the other side of the yard that connected the buildings on all sides in this block, she wondered what it might be that Hedin had found. Something that identified Faust – that was all she could think of. Something that revealed what Otto Rau was called today. And had been called for the last thirty years.

Should she say anything about Hedin's appearance on *A Thousand Answers*? No, why should she? Not right now, at any rate. Even if Hedin had been wrong about Stellan being a spy, she had found all the material that had led to the unmasking of Geiger. And the prevention of what might have been the biggest terrorist attack in European history. And Hedin wasn't the only one to have been deceived by Geiger. That was also true for Säpo, the BND and the Stasi.

Martin's mobile again. Sara rejected the call. Couldn't he just leave it?

When she was almost at the kitchen window, it occurred to her that she ought to have called and checked that Hedin was in before she came here.

But now she was here, she might as well go and tap on the window.

And it was then that Sara saw that Hedin was at home.

Hanging from a noose attached to the ceiling.

The coffee cup hit the ground as Sara dragged over a garden chair so that she could reach better and then she smashed the window with her elbow. She stuck her hand inside, opened the window and crawled through. She didn't even notice that she cut herself on the shards of glass.

She ran over to Hedin and lifted her to minimise the pressure on her neck, but she realised immediately that she was holding a dead body.

So she let her go again to avoid contaminating the crime scene any more than she had done already.

Then she sank down onto one of the kitchen chairs and stared into space.

Suicide? No.

The same murderer as Stiller? Yes.

Rau.

And the hanging was a blatant signal – a discreet signature on the work.

Sara wanted to offer comfort, to hug Hedin, though she knew it wouldn't help. But she took her hand. Her cold, slender hand.

Stubborn Eva Hedin, who had sacrificed everything for her research. Absolutely everything. Would she have lived if Sara hadn't urged her to help pursue the terrorist Faust? She felt guilty and could find no good arguments in her own defence, although she desperately tried to do so. Was the photo that Hedin had found the thing that had cost her life? Had Rau taken it? Would Hedin had given it up?

Sara doubted that. Hedin had probably realised she had no chance. That it wouldn't make any difference if she surrendered the proof. Her life couldn't be saved whatever she did. So Sara thought.

Then she looked around the small flat and noticed right away that someone had rifled through Hedin's papers, primarily the files from the Stasi. Hedin had maintained them in pedantic order, always had every bundle of paper straightened in a way that was almost compulsive. And now the stacks of paper and files with archival copies were in disarray.

Instinctively, Sara knew she couldn't hope to find something that Rau hadn't found.

Then her gaze fell on the fridge and she was at once sure that she knew where Hedin had hidden her discovery. The only question was whether Rau had discovered it.

She noticed that her hand was trembling a little as she reached to open the door.

And there, in the small freezer compartment, was an envelope that hadn't been there last time.

A regular white C4 envelope.

Sara pulled it out, closed the compartment and then the fridge door, looked around and then opened the envelope.

The photograph was old, judging by the seventies clothes and haircuts. But despite the people in the photo being much younger, she recognised them.

Marita Werner, now known as Marita Leander.

Hans Gerlach, alias Bo Enberg, murdered by Rau.

Stefan Kremp, who had attacked her on Västerlånggatan.

And Axel Bielke.

Her boss.

He couldn't have been more than twenty in the photo, he was more than sixty today; he was obviously the missing link in the terrorist cell.

Faust.

He had been given the identity of Bielke by the priest Jürgen Stiller, had most certainly not lived abroad in his childhood, hadn't been the son of diplomats.

He had been raised as Otto Rau in West Germany.

Someone was watching her – she could feel it.

But there was no one there, and no one visible through the kitchen window. She turned her head and looked through the hall and the window on the other side towards Åsögatan instead. Someone was standing on the other side of the street, their gaze directed straight at Hedin's flat.

Sara slowly went closer. She went through the blue hallway into the little room that had been Hedin's combined bedroom, living room and study. Then she came to a halt in the middle of the floor.

Now she could see who it was standing there looking at her.

Bielke.

63

He followed events in silence.

He had difficulty believing it was really true.

The man who had been Otto Rau, who had been working for the DDR and Stasi on Gladio's orders, planning and implementing various acts of terror, who had threatened and murdered, inciting his comrades to go even further. All in the name of freedom and democracy. The man who had been deployed to crush the enemy from within.

He had now succeeded.

He and his co-conspirators. Officially, it would obviously be claimed that the success was the result of their soft tactics. Diplomacy, propaganda, cultural influence. As if rock stars and pairs of Levi's were what it took to bring the Cold War to an end. What a joke! He and all the other secret operatives knew there had only been one way to crush the evil empire. Through violence. By urging them to show their true face, to give peace-loving Western Europeans a bloody nose and make them realise how impossible dialogue was.

He had wanted to share that moment with someone, but both his mission and his personality demanded solitude in the crucial moments.

His wife was 'resting up' at her parents'. She was weak. But it was a good job that she was staying there until the bruises went away. It was a shame that she had to constantly annoy him. It presented a social obstacle when they were unable to participate in the parties and social gatherings that came with his assignment. Or that had been associated with it. Because now it was over.

It was finally happening. Before the eyes of an unprepared world.

The Berlin Wall fell.

It was hacked into pieces by exhilarated East Germans lent a hand by celebrating West Berliners. People helped each other up and began dancing on the Wall which until then it had been potentially lethal to approach.

Grim-faced East German border guards merely stood there. The reporter acted as interpreter for the whole world's surprise at the fact that this was permitted to take place, that the guards weren't dispersing the masses, or opening fire on them.

In Hungary, the border had been dismantled that summer, but in China the popular uprising in Tiananmen Square had been brutally quelled, with tanks and dead freedom activists as a result. The same reaction that had been expected here.

But it did not come.

The anti-capitalist protective rampart fell without anyone defending it and no one had any idea whom they should thank.

Lotta called and was shaken by the betrayal. She was sixteen years old and blinded with hatred and a desire for revenge. He had drilled her well, supplementing the gardener's theoretical instruction with practical exercises. Weapons, explosives, close combat. Sexual prowess. All key to undermining the other side.

And now it was over. He had built a human missile that would never be put to use.

So much power that wouldn't be channelled.

Fanatical Lotta couldn't understand how her world could crumble like this. The Wall was there to protect the DDR and its people. What would happen now?

'Is it over now?' she said, equal parts crushed and furious.

'On the contrary,' he said. 'It's now that it begins. Just lie low.'

Then he had said that she could come over if she wanted. He had realised that if he stuck to his assumed role as a terrorist, he could have fun with Lotta for many years to come while pretending to plan their great revenge in the meantime.

She said she was on her way and hung up, and then he thought about the money.

Fifty million kronor for their big operation – Wahasha. It was to have been spent on pistols, automatic weapons, hand grenades, explosives, cars, safe hiding places in Sweden and abroad, false passports, fees for helpers and flights via many transit points to a well-disposed country in the Middle East. It was an enormous operation that would have resounded across the world.

But now the taskmasters were gone and the Palestinian group didn't know where the money was. Nor did the other members of Kommando 719. Only he did. No one would ever think to ask for it back. Back where?

With the Wall gone, he realised what would happen. The Stasi was dead and the DDR would rapidly vanish – the whole system eradicated by its own functionaries.

Desperate instructions reached him during the evening: 'Destroy everything.'

He realised that the Stasi were burning and shredding files as quickly as they could, that alternative stories were being constructed, that all connections to the opposition were being dug up and invoked.

History was being rewritten. The past was being erased.

That suited him fine.

The fortune they had given him for the operation had no sender any longer. No one he had to report to.

The money was his.

64

Sara slowly emerged from the main door of the block of flats at 189 Åsögatan. Bielke stepped off the pavement on the other side of the street and met her halfway.

So Bielke was Faust?

Bielke had murdered Hedin?

And tried to shoot Sara?

So much for love.

Sara drew her pistol, extended her arm and took aim directly at the face of her boss and passing lover.

She held up the photo she had found at Hedin's.

'You missed this.'

Bielke looked at the photo for a long time and then nodded to himself.

'I was afraid something like this might come up.'

'You tried to kill me. You fired into my own home.'

Bielke looked at Sara with what appeared to be genuine surprise. 'No.'

'And now you've killed Hedin. Was it supposed to look like suicide?'

'Sara, you're mistaken. I'm not who you think.'

'I don't think, I know. You're Otto Rau. Seen in this photo with his friends.'

'I was in the cell. That's true. But I've never met Otto Rau, only heard about him. I was no more than an errand boy,' said Bielke, his eyes widening.

'That's what you say now.'

'I promise. Ask the others. Ask them about Anders Karlsson. That was my cover name.' He swept the street with his gaze. 'I think it's probably best if you lower the gun, otherwise someone will call the police.'

Sara did as he said, but was still prepared to defend herself.

'Go to the edge of the road,' she said.

They went to the pavement just outside Hedin's window.

Should she take him inside and shoot him? As revenge?

No, she couldn't do that.

But she wanted to.

'Was it worth it? Four people's lives on your conscience to protect your dirty little secret?'

'I haven't killed anyone. It's not as secret as all that. It would cost me my career if the past came out, but I would never go so far as to commit murder.'

'So someone else did it? Killed all the people threatening to reveal your identity?'

'Sara, listen to me. I was drawn to the revolutionary groups when I was young, but I was just a hanger on, a foot soldier. I went to places and shopped, acquired weapons, gave people lifts, found places to live. Today I'm ashamed by how naïve I was, but I was never calling the shots in those groups. I've never done anything really awful. I wasn't even part of it for very long. OK?'

'You just happen to be standing here outside Hedin's flat? And you found your way to my house because you've been before, to leave a body, the body of your friend in the photo.'

'Sara, you have to believe me! The only thing I've been hiding is that I was in the cell. I haven't killed anyone. I waited outside your building and followed you here. I just wanted to know whether my secret was going to be uncovered. I knew you wouldn't give in easily – that you were onto the truth.'

Her mobile buzzed again. A message. Bloody Martin. Why wouldn't he ever give up? Sara couldn't take her gaze from Bielke, so she ignored it.

'Sara Nowak!'

The voice was unfamiliar and she didn't want to allow herself to be distracted. She took a half step backwards so that she still had Bielke in the corner of her vision but was able to turn her head to see who had shouted.

She saw a bespectacled man with a grey-flecked beard and grey hair in a ring around an otherwise bald head. He presented police ID.

'Quintus Nyman,' he said. 'Säpo.'

'Have you been following me too?'

'Put away the weapon please,' said Nyman, approaching slowly with the palms of his hands extended to placate the armed Sara.

'No,' said Sara. 'He murdered Eva Hedin. And the others. He's Otto Rau. Faust.'

Nyman blinked. Then he looked at Bielke.

'Him? Are you sure?'

Sara handed over the photo that Hedin had hidden in the freezer compartment. Nyman scrutinised the photo and then looked up at Bielke.

'Finally,' he said.

'I'm not Faust!' said Bielke. 'I've never even met him. He kept me at arm's length. Only a few got to meet him.'

'I didn't expect you to confess,' said Nyman.

Suddenly the Säpo man was brandishing a gun and aiming right at Bielke.

'This is for Alger Nyman.'

The operative fired two shots into the chest of Sara's boss. A couple of teenagers who had been sauntering by and an older woman walking her dachshund panicked when they realised what had happened and ran for their lives.

Sara raised her pistol in reflex, but didn't know what to do. She took aim at Nyman.

Bielke fell to the ground. Nyman took a revolver out of his pocket and threw it onto the ground next to him. The pavement slowly began to turn red with blood.

'He tried to shoot me,' he said, looking at Sara. 'OK?'

'I don't know. Maybe if you say why.'

Sara crouched to see how Bielke was. He was breathing but he was bleeding profusely. He looked at her with panic in his eyes and seemed to be trying to say something, but all he was able to get out was a strange, gurgling sound. The bullets didn't seem to have hit his head, but she couldn't say more than that.

There was still no reply from Nyman.

'Who is Alger Nyman?' said Sara.

'My father. Rau killed him. Pushed him in front of an underground train in 1987 to conceal arms exports to the DDR. Thanks for finding him.'

'You've been following me to get hold of him?'

'I've been looking for Otto Rau my whole life. I knew he was dangerous, so I thought you might need some backup. The BND forbade us to help you, so I suppose we'll see what happens now.'

He pulled out his mobile and made a call.

'Nyman at Säpo. There's a policeman shot in Södermalm, 189 Åsögatan. Immediate assistance required.'

Nyman ended the call and looked at the bleeding body on the pavement with disgust.

'The BND have been shielding his identity all these years, not a thought for his victims. They're probably still in cahoots with him.'

'But now you've got your revenge?'

'Not quite. He's not dead yet.'

Sara noted Bielke's juddering, irregular breathing. How much blood his body was pumping onto the pavement! Nyman went over and took aim at his forehead.

Sara stepped into his line of sight.

Nyman looked at her, then he picked up the revolver he had cast away.

'OK. I'll shoot you with his gun. I'll say I wasn't quick enough to save you.'

Sara grabbed her own pistol and took aim at Nyman.

'Stop it! He should be in prison!'

They stared at each other along their respective barrels, each unsure what would happen. Would the other shoot? Sara didn't want to shoot first, but she definitely didn't want to shoot last.

She fumbled desperately for her mobile – to call for help or perhaps to record Nyman. Her mobile was her saviour, somehow.

She pulled out her phone and was about to enter the PIN to unlock it when her eye was caught by a picture message that had been sent from Martin's mobile. She could see a preview of it on the display. Without a thought for the injured Bielke or Nyman and his revolver, she unlocked the phone and opened the message.

Seven missed calls from Martin's mobile.

But it hadn't been Martin calling. Or sending the message.

The picture showed Martin bound and bleeding.

He was standing on a stool with a noose around his neck.

The caption read: 'Don't you want to save him? Rau.'

Sara stared at the picture.

While her thoughts rushed around her head, another message arrived.

There was a picture of the table with the straps in Warehouse 7.

It was captioned: 'Room for you. You know the address. You have fifteen minutes.'

She looked at Quintus Nyman.

'Get him to hospital! He's *not* Rau. The real Rau has my husband.'

She got up and ran around the corner to Erstagatan and Eric's car that she had parked there.

Now she would have to see how fast a Maserati could go.

Which way was the fastest from here, given the roadworks everywhere? She started the car, switched on the built-in satnav – and froze.

The screen showed 'Most recent searches' and at the top was 'Torpa vicarage, Ydre'.

Suddenly it all made sense.

A terrible realisation pounded inside her head.

Her whole life – the last twenty-five years – flashed before her eyes. How could she have been so blind?

All that time living in proximity to a terrorist. A cold-blooded killer.

And she hadn't even noticed a thing.

But now she knew.

Otto Rau hadn't needed a false Swedish identity from Jürgen Stiller. Eric Titus had needed a false German identity to infiltrate the cell.

Otto Rau had never existed.

It was Eric Titus's cover name. It always had been.

At Titus & Partners, Sara had seen the history of Eric's company. Founded in 1990. Just as the Wall had fallen.

Using what capital?

The money for Operation Wahasha had been the making of Titus & Partners. The group's activities included international shipping, like the company that owned Warehouse 7, where Eric wanted her to go.

She looked at the picture message again.

Was Eric holding his own son hostage? How could that be possible?

Or was Martin pretending? What was Eric's relationship with his son?

Now she spotted a detail that told her something even more important. Something that Eric hadn't thought about. But could she be sure? Otherwise she was risking both her own and her husband's lives.

If she didn't do exactly as Eric said, there was a big risk he would actually kill Martin.

Her father-in-law wanted her to go to Warehouse 7.

And she only had twelve minutes.

Sara started the car.

65

He wouldn't last much longer.

His toes only just reached the stool.

The noose was cutting into his neck and he had to tilt his head to the side to be able to reach down with his feet.

He couldn't think of any more songs to sing.

The powerful lights meant he couldn't see anything more than the contours of his father.

Hear the sound of rats chewing away in the walls.

See the little red light on the video camera. Just like when he had been little. He was back in the hellscape of his childhood, in his parents' basement, the subterranean domain where Eric was the devil.

'Sing!' his father commanded now. 'And dance! Entertain me. Otherwise I'll get bored.'

'What do you want to hear?'

The noose chafed against his skin, and his head had been cocked for so long that he couldn't talk properly any longer.

'You're the artist,' said Eric.

'*He is my song and my light . . .*'

'Nothing Christian!' said Eric, a half-eaten apple hitting the stool with such force that it almost tipped over. Martin was only just able to keep it in position with the tips of his toes.

'Do you think she's coming?'

Eric looked at the screen. The peepshow in Warehouse 7 in real time. His men standing by next to the table. At the very moment Sara entered, he would see it. He would see her overpowered and then his men would rig two cameras to show her struggle to the death in real time. Martin would also get to see that.

'Do you think your wife is willing to swap places with you? Is she the type?'

Martin didn't know what to say. He didn't know what to think. Or hope. He wondered how Olle and Ebba would take it if both their parents disappeared.

'Dad . . .'

'Yes?'

There was a sound from above, smashing glass and then a thud, as if someone had landed on the floor.

Eric looked at the screen where he had been expecting to see Sara and then glanced upstairs in the house.

'Your little pit bull is pretty smart after all.'

'Sara . . . .!'

Martin apparently wanted to warn his wife, but his voice wouldn't carry. And Sara probably wouldn't have allowed herself to be dissuaded, Eric reflected.

He went and stood right by his son, ready to welcome his daughter-in-law with a smile.

'Congratulations,' he said when Sara came down the steps to the basement, pistol in hand. 'Just a small warning. If I fall then I may very well tip over Martin's stool.'

'What makes you think that bothers me?'

'I must say I hadn't been expecting this. Did you look in the freezer?'

'So you found the picture of Bielke?' said Sara. 'And left it there?'

Eric grinned.

'It was perfect for my plans.'

'And it was perfect for your plans to shoot into our home. When Olle was at home. Your own grandchild.'

'I would never hurt him. I'm not that bad a shot. But come, come, tell me how you realised it was me? And that we were here rather than at Warehouse 7?'

'Your satnav. And I recognised the stool that Martin was standing on – yellow with green flowers – from the photo that Marie showed me.'

'Ah, a little luck and a little skill. Well, I suppose that's what it takes. A real pity that the luck ran out.'

'Why the peepshow?'

'I wanted a hobby for when I retire,' said Eric.

'And why Stiller, Enberg and Hedin? To avoid discovery?'

'Naturally. And now you can add Nowak and Titus Jr to that list.'

'You're going to make orphans of your grandchildren?'

'Deep down, Martin has a rather negative perception of me. But with Ebba, I can correct that perception, be remembered as something completely different. As the person I am, the one I have become.'

'You mean the person you're trying to convince yourself that you are.'

'It's always the same with you, Sara. You always have to stick your nose in. I saw the folder containing my file in your hall last Sunday.'

Hedin's folder, that Sara had put down in the hall when they had all gathered for Sunday lunch.

'You've no idea how disappointed I was,' Eric said. 'My own daughter-in-law pursuing me. But I wanted to give you a chance. Well, actually, you got lots of chances. If you had just listened to my warnings. But I can't let you get between me and my grandchildren.'

'You mean my children.'

'They seem to like their grandfather far better. And they can't be allowed to develop the wrong impression of me.'

'Are you that ashamed of what you did? Of Kommando 719? Of Stay-Behind?'

'Everything that I did, I did for my country. So that you and Martin and everyone else could live in freedom,' Eric said, looking at her with a fiery gaze.

'They said you were still in the game.'

'Well, I suppose you might say that. My little corporate empire has its uses. We build bugs into buildings in other countries, ship sensitive equipment to recipients we'd rather not acknowledge, a weapons system to an Arab state at war to secure our oil shipments. We can act as a front in every part of the world. I continue to do my bit.'

'Stirner Shipping SA?' Sara asked.

'One of my companies.'

'And you've built it all up using the money from Operation Wahasha.'

Eric frowned.

'What do you know about Wahasha?'

'That you want to conceal what you didn't do. It's not the murders and the attacks. It's that you didn't build up your company by yourself using your own means.'

'You think that's worse?'

'Yes, for you,' Sara said, taking a couple of steps closer. 'When you finally won your father's respect, it was because you had deceived him. And that realisation torments you. Like all tragic men obsessed with their fathers, your father's recognition is what has governed your life. So you carry on deceiving him and yourself – twenty-five years after he died.'

'Well, well, you're quite the armchair psychologist.'

'But it's true,' Sara added. 'Even though Martin is here with a noose around his neck, it's you who failed in that regard. He actually managed to build something by himself. You never did that.'

'Shut up!'

Sara raised her pistol. She took aim at Eric's forehead. Otto Rau. Faust.

'Cut Martin down.'

Eric smiled and nudged the stool his son was standing on with the tip of his shoe. The stool wobbled back and forth and Martin struggled not to lose his balance, gurgling as the noose cut even more deeply into his neck.

'Take it easy with that gun,' said Eric.

Sara quickly moved towards Eric, raising one hand and striking him on the head with the butt of her gun. At the same time, she was prepared to catch Martin's body if the stool was kicked aside.

Eric staggered back a couple of steps and then straightened up, but now with a pistol in his hand, aimed right at Sara.

'Is this how it's going to end? Seeing who shoots first? Can't we do something more amusing?'

He moved in a wide circle behind Martin so that his son was between them.

'Sara . . . Forgive me . . .' Martin sobbed and cried.

'What do you say? Why don't we lay down our arms?'

A rapid step to the side and then Eric shot the pistol out of his daughter-in-law's hand. Sara let out a shout of pain as the gun flew through the air, landing on the cement floor and sliding off into the darkness.

'I think that makes us quits?'

Eric went over and turned on the video camera.

Sara didn't know whether to lunge after the pistol, throw herself at Eric or try and free Martin from the noose.

Eric looked at her.

He came a few steps closer, then he let the pistol fall to the floor.

'That evens things out a bit,' he said with a smile.

While Sara followed the gun as it fell to the floor, the first blow landed.

A right hook to her chin, shaking her badly.

She hadn't been ready for the attack, but she still managed to get her guard up and shield herself from the follow-up blow.

Right after that blocked blow, there was a quick jab at Sara's face from right in front.

And then a kick from the side to back of her knee, making her collapse to the floor.

Eric was surprisingly agile.

When Sara tried to get back to her feet again, Eric caught her with a kick to the temple. And then a knee to her nose. There was a flash before her eyes and the pain was sharp and intense like a razor blade. She had to think fast.

She lunged at his feet to pull him down, but he danced away and responded with a lash of his foot to her head.

Then he stepped over her back, put his arm around her throat and rolled onto his back with her. He wrapped his legs around her thighs, locked his arm using his other hand and pressed for all he was worth.

Sara noticed that the video camera was aimed right at their fight.

Eric had already made up his mind before attacking where he would kill her. And now he wanted to immortalise her deadly struggle.

Sara tried to scratch Eric's hands, but her nails were too short.

She tried to reach his eyes behind her neck, but he ducked his head out of reach.

Her eyes began to darken.

She knew she didn't have many seconds in a stranglehold like this.

First she would faint and if Eric didn't let go, she would be dead in less than half a minute.

And she knew he wouldn't let go.

Where had the pistol got to?

She tried to twist her head to see where it was, but his grip only tightened.

She tried to reach his crotch, but he pressed against her. And she was unable to get any grip on his fingers so that she could prise free her hands.

Her temples were pounding and her vision was increasingly blurry.

His voice reached her through a tunnel.

She only vaguely understood that Eric was talking to her, but she couldn't understand what he was saying.

Her body began to jerk and cramp.

Her consciousness slowly began to die away, and she knew time was running out.

Whether it was pure reflex or a sudden bolt from the blue she didn't know, but when her body capitulated and became loose-limbed, she tapped Eric's arm softly three times. As if to indicate she was tapping out. Giving up.

And he reacted instinctively and let go.

The half second it took him to realise what he had done was all Sara needed.

She twisted out of his grip and put her hands in his face to push him away. A finger deep in his eye made him scream.

He put one hand over the eye and with the other he reached for her face.

He got hold of her lower jaw, two fingers inside her mouth.

And then she bit.

As hard as she could.

She felt the fingers moving about inside her mouth and she bit down even harder until the fingers suddenly fell onto her tongue and her mouth was filled with warm, sweet liquid.

Eric shouted – more out of rage than pain.

Sara didn't wait for his counterattack. She spat out the bitten-off fingers, grabbed his scrotum and twisted. As far as she could.

Now there was more pain in his shouting, and he curled up in his impotence as she lunged desperately for the pistol.

Both her own life and Martin's depended on her succeeding.

Sara fumbled in the dark for the weapon, struck it but pushed it even further away in her eagerness. She crawled after it as quickly as she could, while at the same time she heard Eric following – back on his feet.

'You little whore!'

Her fingertips found the hard metal.

She extended her fingers, grabbed the barrel and quickly put her other hand around the butt.

Then she rolled around in the same moment that a spotlight was directed at her and a bullet hit the floor, ricocheting from where she had just been lying.

She fired straight at the contours of Eric on front of the bright light.

He fell to the ground and she carried on shooting. She crawled backwards away from him as she shot. And shot. And shot.

Until her magazine was empty.

When Eric collapsed on the cold basement floor, Martin began to sing hysterically.

'*Money, money, money, must be funny, in the rich man's world . . .*'

He was crying even harder now, until he stumbled and the stool fell over.

The fear in his eyes as the noose tightened around his throat and the last of his air disappeared . . .

Sara leapt up. She grabbed Martin's body and held it up so that the noose wouldn't strain at him but she knew she wouldn't be able to hold him indefinitely. She couldn't reach the stool, couldn't even see it in the darkness.

She contemplated the options while panic spread in her body. She had seconds.

At last she made up her mind.

She let go of her husband.

His gaze filled with horror as he thought she would leave him to die. His body writhed with desperation. The anguish. The desolate cry that was reduced by the noose to nothing but a pitiful gurgle.

But she hurried over and retrieved Eric's pistol, ran back and put the muzzle to the rope before firing.

When the rope snapped, Martin fell to the floor. He must have hurt badly, but he said nothing. Not a sound.

He just lay there, completely still on the floor.

Sara looked from Eric's dead body to her bleeding, tear-stained husband.

His whole life crushed.

And hers.

Now it was just them.

They had survived.

But it might have been better to die.

66

No radio, no television, and no internet. Just classical music through the tannoy.

She had no idea what was going on in the world.

Both the guards and the nurses spoke German, so she assumed she was in Germany. And the facility was brand new – that much was clear. If they had dared to bring her to Berlin then she was probably in the BND's new headquarters, but it was far likelier that they had taken her to some secret facility in another part of the country.

They had made her an offer.

She would be allowed to resume her life in return for carrying out a mission for them. a very dangerous mission with no official backup. There was a big risk that it would end her life – but it wasn't as if she had anything to lose.

They said the only catch was that the mission would be carried out together with her worst enemy.

The lock clicked and the door slid open.

The old man who called himself Schönberg came in. He looked at her thoughtfully.

'Have you made up your mind?'

She nodded.

'I'm afraid there is an added complication.' He paused, as if he didn't want to utter the words on the tip of his tongue. 'Sara Nowak has unmasked Rau.'

Sara. Again.

'This will make the mission somewhat more challenging, but we have no choice. And you don't have much choice either. You must stop Nowak too. In addition to the other plans we made.'

She didn't reply. She merely looked at him. She remembered him from when he had been young and full of implicit faith. And had gone by another name.

'So what do you say?'

Her gaze lingered on him. Her head felt as if it might burst as she slowly nodded and accepted the mission.

Schönberg couldn't help smiling. Relieved.

'Good,' he said. 'Thank you, Agneta.'

Acknowledgements

I want to thank my publisher Jonas Axelsson, my editor Annie Murphy, and Ben Willis and the whole team at Zaffre for their brilliant work.

Don't miss out on Sara Nowak's first case . . .

The landline rings as Agneta is waving off her grandchildren. Just one word comes out of the receiver: 'Geiger'. For decades, Agneta has always known that this moment would come, but she is shaken. She knows what it means.

Retrieving her weapon from its hiding place, she attaches the silencer and creeps up behind her husband before pressing the barrel to his temple.

Then she squeezes the trigger and disappears – leaving behind her wallet and keys.

The extraordinary murder is not Sara Nowak's case. But she was once close to those affected and, defying regulations, she joins the investigation. What Sara doesn't know is that the mysterious codeword is just the first piece in the puzzle of an intricate and devastating plot fifty years in the making.

AVAILABLE NOW